A
Brother's Journey

The Tale of the Devil's Kettle

Book 2

By

For His Glory

Available as an ebook

ISBN 978-1-968640-06-4 (paperback)

ISBN 978-1-968640-07-1 (hardcover)

Copyright © 2025 For His Glory

All Rights Reserved. No part of this publication may be reproduced, distributed, or transmitted in any form or by any means, including photocopying, recording, or other electronic or mechanical methods, without the prior written permission of the publisher. For permission requests, solicit the publisher via the address below.

Publify Publishing

Lampasas, TX 76550

contact@publifypublishing.com

Dedication

I would like to dedicate this book to Eileen. Thank you for being the first to read my story and for giving me the drive to finish it. Without your interest in my story, I'm not sure I would have completed it! I hope that as we grow old, you can read these stories and remember all the adventures we had as a youth group. You have become like a little sister to me, and I wish you the best in whatever you do in life!

Table of Contents

Chapter 1 - King Fraust's Dream..1

Chapter 2 - In the Clearing..6

Chapter 3 - Crusade Parade...23

Chapter 4 - Interpretation...35

Chapter 5 - Wishing Well...42

Chapter 6 - A Mother's Plea..59

Chapter 7 - A Farewell Forever...68

Chapter 8 - The Book of Truth..82

Chapter 9 - Dungeon Discoveries..95

Chapter 10 - Decisions, Decisions...116

Chapter 11 - Below Ground Brawl...131

Chapter 12 - Desperation..150

Chapter 13 - The High Priest..160

Chapter 14 - Hector's Help..180

Chapter 15 - Lost in the Castle...201

Chapter 16 - Hay Mound Haven..220

Chapter 17 - Repercussions..240

Chapter 18 - One Last Gift..253

Chapter 19 - The Light..259

Chapter 20 - Castle of Chaos..274

Chapter 21 - The Shepherd Boy...286

Chapter 22 - In Plain Sight...298

Chapter 23 - Mischka's Morning Miracle..308

Chapter 24 - The Rock 318

Chapter 25 - Preparations 335

Chapter 26 - The Lamb, the Bread, and the Doorway 346

Chapter 27 - "I Used to be You, Don't Become Me." 354

Chapter 28 - An Example for All to See.................................... 365

Chapter 29 - I AM.. 375

Chapter 30 - Esok Adams 388

A Note From the Author 391

About the Author.. 392

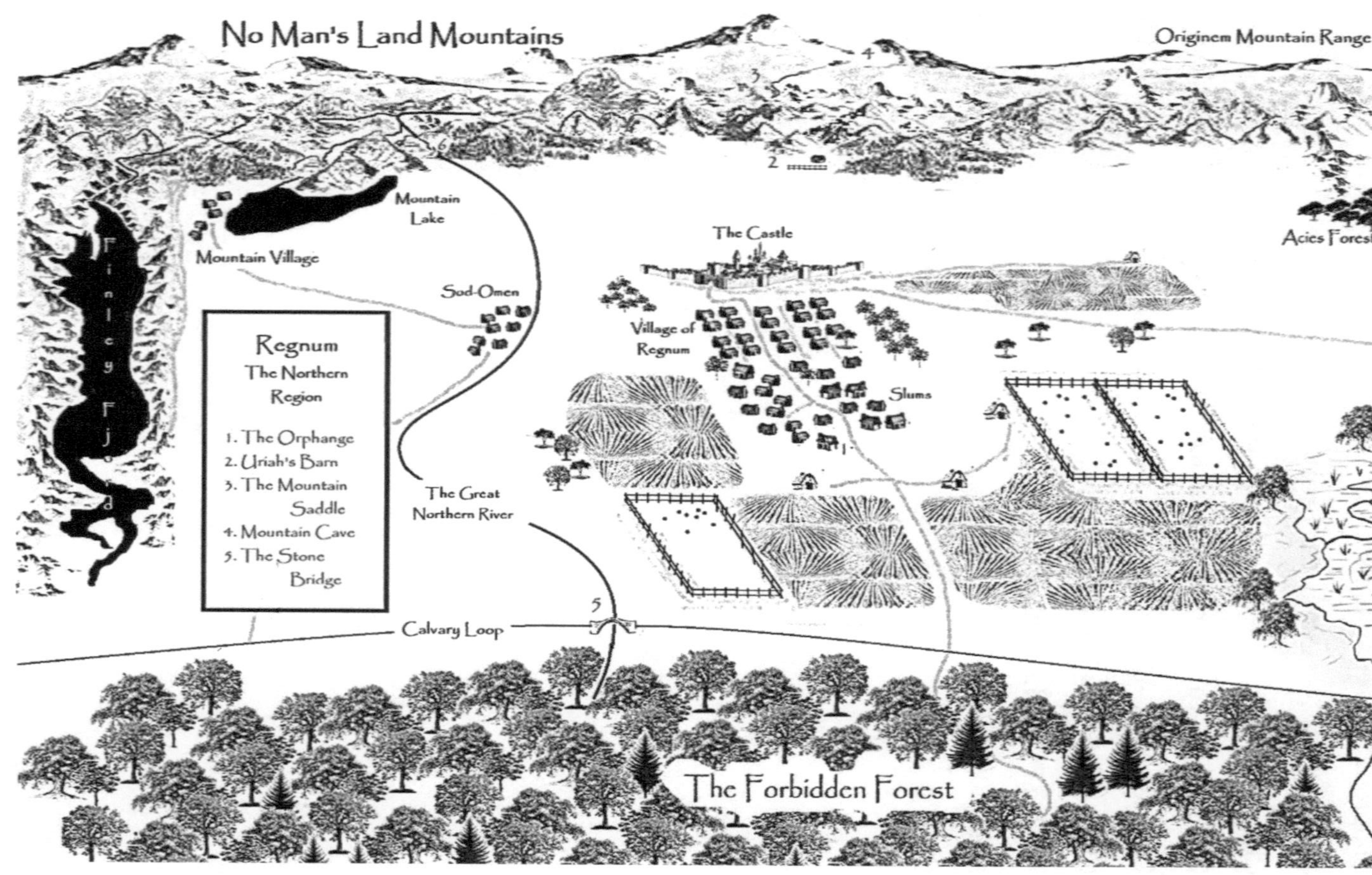

No Man's Land Mountains
Originem Mountain Range
Finlcy Fjord
Mountain Lake
Mountain Village
Sod-Omen
The Castle
Acies Forest
Village of Regnum
Slums
The Great Northern River
Calvary Loop
The Forbidden Forest
Regnum
The Northern Region
1. The Orphange
2. Uriah's Barn
3. The Mountain Saddle
4. Mountain Cave
5. The Stone Bridge

Chapter 1
King Fraust's Dream

"Wake up," a soft voice of a servant girl whispered. She was gently shaking King Fraust, who had been fast asleep in his chambers.

"Have you another dream, your majesty?" The servant girl inquired. She had a damp rag and was using it to pat the King's forehead softly.

As he opened his eyes, he could see the innocent girl caring for him, but his heart was full of anguish, for he did in fact have a dream.

"Off of me!" he ordered in a booming voice, as he pushed the rag from his forehead and shoved the girl back.

Her posture drooped as she was forced back. She stood at a distance with her eyes on the floor and one hand holding her other arm, afraid to make any movements that would upset the King.

"Fetch my brother!" he ordered the girl.

"Yes, your majesty," she whimpered, as she ran quickly from the King's chambers.

The king sat up in his bed and swung his legs over its edge. From there, he could see all of his royal room, and most importantly, the doors that led out to the balcony that overlooked his courtyard and his kingdom.

He fished for his slippers and slipped out of bed, making his way over to the balcony. Before opening the doors, he grabbed his royal overcoat that was hanging on a peg next to the double doors. As he slipped it over his shoulders, the moonlight peeked through the stained windows and flickered off the golden thread that sewed patterns into the cuffs and collar of the coat. The navy blue of the overcoat shared its color with the night sky.

He pushed open the doors and stepped into the cool, crisp air. His long black hair, peppered with gray, hung freely at his shoulders as the wind brushed through it. His beard was full and hung down to his chest.

He rested his hands on the railing carved out of quartz and gazed up at the stars.

All was still but for a few minutes, until the King's brother entered the chambers.

"Brother, can you not find it in your heart to be kind to your servants?" King Fraust's brother spoke sternly from within the room. His face was hidden by the shadows.

"What do they matter? I am King, and I provide them food and a place to stay! They deserve nothing more!" the King barked.

"Oh, whatever!"

"Watch your tongue, brother!"

"Or what, you'll kill me? Ha! Not likely!" the younger brother scoffed as he lifted a bottle of ale to his lips.

"Are you drunk, yet again?"

"Maybe. But you would be too, if you had a brother like I do."

"Oh, stop your sulking. Let go of the past already. We made our choices, and now it's done with."

"How can you let go of all those horrible things?" he asked, followed by a muffled burp.

"Because, brother, I am strong and you are weak. This is why I am King and you are not."

"Please! I let you be King, do you not remember, brother?" He said with sass as he reached for a dagger he had tucked in his belt.

"Put it away! You do not have the courage to face me. Neither did you have the courage to face the Messorems in the Uada Hollow. Do you remember that, brother? How you let your own demons drown you? While you feared them, I made mine my friends."

"Fine." He said as he slid his dagger back into its sheath. "What is it you want at this late hour?" the brother asked, as he tossed his bottle of Ale to the side and crossed his arms.

"I have had another dream. But this one feels different," King Fraust announced.

"Different? How?" asked the brother, still hidden in the shadows.

"I don't know, that is why I've called you here, you are a Lector after all."

"I suppose you're right," the brother said. "Proceed so I can get back to the things I love the most."

"You don't love them. They are just something to do, while you distract yourself from your patheticness."

"Do you want my help?"

"Yes, yes, of course," the King said.

"Then carry on!"

"Okay, the dream was this… A couple planted the seed into the earth."

"Who were they?"

"Already with the questions?"

"Hey, it's probably important! Continue…" the younger brother said.

"Fine, I don't know who they were. I couldn't see their faces, but they felt familiar."

"Okay, go on."

"The seed took root and grew into a Furlope tree. After it had grown up a bit, the Great White Eagle came and cut down the tree with his razor-sharp talons, and then carved out a handle for an ax from that same tree."

"Hmmm, hmmm, hmmm. Then what?"

"The Great White Eagle fastened the handle to a heavy double-bladed axe that was coated in coal dust. At first, I thought it was just a regular ax, but when the Great White Eagle's feathers brushed the soot away, it was revealed that the ax was actually made of gold," the King explained.

"Ohhh fancy!" the brother smarted off.

"Listen to me, this is not like any other dream I've had before. The Great White Eagle grasped the handle with its talons and lifted itself into the air! He then used the ax to cut down a mighty oak tree. When he was done, all that was left of the oak tree was its stump. The Great White Eagle used the ax to split the stump, dividing it into two. Once he had done all this, the Great White Eagle lodged the Furlope handle of the ax into the stump's crack, which held the golden ax high into the sky. Just before the servant woke me up, the Great White Eagle perched itself upon the ax and boomed, 'It is time.'"

"Huh, that's interesting," the brother said, who was now lounging in a chair, fiddling with the King's sword that was leaning against the chair's arm.

"What does it mean?" the King asked.

"I *don't* know," the brother responded, in a sarcastic way.

"You don't know? Why do I even bother with you, brother?"

"Give me a few days to try and understand it better."

"You have three days, or your ale will be cut off," the King ordered.

"Why yes, of course, your majesty," the brother said, in the most sarcastic way possible. Standing up, he gave the King a theatrical bow, turned around, and exited the King's chambers.

"Oh brother," the King grumbled to himself as he turned back to his balcony, and again anxiously gazed into the night sky.

Chapter 2
In the Clearing

Three Days Later...

Gillian raced through the sky, leaving behind him the battle that brought death to Vincent, a former comrade of his. As he sped towards the clearing, the trees bent over from the gusts of wind his wings created.

The thoughts that flooded his head were all of the things that had happened to him in the past few days. He had gained more 'Noble Markings' in the last three days than he had in his entire life, yet felt sick about it. *Those markings are supposed to bring honor... but instead, I feel guilt and shame.* However, this was only one of the many things that weighed heavily on his shoulders. Not only did his markings feel just plain wrong, but during his journey, he had discovered that the Devil's kettle was real and that Malus, the leader of all Pegesi, had lied to him and his comrades all his life. *It was not a made-up story. It's real, all of it!* The sight of the Devil's Kettle raced in his mind, and the image of the Messorems flashed in his head. *Those horrible creatures dragging souls into the Devil's Kettle*, he thought. *And Richard, he was innocent and didn't deserve that.* To make matters worse, his thoughts didn't stop there. For the first time in Gillian's life, he felt the presence of the Great White Eagle.

Now, if you had felt the Great White Eagle's presence, it would have brought you comfort and peace, especially if you had seen the things Gillian had. However, Gillian became confused and scared. His entire life, up until this point, he denied the Great White Eagle's existence. Yet, now, knowing what he felt, he could no longer just dismiss the Great White Eagle and his mysterious power. *Is the Great White Eagle really just a lie, as Malus has told me? But how can it be? I felt his presence! I saw his image in the clouds! And the strange red light, somehow, I could feel it was him there with me. I don't know what to believe anymore, my whole life seems to have been a lie.* Not only was Gillian conflicted on the inside, but if the discovery of the Great White Eagle being real could be proved, Gillian would have to deny 'his truth.' Meaning he would have to give up everything he was taught to believe and go against the very creatures that raised him. It could change the entire course of his life.

As the wind whipped through his short mane, Gillian snapped out of his thoughts. The clearing that the four humans, Andy, Eva, Jessie, and Richard, had first snuck past Gillian in was just ahead of him now, bringing his journey into a full circle.

His heart pounded as his thoughts began to realign with the mission he was on. No longer was he trying to capture Andy, Eva, and Jessie, but now he was going to try and save them.

If you can remember, moments before the battle between Vincent and Gillian, Vincent told Gillian that the King's platoon was waiting for them in the clearing. Vincent was determined to kill Gillian and take the three humans as prisoners. Luckily, before Vincent could, the three were able to escape his clutches. However, unbeknownst to them, they were headed straight for the King and his men.

Now that Vincent had been defeated, with the help of Koden, Gillian's only thought was to try and get to the clearing before his three new friends did. *If I can just get back before them, maybe I can convince the King to bring his men back to Regnum. That way, my friends can escape to the Elves for help.*

However, for Gillian, there was a major problem: he had no plan on how to convince the King of anything. If the King was truly there and waiting, Vincent would have filled him in on his lie and told him how he had gone into the Forbidden Circle without the King's consent. If Gillian were caught lying again, it would make matters much worse for him and the humans.

Gillian finally brushed beyond the last bit of trees, and he could now see the clearing below. His heart sank as he peered down. No longer was the clearing clear, but it was filled by the King's platoon. The Titans below had all their armor on and stood in a common defensive formation. The first row of men was the archers, and they all had their bows at full draw; arrows aimed right at Gillian.

"Hold your fire!" one of the men in the rear of the clearing shouted. He must have been a commander of that platoon, for he stood right beside the horse that the King was mounted upon and shouted orders for his Majesty.

"By order of the King, you are commanded to come to the ground before us!" the commander shouted up at Gillian.

Gillian descended to the ground in front of the Titans. Once on the ground, the front line of men brought their bows to rest. Then the second row of men who were armed with spears swapped places with the archers.

"State your name!" the commander ordered.

"Gillian from the Lineage of Manuel," he said, looking down at the Titan's sharp, pointy spears. From where he stood, he could see four or five rows of Titans. Then spread out in the back were five Pegasi Guards dressed in their armor, ready for battle. Then last, but not least, Gillian could see the commander standing next to the King's brown quarter horse, in which King Fraust himself was sitting atop.

The King had his Golden crown resting on his head. It had twelve points arranged; one tall, one short, one tall, one short, all the way around the band. The tall points had a round head to it and a red emerald centered in it. The base of the crown was lined with white fur, and it fit well on his head.

"Gillian?" a strong, low voice came from beyond the King. The crowd of Titans hushed as Malus himself slowly emerged from around the bend in the road. Malus was the most beautiful Pegasus in all the land. All of his hide was jet black, and it shimmered in the sunlight. It almost seemed to glow. His voice was low but soothing. It sounded comforting like the voice of a guardian, a guardian you could tell anything to.

"Yes, Sire," Gillian responded after clearing his throat. The confidence he had on his way to the clearing had now dwindled into nothing. The presence of Malus weighed heavily on him. Even though he knew Malus had lied to him his whole life, he had still been a part of who Gillian was, and he felt a lot of respect for him in that matter.

Not only did Gillian have a great deal of respect for Malus, but he feared Malus too. For both the things he had seen and the things he had heard had been done to other Pegasi who disobeyed him.

"Just look at your hide!" Malus said, in a curious manner.

"Oh… ummm," Gillian blabbered as he looked at his hide and remembered his markings, "Yes, Sire."

"Noble markings! Splendid. What good deeds in the name of the King have you done?" Malus asked. The crowd roared with excitement, for Gillian had earned 'Noble Markings.' They all believed that a Pegasus' *Noble Markings* come when a Pegasus does a noble deed in the name of the King or for Malus.

"I… I… I don't know." Gillian stammered. However, little did the crowd of Titans know, Gillian's response was a lie. He knew exactly where they came from, but he was ashamed to admit what he had done. Deep down, Gillian knew his first marking came from when he lied to Vincent. In fact, all of his markings came from a moment he was not proud of, moments of shame and regret. Yet, he was not about to admit that! *They would have my wings for such a thought.* Gillian thought in his head.

"It must have been real brave!" one Titan shouted, and the crowd shouted in agreement.

"I bet it was with the highest honor and will be remembered by all!" another Titan hollered, and again the crowd of the King's Titans roared in praise.

Gillian heard the praises from the men and felt pride fill up his heart. It was a feeling of excitement he had never felt before, and he liked it.

At the loss of his control, Gillian shouted, "It was!" fueling the crowd's excitement.

King Fraust and Malus looked at each other and then looked back at Gillian.

"Where is Vincent?" King Fraust's voice boomed, and the whole crowd hushed instantly.

Gillian's joy vanished, and his ears drooped. The simple question shut down Gillian's joy immediately and brought back the terrible memory of the battle that took place moments ago.

"Vincent... He was killed in battle." Gillian said. This was a truthful statement, but there was definitely more to the story than what Gillian wanted to admit. The crowd of Titans gasped at the news.

"A battle? By what force?" the King questioned in shock. There was a peace treaty in place among all the creatures, a battle would be forbidden under its agreement.

"By a..." Gillian paused for a moment. The truth was that the battle began between him and Vincent, but ended when Koden, a great Gladiator bear, sprang into action. If it hadn't been for that bear, it would have been Gillian who was killed, instead of Vincent. "A great Gladiator bear," Gillian responded, knowing that what he said now would be the story he had to stick with, Gillian did his best to make sure his tail was covered. If Malus or the King learned the truth, Gillian knew they would label him a traitor and serve him the Alatum punishment. So Gillian decided to only tell parts of the story, the ones that made him look like the hero. "I barely got away with my life," Gillian pleaded. "Do you see? This wound on my chest is from the bear's claws." Gillain said. Again, the platoon gasped as they focused on the wound that seeped blood from Gillian's chest. Gillian swallowed hard because this was a lie. It was Vincent who struck the blow to Gillian's chest, not Koden. Little did Gillian know, but with each lie he began to tell or fib that he added to his story, a black mark began to seep up the hair of his tail. As if he dipped it in ink, like you would a pen, the black color soaked up his tail, forming a new mark.

"Well, we have ourselves a real hero then, don't we?" the King asked the crowd as he leaned forward in his saddle, resting his arms on the saddle's horn. Gillian was concerned that King Fraust did not seem to be buying his story. The crowd of Titan's however, seemed quite intrigued by it and all cheered for the Royal Pegasus. "But what I don't understand is why Vincent visited me with news that you had tricked him and had been nowhere to be found?" the King asked. Gillian didn't say anything because he could not think of a lie for it. The only answer he could think of was the truth, but he was afraid that if he spoke it, it would cost him his wings. "After all," the King started. "That is why we are here, in this clearing. Malus permitted Vincent to search the forbidden circle for you. We were all here waiting for his report, and you mean to tell me that Vincent's dead, and coincidentally, here you are? Do you see how this leaves me with a few questions…" the King said in a calm voice as if he was confidently driving home a point. Gillian gulped hard. *He's on to me.* Gillian worried.

"I can see it, your Majesty," Gillian said with a heavy heart.

"So, let's hear it! Why did you lie to Vincent?.. What are you hiding?.. And why should we believe a traitor?" the King boomed. The last question caught both Gillian and the crowd of Titans off guard. Gillian suspected the King did not trust him, but this question confirmed it. All eyes became fixed on Gillian.

"I'm not a traitor!" Gillian snapped back at the accusation, although he really was lying to the King, Gillian felt as if he had been backed into a corner and was angered by it. "Yes, I lied to Vincent, but I didn't know what else to do." Gillian started to explain.

"You should have come straight to me. But instead, you chose to lie. Why?" Malus asked.

"Well… I… umm." Gillian started. Gillian felt as if he had nowhere to run, stuck in the corner while the walls began to close in. He thought back to the beginning of the journey when the four humans first snuck past him. Although Gillian thought much differently about the humans now, in that moment, the anger he first felt became refueled inside him, causing him to place blame on them. "Four human traitors tricked me and snuck past me into the Forbidden Circle," Gillian shouted, but instantly regretted his words.

The royal platoon and the Pegasus guards began to murmur, for trespassing into the Forbidden Circle was punishable by death under the reign of King Fraust. A simple lie had now been revealed as much more of a problem than the King had thought.

"Quiet down! Quiet down!" The commander ordered the crowd.

"Why did you not inform the King?" the commander asked.

"I… I panicked. I did not know what to do." Gillian began, "I failed as a Royal Guard, but thought I could capture the humans before anyone found out and restore everything back to order on my own. As a way of proving myself…" he said as he lowered his head.

The crowd began to shout and call Gillian names.

"Traitor," said one Titan.

"Failure," said another.

"Alatum punishment! Alatum punishment!" shouted the platoon.

"Quiet!" the King shouted over the roar of his men.

The King leaned over to Malus and the two quietly exchanged words. In those moments, the clearing was quiet. Awaiting the King's orders. Finally, King Fraust repositioned himself on his horse and cleared his throat.

"Is Gillian the first of the Royal Pegasus guards to have let a creature through, into the forbidden circle?" King Fraust asked, directing his question to the crowd.

The crowd again murmured amongst themselves.

"Is he the first to have made a poor judgment call?" Malus asked. The crowd quieted.

"Answer me this, Gillian. Did you find the humans?" King Fraust asked. Both King Fraust and Malus knew it was of the utmost importance to find the four humans. To play nice with Gillian was their best option at this point in time.

"I did, Your Majesty," Gillian answered.

"And where are they now?" Malus inquired.

"During the battle with Vincent… against the Gladiator bear, of course. They escaped into the very woods behind me." Gillian said, lifting his wing and pointing into the dense forest that stood silently behind him. There was a moment of silence as the King stared at Gillian and then looked into the forest.

"What do you say I should do with these traitors when we find them?" the King finally asked, after he had collected his thoughts.

"I am not worthy of making such a judgment, Your Majesty," Gillian answered, knowing the answer the King was looking for but did not even want to imagine it happening to Andy, Eva, and Jessie. Gillian may have thrown the humans to the wolves, but he had developed a strange bond with each one of them. He would have even considered them to be friends.

"By law, such traitors must be put to death. Do you think that these humans deserve such a steep punishment?" the King questioned, leaning forward in his saddle. Gillian could feel the pressure around him, from both the Titans and fellow Pegasi, as well as the King and Malus. All these questions were becoming more aggressive in tone, and Gillian could tell that the King was trying to trap Gillian in his lie.

"You are the King, Sire. Only you can answer that question." Gillian's answer made the King relax back into his saddle, and the questioning stopped for a moment.

Suddenly, the clearing's silence broke into the rustling of leaves and small twigs snapping under pressure. Behind Gillian, just off to his right, a bush looked to have come alive. Its leaves and branches began to shake and dance as something was making its way through them. The Titans directed their spear heads at the bush, and the swordsmen in the back gripped their handles, waiting to draw their weapons on the King's command.

Then, three small humans plopped out of the bush. Andy, Eva, and Jessie's faces were full of fear. Their eyes grew wide, and frowns formed on their lips. Andy stepped forward, putting himself between the threat of the Titans and his friends, as a way of trying to protect them. Instantly, they all noticed Gillian standing beside them. Unsure of what to think, they frantically looked back and forth from the crowd of Titans and Gillian.

The King lifted his fist above his head and made a casual circular motion with his hand. Instantly, Titans circled around the three and began to grab ahold of their arms to constrain them.

"Bring them before me," the King commanded.

"Yes, Sire!" a swordsman shouted. The armor fitted Titans, drug Andy, Eva, and Jessie through the center of the King's platoon. Every direction the three friends looked, they saw weapons of war. The tips of arrows, the heads of spears, and the blades of swords all encircled them. Slowly, the crowd parted so they could be brought before the King.

Abruptly, the Titans halted. As the three lifted their eyes, they could see before them the King, staring down at them from on top of his horse, and Malus, who was a large Pegasus, that stood tall and towered over even the King's horse beside him. The King's navy garments draped down the side of his horse, and the horse had a golden harness, with braided reins. They had seen the King before in passing and during the Kingdom's celebrations, but Malus was a different story. None of the three had ever seen him, only heard stories or had seen drawings of the majestic beast. The three teenagers stared at him because he was a beautiful steed. He was larger than all the other Pegasi, and his coat was so jet black it seemed to glimmer in the sunlight. His mane was long and flowed down the side of his thick, sturdy neck, and he was well groomed. His snout, tail, and even his eyes were black. Not to mention, his large hooves remained all black. All three were almost sucked into a trance by his beauty and were mesmerized by his hooves. For some reason, they looked familiar, as if they seemed to flicker or glow. Just like the crystals Jessie and Andy held in their hands.

"Gillian! Are these the traitors you speak of?" the King questioned, peering down at the trio.

"Um," Gillian started, again, his ears drooped in sadness. He looked at the three standing before the King, wondering what he should do. Gillian wanted to protect his new friends; however, if he told the King he did not know them, more questions would arise. *If I tell the King that I have never seen them before, he will wonder where the ones I was after are, if they are not these three. Not only would that mean the King would think there are four others still in the Forbidden Circle, but then he would think I let at least seven humans sneak past me. Failing to protect the Circle against four humans instead would be better than letting in seven! I can't have them thinking that, I must be honest…* Gillian decided what he must do, for his own sake.

"Yes, Sire. These are the humans that trespassed into the Forbidden Circle." Gillian answered.

"What! You…" Jessie started in anger before a Titan hit him in the head to shut him up.

"So these three tricked you, and you allowed them to enter into the Forbidden Circle?" the King asked. Eva slowly turned her head and looked over her shoulder at Gillian. In return, Gillian could see tears forming in her eyes.

"Yes, Your Majesty," Gillian gulped, trying to swallow the ball that formed in his throat. He had to push down his emotions, although he could sense tears beginning to form in his own eyes. Gillian's heart weighed heavily because he had just turned in people he promised to help, the people he considered friends.

"And what do we have here?" the king asked as he motioned to one of the guards. The guard the King motioned to approached Jessie and ripped his brother's crystal apple from his hands.

"You give that back!" Jessie spouted. However, the Titan ignored him because Jessie's squirm was no match for the grip of the Titan that held him constrained. The Titan then moved on to Andy and took his crystal from him as well. The Titan delivered the two crystals to the King. However, something strange occurred as the Titan took Andy's crystal.

"Eagle's heart crystals," the King said with much interest in his voice. "Where did you get these?" The king's eyes were fixed on the crystals with a sort of weird desire. Much like the three teenagers' focus on Malus' hooves, the King was mesmerized by the glow of these two crystals.

However, Malus snapped the King out of his daze by stepping in front of the King's horse, forcing his horse to jolt his head up and step back. The King shook his head and then settled his horse. Subtly, he slipped the crystals into a pouch that was tied at his waist.

Malus lowered his head so his eyes were level with Andy's. The intensity of Malus was amplified in this moment, and Andy was shaken with fear. Andy felt as if Malus' stare pierced straight through him.

"*What* did you discover?" Malus said in a very deep voice, pressing into Andy's space. Andy gulped because he could tell that the huge winged beast was very serious about this question.

The three froze in fear, they knew that they had discovered so many things. Things that Malus clearly did not want them to know. *I must play dumb… If they think we know too much, they will kill us.* Andy thought to himself, pondering the world of trouble they found themselves in.

"How far into the Forbidden Circle did you go?" Malus asked again, only this time he was much more aggressive, demanding an answer. Seconds passed, and none of the trio made a peep, and it was clearly agitating Malus. Someone had to do something fast, or else Malus was going to lose his temper.

"To the edge of the Centrum's Core, oh great one." Gillian finally stammered, breaking the tense silence. Malus jolted his head back to his natural standing position and looked at Gillian. Malus squinted his eyes in a way that made it clear to Gillian that he did not believe his answer, so Gillian continued to fuel the lie.

"Once they came to the cliffs of the Centrum's core, they could no longer move at such a fast pace. With no wings, the cliffs halted their forward progress, sir. That is when I caught up with them and captured them the first time," Gillian said.

"But what about the crystals? Where did you find them?" Malus asked in anger, for he knew more about the crystals than most, and he knew that they had a connection to the Great White Eagle. Little did everyone in that clearing know, but Malus was becoming angry out of fear. A fear that stemmed from the relationship those crystals and the secrets of the Forbidden Circle had with the Great White Eagle himself.

"By the time I captured them, they already had them. I thought nothing of them, Sire." Gillian answered.

"How did you come across them?" Malus pressed, shifting his focus back to Andy and Jessie, who were the ones holding the crystals in the first place. It was clear to the boys that Malus was concerned with the crystals. The boys really didn't know much about them except that they could be used as a weapon against Messorems, and that they seemed to glow at different intensities depending on their mindsets.

"We found them in a mine shaft, one evening when we took cover from the rain." Andy gulped, hoping Malus would buy his lie. Malus looked deeply at the three traitors. For some reason, Andy felt obligated to protect the Beavers and he knew that if he told them about Richard's apple, which they found in a magical apple tree in the heart of the Uada Hollow, that Malus would know they ventured beyond the Centrum's Core and Gillian would be caught in a lie.

"There was a dreadful downpour, oh great one." Gillian weighed in on the questioning, trying to show Andy some support.

Malus paused for a moment, then he said, "If you had them captured, then how did they escape?"

"Umm, well, like I mentioned before, Sire, when Vincent found me, we landed in the meadow so I could explain all that had happened. But that is when the Gladiator Bear attacked," Gillian explained. Again, the hair of his tail became more and more black from his lies.

"Well, we have the traitors now," the King butted in trying to maintain authority in the situation.

"Indeed, we do," Malus said with suspicion in his voice. Gillian could tell that Malus was on to him, because Malus' eye never left

Gillian, even when he stepped back, allowing the King to realign himself with the all black steed.

The mood of the clearing was tense and felt by all. Not one Titan of the King's army dared say a word, or even move, for that matter.

"What do you have to say for yourselves?" the King asked the three traitorous humans. "What would your mommy and daddy have to say?" the King asked in a sarcastic manner, lifting his chin and scanning the crowd of Titans, as if to order his men to laugh at his mockery. It was an odd thing to say, but the King felt as if they were just children. The Titans obeyed, and all began to laugh at the King's weak attempt at an insult.

"Don't you dare talk about my mother that way," Jessie said as he pushed forward towards the King. Jessie's mother was a delicate subject, to say the least. Considering she had only passed away a few weeks ago, and then they saw her soul being drug into the Devil's Kettle by a Messorem, Jessie wasn't going to have it.

"Excuse me?" the King barked. Jessie's forward momentum caught the Titan holding him off guard, and he was able to slip out of his constraints. However, the commander standing beside the King reached for his sword, drawing it out and placing its blade against Jessie's throat.

"Tread carefully, boy," the commander aggressively whispered. Jessie slowly lifted his hands as a sign to show he would back down.

"Sorry, your Majesty. It's just that his mom passed away only a few weeks ago." Eva said, trying to calm the situation.

"That is quite unfortunate, but that's neither here nor there. That is no way to speak to me, your King. Do you understand me?" the king said aggressively.

"Yes, Your Majesty," Eva responded.

The king leaned in once again and peered down at Jessie, "Do you understand me?" the King voiced from above.

Jessie looked up at him with anger in his eyes, he wanted nothing more than to pull the King right off his high horse and let him have it. However, before Jessie's emotions got the best of him, Andy's bony elbow pierced his side. Jessie looked at Andy, and Andy began to nod aggressively, telling Jessie to respond respectfully.

"Yes, I understand you." Jessie begrudgingly said. The King leaned back and raised one eyebrow. Then Andy's elbow struck a second blow.

"Your Majesty," Jessie coughed out against his will.

"Very well then," the King said, settling the matter. The King looked over to Malus, who still had his eyes glued to Gillian. "What shall we do with these treasonous pests?" the King asked Malus.

"I have many more questions that I must find answers for, but until then, let us hold them in the dungeons of Regnum," Malus announced to the crowd of Titans. Instantly, the guards around the three comrades tightened their grips. Before any of them could fight to break free, they found themselves with handcuffs latched around their wrists and ankle cuff links chained around their ankles.

"Off to Regnum!" the commander ordered, and all the Titans fell into a perfect row of three. Leaving Andy, Eva, and Jessie in the center of the pack with no escape in sight.

As they began to leave the clearing, two Pegasus guards led the way, followed by the King, Malus, and the parade of Titans. The other three Pegasi brought up the rear. Gillian remained in the clearing. He stood there brokenhearted, unable to collect his bearings on what had really happened. Then suddenly, he heard a shout from the front of the brigade.

"Good work, Gillian. On capturing the traitors. If Vincent had lived to see it, he would have been proud." Malus shouted over his shoulder as he rounded the first bend out of the clearing.

An array of emotions flooded Gillian. *Malus is proud of me? He was just drilling me with questions, I could tell he didn't believe me. I don't understand. Why am I not chained up like my friends? Oh, my friends. What have I done? What will happen to them? All this time, I thought they were the traitors, yet here I am, betraying Andy, Eva, and Jessie.* Gillian's ears drooped at these thoughts. His head hung low with guilt. He watched as the parade of Titans marched on.

Row by row, the platoon of Titans slipped away down the windy road that led to Regnum. Then his human friends reached the bend that would take them out of sight. As they rounded the bend, Gillian could see Eva looking back at him with tears in her eyes.

After a few moments, Gillian was left alone in the clearing. The clanking of the Titan's armor faded into a whisper, and the rustling of the leaves became the dominant sound.

"What have I done?" Gillian whispered to himself and he broke out into tears. With his head held low, the tears streamed down his nose and dripped into the dirt beneath him. He slowly lifted his head and somberly walked home to Regnum.

Chapter 3
Crusade Parade

The walk home was long. The dirt road, which used to be hard-packed, had been broken into soft, loose sand by the cavalcade of King's men. The road wasn't a difficult trek, especially in consideration of the journey they had all taken to the Devil's Kettle; it only gradually lifted in elevation. The road weaved through the forest until the forest halted, and the landscape opened into the fields of the Regnum farmsteads. A combination of fields and pastures spread out before them, and the dirt road straightened out and aimed directly at the castle. They passed many farms where animals, such as cows, goats, sheep, and other animals good for eating, were raised. (Not intellectual animals, of course, only those listed in the scrolls as okay to eat.)

Slowly, the beautiful countryside faded into the slums of Regnum. The grass was trampled down here into a muddy mess, and stray dogs and cats wandered into filthy alleyways. As they were forced forward by the Royal Cavalry, Andy and Jessie could see the orphanage as they passed by it. All of the other children could be seen peering out from behind the curtain-filled windows, and dear old Mrs. Rosewood, the orphanage caretaker, was standing outside the front door holding the youngest orphan in her arms. A tear could be seen on her cheek, and her eyes were filled with fearful confusion. First of all, because two children under her care were being escorted by the Titans, and secondly, because Richard, Jesse's younger brother, was nowhere to be seen. The boys glanced at Mrs. Rosewood and then looked down at their feet in guilt, for they felt that they had let her down, even after all the kindness she had shown them.

With each step they trudged, the gravity of their situation began to pull harder at their feet. The simple walk became more difficult the further they marched. Not because the terrain became uneven or rocky, but because all eyes in Regnum fell upon them. They were in deep trouble, and the whole world knew it.

The cuffs around their ankles and wrists now seemed to burn as they dug into their skin; each tug at their cuffs the Titans made seemed to cut deeper. Yet every time they looked down, there was no blood, just redness of the skin.

"Gillian did this," Andy whispered with a spark of anger.

"Don't blame him," Jessie barked at Andy, defending his winged friend. "If anyone is to blame, it's the Great White Eagle," Jessie whispered.

"How could you say that!" Eva cried out.

Her voice was portrayed louder than she anticipated because one of the Titans turned and ordered her to 'Shut up, and keep quiet.'

Eva gave the guard a deep glare, but obeyed his command. Soon he turned back forwards and she began to whisper softly.

"How can you blame the Great White Eagle? He protected us in the Uada Hollow, and he set us off on this journey to discover the secrets of the Devil's Kettle. Without him, we would have died out there," Eva explained.

"Yeah, and look at us now. Richard *did* die, and we will soon," Jessie said in disgust.

"The Great White Eagle wouldn't have sent us on this journey just to die," Eva said, then she began to question it all. *Would he?* She thought to herself. She felt sick for even thinking it, but after all, Richard had died.

"Jessie, you never *had* to come! The Great White Eagle told Eva to go to the Kettle, and I could read her dreams. I told you in the Hollow that it was your choice to come, not mine, not the Great White Eagle's, but yours. Don't blame me or anyone else for that matter for what happened in the Forbidden Circle. But in the clearing, that Pegasus pal of yours betrayed us!" Andy unloaded on Jessie.

"Oh, get lost! I wish I never met you." Jessie said. Tragically, there was anger and hurt in both Andy and Jessie's hearts, but after what they had been through, who could blame them? As for Eva, she felt defeated for the first time since they began this journey, and she felt unsure of everything. The air filled with silence as they marched the rest of the way to the castle.

The cavalcade brought them through the slums of Regnum and into the village on the outskirts of the castle. The school, the library, and even the street on which Eva lived. Here, the streets were still dirt, but cleaner. There were green grass-filled yards, sharp white picket fences decorating the homes, and there was even an open field where the townsmen kept the grass trimmed so all the kids could play after their schooling and lessons. It was really home to all of them in a way. However, today was different. Normally, it was a cheery place, full of buzzing voices and laughter, as well as kids running through the streets and playing games in the open field. Not today. Today, the lights were low in the houses, the streets were crowded with people who looked concerned, and there was not a child in sight. Their parents made them stay indoors on this grim day. Andy, Eva, and Jessie did not realize this, but this march signified the loss of their old life and the beginning of their future.

Eva's eyes lifted with some hope as they approached her home. She hoped dearly to see her parents. She knew they would be disappointed in her, but she didn't care; she just wanted to see them one last time. The law of King Fraust says anyone who trespasses into the Forbidden Circle may be punished by death. She feared that fate, but the King was a ruthless man; it would be silly to think he would make an exception for a peasant like herself. *If I could see them just one last time.* She hoped. However, her parents were not there. No peeking eyes from their window, nor were they standing next to the street. A cold rush of fear flooded her body like a sudden plunge into the open river on a cold winter's day. *Where are my parents?* She panicked. *Oh, please, I hope the King has not harmed them, not because of me!*

Her pace slowed in hopes that maybe her parents were still in the house and would come out any second, but then a Titan yanked at her cuffs, washing her mind of sorrow and reminding her of the pain the cuffs inflicted on her wrists.

"Keep moving!" he ordered.

The only thing that Eva could do now was hope in the Great White Eagle, that he would have a dream to explain it all and what to do next. *Great White Eagle, if you can hear me, protect my parents. Help us! Please!* She begged silently.

Through the Village they passed, until they stood before the grand gate of the Castle. The gate was a large wooden door that was opened by two chains that, when pulled on, would lift the gate. Through a narrow slot, the gate rose above the archway, into the fortified wall of the castle, allowing travel beneath it. The rest of the castle was protected by a mighty wall that consisted of large stones stacked and glued together by mortar. On both sides of the castle gate, within the outer wall, watch towers stood with Titans posted on watch. The Kingdom's banner flapped in the wind from poles that pointed to the sky out of the roof of the towers. If you looked either left or right, at the far corners of this fortified wall, two other towers posted guard as well, protecting the East and West sides of the castle.

The platoon was met by two guardians of the gate. One Titan and one Pegasus. They each bowed low before the King and Malus. "Arise, open the gate." King Fraust said. With that, they both stood up, and the Titan hollered up to the Titans in the lookout towers.

"Lift the gate. Make way for the King!" he shouted. It was from those towers that pulleys were in place to open the door. The two Titans cranked on wheels that rattled the chains tightly. Slowly, the door began to creak open.

For a moment, the three were excited. None of them had ever seen the inside of the Castle walls before, as peasants were prohibited from visiting. With anticipation, they gazed as the opening beneath the door grew larger and they could see into the courtyard. To their surprise, the ground of the courtyard was not dirt but instead a cobblestone floor. As they crossed the threshold of the gate, they entered into the square courtyard, which was busy with servants and

Titans. At the center of the courtyard, a beautiful fountain with flowers strategically placed around its brim. The fountain shot water high into the air, and it sprinkled back down into the pool, rippling the pool surface. Among the chatter of servants and Titans, the fountain babbled a calming tune.

As they peered around, they noticed that in each corner of the courtyard, there were large fruit trees planted in giant pots, and their branches were trimmed into perfect circles. There was an abundance of fruit hanging on them, and several servant girls were picking the brightest colored ones and placing them into wicker baskets. There was plenty of space on all sides of the fountain. Beyond the fountain was the rest of the Castle. It stood tall and proud as columns supported a large balcony that overlooked the courtyard and all of Regnum. The columns and the railing of the balcony were made of beautiful white quartz, carved to perfection. Directly beneath the balcony, there was a wooden stage. Which gave all three of the teenagers the creeps. It was not clean like the rest of the courtyard, and a great big battle ax was wedged into a stump on the platform. On both sides of the stage, there were archways. Between the passing servants, they could see a shallow hallway in both directions that led into a large open room. *That must be the ballroom!* Eva thought. There was also an archway to the far left where it looked like stairs climbed up into the castle.

Again, their attention was drawn back to the courtyard. It looked like the servants were getting ready for something big and important. Beautifully colored banners were being rolled out and hung over the railing of the balcony, and flowers of all sorts were being arranged throughout the courtyard.

The castle walls wrapped around the courtyard and then lined the castle. A covered walkway was set on both sides of the castle, which is where servants would appear and disappear around the castle's corners. Then a peculiar-looking man walked their way. He had a large belly, a filthy white long-sleeved shirt, brown pants, and suspenders on. When he walked, he waddled, and his belly led the way. His bottom jaw was large, and he had a clear overbite. His lower lip stuck out like a child pouting, and he had a frayed mustache. Thin hair on his head and thick, grubby fingers.

"Take these prisoners to the dungeons!" the King ordered as the ugly fellow stopped before them. The commander of the platoon helped the King off his horse, and as his feet hit the ground, the bristles of his long cloak bounced to the ground behind him. Then a young stable boy ran up from the far right side of the courtyard and grabbed the reins of the King's horse. He bowed to the King and then walked the horse to the covered walkway on the right side of the castle.

"Yes, your majesty!" the large-framed dungeon keeper responded. They both bowed and then abrasively took over control of Andy, Eva, and Jessie. Considering his appearance, they were all surprised at the man's strength. Without any issues, he had a hold of all three of them at the same time.

The King nodded his head, then turned to his Titans. "At ease," the King announced. Suddenly, all the Titans bowed and then turned to go their own way, dispersing in various directions.

"Commander," the King said. The commander of the crusade halted in his tracks.

"Yes, Sire?" the commander asked, as he turned and faced the King.

"Fetch my brother, will you? It's been three days," the King ordered.

"Of course, your majesty," the commander responded. He bowed and ran off.

Then, without warning, Andy, Eva, and Jessie were being tugged toward the left walkway by the dungeon keeper.

"Simon!" The king shouted to the Dungeon keeper. The old oaf stopped, and while facing away from the King, Andy caught him rolling his eyes. However, when he turned to face the King, it was all smiles.

"Make sure they are fed and cleaned up. They have a visitor," the king ordered.

"Yes, your majesty," Simon responded. The old oaf then tugged on their cuffs and directed them to the opposite side of the courtyard. Obviously, their plans had been changed. *I wonder who would be here to see us? We haven't even been prisoners for five minutes yet.* Andy thought. It was odd, to say the least, that someone was here waiting for them.

They were led past the stage and to the covered walkway that hugged the right side of the castle. The King's horse must have left some apples on the ground, because a servant boy was sweeping up the fresh horse apples into a pan. About halfway along the side of the castle, an archway in the great outer wall appeared on their right.

A dirt path widened out into a yard. Patches of grass grew along the buildings and horse posts. It was clear to the three of them that this was the horse stables. Stable boys were leading horses this way and that. Some horses were getting washed, fed, or brushed. One horse off to the left was in a round pen, where the ground was broken and soft sand. The boy had a whip and was running the horse in a circle. At the center of the stable was a well. Green grass stood vibrantly, surrounding the stone well. In addition, three hitching posts for horses to be tied off on were arranged around the well. Beyond that was a large, long building. It was helpful that many horses were being led in and out of it, so that Andy, Eva, and Jessie knew it was the stable barn.

The stable was an elegant barn, painted white to match the castle, and had a straw roof. The three would have liked to explore the stable yard a bit more, but being prisoners put a stop to that.

"Here! Clean yourselves up." Simon ordered as he led them to the water well. At the well, there was a bucket, which had two holes near the brim where a rope was tied to for servants to fetch water. There was also a wooden horse trough with flakes of hay floating around in the water for horses to drink from.

"With what? I'm not bathing in that!" Eva shrieked, looking down at the horse trough.

Simon looked at the young girl, rolled his eyes, and shouted to one of the stable boys.

"Hey, you, come here," Simon shouted.

"Yes, sir?" the boy said nervously. Although a dungeon keeper earned very little respect in regards to the Kingdom's hierarchy, they were cruel, merciless humans, and most of the servants feared their temper.

"These prisoners need something to wash with," Simon said.

"Shall I fetch them a washcloth, sir?" the boy asked.

"No, this will do!" Simon shouted as he reached out and ripped the boy's shirt off his body. Then proceeded to tear it into shreds, handing a piece to each one: Andy, Eva, and Jessie. Simon laughed abruptly at his bully move. For an ugly oaf, he sure was amused by himself.

You could tell the stable boy was beyond embarrassed, but he never said a word. He just stood there, red in the face, waiting for Simon to tell him what to do.

"There you go, little miss princess," Simon said to Eva, mocking her for being ungrateful to even get a bath in the first place.

"Boy, go get a servant girl so she can feed these traitors and bring them some new clothing. By the king's orders." Simon announced. The boy bowed and ran off back into the castle's walls and out of sight.

"Well, go ahead, get cleaned up," Simon ordered.

"Umm, do you think you could give us some privacy? I am a lady after all…" Eva asked Simon softly.

"Echem, Oh yes, of course." Simon coughed, almost slightly embarrassed. He turned and moved over towards the archway near the castle. *Apparently, he has some manners.* Eva thought.

Andy threw the bucket into the well, and the bucket tugged at the coiled rope until SPLOOSH! The bucket slapped the water's surface. Then Andy began to haul up the bucket of fresh water. Once the bucket could be reached, Jessie leaned down and hoisted it up until it could be placed on the well's edge. They weren't excited about using the poor boy's shirt for a quick wash, however, they didn't know the next time they would get a bath would be, so they each dipped the stable boy's ripped shirt into the bucket.

"This is so weird. Using someone's shirt as a washcloth," Andy said.

"It's just downright wrong, that poor boy," Eva said, thinking about how embarrassed that boy must have been.

The three washed up their faces and arms as best they could. But with their hands still being tied up by the cuffs, it was next to impossible to get a really good washing done.

"How are we to wash up with our hands bound like this? We can't even reach our backsides." Andy grumbled to Simon.

"Backsides? Why would you wash your back?" Simon questioned as he strolled back over to the three.

"Because.. Just like your front side, our backsides get dirty too?" Eva questioned the oaf in shock that anyone would even ask such a silly question.

"By the smell of it, he hasn't washed in ages," Jessie said under his breath, while waving his hand in front of his nose.

"What did you say?" Simon squalled at Jessie.

"I said you stink! You big buffalo!" Jessie yelled, being short-tempered.

"You're gonna watch your mouth!" Simon ordered as he raised his hand high into the air to strike Jessie. However, in the nick of time, a soft voice of a servant girl spoke up from behind Simon.

"There is no need for that, Simon. I will take it from here. If you could please excuse us," she ordered. Simon turned to look at the girl, hung his head low, and walked away.

When Simon moved over, Jessie could see the servant girl, and to his surprise, she was the most beautiful girl he had ever seen. Her golden blonde hair with soft curls hung down to her shoulders. She had big blue eyes that looked like the sky, and a smile that could soften the hardest of hearts. Her pale skin was painted with sun-kissed freckles, and her cheeks were rosy red from the sun. She wore nothing fancy. Just a soft green dress that hung to the ground, and a white apron around her waist. She was carrying a woven grass basket with a few loaves of bread and apples. Jessie marveled at the girl, whose soft voice had the power to order the big oaf around.

Suddenly, at her beautiful sight, Jessie felt embarrassed that he had even smarted off to Simon in the first place, for he feared that she wouldn't think it was very gentlemanly.

"Hello," the girl said as she did a small curtsy. "My name is Isabell, but you can call me Izzy," she said.

"Hi!" Jessie blabbered, and as if he couldn't control himself, he stepped in front of the other two, putting out his hand. "My name is Jessie, but you could call me Jess... I mean, maybe just call me Jessie." He said with a giant, awkward grin on his face. He was so flabbergasted by her beauty that he lost all sense of what he was trying to say. His golden brown skin slowly grew redder by the second. Andy smacked his palm into his forehead, he couldn't believe how awkward Jessie was being in front of this total stranger.

Isabell giggled a soft laugh and her rosy cheeks blushed even more than before. She put her hand in his, and they shook. Which was something that had never happened to Isabell before. Although she was held in high regard by all the servants and many of the Titans, she had always been just a servant, a slave really. Jessie was the first stranger to show her respect instead of demand.

"Anyway, I have brought you some bread, it's not much, but it will do," she said. "And my friends here have brought you some fresh clothing," she motioned to the two girls standing behind her to step forward so they could present the clothing.

"Eat what you please, then I will show you to a proper washroom," Isabell said with a smile. "Oh, and here are some cups for water." She removed a white cloth from the basket and exposed three clay mugs.

The three began to devour the bread. Andy dumped out the water that they had used to clean themselves up with and sent the bucket back down for fresh drinking water. Once it was brought back to the brim of the well, each dipped their cups in. The water was so refreshing and crisp to their lips.

Chapter 4
Interpretation

Meanwhile, the King, Timothy Fraust, had made his way back to his chambers and was awaiting the arrival of his brother. Timothy had much to ponder, for the dream he had days ago left chills in his bones, and news of the three traitors concerned him greatly. Not only did those thoughts weigh heavily, but the death of Vincent would surely cause waves amongst the Royal guards. Timothy removed his cloak and began pacing his room, back and forth, until a knock came at the door.

"Who is it?" Timothy asked.

"Your mistress," a man's voice said sarcastically from behind the door.

"Brother?" Timothy questioned.

"Obviously," the King's brother said as he pushed open the door, bringing him into the King's chamber.

"Why must you always disturb my slumbers?" the King's brother asked.

"Do you not see the sun setting? It is quite late for a nap, and much too early for a night's rest." Timothy stated.

"It is quite dark in my chambers, you know that," the brother said.

Timothy let out an obnoxious scoff. "Of course it is! Poor you! I wish you would grow up and get over yourself!" Timothy blurted out.

"Over myself? My hate is fueled by more than the things I have done! Your actions are unforgivable," the brother said.

Timothy turned away and paced towards the doors that led to the balcony, and under his breath, hoping his brother would not hear him, he mumbled to himself: "I should have killed you the night I killed King Keizer."

Then, to Timothy's surprise, his brother had heard him. "I wish you would have," he said.

Timothy turned and looked at him sharply, "Enough chatter, what did my dream mean?" the King demanded, losing his patience. He was angry now and was growing tired of his brother's attitude, not to mention his constant sulking. The King had made peace with the things they did to become rulers over the land, and wished his brother would too. Many times, he could have killed his brother but spared him, and his brother had never been grateful for the hospitality he had given him. *We are Kings! Royalty over Regnum and significant rulers in all the land. What more could he want?* The King thought to himself.

It was clear the two didn't see eye to eye and possibly never would. Although the King had put aside his guilt and basked in the power of being King, his brother could not. Hate and anger wallowed up inside of him, and he could barely live with the things he and his brother had done, and he despised his brother for being so guiltless about it all.

Their relationship was complicated, to say the least. Timothy had become corrupt, ruthless, and cold. He was harsh to servants, willing to put to death anyone for the sake of his name, and downright untrustworthy. Not to mention, it was obvious that the King only kept his brother alive because he was a Lector. If it wasn't for that, the King would have had his brother killed years ago. Since Timothy Fraust was a Somniator, he needed someone he could count on to translate his dreams, and for the time being, his brother would have to do.

"Your dream… is bad news." Timothy's brother started.

Timothy felt his heart sink, but held his composition, for he suspected it meant something horrible from the start. "Go on," Timothy ordered his brother.

"You said in your dream that the Great White Eagle mended together an ax. One whose handle was made of a tree, planted by someone you felt familiar with?" Timothy's brother asked.

"That is correct," The King responded with a nod.

"And you said the head of the ax ended up being made of gold?"

"Yes, that is what I said."

"And the Great White Eagle used the ax to cut down a mighty oak tree?"

"Yes, yes, yes! Now what does it mean!" Timothy barked, losing his temper.

"You are the mighty oak tree, brother."

The King gulped, for no foe has ever threatened his life and lived to tell about it. However, the Great White Eagle was a different story. Timothy knew how powerful the Great White Eagle was, and he knew that he had betrayed the Great White Eagle to serve Malus. Timothy shivered in fear at the thought of the Great White Eagle returning from his long hiatus and seeking vengeance on him. "Who will the Great White Eagle use to cut down…" - he gulped again - "Me?" Timothy whispered. His confident tone had shrunk into a soft quiver.

"The Great White Eagle, he will be your end." Timothy's brother explained. "The Great White Eagle will use the ax himself. So my brother, I would suggest figuring out who the ax represents." By this time, Timothy's brother had made himself comfortable on the chair where he had sat three nights before. He crossed his legs, sank into the chair, and extended his arms outward in both directions along the back of the chair's rest.

"Do you know?" Timothy asked.

"Well, the couple in your dream must be someone we know, that's why they felt familiar to you. And the Furlope tree is their offspring. The handle of the ax will be that child."

"Do you think…" Timothy began.

"Yes, I would have to guess it would be someone from our adventure to the Devil's Kettle."

"You don't have any heirs, do you?" Timothy asked his brother, knowing he had not been the most behaved man.

"I was about to ask you the same thing." Timothy's brother said with a chuckle.

"Not that I know of," Timothy said.

"Well, Emma never made it out of the Uada Hollows…" the King's brother began, but both brothers paused as they remembered the dreadful night. The two of them, along with three friends, had found themselves in the heart of the Uada Hollow on a stormy night. The Messorems had tricked them all, chained them up, and drugged them through the hollow. Before any one of them could come to their senses, it was too late for their friend Emma, who was dragged under the hollow and never seen again. Even though the King's heart had hardened over the years, that memory still brought tears to his eyes.

"Echem… Anyways!" the King said, trying to get them back on track.

"Yeah… right, that leaves Peter and Rachael."

"Well, we know it's not Peter or his son. Cause…Well, you know…" Timothy said, looking away from his brother. "That only leaves Rachael." Timothy began to slowly walk towards the door. As he opened it, he stepped out into the hallway, turned to his right, and walked all the way down to the exterior wall of the Castle, where there was a large window. Timothy's brother followed closely behind.

"That's right, Rachael and her husband did have a kid years ago," Timothy's brother said.

"Isn't it interesting?" Timothy asked.

"What?"

"Three days after my dream, three teenagers are found exiting the Forbidden Circle. And one of them happens to be Rachael Huntsberg's daughter?" Timothy says, as he leaned against the wall and peered out the window, pointing to Eva, who was eating bread by the well near the stables.

"She looks just like Rachael did." Timothy's brother said, reminiscing about their younger years.

The two brothers stood in the window frame and watched as the three friends huddled together in fear and confusion. Andy and Eva could be seen talking, and Jessie focused his attention on the servant girl Isabell. Although the King could not hear their conversation, he only assumed it was talk on how to escape. That's what he would have been talking about. In fact, he and his friends had been in that exact same predicament years before, and that was the only thing they talked about. They watched as Isabell led the three out of the stable yard under the covered walkway, out of their sight.

"What about the Gold Ax head?" Timothy asked as he turned once again to his brother.

"Well…I'm unsure. Could it be something of value to be used to assist the girl? Maybe a weapon of some sort." Timothy's brother said with hesitation in his voice.

"Like these?" The king reached into the pouch on his hip and pulled out Andy and Jessie's crystals.

"Where did you get those?" Timothy's brother gasped. "I haven't seen an Eagle's Heart since," he gulped, "our very own journey."

In one hand, Timothy held the crystal apple, and with the other hand, he grasped Andy's icicle-shaped crystal. As the King's eyes gazed upon them, they flickered black, yet still held a glow in the King's palms.

"Something like this has the greatest value in all the world, more value than gold! Plus, we know they work against Messorems. There is a power within these, a power that no one has ever been able to harness, or understand, for that matter." Timothy said as his eyes pierced the crystals, and his heart filled with greed.

"It very well could be. That the girl will use an Eagle's Heart crystal to… well, you know." However, the King's brother was unsure. He knew the gold blade of the ax meant something significant, but he could not put a finger on it. *Is it something of value? Something of power? Or possibly someone of royalty?* He thought.

"Well, it doesn't matter what the golden ax head is; my solution is simple." The King said.

"What! Brother! You can't, she's only a child." Timothy's brother said. At this point, the King began walking back to his chambers, and his brother pleaded behind him.

"She threatens my reign! I kill her and destroy these crystals, and the threat to me and my kingdom is gone." Timothy said as he entered his room. His brother attempted to follow him, but King Fraust turned abruptly and blocked the doorway.

"There has to be another way! Maybe I misinterpreted the dream, maybe I was wrong about her," the brother pleaded.

"You have yet to be wrong, which is the only reason you're still alive. The girl dies tomorrow night," the King ordered as he slammed the door in his brother's face.

Chapter 5
Wishing Well

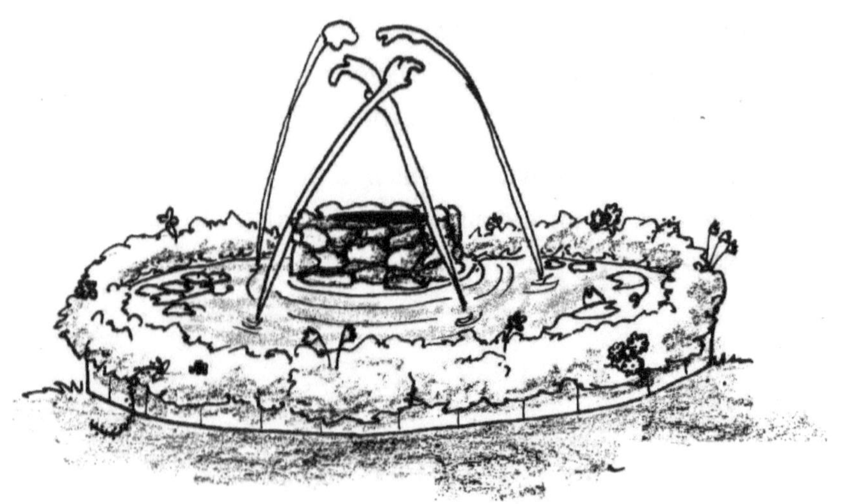

Gillian gazed at the castle gate as it lifted into the air. Normally, he entered the castle over the fortified wall by flying. It was a rare occasion that he entered through the gate, and it was usually for an exciting reason, one with honor. However, this was not one of those exciting times. Instead, he hung his head low in grief and followed the crusade of King's Titans into the courtyard. His limbs and wings were exhausted from the three days of adventure, but it wasn't the exhaustion that weighed down on him. It was the shame and guilt that caused him the most trouble. It was only days ago that life was careless for Gillian. He served the King and Malus proudly with no doubt in his mind that what he was doing was noble indeed. His hide was white, with only a few specks of black hair around his hooves, and he was so blissfully ignorant that he dreamed of earning his black markings and hoped to one day be praised as a noble steed by the other Pegasi guards. However, the last three days had revealed so many things that all those innocent dreams had melted away, and what seemed like a nightmare had taken their place. Over those three days, he began to earn his *noble marks*, the ones he had previously dreamed about. Yet, with every stroke of black that painted his hide, he felt more sick to his stomach. *Where is my joy and pride in these markings?* Gillian questioned. If he looked at his reflection now, he would hardly be able to recognise himself. A black slash across his face, a blob smeared on his side under his wing, and the black stains that climbed his legs and tail. *Who have I become? What have I done to earn these marks? I used to think they were to be praised. But for what? Lying? Anger? Betraying those closest to me? This can't be right.* He worried deeply.

Gillian lingered far behind the others as they funneled into the courtyard, arriving home from their mission. He wished he could hide and avoid everyone. So when King Fraust gave the command for them to disperse, Gillian rushed to the Pegasi Stable to hide in his own straw-stuffed bed.

Panic flooded over Gillian because he knew all his friends would have so many questions about what he had gone through and how he had earned his marks. *If I could just get to my stable. Out of sight, out of mind.* He thought. However, his attempt was in vain. As soon as he rounded the corner into the stable yard, he was met by a small group of Pegasi. Expecting to get hammered with questions, Gillian devised a small plan. *Keep it simple; if it gets too complicated, I am bound to get caught in my own expanding lie.* However, to his surprise, before he was even given a chance to explain himself, things began to change. Instead of being greeted by a hundred questions, Gillian was met with an explosion of praise. This shocking occurrence lifted Gillian's spirits. As he walked towards his stable, his steps became lighter because the praises and cheers seemed to wash his guilt away. Never before had he received such attention and soaked up every second of it.

"It's Gillian!" a Pegasus guard shouted.

"The hero, Gillian, has returned!" another announced.

"How did you find the courage to race into the Forbidden Circle and battle a Gladiator bear?" a young Pegasus asked.

Gillian was taken aback by the many positive reactions. As he walked along, three older Pagesi stood side by side, none of them said a word, but instead nodded in approval. This silent salute was almost better than the verbal praises themselves. A sign of respect and approval.

"Look at the noble markings he has earned!" a voice shouted from afar.

"It takes years to earn that many, and he did it in a matter of days!" another voice praised Gillian.

Gillian's guilt faded away with each praise he received. The thoughts of all the things he had done wrong slipped out of his mind, and thoughts of the things he did well flooded in. Pride in himself became prominent. Each compliment he received seemed to fill his chest with air until his chest was puffed up like a balloon. No longer did his head hang low or his ears droop, but instead he held his head high and mighty.

"How did you do it?"

"Tell us!"

"Please, Gillian!"

A herd of Pegasus ponies surrounded Gillian, begging him to tell the story of his journey. Gillian whined and snorted with excitement right alongside them. He spun around and pranced with the younglings.

"Younglings, in due time!" a deep voice hushed the crowd. Malus was standing at the gate of the stables and smiled at the young Pegasi. "Gillian has had a long journey and must get some rest. He will have plenty of time to tell you all his story tomorrow. Until then, run along, please," the young Pegasi bowed to Malus and trotted off into the pastures to play. The rest of the Pegasi patted Gillian on the back with their wings and gave him a quick 'Good job' of some sort as they went back to what they were doing.

"Gillian, may I have a word?" Malus asked.

"Yes, of course, sire!" Gillian said, almost forgetting all of the horrible things he had thought about Malus just a couple hours before.

Malus led Gillian back to the courtyard in front of the castle. Then, through the archway nearest the west covered walkway, where there were stairs that brought them to the second floor within the castle. Once they reached the top of the stairs, the castle opened up. They found themselves on a mezzanine (indoor balcony) that overlooked the castle's ballroom. This particular mezzanine bordered three sides of the ballroom, leaving the East wall open for windows, banners, and paintings. The East wall contained just that and was filled with gorgeous details. Great images were carved into the stone, and deep red colored banners hung with golden tassels. Unbelievable paintings with incredible detail hung as well. A row of large windows sat at the balcony level. From the ballroom floor below, only the clouds passing by could be seen. However, from the Mezzanine, Gillian could peer out and see the Originum Mountain Range (the mountains in between the No Man's Land Mountains of Regnum and the Nani Mountains of Borrian).

Malus' room was on the north side of the ballroom on the second floor, while King Fraust's chambers were on the south side, also on the second floor. Before the King's chambers, a beautiful spread of stairs stepped down to the ballroom below, connecting both levels of the castle. Gillian could also see that on the opposite side of those stairs, the King's throne rested beneath the mezzanine overlooking the ballroom.

While walking to Malus' room, a white quartz railing rested on Gillian's right, and the black and white checkered floor of the ballroom waited below. On his left, however, the walls were covered in red velvet, decorated with beautiful paintings from all over the kingdom. Each tribe was represented in thick golden frames that hung on the wall. Paintings of Elves, Centaurs, Dwarves, Mankind, Pegasi, and even the Beasts of Terribbia were seen captured by the brilliant colors and brush strokes. The floor, a maroon colored carpet, was spongy and soft.

They rounded the far side of the mezzanine and found themselves standing before Malus' chamber door. Malus stepped off to the side and extended his shiny black wing, as if to tell Gillian to go through the door first.

Gillian lowered his head, as a way of humbling himself before Malus, and pushed open the door with his front hoof.

Once inside, Gillian peered around the room. He had never been in Malus' chambers before, because for the longest time, he was never worthy or trusted enough. *Maybe my journey has earned me just that? If Malus only knew how much I lied, I wouldn't be here at all.* Gillian thought.

Along one wall was a series of feeding troughs. Each filled with a different grain. Oats, corn, soybeans, and even some Gillian didn't recognize. He was amazed at the many options Malus had. This was because Gillian and the other Royal guards only received special grains like these during important occasions. Like the Wing Year or the Feast of Fire, to name a few.

One of the room's corners had a large rack with hay stacked to the ceiling, and in another, there was straw spread out along the floor where Malus slept.

However, even with the impressive setup Malus had in his chambers, Gillian's focus was stolen by the massive glass window on the back wall. From there, Gillian could see the royal garden and the No Man's Land Mountains that were raised up far on the horizon. The royal garden itself was literally a maze. Walkways twisted and turned, splitting into different directions, some even finding dead ends. Each walkway was lined with tall square bushes, and although from Gillian's vantage point, he could see all the pathways, these tall bushes would prohibit any creature consumed within the maze from seeing any other paths except for the one they were on. Gillian traced each path, trying to find a way out of the maze, but each attempt was met with the same outcome. It always brought him to a dead end or to the center of the maze. Each time he tried to escape the maze with his eyes, the pathways led him to one of four archways that opened into the center of the maze. These gorgeous arches were overtaken by manicured vines that had grown up into a leafy canopy with red flowers poking out here and there. Each archway was designed to bring those who entered the maze directly to the maze's heart.

The heart of the maze was marked by a beautiful well, built of stone. This masterpiece was of delicate design. The well was the focal point, however, there was much going on within this hidden gem. Bordering the stone well was a circular pond with four jets shooting streams of water high into the air. Water lilies with yellow blossoms on their pads floated around the outside of this pond. Like the well itself, the edge of the pond was formed by stones that corralled the pond's water, holding it at bay. On top of this border, there was a major arrangement of flowers. Similar to the one found in the courtyard at the front of the castle. It looked so peaceful and calm. The grass was freshly manicured, and Gillian imagined lying in the grass for hours, soaking in the sun, listening to the babble of the four jets trickling into the pond.

Gillian's eyes rose from the maze to far beyond. The ground sloped upwards, and the green grasses faded into rocky grays and browns. There were few trees, but it still remained a magnificent sight. For something as harsh as the No Man's Land Mountains, its beauty was indescribable. His eyes peered at the base of the mountains, but from there the cliffs rose until the mountains formed peaks. Snow covered the pointy tops of the mountain like stocking hats on children in the cold winter months.

"Do you like the view?" Malus asked.

"Yes, of course! It is beautiful. Your chambers are wonderful as well, Your Majesty." Gillian responded without taking his eyes off the gorgeous pillars of rock.

"Please, call me Malus, you've earned it."

"Yes, Sire, I mean Malus," Gillian fumbled out.

"Do you know what they call that mountain range?" Malus asked as he slowly walked to Gillian's side.

"I do, it's called the No Man's Land Mountains," Gillian said proudly for knowing it.

"That is correct," Malus began, "You see, the peaks of No Man's Lands are the highest in all the land and because of the cold snowy mountain caps and harsh weather conditions of the mountain range the existence of life up there has been squandered," Malus informed the young Pegasus. Gillian's hide shivered at the thought of such cold conditions.

"And isn't the maze just as magnificent?" Malus said, directing Gillian's gaze back to the maze just behind the castle. "Did you know that some believe the well in the center is a wishing well?"

"Really?" Gillian asked as his eyes widened with excitement, and he fixed his gaze on the stone well.

"Others believe it only looks like a well, but is instead a magical pot of gold. Some even believe it's a chest of the King's glory. And some think it's a place to find love." Malus explained. Gillian, for the first time, broke his stare and looked at Malus. "However, no matter what it *really* is, every creature dreamed it would fulfill their greatest desire." Malus continued to talk, and Gillian just listened. He soaked up every word that came from Malus' mouth. The fact that he was in Malus' chambers at all was amazing, but the way Malus was talking to him made Gillian feel important. As if he and Malus had a bond that no one else had. "You see, this castle was built by the first ever peacekeeper." Malus continued. "This peacekeeper, Henry Adams, and his wife settled here in Regnum, and he built this beautiful castle. One day, Henry was admiring his work on the castle, but something was missing. Something was needed to really make it feel like home."

"Like a fresh straw bed?" Gillian asked innocently while thinking of what he thought made a good home.

"You could say that, but at first, Henry couldn't figure out what was missing. But, after he thought long and hard, he realized what it was. It was what he missed most about his old home, his garden. That's when he built this maze. He laid all the pathways with flat stone, planted the shrubs and flowers, and pieced together the wishing well at the heart of it." Malus said as he pointed his nose to the maze.

"You said he had an old home? Where was Henry from?" Gillian questioned.

"That is not important." Malus snapped rather quickly at the inquiring Pegasus. Gillian looked back at the maze. Yet, he still could not figure out how to escape the maze.

"This Henry you speak of does not seem too bright," Gillian said while still being confused about the maze. He looked and looked and looked for a way out of the maze and could never find one. Every path led him to the center of it. After always failing, Gillian had convinced himself that the point of the maze was not at all to escape, but to find the center. A task that seemed to be so easy that it would be impossible to fail. "I think a Centaur could figure this maze out," Gillian said, intentionally insulting the Centaurs, who all the Pegasi hated for being half breeds. Malus chuckled at Gillian's statement, but responded much differently than Gillian expected.

"On the contrary, my friend. Henry was a very wise man. Do you know where this maze is supposed to lead?" Malus asked.

"To the wishing well?" Gillian asked cautiously. Although he sensed there was a catch to this mysterious maze.

Malus did not respond, but instead extended his wing out, gently pushing the curtain from the window, exposing the rest of the maze to Gillian's sight. Without even realizing it, the heavy black curtain that draped down beside the window had been hiding the answer to the maze. Immediately, Gillian's eyes found a path that he had not seen before. All the way to the left side of the maze was another walkway. However, this walkway was different. This path had no bends or turns but instead was a straight shot from the start of the maze to the end. As his eyes followed from the entrance of this walkway and traced straight north, he noticed that the walkway gradually became narrower. It became so narrow that he was unsure that he could even squeeze through it himself. Not only was it narrow, but that pathway was not trimmed or taken care of like the rest of the maze; this path looked as if it had never been traveled on at all. The bushes frayed in every direction, and their roots lifted out of the ground and snaked across the pathway. It would be difficult for any creature to travel along if they had tried.

"Oh! So it's supposed to lead out there? Behind the garden, out towards the mountains?" Gillian asked, happy that he had finally conquered the maze.

"Precisely!" Malus said.

"But why? This Henry still sounds like he lost his mind. What good are those barren mountains?" Gillian blurted out.

"Henry told me that he believed those mountains are where the Great White Eagle is," Malus said very calmly. Gillian's ears swiveled sharply towards Malus because what he had said was something Gillian thought would never come from his mouth. It shocked and frightened Gillian all at the same time.

"The... the Great White Eagle?" Gillian gasped. "You don't believe in him... Do you?" Gillian couldn't believe he had even asked that question. All his life, Malus had told him and the others that the Great White Eagle was a lie, just a fairy tale. Yet, during his journey to the Devil's Kettle, Gillian had come to learn that there was more to this so-called fairy tale than Malus had ever let on to. He couldn't deny that he felt deep down inside that the Great White Eagle was real and had somehow been there with him, even when Gillian couldn't see him. Yet, he would have never thought to admit such things to Malus in fear that the all black Pegasus would become violently angry with him. But now, despite all of those thoughts Gillian had, Malus stood before him, expressing that he, too, believed the Great White Eagle was real.

"Of course I do," Malus admitted.

Gillian's jaw dropped to the floor. *I can't believe it. Even Malus believes in the Great White Eagle?* Gillian thought. "You what?" Gillian asked in shock. "But you told us for years that he wasn't real. You lied to us?"

"I was protecting your best interest!" Malus barked.

"But… but," Gillian stammered.

"But nothing. I am not innocent, and neither are you! I know you covered for those kids! I know you lied to King Fraust! And I know your journey did not end at the brim of the Centrum's Core… And *you* have the nerve to call me a liar?" Malus aggressively questioned. As he made each point, Malus crowded into Gillian's space more and more, forcing him into a corner. "You're no better than I am," he snarled. "But that's just it, not one creature in this world is." Malus' tone shifted with this sentence. No longer did he crowd Gillian, nor was his voice heavy or aggressive. It was like a storm cloud had been blown away by the wind, and Malus was once again calm and collected. Which frightened Gillian even more than when Malus sounded angry. "And that's why you must choose."

"What do you mean, I have to choose?" Gillian questioned.

"Will you choose the wishing well? Or the mountains?" Malus asked, looking out over the maze. Gillian walked back over to Malus' side and peered back out the window.

The wishing well or the mountains? What is he talking about… Gillian pondered, not completely understanding what Malus meant.

"Serve me and you can have whatever you desire in this world…" Malus promised.

Gillian gazed at the well and thought of all the riches he could have, the oats, corn, and any other grains he could imagine. He could have anything he wanted if he served Malus. He thought about how good he had it already and imagined how much better it could be. He thought back to all the young Pegasi chanting his name and wondered if he could become one of the greatest Pegasi to have ever lived. Pride swelled up inside of him, and excitement filled his heart. This offer was the Wishing Well. Yet, Gillian did not understand the weight of these two choices.

"What's the catch?" Gillian asked. "Why must I choose between the well and the mountains?"

"You misunderstand, Gillian… The wishing well is me, and the Mountains are the Great White Eagle. You must choose between me and him. You cannot serve two masters."

"Ohhhh…" Gillian said, now understanding the choice he was given. Malus' offer to serve him and be great in all the land was to choose the well. He remembered how Malus described the well. It was always the creature's greatest desire that it provided. Then he thought about the words, 'you cannot serve two masters.' If the Great White Eagle was really a lie, then this choice would have been easy. However, Malus confirmed to Gillian that he, too, believed in the Great White Eagle. Knowing this made the decision all the more difficult. *To be rich and famous. All the grains and grasses I could dream of. Every Pegasus would know my name. Who wouldn't want to be that great? But… If I choose to serve Malus, then will I have to deny the Great White Eagle's existence? Could I really do that? But the truth… It matters. Maybe more than my greatest desires.* Gillian questioned all these things and realized the gravity of the decision he was going to have to make.

Suddenly, his heart jumped. Not from excitement, but like when you get caught doing something you shouldn't be. At the very exit of the maze, a red flicker of light glowed brightly. It was the same red glow he saw at the brim of the Centrum's Core, overlooking the Humilis Pines. Just as suddenly as it had appeared in the Forbidden Circle, it appeared here. As he recalled the night on the cliff, he realized that then and now had one major similarity. You see, the night on the cliff was the first time Gillian had ever doubted Malus, and more importantly, it was the first time he ever thought that the Great White Eagle could really be real after all. And now, the mysterious light appeared when Gillian thought about the Great White Eagle. It was as if it were some sort of sign. Gillian's gaze must have been so heavy on the light that Malus took notice.

"What color do you see?" Malus asked.

"What? I… I don't see anything." Gillian said. He tried to play it off as if there was nothing there. Gillian knew the light had something to do with the Great White Eagle, and he was afraid Malus would become angry if he became distracted by it.

"Can we stop with the lies? I know you see a light, because I do too." Malus said.

"I see red," Gillian answered, lowering his head in shame.

"Ah, believed to be the color of a warrior," Malus said.

"Really?" Gillian questioned, lifting his head back up.

"Oh yes, and rightfully so. Not many creatures would run into the Forbidden Circle without backup. Although it was a treasonous act, your courage is admirable." Malus explained. Gillian drooped his ears at the 'treasonous act' part. "Every creature I have met that has seen red was a great warrior and had been very brave in the sight of danger," Malus explained.

"What color do you see, if I might ask?" Gillian asked softly.

"The light glows black for me."

"What does that mean?"

"To be honest, I don't know. I have given it a lot of thought. The best answer I can give you is that it means I have ignored the Great White Eagle. Or deny the truth if you will." Malus said. The truth of the matter was that the crystals and their colors were a mystery to Malus as well. Their true meaning was unknown. The only advantage Malus had in learning their truths was that he had been around for thousands of years. In all those years, he had met hundreds of creatures who all seemed to have specific colors that they saw. After a while, it was easy for Malus to see which personalities saw which colors.

"I don't understand," Gillian questioned.

"I didn't always see black. A long time ago, I saw white. Back when I too followed the Great White Eagle." Malus admitted.

"You used to follow the Great White Eagle?" Gillian asked in utter shock.

"Yes, I was one of his best. But he never gave me the credit. So I used my skills and broke off. That's when the crystals began to look black to me.

"Would I see black just like you then?" Gillian asked, thinking about what would happen to him if he chose to serve Malus. He thought deeply about his choice. On one hand, any morals he had left screamed to follow the Great White Eagle, but on the other, the shadows of greed and pride loomed around the corner.

"Yes, you would. But don't worry, it is a beautiful black, it goes great with gold, silver, and riches!" Malus said.

"The king? Does he know the truth?" Gillian questioned.

"Absolutely, and he chose to serve me... How do you think he ended up being King?" Malus paused for a moment.

"How many different colors are there?" Gillian asked. He remembered both Andy's and Richard's crystal apple. To him, they both glowed red. *I wonder what color they saw.* Gillian pondered.

"Including the black crystal, seven."

"What did white mean?... You know, before you lost it." Gillian asked.

"Oh no, Gillian, I did not lose my gift. Much like you will not lose yours. Your bravery will not go away when you join me, but instead, your bravery will begin to work for you." Malus explained. Gillian looked puzzled, so Malus explained in more depth. "Let me explain. When I served the Great White Eagle, I saw white. My job at the time was to uphold Truth and be the light of the world. I was expected to share the truth all of the time. Which, in turn, brought forth light, but that never gained me a thing. I wanted more, so I used my knowledge of the truth, twisted it, and forged my own path. In my distortion of truth, my power in this world grew, and so did my riches." Malus explained. "Before I used my skills to serve the Great White Eagle and gained nothing, but once I used my skills to serve myself, I gained the world!" Malus said with a crooked smile.

Gillian did not respond after this; he just gazed out at the maze and wondered what he should do. Serving Malus would fulfill all his dreams and desires. *I could be anything I want to be. What would serving the Great White Eagle get me? A crystal? Dreadfully cold mountain tops? I need to know more about this Great White Eagle before I can make a decision. Who is he really, and if he did care about me, where is he now?* These questions swirled around in his head. *I wish I had more time to think.*

"I tell you what, you have until tomorrow evening to tell me what you decide," Malus said as if reading Gillian's troubled mind.

"Oh, thank you, Sire," Gillian said.

"I also need you to do something for me."

"What is it?"

"I need you to lead a brigade into the Forbidden Circle first thing tomorrow morning."

"You want me to go back?"

"Yes, you know where Vincent's body is. Go and retrieve it. He was a loyal steed and deserves a proper burial. His name will be remembered by every generation to come." Malus requested.

"Oh… yes, sire." Gillian agreed to go, but really dreaded it. He feared that in returning to the meadow, he would have to relive that horrible battle.

"Don't worry, Zolton will be joining you to make sure you don't try and run off," Malus said with a grin. Zolton was one of the fiercest Pegusi that Gillian had ever known. His hide was mostly black now, and he only had a few blotches of white hair left. He was loyal to Malus and always had his best interests in mind. "But until tomorrow, take the day off and relax. Think about your decision." Malus said as he tossed his head towards the door, letting Gillian know he was free to go. Gillian slowly turned towards the door, but glanced one last time at the maze. Taking a deep breath, he turned and walked to the door. As his hoof pushed on the door, Malus called out to him.

"One last thing. If you choose to serve the Great White Eagle… You will receive the Alatum punishment." Gillian's heart dropped. He had assumed that was the case, but to actually hear the word from Malus' mouth was daunting. His head sank, and he felt as if his heart fell to the floor. "Be on your way now," Malus ordered in a low voice.

Gillian left Malus' chambers the same way he was brought in; however, this time, the ballroom and mezzanine were not empty. Instead, on the balcony opposite him, a man stood outside the King's chambers, pounding his fists against the wooden door. Gillian recognized the man as the King's brother, and he looked angry, unlike Gillian, who felt defeated. As he rounded the corner of the balcony, he found himself heading past the man. Although Gillian felt so distraught, he couldn't care less why the King's brother was so angry. He overheard him shouting, "You can't kill her, she's only a child."

Gillian thought nothing of it. The sad reality of the Regnum Kingdom was that the King was constantly executing creatures who disagreed with him. Or if nothing else, he was sending them off to the Dwarves as slaves. It really was just another 'Day in Paradise' around the Kingdom. Not to mention that in Gillian's selfishness, he was more concerned about his own life and choices than those of some random girl.

What am I to do? Gillian wondered as he trotted back to his stable for the evening. Although Malus had given him two options, Gillian felt as if there really was only one choice. If he didn't choose to serve Malus, then he would get the Alatum punishment. For a Pegasus, the Alatum punishment is worse than death itself. The thought of losing his wings and being sold into slavery to the Dwarves was devastating. *How can I choose to serve the Great White Eagle? Sure, it's the truth, but what will I gain? Nothing, in fact, I could lose everything…*

Finally, Gillian stepped into his stable. He stretched out his legs and then lay down in the straw. At least the straw was comforting, he thought to himself, and for the rest of that evening, Gillian pondered his heavy burden.

Chapter 6
A Mother's Plea

After his brother had finally left him be, Timothy removed his crown, took off his royal boots, and settled into his lounge chair. With one leg kicked over the chair's armrest, he leaned back and thought about all that had happened. Not only was his kingdom in shambles, but he feared his life was in danger as well. If his brother's interpretation of his dream was correct, the girl, Eva, and the crystals could end his reign as King, and possibly seek his life. *I must stop the girl, destroy the crystals, and save myself.* The King thought.

What a mess. For once, not by my own doing. The King chuckled to himself as he thought about all the trouble he himself had caused the Kingdom before he was King. *Either way, I have much to do. So many things have happened in such a short time. What will I do? How will I fix this?* Timothy thought. He was right, so many things seemed to be crashing down around him. The first thing that needed to be dealt with was Vincent's death. The reports from the incident all agree that Vincent was killed by a Gladiator Bear. It was important for him to make sure everyone knew that it took place in the Forbidden Circle, otherwise, the people of Regnum might panic, thinking a rogue Gladiator Bear was wandering around the Northern Region, putting everyone in danger. However, Timothy knew that this would raise questions, even more than there already were. It was likely by now that the people of Regnum had seen the parade of Titans, escorting the three prisoners. They would demand answers. Once they learned that Vincent had died in the Forbidden Circle, it would raise even more questions. Some of which would be 'Why was a Pegasus guard in the Forbidden Circle, when it is forbidden?' *If I throw my weight as King, and just tell them it is none of their business, I could have riots on my hands… I've got it! It's so simple.* The King thought. *The law of the land states that no creature shall enter into the Forbidden Circle. And it was because these three prisoners broke the law that Vincent had to go in. Yes, yes! Vincent's death could have been avoided! Their lawlessness was the direct cause of Vincent's death! Therefore, they need to be held accountable! Oh, yes. I will use Vincent's death as a way to justify killing the girl! I will simply tell the Kingdom, because of their treason, I had to send one of my own in to find them. Because he died trying to find them, the traitors must meet the same fate! A life for a life! Brilliant!* The King thought as he slouched deeper into his chair and smiled a crooked smile. Like Malus, the King knew that Gillian and the three traitors had seen more of the Forbidden Circle than they had let on. Knowing this made the King all the more eager to kill the traitors, because if they spoke of what they saw, the truth of the Great White Eagle might get out to the common folk. Although most of them believed in him already, more evidence of it could cause turmoil and rebellion against him and his kingdom. *I cannot have such rebellious waves in my Kingdom. Killing them will solve all of this and set an example. Let's see my dream come true now!* He thought. It was settled, and he had a plan. Now, even for a short moment, he soaked in the quietness of the morning. He had been King long enough to know that when such things occur, there isn't much quiet time until the unrest is put to bed. Knowing this could be the last bit of quiet he would have for the next few weeks, he relaxed, rubbed his eyes, and tried to get some rest.

Unfortunately for Timothy, it was short-lived. Suddenly, an aggressive pounding came from the door.

"Brother! If you've come to change my mind, don't waste your breath. I've made my peace with it, and now you should too." Timothy shouted through the door, assuming his brother had come back again in a flame of anger.

Then, the door flung open, and Timothy jumped to his feet. Rachael Huntsberg stormed through the door, her brown hair was tied up high, and she marched straight towards Timothy, pointing her finger right at him.

"Timothy! Release her!" she ordered. At first, the King was furious that the Titans had allowed such an interruption. As a Titan rushed into the room to contain Rachael and her fit of anger, he did not dare make eye contact with the King after what he had allowed to happen.

However, luckily for the Titan, once the King realized who the intruder was, all was forgiven.

"Ah, Rachael! How are you?" Timothy asked in a charismatic way, acting as if he did not know why she was there. He signaled to the Titan to let the distraught mother be.

"I demand you release my daughter!" Rachael barked.

"You demand? Me? Do you not remember that I am your King?" Timothy asked, slightly irritated.

"Do *you* not remember that you were a scared little boy, who did nothing to save Emma in the Uada Hollows? Do you remember that it was Peter and I who pulled you out from the depths of the Hollows?" Rachael shouted aggressively at Timothy. King Fraust's face flushed red. He became nervous, embarrassed almost, for what she began blurting out were supposed to remain secrets, and she knew that. Years ago, Timothy, his brother, and Rachael had agreed not to speak of those things ever again, yet here she was spilling it all. Timothy grew furious. It was important for his reign as King that no one learned of these secrets, and so he did not want the Titan to hear another word of this.

"Griffin, please excuse us, I can handle her," Timothy said calmly, trying to act as if what she said meant nothing. Quickly, he ushered the Titan out of the room and shut his chamber door swiftly behind him.

"You have no right bringing that up. You may not respect me, but I am your King, and your life is in the palm of my hand. Just remember that!" Timothy said in a stern whisper, pointing his finger directly at Rachael. "Speak of it again in front of my Titans, and I will kill your husband, and everyone else you care about," Timothy said in a louder voice. It was with this threat that Rachael realized she had overstepped and was standing in hot water. Her raging fire of anger was reduced to fumes.

"Timothy, you have to release my daughter. Please," she begged, moving on from his threat.

"Your daughter, along with her friends, are traitors. That is an offense punishable by death." Timothy said.

"Death? Isn't that extreme!?" she asked erratically.

"Their treason caused the death of a Royal Pegasus Guard. They must be held accountable," the King snapped.

"My Eva had nothing to do with that! Everyone said it was a Gladiator Bear," she sobbed.

"Yet, they were the reason he was out there in the first place. It's their fault, she is a traitor."

"Do you not remember we were once those traitors too? You, me, your brother, Emma, and Peter. Don't you remember?" Rachael said forcefully.

"Of course I remember," he said.

"Have you forgotten all the Great White Eagle revealed to us? We learned the truth," she cried.

"I have not forgotten, and yes, I remember it all. We all made choices after learning the truth, and I regret none of them, and now? Well, it's once again time to make more hard choices," Timothy explained.

"But you made the wrong choice, and so did your brother," Rachael grumbled.

"Are you sure? Because of those choices, I became King. How is that the wrong choice?" Timothy asked pridefully.

"Only the Great White Eagle *knows* how much blood is on your hands," Rachael scowled. "None of what you did was good." Then Rachael's voice got really low, "You're a murderer!" she forcefully whispered.

"Oh, stop with that! I did what I had to do," Timothy said casually. However, Rachael became annoyed and scoffed at the arrogant King. "Rachael, my dear, your plea has moved me. Instead of execution, I will give your daughter, and her friends for that matter, the same choice we had. The choice to follow the Great White Eagle, which in turn will receive a just punishment fit for their offense… Which is… well, execution. Or they can serve me," Timothy said, chuckling out loud.

"You can't kill her. Please," Rachael pleaded.

"She broke the law. It's that simple," Timothy said. "If King Kieser would have just killed us all, he would still be King. But instead, he was weak, filled with mercy and compassion! A real King, a real leader, is strong and unmovable!"

"King Kieser was not weak, he was a kind man. Fit to lead the people of Regnum! We didn't deserve to die, and neither did he."

"Malus gave me the chance to be King, and I took it."

"At what cost, Timothy?" Rachael asked.

"This world is cruel, I took advantage of the weak. I deserve to be King!"

"You sound just like that beastly Pegasus. Malus has you wrapped around his finger. Don't you see it?"

"Hush, Rachael. Just shut your mouth. You will never understand, and should be grateful!"

"Grateful? For what?!"

"You're only alive because I promised Malus you would keep your mouth shut. I saved your life. Not my brother, not Peter, I did." Timothy said in a booming voice. Rachael became quiet because she had not known this. She often pondered why Malus had let her live after all these years, but never would have guessed it was because of Timothy.

"Either way, you are not the same Timothy I once knew," she scolded the seasoned King.

"Sorry to be a disappointment, but I must protect my crown."

"Wait a minute! You think Eva will come for your throne? Your nuts, she's not like you!" Rachael said, with a scoff. Never would her sweet baby girl fall into the same murderous trap that Timothy did all those years ago.

"I don't think she will, I know she will. It was revealed to me in a dream by the Great White Eagle himself," Timothy said. Considering she had learned all that Eva had years ago, she knew exactly what Timothy meant. She knew the King was a Somniator, and she knew that his dreams came from the Great White Eagle.

"I don't buy it. She wouldn't hurt a fly. Even if the fly was a cruel, unjust rat!" she sputtered. "Your brother must have interpreted your dream wrong," Rachael sobbed in anguish.

"It's a chance I cannot take. Letting her go would be the worst thing I could do. If she didn't kill me, she would surely cause an uprising among the Great White Eagle followers. You know that," Timothy said, in a way that made it seem like he had no choice but to punish Eva severely.

"Please, Timothy, please spare my daughter," Rachael begged.

Timothy paused for a moment. Her heartfelt cry almost pierced his stone heart. He knew he wasn't going to change his mind. *She must die to protect my Kingdom and my crown,* he thought. However, if Rachael knew her daughter was dead, she would have no reason to keep quiet about anything. She would not stop until all of the King's lies were exposed to the world. So he would have to convince Rachael that her daughter would live, otherwise, his throne would still be in danger, even if the girl were dead.

"You know, I've always liked you," Timothy said in a rather creepy way. "But I have to admit, it's a shame you and Peter never worked out. I always did envy him. Knowing, of course, you loved him…Then again, it's probably best we all went our separate ways. If you and Peter had ended up together, you would have been in that fire with him all those years ago. Then you too would be dead. I guess we can thank the Great White Eagle for that!" Timothy said, mocking Rachael.

She rolled her eyes and crossed her arms. She was offended, but only because it was true. Long ago, she had been in love with Peter, but things changed. He got married, and so did she. Just not to one another. However, Rachael was angry that he brought it up. It was a painful memory for her, and she didn't understand why he would bring it up.

"What's your point?" she snapped. *What game is he playing here?* She thought.

The truth of the matter was that Timothy was trying to be charming but failed miserably. Digging up an old wound never really does the trick when trying to woo a woman. So he shifted back to his plan.

"I tell you what," he said, "I will spare your child, but she must remain here as my servant forever." With this offer, his plan was set in motion. Of course, it was a lie, and he still planned to kill Eva, but as far as Rachael would ever know, her daughter would be alive, and well, living as a servant of the King. This would keep Rachael at bay, avoiding an uprising from the Great White Eagle followers, and he could rid himself of the girl. Rachael would be none the wiser.

"Oh, Timothy, thank you, thank you, a thousand times thank you!" She celebrated. She really hated the thought of her daughter being a servant, but it was far better than her being dead. She would have to allow it, for Eva's sake.

"But you will never be allowed to visit," he said. This made Rachael's smile vanish like the Messorems when smacked over the head by an Eagle's Heart crystal. This was the only way Timothy could mask Eva's death from her mother. By removing all contact, Rachael wouldn't know her daughter's real fate and would assume her daughter was alive. This would also give Timothy leverage. Since Rachael would believe that Eva was alive, the King could threaten to kill her if Rachael ever tried to expose the King for the things he had done.

"But she's my sweet child. My only child," Rachael cried, while tears began to swell in her eyes.

"It's your choice. She will either be my servant or be put to death for her crimes against me," Timothy said, cracking a crooked smile.

"Can I at least see her one last time, before you keep her from me?" Rachael pleaded softly.

"Why, of course, you can. I'm not heartless, I will have her brought to the ballroom immediately!" Timothy said. Rachael couldn't help but roll her eyes. She believed that if Timothy did have a heart, it was stone.

Timothy walked over to the chamber's door and pushed it open. Outside Griffin, the Titan waited patiently. At the sight of the King, Griffin straightened out and waited for his command. "Go fetch the girl. She's down in the stable yard." King Fraust ordered. Quickly, the Titan bowed and raced down the stairs before them. Then the King turned back to Rachael. "Shall we?" He opened the door further and then stood back. With a swoop of his arm, he motioned for Rachael to head out of the room. She quickly rushed down the marble staircase that was spread out before her to the floor of the ballroom. That was where she would wait to see her precious daughter for the last time.

Chapter 7
A Farewell Forever

Meanwhile, Andy and Jessie leaned against the castle, outside the servants' washroom. The boys used the washroom on the left, quickly changing into new clothing. Eva, on the other hand, used the washroom on the right. She was not as quick as the boys were, for she took the time to scrub her face with a clean washcloth that Isabell had given her. She and Isabell began to chat, which was quite refreshing for Eva, who had been lost in the wilderness with three boys who did not appreciate girly things. Things like a good bath and dresses. So when Isabell gave her a servant's dress to wear, Eva was excited to try it on. Something boys would never understand. So, while she took her time in the washroom, the boys had to wait outside.

As they waited, they looked for an escape. As far as they could tell, they were on the rear side of the castle. With the washrooms behind them, an outer wall met the castle on their left, jogged out ten or fifteen feet, and then made a ninety-degree turn and stretched out. It was long and tall, and it bordered the northern side of the horse stable's yard. It looked to encircle the whole stables from where they stood.

"I don't see a way out," Andy whispered.

"Me either, and with that baboon around the corner, we can't even get away to look for one. I wish that filthy dungeon keeper would get lost," Jessie scowled, referring to Simon, who was waiting around the corner for them to get cleaned up.

"Yeah, he is a brute, isn't he?" Andy asked while leaning against the castle.

"What are we gonna do? We have to get out of here," Jessie whispered. It was evident by how they had been treated since their arrival that the King and his crew were not kind, loving people. Isabell was the first, and so far the only, creature who had shown them any kindness from within the castle walls.

"And go where?" Andy asked. "We are traitors, they won't rest until they find us."

"To the Elves! Just like we agreed," Jessie said, surprisingly loud.

"Shhh, keep it down. Even if we could escape, we don't need peepin' Simon over there hearing our plans," Andy said as he pushed off the wall to see around the corner to where Simon was standing. He was picking his nose, so Andy was sure he hadn't heard anything.

"If we run in different directions, they can't catch us all!" Jessie said.

"This is not a story book, Jessie. Do you see how many guards there are? It's not just us running from Gillian anymore. This is us against the Kingdom of Regnum. Besides, I'm not leaving Eva," Andy puffed.

"Well, maybe Isabell can help us. She seems smart and kind. She can get us out of here," Jessie said, floundering over Isabell.

"Maybe she would help us, but if she could get us out, why hasn't she escaped herself?" Andy asked.

Just then, Eva and Isabell appeared outside the girls' washroom. Eva's brown hair paired wonderfully with the robin's egg blue servant girl's dress, at least in Andy's opinion.

"Did you know that Isabell used to belong to the orphanage?" Eva said with excitement in her voice.

"Really?" Jessie almost shouted. He didn't know much about her, but already he found something they had in common. "You know Mrs. Rosewood?"

"Yes, I do. She is a very sweet lady. She took care of me and my sister for years." Isabell said with a soft smile.

"Who is your sister?" Andy asked. He had been there his whole life, it was likely that he would know her.

"Bethany Butler," Isabell said.

"Bethany…Beth… Oh yes! Beth, and that makes you Izzy? You were a year older than I, and she was a year younger, if I remember correctly. Boy, that was a long time ago," Andy said, thinking back to the simpler times. He rubbed the back of his neck and then continued. "I think I was only maybe eight or nine years old when you two were adopted." She smiled at him and then looked at her feet. Andy did not notice that she was uncomfortable before he blurted out his next question. "But wait, how did you end up here? And if you're here, where is Beth?" he asked.

"Andrew!" Eva scolded. She had seen Isabell grow upset and elbowed Andy in the side for asking such a personal question. He turned red with embarrassment.

"I'm so sorry, Isabell, I never meant to make you upset," Andy pleaded.

"No, no, it's okay. You could say I was adopted, but really, I was selected to be a servant of the King. But thankfully, my sister was actually adopted by a loving family who lives on the outskirts of Regnum in the farm country. The family who adopted her has seven of their own kids and has adopted four other children since then. I guess you could say they need all the help they can get on the farm," Isabell said, with a soft chuckle.

"That must be so terrible being separated from your sister like that," Eva said in a sympathetic voice. What had happened to Isabell and her sister began to make Jessie feel uncomfortable. It was only the night before that he had watched his brother fall into the Devil's Kettle. He felt the heavy pain of his loss and felt sympathetic for Isabell because of it. It was another thing they had in common, being separated from their siblings.

"It is. She is allowed to visit me once a month, but only for a few minutes each time," Isabell said, clearly upset but doing her best not to show that it made her sad.

"I...umm, just lost my brother," Jessie said in a very low voice. "Does it get better?" Jessie asked Isabell. Andy and Eva felt hot flashes shoot down their spines. This was a question they themselves could not answer. Sure, Andy grew up without parents, but he never really knew them at all. To lose someone close was something they hadn't yet experienced. However, Isabell understood his question. Thankfully for Isabell, she had only been separated from her sister, however, she still felt his pain.

"Not better, but easier," she said with a soft smile. She reached out and squeezed Jessie's arm as a way to comfort him. They all stood quietly. Andy and Eva didn't know what to say, and Isabell and Jessie both knew there was simply nothing to say. The stale silence was finally broken by Jessie, who desired to escape.

"Hey… Isabell?" Jessie asked.

"Yes, Jessie?"

"Can you help us get out of here?"

"I…I want to… I don't believe you are traitors like the King says. But if I do, I will never see my sister again."

"Come with us!" Eva said.

"I couldn't. The King would bring harm to my sister if I did."

Andy and Eva both wanted to argue with Isabell to try and convince her to help them, but this was because they didn't understand. Isabell's choices had consequences. It would be one thing if she were only endangering herself, but if she angered the King, it could bring the King's wrath down on someone she loved. So while Andy and Eva thought it was selfish for Isabell not to help them, Jessie, who would do anything to get his brother back, understood that Isabell was only protecting her sister.

"I understand Isabell. I would do anything to keep my brother safe. I've failed, but I won't let you make the same mistake. We will figure it out on our own with no hard feelings," Jessie said, comforting Isabell and putting an end to the debate between Andy and Eva.

"Thank you, Jessie," She said with a radiant smile on her face.

Simon had lost complete track of time and was in no hurry. He leaned against the castle walls with his eyes shut, soaking in the warmth of the sun. So the three friends and Isabell took the time to devise a plan of escaping. Although Isabell couldn't physically help them escape, she tried to think of ways they could get away without any trace that she was involved. At this point, none of them knew how, but they were determined to find a way.

"So… Isabell?" Jessie started. "If you're a year older than Andy, and I'm a year older than Andy, that would make us the same age?" Jessie said, baring his teeth with a smile. Isabell's freckled cheeks began to blush red, for she knew Jessie was flirting.

"That we are," she responded with a bat of her eyes. At this point, Jessie was smiling ear to ear. His flirtatious acts distracted him momentarily from the loss of his brother. The joyous moment was shattered by the clanking of a Titan's armor as he approached them. Simon, who was moments away from a quick nap, had been spooked awake by the Titan. Shaking his head, he straightened himself out and acted like he had been alert the whole time.

"The King requests that the girl be brought before the throne," the Titan informed the big oaf, Simon. The two of them poked their heads around the corner of the castle and peered at the four young humans.

"There she is," Simon said as he pointed at Eva. "And the others? What shall I do with them?"

"Take them to the dungeons," the Titan commanded.

"Alright, time to go," Simon said as he cuffed Jessie and Andy's wrists. As Simon began tugging the boys away from Eva, Andy began to panic. He knew that this would separate him and Eva. Only a few minutes before, he had expressed to Jessie that he was not going to leave Eva's side, yet here he was being drug away from her.

"Let me go!" he shouted, "I'm not leaving Eva."

"Stop fighting me, I don't get paid enough for this," Simon said partly to Andy and partly under his breath. Although both Jessie and Andy were strong young men, they were no match for Simon's mass. He was large and round and probably couldn't see his toes anymore. As they tugged against him, Simon simply twisted the cuffs on their wrists, inflicting great pain, and leaned back. Neither of the boys could do much against it.

"Please don't worry, Andrew, I'll be alright," Eva said calmly. He accepted this fate, and slowly, Andy began to give in. He locked eyes with Eva until Simon had pulled him around the corner, and he could no longer see his dear friend.

"Alright, Missy, come with me," the Titan ordered Eva. Then he focused his attention on Isabell. "Be on your way."

Isabell curtsied to the Titan, smiled at Eva, and she too disappeared around the corner.

To Eva's surprise, the Titan did not put any cuffs on her. He just grabbed her by the arm and began directing her. Around the corner they went, following the edge of the castle, under the covered walkway, all the way back to the courtyard. Again, Eva could see the three archways on the face of the castle. Two on each side of the stage, and one to the far left.

The Titan dragged her into the archway right of the stage, bringing her for the first time into the castle itself. The archway was the mouth of a hallway. As they walked along, Eva could see that the hallway would eventually open up into a massive open room far ahead. However, along the hallway, she noticed there were many doors and rooms on both sides of her. Most of the doors were closed, but one room was quite large, and she could see that there were hundreds of cloak hangers lining the walls of the room. *That must be where the guests leave their coats when attending a royal ball!* Eva thought with excitement. As a young girl, she always dreamed of being invited to a royal ball. However, she never imagined seeing the ballroom for the first time would be like this... as a prisoner.

At the hallway's end, the ballroom immediately opened up into a vaulted room. It was beautiful and royal. Directly to her left was a majestic set of stairs that led up to the mezzanine and King Fraust's chambers. To her right was the beautiful Eastern wall, with fascinating carvings and vibrant paintings. She did not know why she was being led into the ballroom before the King, so at the moment she was very interested in the ballroom itself, and did not realize that her mother was there waiting for her. She gazed up at the ceiling, which was high and mighty. Beautiful images were carved into the white marbled ceiling. Hanging from the base of the mezzanine were banners of various colors. They each had golden threading with images sewn into them. Everything from Elves to Dwarves, Centaurs to Pegasi, humans and beasts were represented. Spectacularly beautiful, to say the least.

"Eva?" a familiar voice shouted from across the room. For the first time, Eva realized why she had been summoned. Eva knew exactly who called to her, and it made her heart leap with joy. Without hesitating, Eva broke free from the Titan's grip and ran across the ballroom into her mother's arms. Looking over her mother's shoulder, she could see the King sitting on his throne. It was placed elevated, but beneath the mezzanine, at the head of the ballroom.

"Are you alright?" Rachael asked.

"Yes, Mom."

"Are you hungry? Or hurt?"

"No, I'm okay."

"It's so good to see you," Rachael said to her daughter, and gave her a huge squeeze.

"I missed you, Mom, and I never meant to leave for so long. I... I just," Eva started.

"Hush, honey, I know. Long ago, I too was brought on a journey very similar to yours," Rachael explained.

"Why did you never tell me?" Eva pleaded, misunderstanding.

"It's a journey that brought a lot of heartache and one I hoped you would never have to endure. But by the guidance of the Great White Eagle, he called you just as he called me."

"He called you, too? You're a Somniator?" Eva questioned.

"No, no... But a friend was. The Great White Eagle showed me the truth, just as he has you," Rachael explained to her daughter, knowing time was fleeting.

"You know the truth? All of it?" Eva questioned, hopeful that her mom could direct her next move.

"Yes, yes, my dear, but you must hear me," Rachael lowered her voice to a whisper."You cannot trust the King or his brother."

This was not the answer Eva was hoping for, and it made her even more worried as to what her next move should be. "Why not? He's the King. Am I not supposed to follow the King's orders?" Eva questioned. She remembered back to when she first learned she was a Somniator. She remembered that long ago, the King ordered all Somniators to turn themselves over, to help keep peace among all creatures. At that time, Eva hoped she could be of use to the King to do just that, help keep peace. Until the present moment, she had held onto that hope. Although she was a prisoner, she hoped to sort it all out and be useful to the Kingdom and its creatures. However, here her mom was, telling her not to trust the King. *Maybe I shouldn't admit I am a Somniator… Maybe my mom is right.* Eva thought. "Are you sure? How do you know?" Eva questioned, wanting more clarity.

"Because I know."

"But mom…" Eva insisted.

"Listen to me. The King has promised me to spare your life, but instead you must serve as a servant to the Royal throne," Rachael said as tears began to swell in her eyes. She placed both hands on Eva's shoulders, looking her deep in the eyes. Eva could tell by the tears in her mother's eyes that being the King's servant was not as simple as it sounded.

"And if I refuse?" Eva whispered. Thinking now, it would be best for her and her friends to escape as quickly as they could.

"You have no choice," Rachael cried softly. Eva realized that she would become less of a servant and more of a slave. She was beginning to understand that whether or not she wanted to help the King, she would not get a choice in the matter and accepted the difficult fate.

"Will you come visit?" Eva asked as a tear beaded up. Rachael looked deep into her daughter's eyes and swallowed hard. Doing everything she could to hold back tears.

"Yes, of course, my love," Rachael said. She could not bear the thought of Eva knowing that she would not be allowed to see her again. Eva and Rachael both exploded into tears. The mother wrapped her daughter in her arms and squeezed her tight, knowing that this would be the last time she could ever hold her again.

"Alright, times up," the king announced. "It is time for you to go home, Rachael."

Rachael glanced at Timothy and then again looked Eva in the eyes.

"Do not trust them. I love you more than the world, remember that," She kissed Eva on the forehead, before the Titan pried Rachael away and escorted her from the ballroom.

While all of this was taking place, Jessie and Andy had been locked up in the Dungeons. Each had short bursts of anger as they shook at the iron bars that formed a cage around them. They both knew shaking the iron bars would be in vain, but when you are stuck somewhere against your will, it's sometimes difficult to contain your anger. Simon chuckled at the two trapped in cages and slowly waddled away. His heavy thumping could be heard all the way up the spiral stairs of the dungeon until all was silent.

Quickly, the boys searched every corner of their prison cell for a way out. A loose iron bar, a hole, or a crack, anything to try and escape, but found nothing. Eventually, they both stood defeated. Jessie clung to the iron gate that had trapped them inside. A tear streamed down his cheek as he tried to hold it together. It's bad enough when a loved one dies, but being tossed into a dungeon made it all that much worse.

"Hey Jessie?" Andy said, noticing that Jessie had begun to cry softly.

"Yeah?" he sniffled.

"I'm sorry for snapping at you before," Andy said softly.

"I know you are. And for the record, I'm sorry too. I think I wanted to blame the Great White Eagle for what happened. But after you said it was my fault, the guilt I felt made me angry. But you are right, I made the choice to go with you to the Devil's Kettle. Not you, not the Great White Eagle, but me, I did," Jessie said, choking down tears.

"Well, when we get out of here, we will go to the Elves. They will know what to do," Andy said, trying to encourage Jessie.

"Yeah. Maybe they will," Jessie said. However, as he thought it all over, he pondered a simple thought. *I've lost everything, I have nothing left. Here I am in prison, and the only thing I want is my brother back. What can the Elves do about that?* Jessie thought.

"Jessie," Andy said again, pulling his train of thought back. Jessie turned and could see that Andy had begun to walk towards him. When he came close, he put his hand out and placed it on his shoulder. "I am really... truly sorry about Richard," Andy said. Jessie's eyes flooded with tears, trying to hold back his tears, he pressed his lips together and nodded. Then Andy reached for the compass that Richard had given him back at Maizey's den deep within the heart of the Blackwood forest.

"This belongs to you," he said as he took it off and looped it over Jessie's neck. Immediately, Jessie recognized his brother's compass, and at that moment, he couldn't hold it back any longer; tears swelled and poured down his face. For the first time since his brother had died, he allowed himself to mourn. Andy wrapped his arms around Jessie and squeezed tightly. The two hugged for what seemed like minutes. Tears slipped out of both of their eyes because they shared the pain together.

"I'm gonna find him," Jessie blabbered in between tears.

"Richard?" Andy asked, confused as to what he meant.

"No... The Great White Eagle. I'm going to find the Great White Eagle," Jessie said, knowing that during their journey to the Devil's Kettle that the Great White Eagle's presence was with them somehow. He knew he was real and wanted to find him for answers. Jessie believed that the Elves couldn't help him, but the Great White Eagle could.

Andy let go of Jessie but put both hands on his shoulders. With tears now in Andy's eyes as well, he just nodded. He understood that searching for the Great White Eagle was something Jessie would have to do. Andy himself remembered that dreadful night, standing on the edge of the lake that fed the Devil's Kettle, watching the Messorems terrorize the night. He remembered Jessie saying that just before Richard was swallowed by the Devil's Kettle, that his brother told him to find the Great White Eagle. And that's exactly what Jessie was going to do. They hugged one more time before Andy went to the far wall and squatted to the ground.

Before too long, the two began to hear footsteps coming down the spiral stairs that led into the dungeons.

They wiped the tears from their eyes and straightened themselves up. They wanted to seem tough and unafraid of whatever they would have to face.

Down the poorly lit staircase, Eva stumbled in front of the Titan, who would push her when he thought she was not moving fast enough.

Finally, the floor flattened out, and there was a hallway with prison cells on both sides. Iron bars strung from the roof to the floor. To Eva's surprise, the dungeon was relatively empty. In fact, as far as she could tell, there was no one else besides her and the boys in the dungeon. The Titan forced Eva down to the second-to-last cell. Once she reached it, she peered in and could see Andy and Jessie with redness in their eyes.

"There you go! Your new home sweet home," the Titan laughed as he wiggled the key into the lock. As quickly as it opened and he shoved Eva in, he slammed it shut. The dungeon keys jingled as he relocked their cage.

"Are you okay? Where did they take you?" Andy began to question as he rushed to Eva and hugged her.

"Yes, I'm fine, they brought me to my mother," Eva said, as she wiped the remaining tears from her cheek. "Are you guys okay?" she asked, curious about the redness in their eyes.

"You got to see your mom?" Andy asked, ignoring her question. He was relieved to hear it. He hoped that once the adventure was over, she could return home to her parents. It was obvious that they were not getting out of the dungeons anytime soon, so he was happy to hear that she at least got to see her mom.

"Yes, I did," she said with a soft smile. She still hadn't sorted it all out, and what it meant for her.

"Oh good, that's really good," Andy said. "Do you wanna talk about any of it?"

"Not tonight. I think we should get some rest," Eva suggested. "We have much to figure out and will need all the sleep we can get."

They all agreed and settled onto the cold, hard floor for the night.

Chapter 8
The Book of Truth

Back at the Pegasi stables, birds perched atop the roofs and sang their morning songs. Gillian opened his eyes and felt as if his slumber had gone by too fast. He stood up and stretched out his legs and wings. As he folded in his wings, he shook like a dog ridding the sleepiness from his body.

Although Gillian was grateful to be back in his very own bed of straw, being home felt more like a burden than a relief. While in the Forbidden Circle, he felt free, yet here, the consequences of his journey were crashing down around him. Mainly, the dastardly decision he was being forced to make.

Should I serve Malus? What's there to lose? I will be rich! And famous! I can have whatever grains I desire and graze in all the best fields. Every Pegasi now and to come will know my name. Is that so bad? Gillian pondered, leaning heavily towards Malus' offer. *Plus, I will avoid losing my wings. I would rather die than to allow that to happen. So, my choice seems obvious… but why is it so hard? Why can't I let go of the truth?* Gillian wondered. The truth of the matter was, although Malus' offer was great and benefited Gillian in almost every way, his conscience could not let him let go of the truth. Through his journey to the Devil's Kettle, Gillian had learned that the Great White Eagle was undeniably real and that Malus was not all he claimed to be. *Can I really serve someone like Malus?* He thought, reflecting on everything he had learned.

For breakfast, Gillian munched on hay. Not only was the decision looming over his head, but he would soon be on his way back to the dreadful battlefield where Vincent attacked him and ultimately met a tragic fate. Gillian was not looking forward to his task, for that battle was one of the scariest encounters of his life. The peaceful morning ended abruptly when Gillian heard Zolton calling from afar.

"Gillian?" his royal babysitter shouted. "Time to go, the Royal Titans are waiting for your command."

My command? Gillian thought. He really liked the sound of commanding his own brigade. Not having to follow orders but instead making his own. Gillian winnied with excitement at his newfound obligation. Quickly forgetting all that had been bothering him seconds before.

He followed Zolton back to the courtyard, where fifteen Titans stood in attention, waiting for their orders. They were geared up in armor, and each had a sword tied to their hip. A Titan named Thomas stepped forward to greet Gillian.

"Hello, Sire, what are our orders?" Thomas asked.

"You will accompany me to the Forbidden Circle. We will retrieve Vincent's body and return him home for a proper burial." Gillian explained. He felt proud, for it was his first order he had ever given. Being in charge felt great.

"Very well, Sire," Thomas said with a bow. He then sank back into the line of Titans. Gillian gazed upon his men. They stood silently with stern faces. The sun glimmered off their armor, and they all looked like statues. Gillian was wearing a smile that stretched from ear to ear, but after a few awkward moments, it shrank just a bit. Gillian's eyes looked over the Titans and began to wonder why they hadn't moved. Finally, Zolton leaned over and whispered into Gillian's ear.

"They are waiting for your order, you must tell them to move out."

"Oh!" Gillian said while laughing at himself for not knowing what to do. "Uh… men, MOVE OUT!" he shouted, and with that, the Titans arranged themselves in groups of three and marched out of the courtyard.

Gillian marched the men all the way through Regnum. As he led them, he puffed out his chest, and if anyone passed by or could be seen watching from afar, Gillian nodded in their direction. Pride swelled within him, and again, without realizing it, some of his feathers began to turn black. More and more of these 'Noble Markings' began to appear, and because it was so frequent, Gillian hardly recognized any new ones. This instance was one of those. His sole focus was leading his mission, which he began to enjoy much more than he thought he would. Through the village, the slums, and past the farms, he led them back down the windy road to the clearing. It wasn't until he reached the clearing that he was reminded of just how uncomfortable this mission was going to be. *Back to where it all began.* Gillian thought as he swallowed hard.

Thoughts flashed into Gillian's head. He remembered Richard and Jessie approaching him, and Eva sneezing behind the fallen log. Her sneeze was the signal that started it all. It started Gillian's journey to learning the truth, discovering the Great White Eagle, and witnessing the mysteries of the Centrums Core, all of which led to him having to make difficult decisions. This place was nothing special, just a clearing with soft dirt and a trough full of water, yet it had led to a great deal of trouble for him. A part of him blamed Richard, Jessie, Eva, and Andy for everything that had happened, and this clearing reminded him of that; however, he knew he wasn't innocent either. He would even venture to say that he had grown quite fond of those four and considered them to be friends, despite what they had caused.

Gillian's men stood at attention, waiting for his command. "Titans, straight south from here is where the battle had taken place. The forest is much too thick for Zolton and me to navigate," he started. "You, there." Gillian tossed his nose towards the Titan that first approached him in the castle's courtyard.

Thomas stepped forward. "Yes, Sergeant?"

"Lead these men through the forest. Zolton and I will fly on up ahead. We will scope it out and make sure the coast is clear. Once we land in the meadow, you will be clear to come to us." Gillian ordered.

"Yes, Sire!" Thomas shouted. Then Thomas turned to the rest of the Titans and shouted, "Move out!" He motioned south towards the meadow, and they were off.

"Shall we?" Gillian said, looking at Zolton.

"Hmf," Zolton responded. You could tell by the way he watched Gillian that he wasn't going to give him the benefit of the doubt.

"You don't trust me, do you?" Gillian asked.

"Not one bit," Zolton confirmed.

"Why is that?" Gillian said, not thinking about the obvious reason. Zolton pressed his lips together, squinted his eyes, and raised his nose. A short pause came from the great Pegasus.

"Did you know that Gladiator bears have five razor-sharp claws?" Zolton asked, finally responding to Gillian's question.

"Yeah… so?" Gillian asked. Gillian had been so naive and convinced himself that he hadn't given Zolton any reason not to trust him. He was almost annoyed with Zolton for being cautious. However, Zolton was a very smart steed and had put together all of Gillian's puzzle pieces, catching him in his lies.

"This here is what a real Gladiator claw wound looks like," Zolton said as he lifted his wing. Buried deep in his black hide were five scars stretched out across his side. Gillian's eyes grew wide. Seeing a real Gladiator bear's claw marks sent a cold rush down his neck and made him realize that the gash on his chest looked nothing like Zolton's wound at all. It was evident that Zolton knew Gillian had lied about being attacked by a Gladiator bear and had rightfully suspected Gillian's hand in Vincent's death. "Your wound looks an awful lot like that of a wound inflicted by a Pegasus' cuff," Zolton said cautiously.

Gillian peered down at his chest and then at Zolton's wound. They were nothing alike. Gillian wanted to lie and try to cover his tracks, but he knew it was no use. Zolton had figured it out and called Gillian out on it.

"Vincent attacked me. I had no choice!" Gillian pleaded. "Please don't harm me." Gillian decided that begging for Zolton's mercy was his only option.

"Even if I wanted to harm you, Malus ordered me not to. So you're safe… for now." Zolton said, looking away from Gillian and raising his eyebrow, the way one does when they are not impressed with a situation. Then Zolton asked a very peculiar question. "Am I?"

Gillian was shocked that a Pegasus like Zolton would even ask such a thing. *Why would he fear me?* However, he did not respond to Zolton's question because he was more interested in Zolton's orders from Malus. "Why would Malus order you not to harm me? Why would he want to protect me?" Gillian asked. He couldn't help but wonder why Malus would care about him.

"He believes you will make the right choice. As I have. If you ask me, I think you're too much of a coward." Zolton said. Gillian swallowed hard. "Either way, it's a win for me. If you choose to serve Malus, then I have less of a workload. And if you don't? Off with the wings!" he said with a great laugh. He chuckled to himself as he lifted himself into the air.

Oh man, the Alatum punishment. I cannot bear it. My only logical option is to serve Malus. As much as my heart is telling me not to, I feel like I must. Gillian thought grimly.

"Well, *Serg*. You comin'?" Zolton asked sarcastically, as he hovered in the air overhead.

Gillian stretched out his wings and thrusted them to the ground, lifting all four hooves out of the dirt.

Zolton zoomed off, with Gillian following closely behind. The tree tops bent and swayed as they rushed over them, and the meadow rolled towards them with each flap of their wings. Gracefully, the two of them swooped into a trot upon the ground and gradually came to a stop.

"Oh yeah! I forgot about this stuff!" Gillian said with great excitement as he lowered his head to the ground and took a mouthful of the meadow's luscious grass.

"Can we focus here? For Vincent's sake?" Zolton scolded Gillian. Gillian opened his mouth and let the grass fall to the ground. If his face could have turned red, it would have been because he was quite embarrassed.

"Echem, yes. Sorry," Gillian said, apologizing for getting distracted from their serious mission. "Over here… this way," Gillian said as he began to trot past Zolton towards the battle ground.

Without Gillian knowing, Zolton lowered his head in curiosity and took a nibble of the grass. Satisfied by its flavorful taste, Zolton pressed his lips together and raised his eyebrows in approval. Then he followed Gillian to the battlefield.

The grasses waved in the wind, as if they recognized Gillian and were saying 'Hello.' As they climbed the meadows' natural arch, the Northern river could be seen roaring away in the distance.

The closer they came to the river, the more evident it was that a battle had taken place. The luscious grass became matted down and in some places the sod had been ripped from the earth and dirt was left exposed. Gillian stood before the place where Vincent met his fate. The earth was stained red, and it made him feel sick. Then he looked to the bushes where Andy, Eva, and Jessie hid. It looked like there was nothing left of it. Between the ambush of Maizey's claws and the later battle between Vincent and Gillian, the poor bush was flattened, shattered, and destroyed. Instead of red, the death of the bush was marked by a purplish blue stain; Squished blueberries.

"This is where the battle took place," Gillian said, looking back at Zolton.

"I see that, but where is Vincent?" Zolton asked, looking around. To Zolton's surprise he noticed a Gladiator bears print in the soft sod. However, unwilling to believe any of Gillian's story, he brushed the paw print away with his hoof.

"Honestly… I don't know." Gillian said. Gillian was dumbfounded. *Where was Vincent?* He thought.

"Gillian, don't play games with me!" Zolton shouted fiercely.

"I'm not! I swear!"

Just then, the Titans appeared at the edge of the forbidden forest. Gillian bolted towards them.

"Men! Vincent's body has been taken! We must fan out and find it!" Gillian shouted frantically. Luckily for Gillian, Zolton believed him. Between the paw print he saw, he knew some of Gillian's story was true. *Maybe the bear took Vincent and ate him.* Zolton thought.

The Titans drew their swords and began to spread out. A few went west and a few east. The last group went south towards the Blackwood Forest. Gillian lifted himself into the air and began flying back and forth, looking for Vincent from the sky. It didn't take long, and one of the Titans came running out of the Blackwood forest.

"I think I found something!" he shouted as he waved to Gillian.

The rest of the Titans marched into the Blackwood forest, and Gillian swooped in behind them. Hitting the ground running, Gillian folded up his wings and slowed his run to a walk.

"What is it?" Gillian questioned.

"It looks to be a grave, sir," one of the Titans said.

He was right. Behind a large Blackwood tree was a hump of dirt with a vertical stick jammed into the top of the dirt mound.

"Do you think it's him?" Zolton asked.

"Who else would it be?" Gillian questioned.

"Who would have honored him like this? Out here?" Zolton questioned.

"Looks like… Beavers?" one of the Titans said. He was kneeling down next to the grave, examining footprints in the dirt.

"Beavers? Did you encounter Beavers out here?" Zolton aggressively asked Gillian.

"No, I didn't. But I overheard the humans talking about a colony of beavers. And something about crystals." Gillian said.

"Crystals? Do you know where these beavers are?" Zolton asked.

"Well, yeah, the humans pointed out the lake when we were flying back. The Northern river flows right to their Dam." Gillian answered.

"Men take up arms, let's destroy them!" Zolton ordered. Every Titan present drew their swords.

"Whoa Whoa! Hold on, what are you doing?" Gillian asked. He was confused. The beavers seemed to be honoring Vincent by giving him a proper burial. *Why would Zolton want to destroy them? What have they ever done to him?* Gillian questioned.

"The beavers, specifically the colony of Dux, were chosen by the Great White Eagle to represent all the beasts of Terribbia. Sworn enemies of Malus himself," Zolton explained.

"Shhh, don't mention the Great White Eagle to the Titans," Gillian whispered to Zolton. Gillian had realized that Zolton knew the truth about him, but he assumed none of the others had.

"With all due respect, Sergeant. Did you really think Malus would send Titans who didn't know the truth with you? He barely trusts you, he couldn't afford to send men he didn't trust with. We all believe the Great White Eagle is real."

One of the Titans spoke up from the back of the group. "We have all chosen to serve Malus." Gillian was shocked. It seemed like everyone in the Kingdom knew about the truth except for him.

"We will finally find them and eliminate them!" Zolton shouted. Gillian was sorry he had ever mentioned the beavers' whereabouts. There was no way he could let them harm them. They were innocent creatures. After all, he became a royal Pegasus guard to protect all creatures. The beavers included.

"No!" Gillian shouted.

"No? Have you chosen not to serve Malus?" Zolton questioned, coming nose to nose with Gillian, a much smaller Pegasus.

"No! Malus put me in charge. In charge of finding Vincent. And that's what we have done." Gillian barked. Zolton raised his nose and slowly stepped back. "Our mission is complete. I have done what he has asked. No more and no less. We're going back to Regnum!" Gillian ordered. He was now very worked up and angry at the brigade as a whole. So much so that the whole brigade respected his words. The men slowly sheathed their swords and one by one fell into line. Gillian began counting to make sure all the men were present.

"Thirteen, fourteen," he counted. *Wait, that's not right. I had fifteen men.* He thought to himself. Again, he counted. "One, two… Thirteen, fourteen…" He looked around the Blackwood Forest and then back out into the meadow. "Titans, we are missing a man." The Titans began to mumble amongst themselves, trying to figure out who was missing. Finally, one Titan realized who it was.

"It is Thomas, Sergeant. He is the missing Titan."

Where has he gone? I must find him. Malus will be upset with me if something happens to one of the men. Gillian thought. "Thomas? Thomas? Thomas!" he shouted. To his relief, Thomas responded from off in the distance.

Gillian and the Titans ran towards the voice. What they found was Thomas crawling out of what remained of the blueberry bush. As he tried fighting his way out of the bushes, the branches grabbed at his armor and hindered his escape. Although he was not in any real danger, it was quite an inconvenience for the man.

"I noticed something in the bush," Thomas grumbled as he finally broke free and escaped from the bush's clutches.

Just then, Gillian noticed that in Thomas's hand there was a book. His eyes widened, and his mouth fell open. The familiar book was as beautiful as ever. *It is the book that Eva had, her book of truth.* Gillian thought to himself. *She thought this book was very important, and now it is in the hands of the Titans? This cannot be good…*

"I found this book within the heart of the bushes. It's a very odd book. The inscription on the cover is in a different language, I think. Its leather cover is laced with gold," Thomas explained.

"I bet it is very valuable," another Titan shouted.

"Maybe, but it is locked shut. Looks like you need a key to open it," Thomas said, looking at the leather flap that wrapped around the book, clasping the pages within tightly shut. He pointed to the lock embedded in the leather flap.

"I wonder what this writing is, looks ancient, maybe Centaurian or Dwarvish," Zolton wondered.

"The book cover reads 'Book of Truth'," Gillian said, stepping forward and looking closer at the book.

"How do you know that, Gillian? Are you a Somniator?" Zolton questioned intently.

"Eva…" he started in confidence, then changed his tone to seem like he was uninvolved with the traitors. "I overheard the girl talking about it with the other two."

"The book of truth. Sounds important. Malus will be pleased that we have found this. And the girl, she must be a Somniator! He will be pleased to know that as well," Zolton said, thinking about the book and all the knowledge that it would hold within its covers.

"Did you find Vincent?" Thomas asked. Since he was caught up in the blueberry bush, he had no clue about the grave. They all nodded solemnly. Slowly, they led Thomas to the grave site so Thomas could pay his respects to the fallen comrade.

"The beavers," one of the Titans said, pointing out the tracks in the soft dirt.

"Huh…" Thomas said. When Thomas had chosen to serve Malus years ago, Malus took him under his wing for a while. One of the things he spoke about was his hatred for the beavers. He had convinced Thomas that the beavers were nothing but filthy animals bred to do the Great White Eagle's work, which would only hinder the work and progress of the Kingdom. Yet, here Thomas stood looking down at Vincent's grave. It was done gracefully and with great respect for Vincent. Supposedly by a sworn enemy… *Why would the beavers do something so kind towards one of us?* Thomas began to wonder if the beavers were as bad as he once believed. "What now?" Thomas asked.

"*We* are heading back," Zolton said in a very disappointed voice. He nudged his head towards Gillian, indicating that it was because of him. Thomas sensed that Zolton wanted to hunt the beavers down, but under the current circumstances, Thomas was glad they were not going to.

"Very well," Thomas said, straightening out and giving Gillian his attention. The rest of the Titans followed suit. It was time for them to head home.

Gillian looked one last time at the grave of Vincent. With a tender hoof, he pressed his hoof into the soft dirt of the grave. This was a Pegasus' way of leaving flowers at a grave, or saying farewell one last time; a sign of respect. "If you boys are ready, let's move out," Gillian said very quietly. They all removed their helmets and nodded to the grave, and in groups of three, marched out of the Blackwood forest into the meadow. *It's done.* Gillian thought solemnly.

Following the same manner that they took to enter the Forbidden circle, the Titans marched north up through the Forbidden forest towards the clearing, and Gillian and Zolton took to the sky.

"I will present the book to Malus when we return, and I will inform the King of Vincent's burial," Gillian said to Zolton, who was flying beside him.

"*We* will present the book, and I will make sure you tell Malus the truth of the matter," Zolton ordered. He was convinced that nothing from Gillian's mouth would be truthful, and would be there to make sure that this time the truth was delivered in full.

Landing in the clearing, Gillian waited for his men to arrive. Single file, they paraded from the tangled web of branches and vines until every last one was accounted for. Then, assembling back into rows of three, the Titans marched back to Regnum. Gillian in the lead, with Thomas and the book behind him, and Zolton bringing up the rear.

Chapter 9
Dungeon Discoveries

While Gillian was on his mission, the others were stuffed into the dungeon. It was dark and cold, and heavy shadows filled the prison cells with gloom. The morning brought moisture to the stone floor and made waking up quite miserable. As the first rays of a red sunrise peaked through the small window near the dungeon's ceiling, cool air gushed in, chilling Eva to the bone.

Slowly, she pushed herself into a sitting position and scooched herself back to the rock-faced wall. As she rubbed her blurry morning vision away, she could see the dark silhouettes of Jessie and Andy still passed out on the floor. Unfortunately, the shadows still masked most of the dungeon, but every minute that passed, more light seeped in. Each prison cell had a small window level with the ground outside. It wouldn't be until much later in the morning that the strands of sunlight stood a chance against the long shadows of the dungeon.

If given a chance to enjoy a quiet morning, one sometimes finds peace, but for Eva, this quiet morning was solemn. *A servant to the cruel king?* She thought. Remembering the words of her mother, not to trust the King, she did not like the idea of being his servant one bit. *I must escape, I must.* She had decided.

As she plotted her escape, she watched the rays of light from the window slowly creep across the floor as the sun outside rose higher into the morning sky.

Soon her thoughts were interrupted by a rooster's crow. The loud blast from the rooster startled Andy from his slumber. He raised himself up and rubbed his eyes. Glancing around the room, he noticed Eva against the wall. He scooched along the floor and joined her.

"Good morning, Eva," he whispered.

"Is it good?" Eva asked as she shivered from the cold.

"Well… no. But it will get better," Andy said, with optimism in his voice.

"How do you know?" Eva asked. She was feeling defeated.

"I don't, but I have to believe it will. After all, believing in something brings hope. I'd rather have hope than give up." Andy said.

Eva pondered what he said. She liked that. It brought her comfort in a place that was so uncertain. She really looked up to Andy, and he was always looking out for her in any way he could. He always took charge and followed his heart. Although he may have been a troublemaker, he always had good intentions. She admired that.

Finally, the sun rays overtook the gloomy haze of the dungeon. Enough light had poured in that most of the dungeon was visible. However, something had happened the night before, while Andy, Eva, and Jessie were all fast asleep. A man was put into the cell adjacent to theirs in the late hours of the night. At this very moment, he sat quietly in the deep, dark shadow that still loomed in the corner of the dungeon. It concealed him from sight for the present moment.

This man was quite curious about his fellow prisoners. It hadn't taken long for rumors of their treason to spread throughout all of Regnum, so once he had been placed in the cell and realized the three sleeping beside him were the traitors, he hid himself in the shadows and listened closely to what they had to say. It is always when one thinks they are alone that the truth comes out, and this man was eager to hear their story.

Eventually, Jessie awoke and stood up, stretching out his arms and legs, and he let out a huge yawn.

"What do they got for breakfast in this joint?" Jessie asked while making his way over to the iron bars and trying to squeeze his face between them.

Out of his peripheral vision, he could see Simon sitting on a stool with his eyes closed. When Jessie asked about breakfast, Simon opened one eye, then closed it again, flat out ignoring Jessie's question.

"Fine, if you're not gonna feed me, I'll have to escape and find my own food," Jessie said in a playful voice, trying to convince Simon to bring them food. Simon never opened his eyes, which annoyed Jessie, so with his cheeks pinched between the bars, he stuck his tongue out at the old brute and pushed away from the bar. Jessie gave up his attempt empty-handed but was satisfied by his humor. He put his hands in his pockets, smiled, and kicked at the floor with his foot. Simon, however, thought for a moment about Jessie's request. It reminded him that he was hungry. So, quietly, he got up and went to the ballroom for a royal breakfast.

"Man, the service down here is horrible," Jessie continued jokingly, smiling down at Andy and Eva.

Andy climbed to his feet, giggling at Jessie's shenanigans. "It sure is, we will have to bring a complaint before the King," Andy said, playing along with Jessie's skit. Knowing full well the King couldn't care less about them. They giggled a bit before settling into a bit more serious topics.

"So, Eva. Where did they take you?" Andy asked.

"They took me to the royal ballroom! It was absolutely stunning... I always dreamed of going to a dance at the royal ballroom. Too bad it was under these circumstances..." Eva explained.

"I'm so glad you got to see your mom again," Andy said, smiling at Eva.

"Yeah, it was really good to see her again. I totally bawled my eyes out," Eva said, making light of a truthful matter.

Jessie remained quiet. Thinking about his mom he remembered the painful sight of both his mom's soul, and his brother being sucked into the Devil's Kettle. Storm clouds began to brew in his eyes as tears swelled.

"Yes, but she did tell me one thing before she was dragged away by one of those nasty Titans." She paused for a moment and looked over towards where Simon was sitting to make sure he was still gone. When she deemed it clear, she said, "We aren't to trust the King or his brother either, for that matter," Eva explained.

"I didn't know he had a brother? What's his name?" Andy asked, and again Jessie remained quiet because the reminder of his lost brother caused his eyes to swell with tears.

"Well, apparently he does? And she never said..." Eva said, shrugging her shoulders.

"What else did she say?" Andy asked.

"Well..." Eva said, hesitating. She didn't want to tell Andy that she would have to become a servant to the King. She knew that Andy distrusted the King already and wouldn't stand for her becoming his servant.

"What is it?" Andy questioned. Noticing her hesitation.

"My mom worked out a deal with the King," Eva said.

"A deal?" Jessie finally jumped in. He choked back his tears. He didn't like the sound of Eva's tone and could tell the deal most likely only benefited the King.

"The King promised to spare my life as long as I became his servant." These words from Eva would have been a very solemn moment if it hadn't been for the man hiding in the shadows. With a great burst of laughter, he fell to the ground rolling out of the shadows.

This abrupt outburst scared Andy, Eva, and Jessie. Eva screamed, Jessie jumped, and Andy's heart skipped a beat. The man began to roll side to side and laughed harder and harder. Absolutely shocked to learn that they were not alone in the dungeon, they stood, looking at the man in terror.

Eventually, they deemed the man harmless because he literally rolled around on the floor laughing hysterically like a madman. The terror turned into anger because they did not know what was so funny about Eva becoming a slave of the King. Andy finally got a good look at the rolling mess of a man and noticed that in his hand was a bottle of rum.

"He's not mad, he's drunk!" Andy shouted in anger.

"And what is it that you find so funny, mister!" Eva barked as she walked over to the iron bars that separated her from him. She stood there with both hands on her hips and a fierce frown on her face.

"Oh no! They've spotted me," he squealed. It seemed as if the man had giggled the words to himself. Soon, the man scrambled to his feet and darted back into the shadows.

"I think he's drunk and has gone mad," Jessie said.

"I think they are talking about me," the man said. Jessie and Andy peered around the dungeon, looking for anyone else that he could be talking to, but there was no one. It seemed that he was clearly talking to himself.

"Hey, mister! She asked you a question!" Andy said as he walked towards the iron bars. "Are you insane?" he questioned.

"They think I'm insane!" The man giggled as he rolled back and forth. It was really rather an awkward thing to encounter. "I'm not insane, but you are." Slowly, the man lifted himself out of the shadows and walked over to the iron bars. Eva became frightened and began to back away.

"Leave her alone!" Andy commanded, stepping in front of the deranged man.

"Should I tell her?" the man again asked himself. He then paused for a moment. Using his eyes, he looked up and to the right, but he never moved his head. Soon, his hands clasped the iron bars.

"Tell me what, you lunatic?" Eva asked, distraught. Then, as if the craziness was all an act, the man dropped his hands to his sides and used a very plain voice.

"I'm not crazy, but you want to know what is?" he asked.

"What?" Eva asked, biting the bait.

"Believing the King makes deals!" Then he laughed hysterically once again and took another gulp of his rum.

"You're drunk. What do you know?"

"Fine, don't believe me," the crazy man said calmly, as he sank back into the shadows.

"I don't! My mom said the King would spare me if I served him," Eva cried.

"Sorry, sweetheart, but your mom was lied to," he said.

"How do you know he will not spare her?" Andy said, very angry at the thought of Eva being killed.

"Look around, my friend. Do you see any signs of sparingness?" the man asked.

Again, the three scanned the dungeons, but there were no other prisoners, just them and the odd drunken man.

"So why are you still here then?" Andy questioned.

"Well, you see, the King and I have an arrangement," the drunk man said.

"And what might that be?" Jessie asked.

"That doesn't matter. But fear not, I hate the man, so we have a common enemy. Which, by logic, makes us friends?" the drunk man said. Then came back out of the shadows and waltzed over to the iron bars. Carelessly, he extended his right hand over to their side in hopes of a friendly handshake.

Eva looked at Andy and Jessie, raised her eyebrows, and slowly approached the man. She extended out her arm, and her hand met his. He gripped her hand firmly and then gave it a violent shake.

"Phillip is my name."

"My… My name is Eva," she said cautiously.

"I'm Andy, and this is Jessie," Andy said, pointing to himself and then Jessie.

"Pleasure to meet you," he said, as a burp followed.

"So, how did you end up down here?" Jessie asked, cutting right to the chase. The man looked at Jessie with one eyebrow raised much higher than the other. He then took a swig of his rum.

"Let's just say, I lost something dear to me, and went looking for it in all the wrong places," he said.

"Did you find it?" Eva asked.

"Does it look like he found it?" Jessie said sharply.

"What do you mean by the wrong places?" Andy said.

"Well, to be straight forward, I had to take something that wasn't mine, to trade for what I was looking for in the first place," Phillip said with a deep sigh.

"So you're a thief?" Jessie blurted out.

"It's much more complicated than that. But sure, let's go with 'thief'," he said.

"What did you have to take?" Eva innocently asked.

"It doesn't matter, all that does is that I know I was wrong. I would give anything to go back and change what I did," Phillip said as he slowly stepped away from the iron bars and submerged himself back into the shadows.

"Well, I'm sure that if you ask the Great White Eagle, he will forgive you. No matter what you have done," Eva said with a smile. She knew that whenever she had gotten in trouble as a child, her mother told her to ask the Great White Eagle for forgiveness, and if she truly felt sorry for what she had done, the Great White Eagle would forgive her.

"When I see him face to face, I'll ask him. But until then, I'll just rot down here," Phillip said as he turned his back towards them.

Jessie senses something in the man at that moment. It was the first time that he had felt the man was being truthful. Jessie sensed his pain and his regret for all that had happened and could relate. Jessie remembered his brother telling him to find the Great White Eagle, and that was what he planned to do. *I want answers, and this man wants forgiveness. Together we can find the Great White Eagle. I'll help him move on, as I hope to do myself!* Jessie thought with compassion for the man. Jessie walked over to the iron bars and pressed in.

"Come with me," Jessie whispered. Phillip never said anything, but Jessie could tell by the way he looked at him that he had interest in going with him. "Help me get out of here, and we will go find the Great White Eagle together.

"Jessie! What are you saying? You barely know the man," Andy said.

Phillip took no notice of Andy's disapproval and came back out of the shadows. "Even if I could get us out of here, what makes you think that we could find him? Many have looked before us, and no one has ever found him."

"Eva's dream. Her first dream!" Jessie shouted.

"Jessie! Quiet, we barely know him. The last time we opened our mouths, we ended up here," Andy scolded him.

"Ahh, so you're a Somniator?" Phillip asked, turning his attention towards Eva. "Does the King know?"

"No, not unless the Pegasus told him," Eva said softly. She was almost embarrassed.

"Good, good. The less the King knows, the better. Your mother was right, the King is not to be trusted," Phillip stated.

"You know about Somniators?" Andy asked. He was shocked that a poor man living in the dungeons of the castle would know anything about such things.

"I do…" Phillip admitted.

"What else do you know?" Andy pressed the drunk man.

"I think you'd be surprised at what I know and what I've seen," Phillip said grimly.

"Try me," Andy snapped.

"My story is quite complicated, I'm afraid," Phillip said.

"Complicated? How so?" Eva questioned.

"Let's just say, if you really did go to the Devil's Kettle as the rumor says, we both know you learned a lot along the way," he said mysteriously.

"So you know about the Devil's Kettle?" Jessie asked. His interest in Phillip was growing deeper and deeper. He sensed that Phillip had a wisdom much greater than himself and because of that, Jessie had so many questions for him.

"Sure, I may know a thing or two," Phillip said.

"You're bluffing," Andy said, then turning to Eva and Jessie. "He's just trying to get us to spill our guts. He wants to know all about our journey," Andy said, then turned back to Phillip. "What a crook!"

"Would a crook know about the Messorems? Would a crook know that from the brim of the Centrum's Core, you can see the fog rising up into the sky from the Uada Hollow? Would a crook know what the screams of creatures past sounds like as they are dragged into the Devil's Kettle?" Phillip said with such aggression that Andy turned red as a tomato, and caused him to be embarrassed that he doubted the mysterious man.

"So you've been there?" Eva questioned.

"I didn't say that..." Phillip said with a smile. Jessie now had great faith that Phillip had been telling the truth the whole time, and was eager to pick his brain about the mysteries of the Devil's Kettle.

"Are the legends true?" Jessie questioned.

"Hmmm, not all of them," Phillip said suspiciously. He was curious as to why Jessie was asking such questions. However, Jessie was asking for a specific purpose. He had a specific legend in mind. Jessie felt a warm feeling flood his body. It was hope, something he had not felt since before his brother fell into the Devil's Kettle.

"Really?" Jessie asked joyfully.

Phillip realized that Jessie had a reason, and because Phillip knew quite a lot about the Devil's Kettle and its true nature, he decided that until he knew more about these three that he better shy away from answering this young man's pressing questions. Backpeddling, he directed their conversation back towards Eva's dream, the one that Jessie had mentioned before.

"Let's just focus on the task at hand. You said Eva had a dream. One that proves that we could find the Great White Eagle?" Phillip questioned. This made Jessie a bit angry, and as a reaction, he crossed his arms. He wanted to know more about the Devil's Kettle and not focus on Eva's dream, which in his mind was old news.

"In my dream, I saw the Great White Eagle. He used a sickle and cut down the weeds in a field. All of the good crops were bent over by the sickle, but once passed over, they were not harmed. But all the weeds were cut and destroyed by the blade." Eva explained her first dream.

"Your dream is quite common. In fact, the King has had the same dream and many other Somniators have as well." Phillip said. "It refers to a prophecy of old. The scrolls talk of the prophecy. They say that one day, the Great White Eagle will return. He will cut down all evil in the world, and the good will live in harmony."

"Hold on. The King what?!" Andy asked. "The King is a Somniator?"

"Oh yes," Phillip said.

"How does a drunk man like you know all of this?" Andy asked, questioning who he really was.

"Like I said, the King and I have an arrangement," Phillip said.

"You sound like friends, if you ask me," Andy said.

"Do you think the King would keep his friend in a prison cell?" Phillip snapped.

"I suppose not," Andy said, relaxing his suspicion a bit.

"Anyways, many creatures have had that dream, but it has never been revealed as to when he will return," Phillip explained.

"Well… Um, I think he might have… In my dream, he said, 'It is time!'" Eva explained humbly.

"It's true, I sensed it meant now… That's what made me most concerned with her dream. It seemed like something big and dangerous was going to happen, and we would be a part of it," Andy explained.

"Wait, he really said that to you?" Phillip asked Eva intensely.

"The Great White Eagle? Yes, he did," she responded.

"Then it is time!" Phillip began to shout. "Now is the time, he is going to return!" He began to jump up and down in his cell with excitement. As if he had been awaiting the return of a long-lost friend and could finally see them coming over the horizon. The three looked at each other with wide eyes and then back at the dancing man. Then, as instantly as he began to dance, he stopped and pressed into the iron bars.

"When you say 'sensed danger', would that mean you are a Lector?" Phillip asked Andy.

"I have been told that I am," Andy admitted.

"Told? By whom?" Phillip asked oddly.

"A gladiator bear…" Andy said.

"My my! You two are a pair!" Phillip said with glee. Referring to the fact that Eva was a Somniator and Andy was a Lector.

"You know about Lectors as well?" Andy asked.

"Listen, kid, I know lots. Better if you just accept it, instead of fighting me along the way," Phillip said. Andy looked at him with a bit of shame. It was obvious Phillip knew what he was talking about, but Andy wouldn't let up his reins on the grubby fellow. "Heard from a Somniator and confirmed by a Lector! Warn the cavalry! Warn the people! The Great White Eagle is coming back!" Phillip said as he danced once again with great joy. Suddenly, he stopped his dancing and ran back into the fading shadow of his cell. However, the three in the cell next to him watch intently. To their surprise, Phillip again began to talk to himself.

"Did you hear that? He is coming back!" Phillip said giddily. "I can finally face my faults, my mistakes. I can ask for forgiveness!" Phillip said in a low but joyful whisper. However, in Phillip's excitement, his voice was not at a whisper's volume, and the others heard him loud and clear.

"How can you be so certain that he really is coming back?" Jessie asked, wanting to make sure that when they set out on their journey to find the Great White Eagle that they would really be able to find him.

"Look, I have talked with many Somniators over the years, and most of them had that exact same dream. However, no one ever heard the Great White Eagle say anything. That was until you did." - Looking at Eva - "Now, if you pair her unique dream with the prophecy of the scrolls, it's clear that the Great White Eagle's return is near!" Phillip shouted and began dancing around again. Phillip then took his bottle of rum and chugged the remainder of it and then chucked the bottle at the floor. A loud crashing occurred as the jug shattered into a million pieces.

If Phillip had been sober-minded and had not been filled with such excitement, the next question would have caused a rush of great concern to shoot down his spine. However, as Jessie asked, Phillip's clouded mind answered without thinking.

You see, Jessie desperately wanted to save his brother. Although the legends all said once you fell into the Devil's Kettle, you would never return, he refused to believe it, especially after Phillip assured him that not all the legends were true. Jessie knew he had to find the Great White Eagle; his brother told him so. However, instead of seeking the Great White Eagle in hopes of finding answers, as his brother intended, Jessie wanted to find the Great White Eagle for his own benefit.

"If we find the Great White Eagle, could he bring someone back from the Devil's Kettle?" Jessie asked. His mission was to find the Great White Eagle, but out of grief, his mission changed from finding the Great White Eagle to saving his brother.

"I'm sure he could. Plus, that *would* be a better option than asking Malus to retrieve him," Phillip said, distracted by the good news of the Great White Eagle's return.

"Malus?" Jessie asked himself quietly. Suddenly, Phillip stopped dancing and looked as if to be listening very intently.

He realized that he should have thought about Jessie's question and answered more carefully. Then he said, "Did I say Malus? I meant, ahh… I." Phillip began to stutter and was failing to think of something to say.

"You said Malus!" Jessie said with a shift in his tone.

"I must have said it mistakenly. I meant nothing by it," Phillip said. Then, as if he were talking to himself again, he began to whisper in the dark corner of his cell. "I know, I know. Keep my mouth shut."

"Who are you talking to?" Andy asked, annoyed at the crazed man. Phillip stopped talking and, with a stern look, stared at Andy. Suddenly, his eyes darted to the right.

"Okay, I'll ask them," Phillip said, as if talking to himself once again. His eyes darted back towards Andy and the others. "When you guys got to the Devil's Kettle, did you happen to find a book?" Phillip asked in a peculiar way.

"We never said we made it there…" Andy snapped, still unsure if they could trust him.

"What if he did?" Jessie blurted. At this point, Jessie was almost willing to tell Phillip anything he wanted to know. He was beginning to believe that Phillip knew exactly how to save his brother.

"It's a really fancy book, quite beautiful in fact, with gold stitching and a lock on it?" Phillip asked, showing its size with his hands.

"Ummm… No, we didn't," Andy said, stepping forward. He had decided that he did not trust him one bit. It was obvious that Phillip knew a lot about the mysterious Forbidden Circle, and secondly, he had admitted himself that he worked with the King. *How can we trust him? Who is to say he isn't a spy for the King this very second?* He thought.

"Ahh, that's too bad," Phillip said as he slapped his knee and resumed being jolly about the Great White Eagle's alleged return.

Eva looked at Andy with confusion. She didn't feel there was any need to lie to him, but trusted his instincts.

"Ummm, Phillip... Why is it that you talk to yourself... Do you hear voices?" Eva asked. When he spoke to himself, it made her very uncomfortable. She worried that he was crazy or worse, that a ghost haunted the dungeons, and that he was friends with it.

"I am talking to Mischka," he said proudly. The three again looked around the dungeon, and there was no one else, even the Dungeon Keeper was gone.

"Is Mischka a ghost? Or a spirit?" Jessie asked, saying what Eva feared could be the case.

"Of course not, but wouldn't that be something?" Phillip said, crossing his arms and looking off in the distance, thinking about having a ghost friend.

"Mischka is a..." and before Phillip could answer, a tiny little creature darted out from Phillip's pant leg and dashed across the dungeon floor. Causing a hurricane of panic in the adjacent cell. Eva screeched at the top of her lungs and jumped behind Andy.

"A mouse!" Eva screeched. Even though the fuzzy little mouse had terrified her to the bone, it was not going to bring Eva any harm.

"That's right! Mischka is a mouse!" Phillip said.

Jessie bent down to the ground and put out his palm. Mischka pranced onto his palm and sat back on her hind legs.

"Ahh, she's cute!" Jessie said, looking at her long whiskers, which twitched at the wiggle of her nose.

Eva cautiously peeked over Andy's shoulder. From a safe distance, and with Andy to keep her safe, Eva began to examine the little mouse closer. Her little nose was a soft pink, and her ears were large in comparison to her body. She had fuzzy brown fur coating her with long whiskers and a sharp snout. She had a long pink tail and cute little paws. Still at a distance, Eva could hear a soft squeak coming from her. Eva could hear the mouse squeaking. From where she stood, Mischka spoke too quietly to hear. However, soon Eva saw Jessie lifting the mouse near his own ear. *Can Jessie understand her? That would make her like me?* With this thought, she just had to get closer to hear what the little creature had to say.

"Her faint voice sounded like a squeak at a distance, however as Eva got close to the little mouse, she could understand Mischka perfectly. In the tongue of man the mouse rambled, "...fortunately the Great White Eagle spoke to me in a dream, I had no clue what the dream was about, but luckily I knew of a lector nearby. The only problem was that the Lector was a cat! Can you believe that? The Great White Eagle made *me* a Somniator, a mouse, and then made the closest Lector to me a Cat! Good gravy and biscuits. Anyway, that's when I learned I was supposed to come to the Castle. But I still didn't know why, just that I was supposed to be here..." Finally, the little mouse took a breath, and Eva stepped in. Eva decided that if she were going to have any chance at asking the little mouse a question, she would have to interrupt her. It was evident that Mischka could have talked forever if someone was willing to listen.

"Forgive my interruption, but you said you're a Somniator? Like me?" Eva asked.

"Yes, ma'am! That's why I can speak your language," she responded.

"That makes sense, as to why I can understand her as well," Jessie added.

They all looked at Andy, who was still standing off to the side. He shrugged at their discovery because to him, the mouse was so quiet, all he heard was squeaking. He assumed this was a situation much like when Eva spoke with Maizey on their journey within the Forbidden Circle. He would be left out and filled in later. But learning that Mischka was speaking their language, he leaned in closer until he too could hear the little creature.

"The word around Regnum is that you three found the Devil's Kettle. Not only that, but you survived a night in the Uada Hollow? That must have been scary! I couldn't imagine fighting those dreadful creatures. What was it like? What did they look like?" Again, she took a deep breath, and Andy stepped in.

"We did make it to the Devil's Kettle. We fought the Messorems, but we had weapons. They were these crystal-type rocks that glowed."

"The Messorems were terrified by them!" Eva said.

"Yeah! We sure gave them a taste of their own medicine! We struck fear into them!" Jessie said pridefully.

"What you speak of is called the Eagle's Heart Crystal. They are mysterious crystals. They seem to hold great power, but the truth of their purpose is unknown." Phillip added in, again, he seemed to have a great knowledge that surpassed all three of theirs combined.

"Well, they work well against the Messorems," Jessie said, recalling the moment he saved his brother with the help of Andy's crystal.

"That they do," Phillip said as if he, too, had used one to protect himself from the Messorems long ago. "Say, when you look at a crystal, what color do you see?" Phillip asked.

All at once, Andy, Eva, and Jessie blurted out colors.

Andy said he saw Blue, Jessie saw Yellow, and Eva saw purple.

Then, all at once, Andy, Eva, and Jessie blurted out "What?!"

"The crystals are clearly blue," Andy said, recalling the blue glow in the cave where he first obtained his crystal.

"Um, no, the night we fought off the Messorems, the crystal was yellow. Not to mention Richard's Apple was also yellow." Jessie argued.

"You are both wrong. Both crystals were purple. The cave was filled with purple crystals, and the apple flickered a bright purple!" Eva added.

The three stood in a circle, confused. Each one of them had seen a different colored crystal, even when they were looking at the same one.

"Ha ha ha. Was a shock for me too when I learned this!" Phillip chuckled.

"All we know about these mysterious crystals is that they are somehow connected to the Great White Eagle. Any time one appeared, there was a moment before where we felt as if the Great White Eagle was with us somehow!" Mischka added very quietly.

"You guys have crystals?" Eva asked.

"Well…no," Mischka admitted she had never actually seen an Eagle's Heart crystal, but heard many stories from Phillip and others whom she had spied on.

"I used to have one long ago. But it's gone now." Phillip said with a sigh, remembering all that had happened to him.

"What happened?" Jessie asked.

"That, my friend, is a long story," Phillip said.

"Hmmm, I know what you mean, though, feeling as if the Great White Eagle was with us somehow," Andy said. He remembered the night they spent in the Uada Hollow, and how he tried and tried with all his might to start a fire, but couldn't. That was until the raven showed up and a great wind arose and dried up the fire pit. Every one of them felt as if the spirit of the Great White Eagle was with them somehow. It was the very next morning that the mysterious tree with pink flowers blossomed, and full-grown apples appeared. "It was the morning after we felt as if the Great White Eagle was with us, that a crystal apple appeared," Andy said. Although he did not explain much of that night to Phillip or Mischka, Eva and Jessie remembered it vividly. They all thought of the fond memory until Eva asked another question.

"What do the colors mean? Why do we each see a different color?"

"That is a very good question, and I'm afraid we cannot answer it. The only hope in finding out these answers is in the book Phillip asked you about. Without it and the key, it will all remain a mystery," Mischka said.

The three looked at each other again. Still sticking to their gut feeling, they refrained from telling Phillip about the Book of Truth they once had, but had lost during the chaos that involved Vincent.

"Where are your crystals now?" Phillip asked.

"The King took them from us," Jessie said. The thought of the King taking his brother's crystal from him angered him.

"Ahh, yes… the King. What a dreadfully cruel man," he said in an odd way. Odd enough that Andy and the others all took note of it. "The King will probably sell your crystals to the dwarves, they are of great value and they are very rare," Phillip explained.

The five of them remained quiet for some time after this. They all had thoughts to process. Like, *what were these crystals really?* And, *what did the colors mean?* They also thought about the Book of Truth. *Was it still in the blueberry bush?* And w*hat unknown knowledge was within the pages of the mysterious book?*

Each one also pondered separate thoughts.

Will I ever see my family again? Eva thought.

Can Malus really retrieve someone from the Devil's Kettle, like Phillip said? Jessie pondered.

How will I get my friends to safety? Will we get to safety? Andy worried.

Even for Phillip, questions and thoughts flooded his head. He had been in the dungeons for a very long time. He had seen many things concerning the Great White Eagle: prophesies, dreams, understandings, and various creatures. Most of his later life had been submerged in discovering the truth.

Has the Great White Eagle really returned? Will he save us all from Malus? Can the Great White Eagle forgive me for what I have done? Phillip cried out in thought.

Their silence was broken when Mischka finally spoke briefly.

"I must be off, I have much work to do, but I will return tonight." She said as she scampered up Jessie's arm, and then down his side to the floor and disappeared into a crack in the dungeon wall.

They all watched her leave in silence, and no one said another word for a while. Each ended up wandering to their own corner of the dungeon cell to ponder the great burden that rested upon their shoulders. These burning questions were all they could think about.

Chapter 10
Decisions, Decisions

In a tight formation, the Titans stood at attention. The sun had risen well into the sky, and it was a warm afternoon. Beads of sweat rolled down the back of the Titans' necks, and even Gillian had a glisten of sweat on his hide from their trek back from the Forbidden Circle. "Titans, at ease. You are free to go. Thank you for your assistance on today's mission, but I will take it from here."

All of them bowed to Gillian, and as they disbanded, Gillian let out a sigh of relief; the mission was completed. During his trip to the

Forbidden Circle, he forced himself to commit to the mission, but now that it was over, he wished he could hide from everyone.

I still don't know what I'm going to do, but I don't want these humans following me around anymore. Gillian thought to himself. *I wish I had more time to think, to escape it all. But I know Malus wants an answer, and soon!* Gillian trembled at the burden on his shoulders.

"Thomas!" Zolton shouted, breaking Gillian's train of thought. Gillian's mane stood on end, and his ears drooped. Just when Gillian had thought he could run off to his stable to hide, Zolton reined him back to reality. Just hearing Zolton's voice, the weight on his shoulders grew heavier.

Thomas was just about to enter the castle's archway on the left. (Which leads to the mezzanine above the ballroom.) He stopped and turned about. "Yes, Sire?" he asked.

"Straight to Malus with that book," Zolton said, referring to the Book of Truth Thomas clutched in his hands.

"Yes, Sire, on my way now, Sir," Thomas said with a bow.

"Carry on!" Zolton barked, lifting his nose high into the air. Thomas quickly turned and vanished into the castle. Then Zolton turned his attention to Gillian.

"We will visit with Malus now..." Zolton ordered in a very low and serious tone. Gillian's ears flattened out.

"Malus will call for me when he is ready. We will go then..." Gillian stammered, trying to buy himself time to think. His false sense of leadership still loomed from his mission, but Zolton was no longer playing along.

"You only had my obedience because Malus ordered me to follow your directions while on the mission he gave you. But your mission is done, and now once again you will follow my orders… we go now," he scolded, as he snorted and stomped his foot.

Gillian lowered his head. He knew that the power once granted to him by Malus was gone. Now he must obey Zolton and face Malus.

What does the discovery of this book mean for me? Maybe I should just come clean about everything I know. He thought as he was led back into the castle, up the stairs and around the indoor balcony that overlooked the ballroom and the King's throne.

Zolton used his front hoof and pawed at the door. It was the way a Pegasus knocked.

"Who is there?" the voice of Malus asked from inside.

"It is I, Zolton, your Highness. I have brought Gillian with me and have much to discuss."

"Very well," Malus said, opening the door.

Inside, Malus had the curtain pulled over the window, and it was very dark. For as bright as the midday was, one could not tell if it was day or night from within his chambers. Flickering candles illuminated the room, however, long shadows stretched out along the walls. It was a low-lit and hazy room.

"I see you have brought me a gift?" Malus said as he flicked his nose toward the wall next to the chamber's door. Behind Gillian and Zolton, they could see a short shelf with the book resting upon it.

"We have, I hope you are pleased by it?" Zolton said, trying to get on Malus' good side - if he even had one.

"Did you find Vincent?" Malus asked Gillian, completely ignoring Zolton.

"We did. The beavers buried his body," Gillian said.

"The beavers! Did you hunt them down and destroy them?!" Malus shouted. Lifting his wings from his body. The large gust of wind generated by his wings extinguished a few of the candles, dimming the room.

"We did not, Gillian ordered us not to," Zolton said with a low and calm voice. Zolton hoped this would anger Malus enough that he would become fed up with him and send him away.

"You did what?!" Malus yelled. As Zolton hoped, he was very angry. His nostrils flared, and he pressed Gillian. Malus was much bigger than Gillian, so he was able to peer down with piercing eyes. He began to paw at the floor in anger.

"Oh Great One, I am dreadfully sorry. But you charged me with one mission. Find Vincent, and that we did." Gillian said, gulping in fear. He hoped Malus would have mercy on him.

"Don't worry, Sire. Gillian has informed us of their whereabouts. Finally, we can squash them. After all these years, we have found the pesky varmints." Zolton said, ensuring Malus that he would clean up this tragedy.

"Very good, Zolton," he said, then he looked Gillian in the eye. "So, it seems you have chosen to serve the Great White Eagle?"

"I have not made any decision yet!" Gillian said, defending himself.

"Clearly, you have chosen to protect the Beavers, allies of the Great White Eagle and my sworn enemies."

"Sire, please understand, I only did as you asked. Nothing more, nothing less. I'm sorry if that was wrong of me. But am I not already on trial? I would not dare try anything to upset you," Gillian pleaded.

"I suppose you are. I did give you a mission, and you did complete it... just know, Gillian, I am watching your every move." Malus said with squinted eyes. The mighty black Pegasus was not dumb; in fact, he was very wise. It was the reason he had gained so much power in the first place. He used his wits and schemes to manipulate everyone. So, he had almost seen it all. The situation at hand with Gillian had played out hundreds of times before with many other creatures. However, what Gillian was going to decide was uncertain, which made Malus angry and skeptical of the younger steed. Yet, Malus knew, if there was any hope of converting Gillian to his side, he must play nice until nice was no longer an option.

"Thank you for understanding," Gillian said, trying to show Malus that he was grateful.

Malus eyed the young Pegasus with distrust, but accepted it. Gillian felt relieved for a moment as the tensions in the air seemed to break; however, the burden he felt remained. Gillian had not arrived at a decision, just yet. He knew he wanted to live freely and desired to be praised by his peers, but everything inside of him screamed that serving the Great White Eagle was the right choice. *Is losing my wings worth it?* Gillian questioned.

"I would demand an answer from you, Gillian; however, we have more important matters at hand," Malus said. Gillian became visibly relieved, and Malus, catching sight of it, assured him that the choice still had to be made. "However, at sunset, I will have my answer!"

"Yes, sire," Gillian said with drooped ears.

"Now! Where did you find the Book of Truth?" Malus asked, trotting over to the lowered shelf that held up the book. He peered down his snout at the beautiful golden thread that sewed the image of the Great White Eagle into the cover. The low flicker of candlelight added an eerie feel to the air. It was very evident to both Zolten and Gillian that Malus was pleased to see the mysterious book.

"I knew you would be pleased!" Zolton whinnied, "I made sure you received it, Sire!"

"You found it?" Malus asked.

"No, Sire. Thomas the Titan did," Zolton responded.

"Very well, he shall be rewarded greatly for this find!" Malus said with a smile. "Tell me more."

"That's all I know about it, Sire," Zolton said, with disappointment, that he could not give his master any more information.

Malus turned and glared down at Gillian. "*What about you*?" Malus asked, putting extra emphasis on each word. Gillian gulped hard. He knew a lot about it, and Eva and Andy had told them the whole story. However, he wasn't certain if he should reveal it all.

"The traitors had it when I found them. I don't know where they got it." Gillian said.

"Why then, did they leave it behind?" Malus questioned. He knew the importance of the book and could not fathom why anyone would leave it behind.

"I do not know, Sire. Maybe they panicked when Vincent attacked... was attacked." Gillian said, slipping a bit on his story. Luckily, Malus was so excited about the book, he didn't notice.

"And the key, where is the key?" Malus questioned with excitement in his voice.

"There was no key found, Sire," Gillian said. However, this answer caused Malus' tone to shift. Storm clouds began to brew in his eyes. His nostrils flared, and his teeth began to grind.

"Unbelievable. I have searched for this book most of my life. I finally found it, and there is no key?" Malus said, with an elevated tone.

"Sire, we will find it! Maybe there is a key around the castle that will work?" Zolten suggested, however, Malus disagreed.

"You buffoon! This book is special! No ordinary key will do!" Malus barked.

"I'm sure there is a way," Zolton said, trying to comfort Malus in his abrupt outburst.

"You fool! Without the key, this book is useless! How will I learn the secrets of this book?" Malus began to panic. He began to pace the room viciously. This was the first time that Gillian had ever seen Malus lose control. Sure, he had seen him in angry outbursts, however, this seemed to be as if Malus was filled with despair and hopelessness.

"What's the big deal?" Zolton asked, shocked to see Malus in such a way.

"The big deal? The big deal is that this book holds the answer to breaking my curse!" Malus shouted as he spread his wings out in anger. The room was down to only one candle burning now, for his wings extinguished the others. It was dark and volatile, and Gillian feared Malus even more while he was in this craze.

"Curse?" Zolton whispered under his breath. Malus had never told him of any curse.

"Yes! I am cursed! I will break my curse, I must!" Malus vomited in anger. Even though it was dark in the room, Malus could see the visible terror, fear, and confusion painted across Zolton's face. Malus' biggest secret had slipped out. Malus became embarrassed, which angered him all the more. "Out of my chambers! Out!" Malus screamed at Zolton. Zolton was shocked, he was loyal to no one but Malus. Yet, here it seemed as if Malus had turned on him.

"But.. But," Zolton stammered.

"Out!" Malus shouted as he pressed Zolton's space, "Get out!" With that burst of aggression, Zolton was forced from the room. Almost chasing his most loyal subject out of the room, Malus stopped just short of his door. If he had gone any further, the door would have clobbered him right in the snout when it slammed shut behind Zolton's tail.

Malus was done playing nice. His rage had grown to the point that he wanted answers and wanted them now. As soon as Zolton was out of his chambers, he sharply spun around and crowded Gillian.

"Enough with your games! Enough with your lies! You are going to be straightforward with me and answer every single question I have," Malus said in a low and aggressive voice.

"Ye...Yes, Sire," Gillian said. Malus, in a desperate attempt to discover information, had completely lost his composure. Much like the King, Malus seemed volatile, which was a very scary thing for Gillian, who was stuck in a room alone with the beast. "If you lie to me one more time, off with your wings! Do you understand me?" Malus questioned as he pressed in.

"Yes, Sire. I understand you," Gillian cried. As Malus pressed in, Gillian backed up until his rump ran into the wall behind him. He knew that there was no way out. He had to do everything Malus said or else it would be the end of him.

"Where did you find the book?" Malus questioned.

"The girl had it when I found them," Gillian said, which was true.

"Gillian! Enough! I know you know more. Let it out!" Malus scolded.

"It's true! The girl had it when I found them. She told me she found it in a house."

"A house?" Malus asked.

"Well, what was left of it. It was falling apart. At least that's what she told me," Gillian stammered.

"You must bring a squad to the Centrum's core. You must find the key. It has to be in that house," Malus ordered.

"I never saw the house. I don't know where it even is," Gillian said. He flinched as he said the words. For he feared Malus would strike him in anger.

"It's the peacekeeper's house. It must be!"

"Peacekeeper?"

"Never mind that, you are useless, I must speak to the girl. If she found the book, she might know where the key is!" Malus shouted with hopefulness in his voice.

"Forgive me, Sire. But what is so important about this key? Why can't you just bring the book to the Dwarves? They have many tools that cut rock, surely they can cut the simple leather strap that binds this book shut," Gillian suggested.

"This book is a special book. It is true, the cover of this book and the strap that holds the pages shut are made of leather, just as are many other books. But this book is different. Its cover is actually sewn with two layers of leather."

"Why?" Gillian questioned.

"Because, flowing between the two layers is a pool of poisonous ink."

"Really?" Gillian asked.

"If the book is damaged, or cut open, as you are suggesting, the ink would burn the pages in an instant, and the pages that escape the ink's poison would be stained black. Making it impossible to read, leaving the secrets of the book lost forever. We must not allow that to happen!" Malus said.

"How do you know that there is this ink within the cover?" Gillian asked. "It looks and feels just like a regular book."

"The Great White Eagle told me himself…" Malus said. For the first time, Gillian had noticed fear in Malus' voice.

"You have actually met the Great White Eagle?" Gillian asked softly.

"Long ago. I used to serve him," Malus said.

It was information like this that made Gillian's decision all the harder. He gasped at the news. *Not only does Malus believe, but he has actually laid eyes upon the Great White Eagle?* Just when he thought his choice was clear, Malus' lie cut deeper. Gillian felt so much distrust for Malus that he began to wonder if he could ever come to trust him. It would have been one thing to say you don't believe in a creature that no one has seen, yet Malus had seen him, even served him, and pretended as if he never existed. His lie was grave. *How could Malus deny something so real? How can I ever trust such a heartless beast?* Gillian asked himself with great distress. Gillian decided that in order to make his decision, he should dig deeper, hear Malus out.

"What… What happened?" Gillian stuttered.

"The Great White Eagle would not share his Kingdom with me," Malus began.

"Why would you expect him to?" Gillian asked, but the nasty look he received from Malus caused him to bite his tongue.

"I was his most loyal subject! Not to mention the greatest Pegasus that ever lived. I deserved a share of his kingdom. When he refused to reward me, I rebelled," Malus explained.

"You rebelled against the Great White Eagle?" Gillian asked in shock.

"Indeed, I gathered allies, and there was a great war," Malus said.

"Oh dear…"

"A great battle took place in the skies, but we were forced to this land," Malus explained, before Gillian cut in.

"Forced? But all the stories said you and your followers came here to create the land. Are you telling me that you were at war with the Great White Eagle and only came here to flee? You said the others were like stars, but upon their journey to our land, their vessels burned up. Not because they were defiant to the Great White Eagle!" Gillian said, confused and angry, that what Malus had once told him may not be true.

"Oh Gillian, the sooner you accept that nothing is what I made it out to be, the sooner you can accept reality." Malus scowled. "We didn't come to this land by choice, during the war we fell here. My league of warriors didn't burn up on the way here as I first put it, but they did perish! We lost the war, that's why only I and six other Pegasi landed here." Malus explained, but Gillian was silent. His eyes remained wide open, and his mouth dropped. He couldn't believe what he was hearing. "The Great White Eagle sent a few warriors to find us, and they did, but I used the Great White Eagle's precious little creatures as shields."

"You did what?" Gillian gasped.

"I survived!" Malus boomed. "That's what I did! Anyways, since the Great White Eagle knew hunting me and my comrades down would cause the death of many of the creatures he had created, he let us be."

"Wow…" Gillian said out loud, and the rest of his thoughts babbled in his head. *The Great White Eagle loved us so much that he let his enemies get away? Unbelievable… Malus would let us all die to protect his own power…*

"We lived in the shadows for a few years, but eventually I took what was mine," Malus said. "It took thousands of years, wars, and lies, but now his beloved creatures answer to me!"

"So my lineage, my ancestor Manuel, was a rebel?"

"Oh yes, a great ally of mine!" Malus said, thinking highly of his former comrade. However, Gillian did not think too highly of his lineage. To think that his ancestor rebelled against the Great White Eagle made him feel as if he were ripped in two. He was once proud of his lineage, but now it felt tarnished and tainted. "Eventually, I gained power over his little creatures, which angered him. Luckily for me, even though he was very angry with his creatures, he withheld his wrath."

"Why was he angry?"

"Because they began to follow me. They betrayed their very creator!" Malus laughed. "If I were him and my subject betrayed me, I'd have them all killed!" Gillian received this statement from Malus as a warning.

"Wh… Why didn't he?" Gillian stuttered.

"Because he *loved* them, yuck!" Malus said mockingly.

Unbelievable, the Great White Eagle is nothing like Malus, and in all the best possible ways… How could I ever serve Malus? Gillian thought.

"So, he just let you go? To protect his creatures?" Gillian asked.

"Kind of, this is where my curse comes from… When I was able to get his most trusted creature, Henry Adams, to betray him, he put a curse on me and drove Henry away from his presence." Malus explained.

"What's your curse?"

"Oh, Gillian, not even Zolton knows that," Malus said with a wicked smile. Gillian just looked at Malus. The flame of the single candle left burning in the room danced and swayed about. "All you need to know is that I want my curse broken, and I need the Book of Truth opened to do just that."

"I understand…" Gillian said.

"Now, if a word of this is spoken to anyone, you will never speak again! Do you understand me?" Malus threatened.

"Yes, Sire," Gillian said with a shiver.

"Now do you see? This is why I must speak to the girl! She must tell me where the Key is. I must have it! I will finally be free from this stupid curse!" Malus said.

Gillian didn't say a word, there were so many things going through his head. When he finally landed on a thought, he looked at Malus.

"When would you like my answer?" Gillian said, referring to his decision to serve Malus or the Great White Eagle. Malus' response made Gillian's blood run cold.

"Don't you get it? You never had a choice. You will serve me, or lose your wings. It's that simple. Like the rest of the creatures before you, you will choose me." Malus said. He then turned his back on Gillian and softly walked over to the curtain that draped over the large window in Malu's chamber. Extending out the tip of his wing, Malus pulled the curtain over, allowing light from the afternoon sun to burst into his chambers. Gillian had to cover his eyes with his wing; The light was so bright and *so* abrupt. Slowly, the light that filtered through his feathers helped his eyes adjust, and he could see the grand No Man's

Land Mountain range resting on the horizon. Even in the vast flood of sunlight, the red glow at the edge of the maze glowed steadily; however, at this particular moment, he did not take much notice.

Gillian's heart was filled with sorrow. *Do I really have a choice in any of this? My fate is set either way. I'm a slave to Malus either way. However, as a loyal servant, I will be praised among the other creatures of Regnum, which would be better than losing my wings and being a slave in Mount Nani to the dwarves. I hate both options, but one would be better than the other.*

With this grave thought, Gillian noticed the crystal. Not because of its glow, but instead because it grew dim. With each flicker, the brightness of the crystal faded. Simultaneously, as Gillian lost hope and his heart sank with despair, the crystal lost its shine. Like before, each candle that went out in Malus' chambers allowed the darkness to creep in, and now Gillian felt that same feeling flood over him as he began to accept his crushing fate.

"Have you ever completed the maze?" Gillian asked Malus.

"I have not…" Malus said. He said it in a way that Gillian took notice of. Malus almost sounded shaky, like when fear is in your heart. Malus could see that Gillian wanted to ask why, and in this moment, he felt frail, as if he needed comfort, so he confided in Gillian, which was a rare thing for him to do.

"There is nothing in this world that I fear. But the Great White Eagle is not of this world."

"Oh…" Gillian said softly, understanding that Malus had just admitted that he was afraid of the Great White Eagle.

"The scrolls predict that he will one day come again, and there are a few references that claim he will come from the Mountains of the North. 'In completion of the Maze, I will return.' One verse says. I refuse to be the creature that completes the maze. I don't want to know what is at the other end, and I don't want the Great White Eagle to return." Malus said grimly.

The two stood in silence, gazing out the window. Looking at the snow-covered mountain tops and the glowing crystal that was mysteriously placed at the end of the maze. Gillian pondered his options and everything that weighed heavily on his wings. When he looked at his reflection in the glass window, he was reminded of his 'noble markings': the black slash across his face, the blotch under his wing, and his dipped feathers. Each one was like a scar that reminded him of a painful memory. *All at what cost? Being rich and famous? What should I do?* Gillian thought. It was a quiet and solemn moment for both of them, but after taking notice of the young Pegasus's gloom, Malus changed the subject.

"But we must not fret! We have the book, we just need the key! The girl will give it to us. She must! Bring them in, would you?" Malus asked Gillian.

Suddenly, Gillian's hair stood on end. It was at this moment that Gillian realized he had to decide. Malus was testing him to see if he would refuse or accept his request. One that involved the three humans he had grown very fond of. *If I refuse, Malus will take it as me disobeying him, but if I do it, I will seal my fate as his minion..."*

Gillian took a deep breath and could feel sweat beading up on his forehead. He didn't know what to do. In a slow burn of agony, Gillian responded, "Yes, Sire."

Disappointed in himself, he slowly turned and exited Malus' chambers. This was the beginning of his treacherous walk to the dungeons, where he would once again betray his friends.

Chapter 11
Below Ground Brawl

Deep down in the Dungeons, the three prisoners sat in silence. Each with their own thoughts racing in their heads. Beside them, Phillip sat in the shadows doing the same.

At the top of the stairs, the four could hear the muttering of words. Although they could not make out what was being said, they knew it was of some sort of importance, for the voices sounded like commands.

Suddenly, the voices stopped, and in their place, the sound of clanking armor echoed down the stairs. At last, there appeared a Titan. His face was stern, as if he meant business. Turning towards Simon, he began to whisper something to the ole brute. Jessie made his way to his feet and walked over to the bars. Pressing against the cold iron, he leaned an ear in the direction of the Titan. Despite his efforts, it was unclear as to what they were saying.

Although Jessie could not hear a word they said, he watched as Simon rose to his feet. The mysterious Titan then casually turned away and began making his way back up the stairs.

With thick fingers, Simon fished for the key chain looped at his belt. The jingle of the keys gave Jessie a feeling of excitement. Realizing that Simon was coming to open their cell door, Jessie's heart began to thump within his chest. *This is our chance*! He thought. He turned and looked at Andy, "Follow my lead." Jessie stepped back from the iron bars and put his hands in his pockets, as if he wasn't paying any attention to what was going on. Andy sensed that Jessie had a plan and that something was about to go down, so he leaned forward and clinched his fists with eagerness. As Simon squared up on the prison cell door, Andy knew exactly what Jessie was thinking.

We can make a break for it! Andy thought. He slowly worked his way to his feet, not trying to draw any attention to himself, and Eva followed suit. Even Phillip, noticing the three subtle movements, realized that something was about to go down. The older gentleman leaned out of the shadows of his cell and watched closely at what was about to unfold.

As Simon inserted a key into the lock, the jingle of keys was like music to Jessie's ears. With his eyes glued to Simon's wrist, Jessie waited for the perfect moment to pounce. Effortlessly, Simon twisted the key, and the lock clunked open.

Like an arrow leaving the bow string, Jessie shot forward, kicking the dungeon gate open. Dazed, Simon was knocked back. Then Jessie lowered his shoulder and tackled the ole brute. As if planned, the cell directly across the hallway had been left open. Which worked well for Jessie, who was able to catch Simon off guard, tumbling into the open cell. It all happened so quickly that Simon never pulled the key out of the lock, so as Jessie scrambled to his feet, Andy was able to get to their cell door and remove the key from the lock. Simon was no small man, so like a turtle teetering on its shell, Simon swung his arms trying to catch Jessie as he backed out of the cell. Before Simon could roll onto his knees, Jessie slammed the cell door closed. Using the key, Andy locked Simon in the cell. For the moment, the three of them were free. However, before they could celebrate, the Titan had heard the commotion and raced back into the dungeon. With a fierce look in his eye, he drew his sword and took his fighting stance.

The Titan tiptoed towards Jessie and Andy. The Titan sliced his blade through the air, aiming to take off Andy's head; however, with quick feet, Andy slipped back into the prison cell with Eva. The Titan's blade followed closely behind Andy, but with luck, it was halted by the iron bars of the cell that Andy now used to hide behind. Furious, the Titan slammed the cell door shut; it did not lock Andy or Eva in, but for the moment would serve its purpose. The aggravated Titan turned his attention towards Jessie, who had sunk down the hallway, pressing his back into Phillips' cell door.

The Titan pulled back his arm, aiming the tip of his sword directly at Jessie. With great force, the Titan thrusted it forward, attempting to pierce the escaped prisoner. Again, with luck, Jessie escaped the blow. He flinched, moving his whole body to the left, which allowed the Titan's sword to pass by him without a scratch. The Titan tried to swing his sword in adjustment to Jessie's dodge, but because of the iron bars of the prison cell behind Jessie, the Titan's initial poke trapped the sword, preventing any side-to-side movements.

Realizing this, Jessie took the opportunity to cling to the Titan's arm. With the Titan's arm pinned down, Jessie was able to render the sword useless, at least for the moment.

Andy acted fast, with great might, he gripped the iron bars of his prison cell and rammed the door forward. Because the Titan had only closed the door, never actually relocking it, the door swung open on its hinges. It swung out and around until it collided, with great force, into the back of the Titan. The massive blow sounded as if pots and pans had been dropped because the Titan's armor and the iron gate echoed throughout the dungeon as they clanked together. Slightly dazed, the Titan had been forced forward, squishing Jessie between himself and the iron bars of the prison cell. The sudden blow from behind not only dazed the Titan but also caused him to drop his sword to the floor inside Phillip's prison cell. Now unarmed, the fight became a bit more even for Jessie.

Jessie's eyes grew wide as he peered over the Titan's shoulder at his friend, but he had not given up. If he wasn't going to get out, his friends should at least have the chance.

"Go!" Jessie shouted. "This is your chance!"

Andy did not have time to think, so he grabbed Eva's hand to lead her out of the cell. As he was about to leave, he noticed Phillip watching intently as the three of them tried to earn their freedom. Andy, having compassion on the odd man, tossed the set of keys he still clutched in his hand through the iron bars that separated them from Phillip. Andy made eye contact with Phillip as the set of keys plopped on the floor, and he gave him a nod. Then he and Eva turned and raced out of the cell and up the spiral stairs of the dungeon.

As all of that occurred, Jessie had a small window of time where he overpowered the Titan. With all his might, Jessie leaned into the Titan, forcing him backwards. In an attempt to escape himself, he forced the Titan off to the side and made a break for it. However, in a last-ditch effort, the Titan reached out and grabbed hold of Jessie's arm. The sudden jerk spun Jessie right back around, bringing him face to face with the Titan once more. The last thing Jessie saw was the Titan's armored fist gliding through the air straight towards his nose. Then, only pain, before the room went black. Jessie collapsed to the floor.

"Whoa! What a show!" Phillip chuckled. He hadn't seen such excitement since his younger years when he used to get into fights himself. "Bruce! He almost had you! Getting rusty, are we, Bruce?" Phillip laughed. If Jessie had been awake, he would have been thoroughly offended by Phillip's remarks. As a fellow prisoner, Jessie would have assumed that Phillip would take their side, just as Andy had. That is why Andy had tossed Phillip the keys before he made for the exit. However, Phillip's condition was complex. Sure, Phillip was rotting away in the dungeons, but he had been around long enough to know the Titans personally. In his younger years, he had even sparred and jousted with them. Although time had changed Phillip, he still had an occasional joke for his old friends. Not to mention that he had seen prisoners come and go many times and learned to never get attached. At this present moment, Jessie, Eva, and Andy were no different. Except that they provided a fantastic show for Phillip as he watched a young kid give his old friend Bruce the what-for.

Bruce, red in the face and breathing heavily from the tussle, did not think the situation was as funny as Phillip thought, and rolled his eyes at him in response. Adjusting his armor, Bruce straightened himself out. Jessie lay unconscious on the floor, but Bruce knew it was only temporary, so he rolled Jessie onto his stomach. He walked over to Simon, who was still trapped in the cell, and pointed to his belt. In a leather pouch fastened to Simon's belt was a pair of iron cuffs.

"Oh yes! Good work, Bruce! Such a noble warrior," Simon chattered, the way one does when trying to suck up. Fishing out the cuffs, Bruce snatched them from Simon in a way to show he was annoyed with the useless dungeon keeper, and clasped them around Jessie's wrists.

What happened next was truly unexpected. Phillip, who had been watching it all unfold, stood in his prison cell with the keys Andy had tossed him. However, while Jessie lay unconscious, Phillip simply pushed his prison cell door open. It was never locked. Causally, the mysterious man bent over, picked up Bruce's sword, and then walked out of his cell over to the Titan. Phillip dangled the keys before Bruce, who opened his hand. Phillip calmly plopped them into the Titan's palm. "Better sharpen up!" Phillip said as he patted Bruce on the shoulders and handed him back his sword. With a quick turn and a few short steps, Phillip had returned to his cell, slamming the dungeon door behind himself. Never once did the key touch the lock on Phillip's prison cell door. And none of the three, Andy, Eva, or Jessie, were able to witness it.

"Go get a bucket of water," Bruce ordered, as he wiggled the key into the lock to open the cell that contained Simon.

Free once again, Simon did as Bruce asked and ran off to fetch a bucket of water. Bruce propped Jessie up against the iron bars. Jessie's face began to bruise. Within seconds, his cheek swelled, turning his soft brown skin into a puffy pink flush. Soon enough, the rosy color dissipated and settled into a deep purple bruise just below his eye.

"Where were you taking them?" Phillip asked Bruce.

"Frankly, Phillip, it's none of your business," was his response. Clearly, he was quite annoyed.

"To the King, I suppose..." Phillip said casually. He ignored Bruce's attitude, he had been in the castle long enough that he knew prisoners only left their cells for two reasons. One, to see the King or Malus - usually the King - or two, for execution. However, usually

Mischka would report such grave plans, so Phillip assumed the King wanted to speak to them. "Well, either way, I would get going if I were you. By the looks of it, you're out of shape. You might never catch two young kids on foot!" Phillip said with a belly laugh.

"No way they made it past Gillian at the top of the stairs. And for the record, Phillip." - Bruce said in an aggressive tone - "Malus has requested their presence, not the King." Bruce spouted off, proving Phillip to be incorrect.

Phillip grasped the iron bars and pressed his cheeks between two bars.

"Really?" he asked sharply. It was then that Phillip began to connect the dots. He recalled the pressing questions Jessie had, his interest in pulling someone out of the Devil's Kettle. Phillip knew Malus, and he knew that Malus never had any interest in the King's prisoners unless it somehow benefited him. Knowing that these three prisoners had all come from the Forbidden Circle set off an alarm within Phillip. *What does Malus want with them? Does he know something about their journey that I have yet to learn? This could be bad. Just like last time...* Phillip thought. Phillip had been around years before, during the last time Malus spoke directly with prisoners, and the result of that was blood. *Did these three lose someone in the Devil's Kettle? Did they find the Key to the Book of Truth? Either way, none of it could be good...* Phillip paused deep in thought. His lightheartedness jabs toward Bruce moments before vanished, and his face turned to a cold stare. Something serious was about to happen; he could sense it and began to relive what happened all those years ago that led to his mysterious imprisonment, which was his own self-punishment. This moment brought a sort of panic to him, and he began to worry and question what had truly happened to these three. If it hadn't been for the conversation he had just had with the prisoners about the Great White Eagle's return, he would have never dreamt of doing what he was about to, but in this moment, it was the only thing he could think to do. Quietly, in the corner of his cell, he pressed his back against the cold stone of the dungeon wall, slumped to the floor, closed his eyes, and bowed his head. *Great White Eagle… I… I have no right to even call out to you, but… if you can hear me. Protect us all from Malus.*

The dungeon remained quiet for a few minutes after that. Bruce could tell that Phillip had lost his desire to talk, and frankly, he was so annoyed at Jessie that he just stood over the unconscious boy while waiting for Simon to return with a bucket of water.

Simon had returned, but the oaf was so clumsy that with each step he took, water splashed out of the bucket, leaving a trail of water down the stairs of the dungeon. By the time he had returned, the bucket was less than half full. Bruce signed deeply in annoyance, but took what was left of the water and splashed Jessie's face.

The sudden burst of cold water sent a shock to Jessie's core, waking him from his unconsciousness. As if waking from a bad dream, Jessie straightened out. Gasping for air, he tried to bring his hands forward to wipe his face, however, it was at this point that he realized he had been cuffed. Water dripped out of his springy hair and fell into his lap.

"What's going on?" Jessie spouted.

"You're being detained," Bruce said.

"You tried to kill me!" Jessie spouted.

"What did you expect pulling a stunt like that?" Bruce asked. Jessie just looked up at the Titan who towered over him.

"I had to try…" Jessie admitted.

"Look, kid, I got no beef with you. Just doing my job," Bruce said. Jessie paused for a moment. He believed him. If the King was as ruthless as Jessie believed him to be, he knew that if he escaped, Bruce would have to face the consequences.

"...So, did my friends escape?" Jessie asked hesitantly, but because Bruce had been so straightforward with Jessie, he felt as if he could ask without irritating Bruce.

"What do you think?"

"Hmmm, I was afraid of that," Jessie said, looking down at his feet that were sprawled out in front of him. "Where are they? Where did you take them?"

"I'm not at liberty to say. Sorry," Bruce said. He then knelt down beside Jessie, gripped Jessie's arm at his elbow's crease, and yanked him to his feet.

With great force, Bruce directed Jessie back into the prison cell and slammed the door shut. Still bound by the cuffs, Jessie did not resist. Instead, he just turned and watched as Bruce locked him in his cell. Phillip also sat quietly. Considering all that had happened and knowing that Malus wanted to speak to Eva, he was very nervous about what was going to unfold next. He just hoped that Malus had not discovered anything pertaining to the Book of Truth or the whereabouts of the key. If he did, destruction lay ahead for them all.

Bruce left the dungeon, and Simon eventually settled back into his chair and closed his eyes.

"What do you think they did with them?" Jessie asked Philip. However, Phillip didn't respond. He wouldn't even look at Jessie. "Phillip?" Still nothing. Before Jessie could press Phillip with any more questions, Bruce returned down the stairs. Without a word, he retrieved the keys back from Simon and came before Jessie's cell. Surprised, Jessie stood waiting for instructions. It was obvious that Burce was going to take him somewhere.

"Where are you taking him?" Phillip said, leaving his post in the corner. Jessie could sense desperation in his voice.

"To Malus," Bruce said.

"Jessie! Listen to me!" Phillip said dramatically. He rushed to the iron bars between them, gripping the bars and pressing his face into the space between, he pleaded with Jessie. At this point, Jessie had been taken by the arm and directed towards the stairs. As Jessie was about to disappear up the stairs, Phillip shouted, "Do not trust Malus. Whatever he promises you, it's not worth it! Trust me!" Feeling defeated and hopeless, Phillip began to pace anxiously around in his cell.

The castle seemed quiet. Not because there was no one around, but everyone seemed to be relaxed and at ease. Bruce led Jessie along the castle, under the covered pathway, and out into the courtyard. With a sharp U-turn, Jessie was directed through the first archway and up the stairs to the Mezzanine that overlooked the ballroom.

At last, Jessie stood before a door. Behind him was the marble railing that overlooked the ballroom. Bruce pushed the door open. And what Jessie saw filled his heart with dread. Standing in the center of Malus' chamber were both Andy and Eva. Each had their arms tied behind their back.

"Ah, Jessie, is it?" Malus asked with a smile. "Glad you could join us."

"It was worth a try?" Jessie shrugged towards Andy, referring to their attempted escape. However, Andy did not respond with words, instead, he just nodded his head towards the corner of the room. To Jessie's dismay, he saw Gillian standing in the corner. Once eye contact was made between Jessie and his Pegasus friend, Gillian felt the weight of guilt crush him. His ears drooped, and quickly his eyes darted to the floor. Jessie, in that moment, realized that Gillian was the one who captured Andy and Eva as they tried to escape. He was the one who brought them before Malus.

"How could you? You betrayed us! They could have escaped, but you stopped them?" Jessie cried out in a red-hot flash of anger.

Gillian's heart sank deeper than it had ever sunk before. All he could do was look away. His ears pinned back more with each word Jessie flung at him, and they stung more than any stick, stone, or sword ever could. "And to think I stood up for you when Andy doubted you. I was wrong about you!" Jessie said. He was so angry that a tear had formed in his eye and rolled down his bruised face.

Jessie lurched forward toward Gillian in anger, but Bruce was able to grab onto the cuffs around Jessie's wrists and rein him back in.

The cuffs dug into his wrists, which forced him to calm down and stop resisting Bruce.

"What a ball of fire!" Malus said with a large grin. He always did enjoy a good betrayal. Jessie turned sharply and gazed at Malus. Bruce walked him forward so he was standing beside his friends. The big window was open to the mountains behind them, and Malus stood in front of that, with the King slouched in an armchair beside him.

King Fraust looked upset. He sat with one foot on the ground and his other leg crossed over his knee. As one hand tapped its fingers impatiently on the arm of the chair, the other was firmly planted in his cheek as one does when they are irritatedly bored or unhappy to be somewhere; and it was clear he was unhappy, considering there was a frown painted across his face.

"What do you want from us?" Jessie scowled.

"I have called you here to seek your help," Malus said.

"Why should we help you?" Jessie spouted. Andy and Eva stood quietly, for they had already talked to Malus and learned all they cared to know.

"Well, for starters, because I have the power to release you from prison, or to have you hanged," Malus said casually. "But… sometimes, creatures like you seem to be a bit more stubborn than I'd like, and threats of death don't always get me what I want. So, the real question is, what is it that you want?"

"What do I want?" Jessie asked, then his mind became clouded with only one thought. His brother. Jessie wanted more than anything to have his brother back, and the more the thought of his brother pressed, the more willing he was to do anything to get him back. Even if that meant striking a deal with Malus.

"Your friends here are pretending to be noble, unwilling to even make a deal with me. So that is why I called you here. Maybe… just maybe, you would be wise enough to help me out," Malus said in a convincing way. As if Malus had some sort of control over Jessie's mind, Jessie ignored Phillip's warning not to trust Malus and listened intently to the Black Pegasus's words.

"Jessie, don't," Andy said, but instantly received a blow to the back of the head from a Titan standing behind them.

"Quiet!" the Titan ordered.

"What is it you think we can help you with?" Jessie asked.

Malus nodded towards King Fraust. Slowly, the King reached down next to his chair and picked something off the ground. In a careless way, he presented a book with a limp hand and rolled his eyes.

Eva let out a gasp, realizing what it was. It was the Book of Truth. The same book she had forgotten within the blueberry bush.

"Oh, so you have seen this before?" Malus said. Eva's reaction to seeing the book was a sure tell that they had, and proof that they lied when first asked about it.

"I…I…" Eva began to babble, realizing that her reaction gave it away. She was saddened to see that the evil King Fraust had gotten his greedy fingers on it. Andy remained silent.

Jessie, however, was determined to hear Malus out. Remembering what Phillip had said about Malus being able to bring creatures back from the Devil's Kettle, he was interested in hearing what Malus would want in return for getting his brother back.

"What about the Book of Truth?" Jessie asked confidently, overpowering Eva's fear and getting straight to the point.

"I want the key that unlocks it. If you give it to me, I will give you whatever you want… and I would guess that because you've already considered helping me, that you have something in mind?" Malus said, side-stepping so that he was looking right into Jessie's eyes. "What is it that you want?"

Andy could feel that Jessie was being pulled into Malus' trap, so in a desperate attempt to save his friend from the evil one, he blurted out, "It doesn't matter we don't have the key!"

"Quiet!" King Fraust shouted in annoyance.

"Is this true?" Malus asked, gazing deeply into Jessie's eyes.

"I'm afraid so, but isn't there anything else I can do? I know you can help me," Jessie said in desperation. Standing here in front of Malus made him completely forget all about the Great White Eagle and his mission to find him. Instead, he was now pleading with Malus, a well-known liar.

"Hmmmm, I believe you, Jessie," Malus said in a disappointed tone. "Where did you find this book?" he then asked softly.

"We found it in the Forbidden Circle," Andy said, trying to stay as vague with his answers as possible, however, it was clear that Malus knew they had lied before. If they were caught in a lie again, the beast might become furious with them. So he told the truth, but only in small doses.

"Clearly… you found it in the Forbidden Circle. But where specifically?" Malus said patiently, trying to get his answers truthfully.

"In a pile of rubble," Jessie said. Jessie thought that his answer would confuse them, make them wonder what he meant, however, it did the exact opposite for King Fraust. The description of the house of rubble that Jessie and his friends had discovered in the meadow just outside the Corkscrew Canyon told King Fraust exactly where they found the book. His eyes grew wide, and for the first time since the traitors had been brought in, he began to take interest in what was being said. The King uncrossed his legs and leaned into the conversation.

"Where was this pile of rubble? In the Superior Pines? The outskirts of the Centrum's Core?" Malus asked. It was clear that Malus did not know what they were talking about, but all the pressing questions made them all nervous. Yet, before any of them could think of what to say, King Fraust stood up slowly.

"My Lord. The pile of rubble they speak of is the house of Henry Adams on the outskirts of the Devil's Kettle itself." King Fraust said. The fact that King Fraust knew exactly what they were talking about shocked them all. It made them realize that Malus and King Fraust knew much more about their adventure than they ever dreamed possible. Even Jessie, who was tempted to trust Malus, began to worry they had *really* gotten themselves in over their heads.

"How did you…?" Andy said, shocked at the King's great knowledge.

"This is where you found the book all those years ago yourself?" Malus asked, cutting off Andy and turning towards the King.

"Yes, Sire. But I don't understand." The King said in response to Malus, then he continued softly, as if speaking his inner thoughts out of shock. "I thought the book was lost forever." Then the King turned to the three prisoners. "You're sure it was in the house?"

"I'm sure…" Eva said softly, admitting that the King was right about its location.

"So, you've seen the Kettle? You know the truth?" King Fraust said.

"You mean that the Devil's Kettle is real? And that the Great White Eagle is real, despite your efforts to hide it from the creatures?" Andy said angrily.

"Hmm." King Fraust said, seemingly satisfied with Andy's response.

"That's all you have to say for yourselves? Hmm?" Eva spouted. You've known the truth this whole time, but you lied to everyone?"

"Yes. And now we must keep this secret," King Fraust said with a conniving smile.

"Don't count on that!" Andy said. However, King Fraust went toe to toe with Andy and bent down to his level.

"When I'm done with you, you won't have the chance to say anything," King Fraust whispered.

"Enough, Timothy," Malus intervened. He was still concerned with the key, more than he was about silencing the three of them. "Where is the key?" His patience was growing thin.

"There is no key. Not in the house at least." Eva said.

"Do you know what this book is?" Malus asked. At this point, he did not realize Eva was a Somniator, so he greatly underestimated their understanding of the book and its importance.

"It's called the Book of Truth," Eva said.

"So its pages hold the truth that uncovers all the lies you have poisoned this world with!" Andy barked.

Malus stepped back and jolted his head up and down, surprised to learn that they did know what the book was.

"You're a Somniator?" Malus asked. "Interesting…" King Fraust also took a surprisingly large amount of interest in this, but for a different reason than Malus'.

"Have you received any dreams about a tree? And an Ax?" King Fraust asked quickly. He remembered the dream he had received from the Great White Eagle, the one that his brother interpreted to say that this young girl, whom he had just learned was a Somnaitor, would be the end of him. King Fraust wanted to know if she, too, had received the same dream.

"No?" Eva responded. She found herself not trusting the King, yet, was curious as to why he was so specific about a dream.

King Fraust squinted at Eva, processing what that could mean. His questioning halted as soon as he caught a glare from Malus, and he straightened himself out.

"So you know its importance?" Malus asked, redirecting the conversation back. "You know what truths are held between these covers?" Malus asked.

"Well… No, not exactly. But I'm sure there are plenty of truths that you've lied about that would be revealed in here." Eva barked.

"You are very correct," Malus said. Which surprised Eva. She figured he would have denied ever lying. Yet, the truth of the matter was that Eva and the others knew too much; lying to them was no longer an option for the evil Pegasus. "Don't you see? We are on the same side here."

"No, we are not!" Andy barked.

"Sure, we are. You want to know the book's secrets, and I want to know the book's secrets," Malus said.

"Yes, we want to know them to expose you!" Andy said.

"Minor details!" Malus said, "You can cross that bridge once we figure out how to open this thing."

"If we can figure out how to open it, then what?" Eva asked.

"You can help translate it, of course!"

"Let's say we know where the key is... which we don't," Andy began, "If Eva can translate the book because she is a Somniator, then what do we need from you?"

"Why you little!" King Fraust said as he raised his hand to smack Andy.

"Halt!" Malus shouted. "Contain yourself, King. His question is fair... Clearly, neither of us has the key. However, even with the key, the book is believed to be written in all of the native tongues. Tongues of Centaurian, Elvish, Dwarvish, mankind, and possibly even the lost language of the beasts of Terribbia. Although I have never seen such writing."

"Yeah, so? I can speak to bears, I would guess as a Somniator, I can speak all of those other languages as well." Eva said, still not understanding why they would need Malus or the King's help.

"But can you read it? How long did it take you to read these three words? Book of Truth," the King asked as he pointed to each word on the book's cover.

"You have a point. Written words are different for some reason. I have to sound out the word, and hear it verbally before I can understand it," Eva said, beginning to realize that translating the Book of Truth might be a larger task than she first thought.

"Exactly, you have only been a Somniator for what? Days?" King Fraust asked, as if she barely counted as a real Somniator.

"Well, yeah… but - " Eva began.

"But nothing, you need my help. I have been reading lost languages for years," King Fraust said. "You need me to translate, or else it may take you years to discover the secrets on your own," Eva said, looking at Andy and then at Jessie. In her mind, she thought that as long as she could keep the truth out of Malus' hooves, she didn't care how long it would take her. However, Malus revealed a promise that startled them deeply.

"Do you understand? Without us, it will take you years to understand the book. And know this, if you are not with us, you are against us." Malus said, threatening their lives if they did not conform to their deal.

"We don't have the key. So even if we were to consider helping you, we cannot do anything now. Let us go and we will help you find it," Andy said, trying to secure an escape. However, both the King and Malus burst into laughter.

"Let you go? Good one!" The King blurted.

"Here's what's *really* going to happen. You will stay in the dungeons while we find the key. Once we do, you have two options. Rot in the dungeons or help us," Malus said. Then he nodded to Bruce, indicating that he was to take them to the dungeons. Quickly, he grabbed hold of Jessie, while a second Titan who was present took a short chain with clasps at each end. One end he hooked to the cuffs around Andy's wrists, and the other end he hooked to Eva's. With it, the two of them could be controlled by one Titan. They were brought abruptly back to the dungeons.

Eva was grateful for the opportunity to talk with Andy and Jessie in private once they reached the dungeons. She wanted to make sure that they all remained on the same page. In her mind, helping the ruthless King and Malus was not an option. She trusted that the Great White Eagle had a plan for them, and serving Malus was not a part of that plan. She was hopeful that they could escape and flee from the King as quickly as possible. She remembered thinking she would have to be a servant of the King and how much she hated the thought, but to work with him on her own accord would be a disgrace to everything she ever stood for. Her hope of being able to talk it all over with her friends came to an abrupt stop when Jessie cried out, "Wait!" Eva's heart jumped into her throat. *What is he doing?* She thought. *Is he really considering serving Malus? Jessie, please don't…* She pleaded in her mind.

Chapter 12
Desperation

"I would like to speak with you, Malus… alone," Jessie said calmly as he stared into Malus' eyes. Bruce stopped tugging at Jessie, awaiting his master's response. Even the Titan pulling at Eva and Andy halted. But the look on Andy and Eva's faces was that of pure concern.

"Very well," Malus said as he lifted his wing to command all the others to leave. One by one, Jessie watched everyone exit. Bruce let go of Jessie and followed Eva and Andy out as they were led by the other Titan. Then Gillian tiptoed towards the door. Before leaving, he glanced towards Jessie, but his human friend refused to look at him.

Dropping his head, Gillian left the room. Now it was only Malus, Jessie, and the King, who had slouched back into his armchair, thinking he was exempt from Jessie's request to be alone with Malus. However, with an "echem," Jessie indicated that he was not. Malus flicked his nose to the door, and the King begrudgingly obeyed, leaving them alone at last.

"What is it, Jessie? Have you come to your senses? I had hoped that you would," Malus said.

"The Legend of the Devil's Kettle." Jessie began, cutting right to the chase.

"Which one? There are many legends, most untrue," Malus responded.

"The legend that says 'Anyone who falls in will never return,'" Jessie said.

"Ahhh, yes. A wonderfully false legend. I sense that you lost someone, specifically lost them to the Kettle?" Malus asked slyly.

"My brother, his name is…was Richard…" Jessie said in a shaky voice.

"And you're here because…?" Malus asked, allowing Jessie to spell it out.

"The man in the dungeon, he said, you can pull them out. You can save them." Jessie said.

"Ahh, he did now, did he? Such a peculiar man isn't he?" Malus said, bypassing the answer Jessie was searching for.

"Is the legend true, or can you save him?" Jessie said, trying to get a straight answer from the steed.

"I have retrieved a man from the depths of the Devil's Kettle once before," Malus started. A grin grew across Jessie's face, and his eyes almost twinkled. "But it comes at a cost," Malus finished, and the twinkle in Jessie's eye sank into a stern stare.

"At what cost? I'd do anything to bring him back," Jessie begged, and at this moment of desperation, a kindling of hope sparked in his heart; the hope of getting his brother back caused Jessie to fall weak to Malus' temptation.

"Anything?" Malus asked with an uncontrollable grin.

"Yes, I would do anything. He's all I had left, and now he too is gone," Jessie said, choking down tears. Malus watched as Jessie's eyes welled with tears. Things were playing out better than Malus had imagined. Malus knew that every word he spoke to this grieving human would have to be placed carefully in order to properly trap him in a deal.

"Losing loved ones is a very difficult thing," Malus said, as if he cared. Jessie just nodded with soft eyes. "There may be something I can do about it. In fact, I have done it before."

"Oh, that is wonderful!" Jessie said, wiping the tears from his eyes.

"But are you prepared to do what I ask?" Malus asked.

"Yes, of course, what is it I can do?"

"You understand that the task you desire from me is not easy. It is dangerous and very difficult," Malus said.

"I imagine it is."

"Then you understand that just any old request will not do. Instead, when I ask you for something, it will be grave," Malus explained. Still, Jessie's mind was clouded with a dangerous hope. Wishing for something unnatural.

"You mean it could be a dangerous task?" Jessie inquired.

"Sure…" Malus said, keeping things vague. "However, at the moment there is nothing worthy of such a deal, but if you're patient, I'm sure one will arise."

"How long must I wait?" Jessie asked, beginning to see through the veil of deceit.

"As long as it takes," Malus said. Jessie was right where Malus wanted him, desperate and sad. Willing to do anything Malus wanted. Every creature that had ever been stuck in this trap before had always been met by dangerously evil requests, and unfortunately, many of those creatures had followed through on Malus' requests. Despite this, very few creatures had ever been in a situation like Jessie's. Considering the Forbidden Circle was forbidden, most of Malus' deals did not include the Devil's Kettle, therefore, most of his deals were on a smaller scale.

The truth was that there was something different about the Devil's Kettle, something that would make what Malus would request all the more daunting for Jessie. You see, Malus had no power to bring anyone back from the dead, but if someone was swallowed by the Devil's Kettle and survived, Malus could retrieve them. Making Jessie's situation a rare opportunity that Malus could not let slip away. Therefore, the deal made with Jessie would have to be worthy of what was required. Jessie would be asked to trade a life for a life. Someone of Malus's choosing would have to die in order for Richard's life to be restored. One of the most evil trades ever imagined. However, knowing that he had no particular creature in mind, Malus refrained from explaining the nature of this deal with Jessie. Knowing full well that if he were given time to think it over, he might come to his senses and refuse Malus. So until then, he held the deal in front of Jessie like a carrot, tempting him.

"Fine…" Jessie settled for the current terms, and unfortunately, at this point, Malus seemed like his best option. He had no earthly idea how or if he even could escape the dungeons, so finding the Great White Eagle seemed like an impossible task. So, if that was out of the question, Malus would be his only chance. Jessie accepted things as they stood, hoping that things would change sooner rather than later.

Malus stretched his wing over Jessie's shoulders and began walking him out of the room. Oddly enough, Jessie felt comforted and hoped to one day wrestle with his brother again. He imagined them laughing, fighting, and playing tricks on everyone else as they had done before.

Outside of Malus' chamber, there was a Titan waiting to take Jessie back to his cell. This time, Jessie didn't fight him, but walked calmly around the balcony and down the stairs out of Malus' sight.

Finally alone, Malus quickly trotted over to King Fraust's chambers. The two of them had much to discuss. As Malus came to the wooden door, he pawed with his hoof.

"Who is it?" King Fraust asked angrily, from inside his chambers.

"Open the door!" Malus ordered.

King Fraust opened the door with a frown fixed to his face. He was quite upset that Malus made him leave the room upon Jessie's request. A prisoner of all creatures. "I can not believe you forced me to leave like that. I am the King after all!" King Fraust announced.

"Oh, quit your crying, you big baby. You're only King because I gave you the opportunity to become King," Malus said, annoyed with the King's arrogance.

"Even still, I had to do many awful things to obtain it. I deserve some credit." Timothy said as he flopped into his chair and sank into the cushions, pouting.

This conversation would have been private, and both the King and Malus believed it was, but luckily for our prisoners, Mischka was listening in. In fact, she had heard it all. While they were packed into Malus' chambers, she was there. Hiding deep within Malus's trough of corn, she listened in on all of Malus's conversations that afternoon. Including his chat with Gillian, as well as both the group conversations and Malus's one-on-one talk with Jessie. Even now, as Malus made his way to King Fraust's chambers, Mischka scampered as quickly as she could behind him. As Malus entered the room, Mischka made her way to the window at the end of the Mezzanine, scampered up the curtain, and burrowed herself into a crack on the wall. By that hole, she found herself inside the King's chambers. Carefully and quietly, she scurried to the top of the King's bookshelf and hid herself behind some of the King's trinkets he had on display. Winded, she settled in and tuned her large mouse ears into the conversation.

"Yeah, Yeah, Yeah. You already have a crown, what more do you want?" Malus said.

"Some recognition would be nice! Some respect!" Timothy pouted.

Mischka quietly scoffed to herself at the King's greed. *Me, me, me!* She thought. *That's all the King ever thinks about.*

"We have bigger problems. But some good news," Malus said.

"What's the good news? Will the boy help us?" King Fraust asked.

"Not with the book… But, I do have leverage over the boy," Malus said.

"And what leverage is that?"

"The same leverage I had over your brother all those years ago," Malus said with a devilish smile. King Fraust's face turned pale.

"You mean…"

"Yes, Jessie had a brother."

"And he…"

"Yep, right into the Devil's Kettle. Just like you, Timothy."

"Oh wow…" Timothy paused for a moment to remember the dreadful time he had while in the Devil's Kettle. Then he softly asked, "With the bloodline gone, what will you ask of him?" He remembered what was required of his brother for his own life all those years ago.

"I am not sure yet. But it will have to be big. It's not too often that some kid falls into the Kettle, is it?" Malus said with a smile and a wink towards Timothy. Timothy laughed anxiously, even though he did not think anything about The Devil's Kettle was funny.

Timothy sank deep into his chair. Dreadful memories that he had spent years suppressing began to flood back into his mind. For the first time in a very long time, King Fraust felt sympathy for another creature. *That poor boy… The torment the Messorems inflict, and the darkness. It's so cold and so lonely.* Timothy thought, recalling what it felt like for him all those years ago.

"Cheer up, would you! This is a good thing for us." Malus said, seeing the worried look on King Fraust's face.

"It's just… The Messorems…" King Fraust said as shivers went down his spine.

"Such wonderfully dreadful creatures! Really, Timothy, the Messorems are not so bad once you get to know them!"

Timothy rolled his eyes, considering he actually knew them well and was not fond of them at all. "Malus, what use do you really have for the boy? The Great White Eagle's bloodline is gone; there is nothing he can offer you. I'd much rather kill all three of the traitors."

"Timothy, you know I will not allow you to kill Jessie. Sure, I had your brother end the Great White Eagle's beloved bloodline, but I'm sure I will find a good task for Jessie. It is an order that he remains alive. Do you understand me?"

"Fine! But the girl must be dealt with. You know about my dream, you know the Great White Eagle intends to use her to eliminate me. I must rid myself of her." King Fraust pleaded.

"What are you suggesting we do? Execution?" Malus asked.

"Yes!"

"Hmmm, what if they choose to help us? What if they know where the key is?" Malus asked, not wanting to risk losing knowledge of the key's whereabouts.

"Do you really think they know where it is?"

"I suppose I don't."

"Then we don't need them. Did you really intend on working side by side with them?" King Fraust asked.

"No, it was just a charade. To get them to trust me." Malus said calmly, knowing the tactic failed.

"Well then, I say, off with their heads! The girl and the other boy!"

"Hmmm, considering they give us no advantage in opening the Book of Truth and we don't need the girl to translate because we have you, I guess, I have no opposition to your desire for execution," Malus said, compromising with King Fraust.

"Thank you, Sire! Thank you!" King Fraust said joyfully. He stood to his feet and clasped his hands together the way one does when they are overjoyed, but in a calm manner.

Oh dear, those poor children. I must warn Phillip, Mischka thought. Knowing King Fraust's intent brought sadness to her heart. It was only hours before that Eva told everyone that the King was planning to make her a slave, but now Mischka knew that was all a lie. He never intended to keep her alive. Her only hope would be to warn Phillip and hope that he could devise a plan to save them. After all, Mischka knew all of Phillip's secrets. Who he was and why he was in the dungeons with his cell door unlocked. If anyone could save Eva and Andy, she believed it was him. Quickly, she darted off to the dungeons to warn her friend.

"Please, Malus, I ask just one more thing…" The King said, calmly standing cautiously before Malus.

"What is it?" Malus asked in a surprisingly calm way.

"When you brought me back… You made a deal with me. Do you remember that?"

"Of course, I made you King."

"Yes… You asked me to kill King Kieser." Timothy said quietly. It was the first malicious thing Malus had ever asked of Timothy Fraust.

"Oh. I see. You're wondering if I will request the same from Jessie's brother?" Malus asked, piecing King Fraust's concerns together.

"I have no need to get rid of you. King Keiser was a follower of the Great White Eagle, I had very little influence over him, therefore, I needed him gone. Which is why I brought you into the picture. You have my word, no harm will come to you, when the boy returns," Malus assured him.

"Thank you," King Fraust said.

"You know it's funny, I encouraged King Kieser to kill you and your brother. Haha!" Malus said with a smile.

"You what?!"

"Oh, stop it! That was long ago, you knew too much, and I wasn't sure I could trust you. But it didn't matter. He was weak. So I flipped it on him."

"Well, I won't make the same mistake as him; those two traitors die tonight!" King Fraust said, making a fist with his hand.

"Very well, I will be back before then," Malus said.

"Where are you going?"

"To visit a few old friends, there is something I must check on," Malus said, and with that, he exited the King's chambers.

Chapter 13
The High Priest

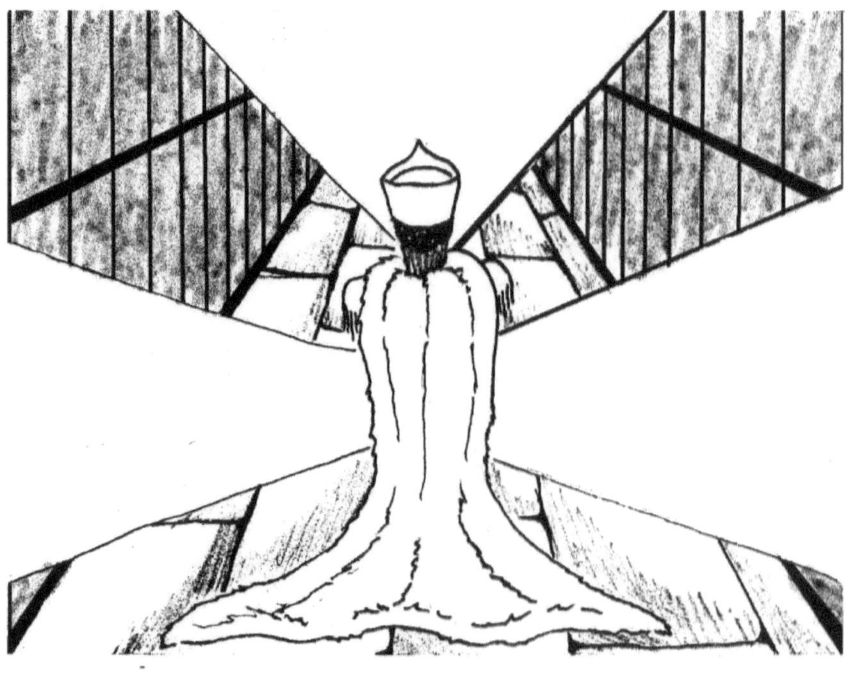

Jessie walked down the stairs to the dungeon floor. Part of him had hoped that he would one day have his brother back again, while another part of him felt shame for even considering working with Malus. However, at this moment, his desire outweighed his guilt, and he was in fact willing to do what Malus wanted, even if he had no clue what that could mean for him.

As the Titan led him down the hallway, Jessie turned to be escorted into the cell with Andy and Eva, who looked out at him with grave looks of concern on their faces. Jessie just looked down at his feet, unable to look his friends in the eye. But then, to Jessie's surprise, Simon waddled over to him and instead of unlocking the door that would imprison him with Andy and Eva, Simon unlocked the door directly across the hallway.. As Jessie turned to look, the Titan jolted him, forcing him into a lone cell.

"What gives?" Jessie asked as the cell door slammed.

"Malus' orders," the Titan barked. Then quickly he turned and left the dungeon. Simon, of course, locked the door. It was nearing mid-afternoon. Concerned about his stomach, Simon waddled up the stairs in search of a snack.

Jessie turned and looked across the hall, and pressed against the iron bars was Andy.

"What was that all about?!" Andy questioned.

"You didn't agree to help them, did you?" Eva said with fear as she too came forward and gripped the cold iron bars. "Jessie?"

Jessie didn't say anything. He just hung his head and found a corner to sit in. He was ashamed that he agreed to form a deal with Malus when the time came, especially when he knew his friends would not approve. *But they don't understand. I have to get my brother back. He's gone, and now I have nothing…* Jessie was so blinded by his pain that he could not see the friendships he had and just how important they would prove to be for him. *If we cannot find a way out of this dungeon… If there is no escape, then there is no chance at finding the Great White Eagle. So, if Malus could bring back my brother, I would have to consider it.*

Andy and Eva became impatient, but knew Jessie would not speak unless he wanted to. So until then, they wriggled restlessly across the hallway. Phillip sat in silence, for some reason, he cared what happened to these three. Maybe they reminded him of when he was younger, or maybe because he hoped to meet the Great White Eagle, just as he and Jessie had made a pact to do. Either way, these three prisoners were different from all the other creatures he had come across down in the dungeons. He felt a part of their journey even though he barely knew them. Although in words, Phillip was silent, his inner voice babbled many questions. *What did they talk about? I hope it's not what I think it is… What terrible thing will Malus have him do if it is true?* Phillip had a funny feeling tingling inside, one that really wasn't funny at all. He sensed that he knew exactly what the meeting with Malus was about, but hoped he was dead wrong.

Suddenly, they could all hear the exhausted squeaks coming from Mischka. She hadn't scampered that hard in years, so Phillip knew she brought important news into the depths of the dungeon. Darting out of the hole in the wall, she scampered along the cold floor. With ease, she weaved around the iron bars created to contain much larger creatures than her, and found herself at Phillip's feet. Wasting no time, she climbed up his leg and scurried all the way to his shoulder, where she could speak into Phillip's ear.

She panted heavily. Trying to catch her breath, even wheezing with each exhale.

"What is it?" Phillip asked quietly. He turned his body away from the others to try and keep their conversation quiet.

"It's…" she breathed in, "The boy!" she squeaked out.

Philip turned his attention back towards Jessie. But quickly turned away again. "What about him?" He whispered.

Andy and Eva stood pressed against the iron bars that separated them from Phillip. Doing everything they could to hear what the mouse had to say. But it was no use, they couldn't hear anything of what Mischka said, and only bits and pieces of what Phillip said.

"What is she saying?" Andy asked, wanting to know what was so urgent. Everyone in the dungeon knew Mischka was worked up.

"Shhh!" Phillip scolded Andy.

In a quiet yet desperate voice, Mischka spilled the news. "He had a brother, but he was lost to the Devil's Kettle," Mischka explained.

"What!" Phillip shouted in fear. What he feared had been confirmed. Knowing this for certain left Phillip in a state of despair. The look on Phillip's face as he turned to look at Jessie made it all clear to Jessie. Tears formed in Phillip's eyes, and a frown appeared upon his lips. Jessie realized exactly what Mischka had said. He remembered when she first scampered off, claiming that she had work to do. Jessie realized now what that work meant. She spied on Malus. She spied on him. Guilt seemed to be loaded upon Jessie's shoulders heavier than ever before. Now that Phillip knew, it was only a matter of time before his friends realized just how desperate he was to get his brother back.

"What did Malus want in return for his brother?" Phillip asked Mischka, still not taking his eyes off of Jessie.

"Malus had not decided, but Jessie said he would do anything to get his brother back," Mischka squeaked.

"I was afraid of that... But I can't blame him," Phillip said.

"Who are you talking about? Who can't you blame?" Andy said. He was being impatient and wanted to know what was going on. Only being able to hear Phillip's side of the conversation left him with many questions. This time, Phillip just ignored him. Focusing on Mischka and the news at hand, he continued.

"What else did he say?"

"Once Jessie left, Malus went and talked with Timothy," she started. "Timothy wants them all dead."

"The boys, too? Not just the girl?"

"What about me?" Eva shrieked with concern.

"At first, but Malus convinced the King to let Jessie live, because they had leverage on him. They could get him to do whatever they want," Mischka said quietly.

"Well, I know that to be true… all too well," Phillip said, regretting his own past choices. Mischka didn't respond, for she did not like bringing up the past. "When? When will he?" Phillip asked. He knew the other could hear his side of the conversation, so he refrained from saying execution.

"Tonight. He plans to kill them tonight. Oh, Phillip, we have to do something," Mischka cried. She, too, realized that these three prisoners were something special. Being a Somniator herself, she had a special interest in Eva, and considering Eva's dream, the return of the Great White Eagle seemed to be at hand, and Eva was that chosen messenger. Mischka felt called to do something to help her.

"But what can we do? I'm too much of a coward," Phillip said sadly.

"But you can escape, you're not even locked in your cell…" Mischka explained softly, so the others could not hear.

"I know Mischka, but Timothy would kill me if I betrayed him like this," Phillip said with fear in his voice.

"Phillip! This is bigger than you. You of all people know what Malus is capable of, and you of all people know what someone like Jessie is willing to do in this exact situation!" Mischka pleaded. However, before Phillip could respond, an unexpected visitor arrived in the dungeons.

It was Isabell. She wore the same robin blue servant girl's dress as Eva, but her soft smile seemed to bring a much-needed light into the dungeon. Everyone's mood was brightened ever so slightly because of her innocent presence. She carried with her a bucket, and a white washcloth was draped over the bucket's lip.

"Isabell?" Phillip asked, causing Jessie to scramble to his feet. Jessie straightened himself out and tried to look presentable. He had such a big crush on Isabell that in comparison to his actual friends, he cared about what she thought most of all. If she was going to discover his intentions, he hoped to present them in the best way possible. That way, she just might understand.

"What are you doing down here?" Phillip asked as he pressed the dungeon cell bars.

"Phillip." She said as she curtsied in his direction. She then turned sharply to Jessie. "Jessie, are you alright?" Isabell asked. She set the bucket on the floor. The warm water inside splashed from side to side. She dipped the washcloth into the warm water and looked at Jessie. His brown eyes met hers. Her sapphire blue eyes rendered him powerless. Looking at her made Jessie's hard outer shell melt into a sappy mush. Now he felt all the more shame for even considering Malus' offer. He remembered that it was King Fraust and Malus who forced Isabell to be their servant, and it was them who separated her from her sister. *How could I work with the ones responsible for all her pain?* Jessie began to think. Regret began to build a case within his heart. After being so confident that working with Malus was his only option, one look into Isabell's soft eyes was all it took to change his thinking. His hope began to shift from hope in Malus to hope in something better.

"I'm better now," he said, cracking a smile. Although a small tear had emerged from his eye and was running down his purple cheek.

"Malus told me that your face was bruised pretty badly," Isabell said as she reached in and gently wiped the tear that rested on his puffy cheek. He winced a bit because his face was very tender, but embraced the pain because it was a genuine act of care from Isabell.

"Malus? Why would he care about you?" Andy snapped. He had a look of disgust on his face. "Malus and the King are the ones keeping us locked up. We refused to help them, so why would he help you?" As Andy said those words out loud, he and Eva both realized that something had happened during Jessie's private chat with Malus.

"You didn't?" Eva cried.

"You promised to help Malus discover the truths of the Book?" Andy asked. Furious at Jessie, Andy began to clench his fists. *How could you, without us agreeing?* Andy thought.

"No! I didn't." Jessie said as he shifted his gaze from Isabell to Andy, ready to defend himself.

"I'm afraid it's much worse," Phillip said solemnly. Everyone, including Jessie, looked at Phillip.

"What do you mean?" Andy asked.

"Jessie, what's your brother's name?" Phillip asked.

"How did you know he had a brother?" Eva said.

"Mischka overheard their conversation. Trust me," Phillip looked directly at Andy and Eva, "I don't know if you have any siblings, but if you were in Jessie's shoes, would you do anything to save them if something happened to them?" Phillip asked.

"But a deal with Malus? The leader of the Pegasi?" Andy gasped. "What about every cruel thing a royal Pegasus guard has done. It all comes from him!"

"And the King, it's no secret! He's a cruel man." Eva sobbed, understanding that some very dangerous things could come about if Malus gained access to his greatest desires. Although they did not know what that was exactly, neither the King nor Malus had ever set a good example and had been known by all the Kingdom as cruel and unjust. Even more so now that Eva, Andy, and Jessie understand just how true that was. Now that they had learned the secrets of the Devil's Kettle, and were being kept as prisoners.

"You don't get it! None of you do! What choice do I have?" Jessie cried. Andy and Eva both crossed their arms in anger. Jessie looked to each one, hoping for some sort of assurance that they would understand. Lastly, he looked at Isabell. She seemed shocked, but could tell Jessie was desperate to get his brother back. She thought of her own sister and realized that she would go to the ends of the earth for her. She would do anything to keep her safe. Understanding Jessie's predicament, she empathized with him and comforted him. "Jessie, I don't blame you. I don't know what I would do if something happened to my sister," Isabell said. I know that the rumors among the servants have said that Malus can get people out of the Devil's Kettle, but the cost is truly dreadful."

"Do you really think it will be that bad?" Jessie asked softly, not understanding the multitude of Malus and his deals.

"Oh, I know it's that bad. I've seen it with my own eyes." Phillip said in a serious tone.

"Oh..." Jessie said, lowering his head in shame.

"Promise me... Before you accept anything from Malus... Think it through. Make sure you don't become one of them..." Isabell said softly as she placed her hands gently on Jessie's hands, which were wrapped tightly around the iron bars.

"I promise..." Jessie said.

"There has to be a better way than Malus... There has to be. We will find a way." Isabell assured him, not willing to settle for a deal with Malus.

"The Great White Eagle!" Phillip shouted. "He can help us."

"Do you really think he's somewhere out there?" Jessie asked.

"It's all in Eva's dream. I believe he is coming back. If not now, soon!"

"I believe it too. I can feel it." Isabell said with hope flowing in her voice. Jessie peered into her eyes. He felt so much better when he did that. She brought him pure comfort even in a time of distress. Because of her, he began to believe that there was a better way to save his brother than becoming Malus' slave.

"How do we find the Great White Eagle?" Andy asked, seeing the change in Jessie's heart, he was ready to spring into action. Trusting in the Great White Eagle seemed like a much safer plan than trusting Malus.

"Well, first we have to escape," Eva said, tapping her foot on the ground as she thought about how they could escape.

"Isabell? Can you get us out?" Andy asked.

"Andy! No, I will not allow her to get involved. She has a sister to protect," Jessie snapped. Isabell felt relieved. She knew that if she got caught helping them escape that the King would not tolerate it and harm her little sister Beth as punishment for it. She really appreciated Jessie standing up for her. It was obvious that he liked her, but if she was honest with herself, she was developing feelings for him as well.

"Thank you, Jessie," She said as she looked down at her feet.

"What about Gillian?" Jessie asked.

"He betrayed us!" Andy snapped.

"I know he did, and I don't know if I can ever forgive him for it. But he's our only hope. Don't you remember all the things he has done for us? After all, he saved me from the Devil's Kettle. He did what he could..." Jessie explained. After Jessie's moment of weakness with Malus, he started to understand Gillian's actions a bit more. At first, he hated Gillian for betraying them, then moments later, he himself was trying to make a deal with Malus. *Maybe Gillian felt like I did. Like he had no other option. I can't blame him for that, especially considering I just did the same thing...* Jessie thought. Jessie understood that if he expected Andy and Eva to forgive him, he should forgive Gillian.

"Not to mention, Malus is very wise. I would bet he knew Gillian was lying from the start. He probably threatened Gillian with the Alatum Punishment, and that's why he betrayed you." Phillip added.

"I guess that makes sense. The same way you," Eva said to Jessie, "felt there were no other options."

"Even if that was the case, how could he help us now? And if he wasn't willing to help before, who's to say he would now?" Andy asked.

"I have an idea!" Phillip said. Suddenly, he turned around and began to whisper to Mischka again. "I need you to find Gillian and convince him to help us, or at least find others to help us."

"Um... who is he talking to?" Isabell asked, she had not yet met Mischka the mouse, and was completely unaware that a talking mouse was perched on his shoulder. Phillip's peppery hair hung low enough that between it and his bushy beard, Mischka remained out of sight.

"It's a long story," Jessie said, as they waited for Mischka and Phillip to finish their conversation.

"I do not know who Gillian is, nor what he looks like! How will I know where to find him?" Mischka squeaked with concern. Phillip thought to himself for a second, wondering how they could overcome this roadblock. Mischka had never seen Gillian, and until a few days ago, his name had never been brought up in any important conversation. *He was just a regular old Pegesus guard, so why would I have known of him?* "Even if I find him, do you think he will help?" Mischka interrupted Phillips' thoughts. "The little bit I have overheard from Malus and King Fraust is that they believe he will choose to serve them..."

"We have to try. Timothy cannot get away with this," Phillip said, almost heroically. However, if Phillip could have seen the look Mischka gave him, he would have humbled himself. She was slightly annoyed with her dear friend because he was, in fact, free to come and go from the prison as he pleased. It would be easy for him to overpower Simon and help them escape, but out of fear of the King's wrath, Phillip refused to make a scene of rescue. Overall, Mischka did care about Phillip, which is the only reason she did not encourage him further to save them himself; she worried that he was right and that King Fraust would make an attempt on Phillip's life if he was caught helping the fugitives.

So, because Phillip was unwilling to expose himself to the traitors as a free man and unwilling to openly betray the King, Phillip needed to overcome Mischka's dilemma of not knowing who Gillian was. He thought hard on it until finally he had an idea.

"I've got it!" Phillip finally said. He turned his attention to Isabell. Brushing his hair away from his shoulders, the small mouse that was Mischka was exposed to the room.

"Isabell? Do you know what Gillian looks like?" Phillip asked. Hoping she had at least heard of him or had seen him since she spent time in the stable yard.

"I don't..." Isabell said. Phillip's hope in the plan began to fade, but then Isabell spoke again. "But I know someone who would. He can point him out to me."

"You must take Mischka to Gillian! She will do the rest. Can you do this for me?" Phillip asked the servant girl.

"A mouse?" Isabell said with wide eyes.

"She's a Somniator. You know what those are, don't you?" Eva questioned Isabell.

"Of course, I've heard many stories about them. Just never actually met one." Isabell said, intrigued by Mischka.

"Well, now you have met two of us," Eva said with a smile.

"You are… and she is?"

"Yep! Nice to meet you, I'm Mischka. No time for small talk! We'd better get moving!"

Isabell approached Phillip's cell to get an up-close look at Mischka. With a great leap, Mischka jumped from Phillip to Isabell. "Oh!" Isabell said as the little mouse landed on her arm.

"So you will help me?" Phillip asked Isabell, who in turn looked down at Mischka's beady little eyes.

"I'm not doing this for you… But I'll do it for Jessie," Isabell said softly.

"Oh! One last thing!" Mischka said, turning back towards Phillip.

"What is it?" Phillip asked as he pressed himself as close to his friend as his cell would allow.

"The Book of Truth, I believe it's the one you spoke of. The book that drove you and Timothy apart. Timothy has it in his chambers." Mischka informed Phillip.

"Mmm, good to know. Thank you, good friend. Be on your way." Phillip said.

"Wow. Is this really happening right now? A talking mouse?" Isabell asked.

"Shocking, I know," Mischka said with a smile that lifted her whiskers up.

"Well, it's very nice to meet you."

"Likewise, I have seen you many times throughout the castle. Hardworking and trustworthy, you are. I have always admired your willingness to help other servants with their needs. Even above your own," Mischka said. Isabell smiled down at the little mouse. Her soft words brought encouragement now, when she needed them more than ever.

"Shall we?" Isabell asked. Mischka nodded in agreement. Isabell looked to Jessie, then to Eva and Andy. Then looked back at Jessie. "We will find a way…" Then, just as quickly as she first appeared, Isabell and Mischka had disappeared from the dungeon.

This moment was tense for Eva, Jessie, and Andy. Like when you are a young child and a nasty storm is rolling in. The sky is dark, the wind is howling, and thunder is echoing outside. As a child, you could sense something scary. You could see the look of worry on your parents' faces, and could tell that the weather outside was not comforting. Yet you did not really know how bad it was going to be. Not like your parents did, they had seen storms before, lived through them. Maybe they had seen much worse. Andy, Eva, and Jessie were like these small children. They could tell something was coming. A storm was brewing, yet they had no clue exactly what. However, Phillip's worried face, and the apparent hurry Mischka was in, caused the three prisoners to become uneasy.

They were locked in the dungeon and could sense danger, but still, they began to hope in Phillip's plan. They hoped that Gillian would help them. However, this too was a gamble because it seemed one moment Gillian had their backs and the next it seemed as if he turned his back on them. Although a gamble, Phillip knew it was a risk they had to take. With knowledge of the King's plan and fearing for his own life, Phillip believed there was no other option.

Anxious, the four left in the dungeons sat quietly. Eva huddled into the corner of her cell, while Andy paced back and forth. Phillip sat in his shadowy corner and watched the sun rays that had stretched across the floor that morning as the sun rose, now beginning to seep into the dungeon from the other side, for now the sun was setting on the other side of the land. Leaving long pillars of light along the floor. Jessie sat with his back against the iron bars and stared up at the small windows along the ceiling of the cells, where the light flooded in, and gazed at the evening colors of the sky.

By now, Simon had returned from his search for dinner and made himself comfy in his chair. Entertaining himself by biting his nails, picking his nose, or pulling out his arm hair. Every second Phillip waited, he grew more anxious. He began to wonder what he should do. At first, he tried to convince himself to act. To find the courage within himself to fight Simon and get the keys. With the keys, he could release them all and escape. However, Phillip clung to the fear of losing his life. He hoped desperately that Mischka would convince Gillian to help. That way, he would be free of punishment. Yet, he felt sick, knowing that Gillian would be blamed instead of him. *Maybe I should do something. Maybe I should help them escape… What do I have to lose? My life? I live in the dungeons… What life? That's it, if Gillian does not come soon, I'll save them. I'll run away with them and help them on their mission to find the Great White Eagle.* Phillip arose from his corner and made his way to the cell door. He gripped the iron bars tightly and paused. Taking a deep breath, he realized that by opening his unlocked door, the others would know something was off. His secret would be made known, and everything would change. As he exhaled slowly, something halted his plan.

Tap…Tap…Tap. Slow, even steps made their way down the dungeon stairs.

The four all quietly moved to see who was coming. Each with their own fears about who it could be. Would it be the King? Or Malus? Maybe it was Gillian. But they were all wrong. Soon, a man was standing before them. The man was dressed in white, which seemed to glow so brightly that Phillip covered his eyes at first. He had white pants with a crease down the front and golden shoes. Upon his head, a rigid white cap rose tall with golden markings embroidered on its face. His shirt was white and had puffy shoulders and big golden buttons down the center, and each shoulder had golden tassels. His black hair and dark skin contrasted with the white in a beautiful manner that is hard to describe unless you have seen it yourself. Around his neck, a long fur cape was fixed, and its end trailed to the floor behind him. Remarkably, the white fur stayed spotless as it dragged across the filthy dungeon floor. Finally, the man held a golden scepter in his right hand. Fixed to the top of the scepter was a golden eagle.

"Who are you?" Phillip demanded. He had been around the castle for many years. Inside the dungeon and out, but he had never seen this man before in his life. The way he was dressed indicated the utmost importance. Something only the Holy men would wear on special occasions, like weddings or the anointing of a Knight or King. Yet even those holy men could never look as remarkable as this man did.

"I am *the* High Priest," the man said.

"Have you come to give us our death wishes?" Jessie said. He only ever met a priest the night his mother died. He asked her what she desired most before she passed away. So that's what he thought this man was here to do.

"On the contrary, Jessie. I have come to show you life," the High Priest said.

"How do you know my name?!" Jessie exclaimed.

"I know you all. Andrew." He said as he nodded to Andy. "Eva," he said, doing the same for her. Finally, he turned his attention to

Phillip. "And Phillip, you must not spend eternity down here," he said, extending his arms outward with a smile.

"What do you know! I'm getting what I deserve… Besides, if you are some high priest or whatever, why have I never seen you here before?" Phillip questioned the stranger.

"Because I have never been in this castle before. It is quite the establishment… And as for you, Phillip, I know that you are punishing yourself. But you *do* know it is not your job to do so," the high priest said.

"Then whose job is it?" Phillip asked.

"It's the one who sent me," the High Priest responded.

"And who might that be?" Phillip asked angrily.

"The Great White Eagle, of course. He is the only one who can properly judge you," he responded.

Phillip sank into a puddle. He was ashamed of his past and knew that this strange man was right. He had done so many terrible things, things he wished he could take back, things that would haunt him til the day he died. On any other day, Phillip would have doubted that this man had really been sent by the Great White Eagle. However, Eva's dream indicated that the Great White Eagle was going to return soon. Meeting this mysterious man who claimed to be sent by the Great White Eagle himself sealed it in stone. The prophecies of old were coming true, and Phillip became terrified because of it. Soon, he would have to face everything he had ever done before the one creature whose judgment mattered the most. Even more now, Phillip realized that he must help his new friends, and he must go with Jessie to find the Great White Eagle. There was no longer a choice in the matter. He knew he couldn't face the Great White Eagle seeking forgiveness while he watched his friends be murdered by the King. Not when he had the opportunity to help, but refused out of his own cowardice. He would make his move and try to help his friends escape.

"Why have you come?" Jessie asked bluntly.

"To warn you," he said.

"To warn me? Of what?" Jessie asked. He obviously knew the trouble they had all found themselves in; what more could this man possibly tell him?

"If you seek the things of this world, you will find death. But if you seek the Great White Eagle… you will find life," the High Priest said.

"What do you mean?" Jessie asked. He was confused by the man's response. So he looked over towards Andy and Eva. But to his dismay, they were gone. As if they had vanished into thin air, Jessie was alone in his cell. The high priest was gone, Andy and Eva were gone, even Simon had vanished. Jessie shrieked and turned to look for Phillip, but as he turned out of the corner of his eye, he caught sight of someone sitting in the corner of the cell across the hall. It was Eva, in fact, there was Andy again, and back in his chair, Simon the big oaf was sloughed over again.

The oddest part of it all was that none of them looked disturbed. Each one looked as if nothing had happened. Like none of them had seen the strange High Priest from only seconds before.

Jessie quickly scanned the room for the man, but there was no sight of him. Only the fleeting rays of sunlight were left. The man and his white garments that shone brightly like the noontime sun were gone.

"Where did he go?" Jessie asked.

"I was wondering the same thing!" Phillip said from his adjacent cell.

"Where did who go?" Eva asked.

"The High Priest!" Jessie exclaimed.

"He was standing right there," Phillip added as he pointed through the iron bars into the hallway.

"I don't know what you're talking about," Andy said. "No one has come down here since, Simon. And he hasn't moved from that chair."

"You didn't see him?" Jessie asked. Both Andy and Eva shook their heads. Jessie's mouth dropped open because he was in shock. *How could they have not seen him? Was I dreaming? But Phillip saw him, why couldn't the others?*

"How did Jessie and I see it, but not you two?" Phillip questioned partly out loud and partly to himself.

"You saw it too?" Jessie asked.

"Yes… You guys really didn't?" Phillip asked. In all his life, he had seen many things. He had met many creatures, but now it seemed as if they had just had a conversation with a ghost.

"Really…I didn't see a thing. Did you finish another bottle of rum or something?"

"Well, what did this… Ah, man, say to you?" Eva asked, curious as to what Jessie and Phillip had seen.

"He left us with a warning," Jessie said.

"A warning?" Andy asked.

"He said, if I seek this world, I will find death. But if I seek the Great White Eagle, I will find life," Jessie explained.

"Weird. I have no clue what that means," Andy said.

"Do you think it was a dream?" Eva said.

"I don't. It seemed so real. Plus, I never laid down or passed out, did I?" Phillip asked.

"No, you just stood at your cell door and stared into the hallway for a bit," Andy explained.

"Could it have been a daydream?" Eva asked.

"That we both saw? Unlikely…" Jessie said. "Someone… or something, really came here."

"Well, if it's not a dream, then that would make sense as to why you cannot understand it, Andy," Phillip said.

"I guess we have to put our thinking caps on for this one…" Andy said. However, what he did not understand was that this message from the mysterious high priest was not for him to discover; instead, the message was specifically for Jessie and Phillip.

Although Jessie and Phillip had no knowledge currently, they would soon learn the meaning of this encounter.

"Seek the Great White Eagle," Jessie said out loud, pondering the phrase. He crossed his arms and then used his hand to rub his chin as he thought about what that could mean.

"I think we must find the Great White Eagle. If he really has returned, this High Priest must be telling us to go find him," Phillip said.

"Maybe, if we seek the Great White Eagle, the life we will find will be my brother!" Jessie said excitedly.

"Maybe… but even so, how? We are stuck down here?" Andy said.

This was Phillip's moment. He had decided that he needed to act. If he was even going to stand before the Great White Eagle and beg for forgiveness for all that he had done, the least he could do was try and save Andy and Eva, even if it put himself at risk.

"I have a…" Phillip began, but again, his plan in motion was shut down by the tapping of feet down the stairs of the dungeon. This time, however, the tapping of footsteps was accompanied by the clanking of Titan's armor. Phillip gasped because it was too late. Appearing at the bottom of the steps were three Titans. All dressed in battle gear for the ceremony that was planned for Eva and Andy. Each with their own sword tied at the hip.

If I try for the keys now, I will be outnumbered, four to one… I've missed my window… Such a coward I am. Phillip thought as he hung his head and gripped the iron bars tightly in his hands.

Chapter 14
Hector's Help

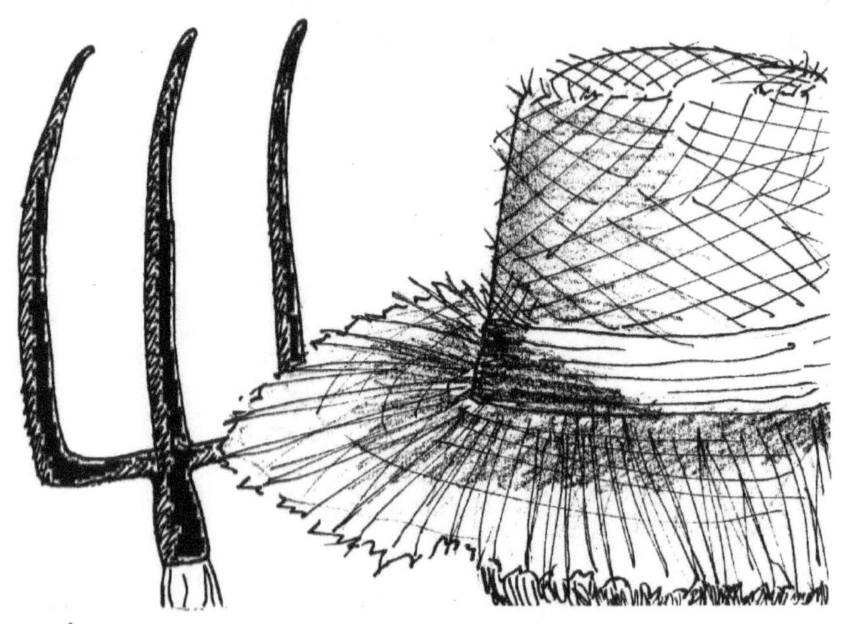

Andy and Eva's fate began to close in. As the vibrant colors in the sky began to fade, the sun was sinking fast beyond the Western Mountain peaks of Gravis Terra. King Fraust's plan had been set in motion. All day, he spent making preparations for the execution of his two prisoners. He feared the meaning of the dream that he received from the Great White Eagle, and believed that Eva would be responsible for dethroning him. If he had it his way, he would kill all three prisoners, Jessie included, however, Malus had other plans for him. So, King Fraust would settle for the other two. With Eva gone and their crystals in the King's possession, nothing could stop him.

Meanwhile, Isabell swiftly made her way through the castle. She had personally never met Gillian, because most of her time was spent attending to the King or helping in the kitchen. She knew that in order to find Gillian, she would need help. However, she would need to find someone she could trust, someone who wouldn't ask too many questions, and someone who would know exactly who and where Gillian was. The servant boy she had in mind was named Hector. The biggest downside to Hector was that he was the laziest servant the Castle had ever seen. It was honestly impressive the amount of work he put into not having to do any work. He spent countless hours studying the Titans, so he could move about the castle without being seen, all so he could avoid any work, find places to hide, and take naps. He only did the bare minimum to keep King Fraust happy. This meant Isabell would have to check all his hiding spots in order to find him. Isabell did not want to look suspicious, nor did she want to get Hector in trouble. So, checking throughout the castle was a timely process, and Mischka was growing impatient. You see, Mischka knew exactly what the King planned for Eva and Andy, but Isabell did not. So, after Isabell checked a few spots within the castle, Mischka, concealed by Isabell's long blonde hair whilst being perched on Isabell's shoulder, whispered the importance of finding Gillian in her ear. This time, Mischka told Isabell exactly what King Fraust had in store for poor Andy and Eva.

The news made Isabell sick to her stomach, but gave her the motivation to quicken her pace. *Oh dear, this is life or death! I must find Gillian. Please, Great White Eagle, if you can hear me, help me find Hector, help us find Gillian!* She thought to herself.

Isabell ran swiftly to the courtyard. Not wanting to draw any attention to herself, she slowed to a fast walk as she passed by the stage where a few Titans and servants were making preparations for the evening's activities. Any other day, Isabell loved speaking with everyone, seeing how their day was and what they were up to, which was why she had become one of the most respected servants in the kingdom. So as she moved along, she tried to keep her head down, but each servant she passed called out her name and waved, and every Titan tipped his helmet towards her. She knew if she ignored them, they would know something was wrong, but she didn't have time to get caught up in any conversations. So she quickly smiled or waved back to each one and rushed around the corner, which brought her to the pathway along the east side of the castle.

Trying to find Hector was proving to be difficult. *He is a stable boy, and he deals with the Pegasi. He will know where I can find Gillian. Plus, he owes me one!* Isabell thought as she made her way into the horse yard.

Straight ahead of her was the well in which she first met Jessie, Andy, and Eva. This time, however, a young servant girl knelt down beside it, fetching water for a small tan pony that was tied off to a post, munching on tufts of grass growing up near the base of the well itself.

"Katy, have you seen Hector? It's important," Isabell asked. If Katy had been paying attention, she would have seen how nervous Isabell looked. But the young girl seemed to be off in her own little world, peacefully fetching water for her pony. Isabell rocked back and forth from her heels to her toes, and kept fiddling with her fingers.

"No, I haven't, Izzy. Why?" Katy innocently asked, not really caring for an answer. The small girl grunted as she tried pulling the bucket of water out of the well.

"It's nothing you need to be concerned with! Thanks, though," Isabell said as she moved on. She began to head for the barn. *Maybe he's tending to the horses. Or cleaning their stables. It would be like him to push off his duties until evening.* Many other stable boys were busy at work. The sun was dropping, and the horses needed to be tended to before being locked up in the barn for the night. Isabell, in a great hurry, frantically weaved in and out of traffic. Many horses were being led about the horse yard after being worked with by the stable boys, others were being brushed, and some watered.

She hoped she might spot Hector with one of the horses he was assigned, but she did not see him or any of his horses. Once she reached the barn, she peeked her head inside.

Franky, William, and Fredrick were cleaning the horse stalls, and Jessica had just entered the far end of the barn, leading a horse in from the pastures. While the boys pitched manure, Jessica brought the horses in from the pastures to freshly cleaned stalls for the night.

"Have any of you seen Hector?" Isabell asked. She was beginning to panic more and more with each passing moment. *Please know where he is, please.* She cried to herself.

"I haven't seen him," William said, as he pitched manure out of the stall onto a pile that was in the center walkway.

"I haven't seen him since yesterday," announced Franky, who was pitching the pile from William onto a skid that was fastened behind a horse, to be dragged out of the barn to the compost pile.

"Have you checked the round pen? I think he was going to work, Lucky, this afternoon," Frederick said from the stall opposite William's.

"I haven't, but I'll check there next. Thank you!" Isabell said as she ran quickly out the back of the barn and around the corner.

"What did she want?" Jessica asked.

"To know where Hector is," Franky said.

"I just saw Lucky standing back by the hay shed. I would assume Hector is close by," Jessica said. Unfortunately, by the time Jessica had said this, Isabell was well on her way to the round pen and out of earshot.

"Oh well, she'll find him eventually," William said, and he went back to pitching manure.

And it was true, she had begun to panic so much that Isabell no longer cared if people knew she was worried. She was in a dead run now, and in no time, Isabell approached the round pen. Running around the circular pen was a beautiful horse, trotting the perimeter with a young stable boy working it with a whip. The horse's black mane and long tail were streaming behind her as she ran. She was half white and half brown with no particular pattern to her hide. As she trotted, she kicked up sand and whinnied. The round pen itself was made from iron gate panels, which made it easy for Isabell to climb and peer in.

Stepping up the first rung and then the second, she leaned over the top of the fence and called out to the boy.

"Have you seen Hector?"

The boy lowered the whip, and the horse slowed to a walk. He reached into his breast pocket and pulled out some pellets and put out his hand for the horse to scoop up with her bottom lip.

"Yeah," the boy answered.

Yes, finally! Someone knows where he is. She thought joyfully to herself.

"Do you know where he is?" Isabell asked.

"He worked Lucky here about an hour ago, said something about giving him fresh hay before bringing him to the stables," he said.

The hay mound! That's where he is. Isabell said to herself. "Thank you!" She hollered with a big smile. She waved to the boy and hopped off the gate to the dusty ground. Off she ran, kicking up dust, just like the horse had done in the round pen. She ran across the stable's yard all the way to the back, where there was a three-sided building specifically built to store hay.

The open side of the building faced out to the pastures, so it was hidden from view for anyone in the stable yard, or the castle, for that matter. As she peeked around the building's corner, she was surprised to see a horse unattended. It was calmly munching on the hay, from the mound which piled nearly to the roof of the hay shed.

"Lucky?" Isabell asked. Although the horse could not understand her, it recognized its name. Pulling some tufts of hay from the mound, it lifted its head and looked at Isabell. The horse looked as if it didn't have a care in the world. It just stared blankly at Isabell and munched on its hay. Lucky had a halter on with a lead rope tied under his chin that was coiled up nicely on the ground. If the horse had been anywhere else, the lead rope surely would have needed to be tied off; however, considering the abundant source of hay, Lucky had no interest in wandering off.

"Have you seen Hector?" Isabell asked the horse. But it didn't change at all, just looked contentedly at her and kept chewing on the hay.

She turned to the east. In front of her, she could see the pastures that extended out into the green hills that rolled out. The Mountains to the north extended out to the East and slowly curved in, corralling the land. These pastures were vast, but not endless. Beyond them, the mountain's arms reached down into the foothills where small farms took root. Further south of the foothills, fields stretched out East and West, and to the South, until they were met by the Quattuor marshes.

Isabell scanned the pastures for Hector. She had found the horse that multiple sources claimed he was with, but still, she could not find Hector. *Maybe he is out rounding up another horse?* She thought.

"We have to find Gillian!" Mischka squeaked, reminding Isabell of their mission. Mischka was growing very impatient. She could see the darkness falling on the land, and only the glow of the sun shining from behind the castle.

"I know! I know!" Isabell frantically said.

"What does Hector look like? I'll climb to the top of the hay barn and see if I can see him anywhere."

"He has black wavy hair. Just enough to cover his eyes. And he is maybe a few inches taller than me? He usually wears a baggy brown shirt and runs around barefoot. Ummm, oh, and his skin is almost golden brown, lightly tanned from the sun," Isabell said, trying to describe her friend Hector as best as she could.

"Okay! I will go up there and look." Mischka said. She shimmied down Isabell's side and hopped to the ground. As she started running towards the hay shed's corner post, Lucky caught sight of the little mouse. His lack of interest before suddenly changed drastically. Little old Mischka terrified the much larger horse to the bone. His uncaring eyes now widened to an unnaturally large size. His jaw dropped open, and all the hay that was inside his mouth fell to the ground. Finally, he reared up and began running away. In exchange, the lead rope that was tied to his halter began unraveling from its coil as the horse galloped away. Before too long, the rope had straightened out and for the first time, Isabell knew where Hector was.

Apparently, Hector had finished working Lucky in the round pen and brought him back to the hay mound to let him munch on fresh hay. He gave the horse this treat, only so he could bury himself in the hay mound and sneak a nap. Making sure Lucky wouldn't get away, he tied the lead rope around his wrist. Napping was much more enjoyable when he didn't have to worry about Lucky getting away from him.

But once Lucky saw Mischka, he had had enough of that. He took off like lightning. Once the rope reached its full extension, poof! Hector was yanked out of the pile of hay.

Remarkably, as if he planned the whole thing, Hector was awake and on his feet before Lucky could run off too far. As hay floated to the ground in all directions, Hector was trying to calm Lucky, who was fighting to run away.

"Eeek!" Mischka screeched, and she bolted to Isabell, who reached down to catch the frightened mouse and placed Mischka back on her shoulder. Luckily for Mischka, Hector did not see the mouse dart back to Isabell, so she safely hid under Isabell's hair out of sight.

"Lucky! It's fine, it was just a mouse," Hector said calmly. He was trying to get Lucky to relax, but Lucky just kept rearing up, causing a major scene. Finally, Hector was able to settle him down.

"Hector! I need your help!" Isabell cried, wasting no time. She was relieved that she had finally found him, but was worried that they were running out of time.

"Hey Izzy, I was just… giving Lucky here some hay!" he said as he scratched his head and began to yawn.

"I don't care what you were doing, I need your help," Isabell said.

"Oh, phew, so you won't tell?" Hector said.

"Have I ever?" Isabell scolded.

Hector shrugged in agreement. "What can I help you with?"

"You must bring me to Gillian. He is a noble Pegasus. The one involved with the prisoners in the dungeon!" Isabell explained.

"What for?" Hector asked.

"I can't tell you. But it's important," Isabell said.

"I would bet he is in his stable. I put fresh hay in there early this afternoon," Hector said. He looked back at the mound of hay and wished he were still sleeping in it.

"Take us to him," Isabell demanded.

"Why? Why must you see him?" Hector asked. He didn't want to have to leave his nap unless he absolutely had to.

"Do it, or I'll tell the King you take naps back here, when we both know you're supposed to be tending to the Pegasi," Isabell threatened.

"You wouldn't!" Hector gasped.

"I would. And will. Now come on, this is time sensitive," Isabell said.

"Hmmm, fine, but then we are even! Okay?" Hector said. Trying to get out of the favor he owed her from before.

"Yeah, okay. Now let's go," Isabell said.

Realizing that Isabell was in a hurry, Hector did not have time to put Lucky in his stable, so instead he would release the horse back into the pasture for the time being. Hector led Lucky around Isabell and Mischka. Although Hector did not know Mischka was hiding on Isabell's shoulder, Lucky did. Still terrified that Mischka would leap out and attack him, Lucky kept the lead rope tight, staying as far from Mischka as possible. Until Hector unclipped the lead rope from Lucky's halter, the horse's eyes remained glued to Isabell's shoulder. Once the horse knew he was free, he bolted out into the pasture.

"Okay, to the Pegasi stables!" Hector announced as he latched the gate shut and began walking back west towards the castle.

Mischka and Isabell followed closely behind Hector as he led them back through the horse yard. As they approached the castle, Isabell suggested, "Let's go through the castle, it will be quicker." So, instead of a sharp left turn down the covered pathway of the castle, they went straight. Through a heavy wooden door, they went and found themselves in a gloomy hallway. Although it was dimly lit, this was where they called home. This hallway had several doors, all of which led to the rooms of the servants. Isabell's included.

It was a good thing they went this way, for one, it was shorter, and two, the courtyard had flooded with creatures and servants all preparing for the execution this evening. The stage was being swept, the flowers were being removed, and the bright colorful banners had been taken down and replaced with the Royal Banners of war. Blood red in color and the image of a black pegasus reared up was fixed in the center. If Isabell had tried to go through the courtyard, she would have been slowed down by the traffic of creatures, and her spirit of hope would have been crushed at the sight of these banners, only ever used during an execution or act of war.

Quickly, they rushed through the castle, which brought them to another wooden door. With a cautious push, they opened it up and peeked out. The sun was now beginning to drop so low that servants had begun to put out the torches in their sconces for the evening. The heavy glow of the flame stained the cobblestoned floor and rocky face of the castle.

"We must hurry," She whispered to Hector.

This door opened up to the western covered pathway. Directly across from it was the archway that would bring them into the Pegasi yard. And to the right of where they peeked out, was the dungeons down the hall. With no one in sight, Hector slipped across the pathway and stepped into the open evening air of the Pegasi yard. Isabell and Mischka followed closely. Once inside, they pressed their backs against the stone wall to their immediate left.

"Here, grab this," Hector said. Beside him rested a pitchfork, which was leaning against the castle's exterior barrier wall. Hector then grabbed a second pitchfork. This pitchfork, also leaning against the wall, was wearing a straw hat on top of its handle. Hector placed the straw hat on his head and pulled the brim down, snugging its fit on his head and concealing his face a bit more from the world around him. It was a worn-out hat, and had seen a lot of use, and Isabell thought it was time for him to find a new hat. Yet, Hector seemed to love the hat; his eyes lit up with a bit of pride when he wore it, and his body language perked up a bit as well. He pinched the brim of his hat with two fingers and traced its edge. Apparently, he was looking for a loose stalk of straw because once he found one along the brim, he pulled at it. Like a farmer, he put the piece of straw in his mouth, completing his desired look.

"All right, let's find Gillian," Hector mumbled. He sounded funny because he kept his teeth clenched so he wouldn't lose his piece of straw.

At first, Isabell hoped the hat was a disguise, but unfortunately, it was the exact opposite. Apparently, that hat was Hector's chore hat, meaning every time he did chores, this was how he looked. This seemed to draw more attention to them, when she had hoped for a more sneaky approach. Hector was well-loved by the Pegasi. Each one they passed by had something to say to him, like "Hey Hector!" or "Who's this? Your girlfriend?" They would ask. He would laugh or smile or chirp back, with a "Oh yeah, ain't she lucky?"

Isabell turned a bit red because she had never thought of Hector that way, but she never said anything. Although she hoped to sneak below the radar, Hector's nonchalant attitude about the situation seemed to be causing no harm. No one stopped them, and no one questioned what they were doing, so she just went with it. Everyone just assumed he was doing his chores. Even considering how late it was getting, no one questioned him because he rarely did his chores on time as it was. Isabell just hoped they would reach Gillian soon, because each Pegasus they spoke to caused her stomach to turn.

With her head down, she anxiously followed Hector as he waded through the stable yard. Every step felt as if she was crawling into the enemy's territory, and the weight of being found out followed her like her own shadow. She knew that if King Fraust found out about her aiding the prisoners, he would punish her severely, most likely taking aim at her beloved little sister. However, her heart ached at the thought of innocent people being murdered. She had to help her new friends.

Isabell had rarely ever entered the Pegasi stables, and never late at night. The Pegasi always seemed to be the serious type when she was around. They took their roles within the Kingdom very seriously and with great pride. However, at dusk, the atmosphere of the Pegasi yard was surprisingly light and almost joyful. The Pegasi foals were prancing around. Running, jumping, and learning to fly. While the older Pegasi seemed to be gathering together, telling stories, and filling the air with laughter. Something she had never seen them do before. It was odd seeing them relaxed and not all about business.

Another thing began to make her nervous as well. As she passed by the Pegasi, Gillian's name began to echo out of the Pegasi clumps. She was not surprised, considering Gillian had been lifted up as a hero among their community. As far as they knew, Gillian had captured three traitors and fought off a gigantic Gladiator Bear. Some even called him the Great Gladiator Slayer. Rumors flooded the castle, including the many stories she began to overhear now, and they all painted Gillian to be a great warrior, which added to Isabell's nerves. She, too, began to think of him as a fearless soldier and began to wonder how she would ever stand before him.

It felt like forever, but finally, they reached Gillian's stable. Unlike the horse stable, which was one large building with multiple stalls inside, the Pegasi stables were individual buildings with only one stall in each, spread throughout the yard. The Pegasi, being intelligent creatures, desired more privacy. Each building was constructed with three sides. The fourth side was left open for fresh air and the ability to exit quickly in case their services as warriors were needed. They had a bed of straw made daily by servants like Hector, and fresh hay stocked in a trough along one of the walls. In addition, each stall had a pail of water. Servants would take shifts and make sure the hay and water were always properly stocked, and each morning, the stalls were cleaned while the Pegasi was either on duty or out in the pasture.

As Isabell rounded the corner, her heart sank for she could see four young pegasi standing in a half circle around the open side of Gillian's stall. *He's not alone…* she thought. The young Pegasi listened intently as Gillian spoke of his adventure into the Forbidden Circle.

"And then a ferocious Gladiator bear sprang out of the Blackwood Forest and began slashing its razor-sharp claws this way and that. I was terrified for my life!" Gillian said, as all the little pegasi oohed and awed. Little did they know, it was all a lie. In fact, it was the Gladiator bear who saved Gillian's life. In reality, Isabell did not know Gillian's truth either, but Gillian did. At first, he hesitated to tell his stories. However, with each fib he told, the more praise he received. So by now, Gillian had become submerged in the lie and began to enjoy the attention he received from his comrades. *I know it's all a lie… but, if I have to serve Malus, I might as well bask in the glory of it. Besides, who was going to find out the truth now?* Gillian thought on the matter.

"Gillian! We know the truth!" Isabell said, interrupting both his story and his thoughts. Her soft voice shattered the atmosphere and caused the hair on his hide to stand on end. Isabell didn't actually know much of anything with regards to Gillian, but she knew Mischka did. With the sun down to the horizon, Isabell panicked, and the words blurted out of her mouth.

Gillian gulped hard. Jumping to his feet, he stared at Isabell. He had never seen her before, except maybe in passing. Her words left a heavy aroma in the air, which caused all eyes to fall on her. Gillian, the young Pegasi, and even Hector all stared at her.

"Run along now, I'll finish the story later," Gillian said to the crowd of young Pegasi. The group of foals whimpered in disappointment but slowly dispersed from his stable out into the crisp evening air.

Gillian then turned his attention sharply to Isabell and Hector. Peeking around the corners of his stables, Gilian checked for anyone who could be nearby. He was afraid that someone might overhear them.

"What do you know?" Gillian asked. This question floated through Hector's mind as well. He was in the dark on everything, but now desired to know all the details of Isabell's secret mission.

Hector stepped sideways and turned towards Isabell, putting himself next to Gillian. "Yes, what *do* you know?" Hector said lightly, crossing his arms and lifting his chin high into the air, and then settling it back down so he had to look up at Isabell to see her. Gillian became annoyed with Hector. You see, Hector was making light of this secret mission, but for Gillian, if any of his secrets became exposed, it could be the end of him.

"Hector, you must leave us," Gillian ordered. Gillian could tell by his playful tone that Hector knew nothing of what Isabell wanted to talk about. He would only talk to Isabell if Hector was out of earshot.

"What?" Hector said excitedly. "I brought you to him, and now I have to leave?"

"It might be best if you do," Isabell said softly. She felt bad for Hector, but knew it was the right thing to do. The less that he knew about their plan, the better.

"Really? Isabell! Pal! Come on," he begged.

"No, Hector. Not this time. Consider us even. I'll see you tomorrow," she said firmly. She was a sweet girl, but she was strong-willed, and Hector knew he wasn't going to convince her otherwise. So, he lowered his head and began walking away.

"Remember! Tell no one," Isabell said to him before he was too far off. He looked back over his shoulder and gave a quick nod, and disappeared around the corner.

Isabell quickly shuffled to the edge of Gillian's stable and watched Hector mope around the corner. She watched as he slipped out of sight at the entrance of the stable yard, back into the castle. As she swiveled her head towards Gillian, she was startled because Gillian stood peering down at her. Almost nose to nose.

"What do you know?" Gillian demanded. He became angry only because he feared the punishment that would befall him if his secrets were exposed.

"Well… It's not what I know, but what she knows," Isabell said as she pulled her golden hair back from her shoulder, exposing little Mischka, who was perched on her shoulder.

Gillian jumped back, bobbing his head up and down. He had always been afraid of mice, ever since he was a pony.

"Do not be afraid, Gillian." Mischka squeaked. "Forgive me, but we have very little time, so I must speak quickly."

"Are… you, a Somnatior?" Gillian asked, recognizing that the little mouse was speaking.

"Yes, Gillian, I am a Somniator and my name is Mischka Meese," she began. Knowing this helped Gillian relax a bit, even though he was in the presence of a mouse. However, he remembered how sweet young Eva was, and assumed that this Somniator would be very similar. "We don't have much time. I must speak to you concerning your friends."

"Did you have a dream? Is that how you know about me? About it all?" Gillian asked, assuming Mischka was talking about all his lies. Gillian's anxiety began to get the best of him. Unaware of what Mischka knew about him, all his mistakes began to swarm like the Messorems in his head. He was tricked by four teenagers and then befriended the traitors. He also had learned about Messorems and the Devil's Kettle, which was supposed to be a made-up story. His markings and the lies he had created all added weight to his wings. If word got out about any of these things, the axe would fall on him.

However, despite Gillian's concern, Mischka knew nothing about his lies. She had yet to hear any of the stories from their adventure to the Devil's Kettle; all she knew was the dangers that lay ahead. Especially the daunting fate that was planned for Andy and Eva.

"No dreams. I only bring with me a very important message about Jessie, Eva, and Andy."

Gillian felt a cold rush of relief fall over him. *She doesn't know!* His dire concern faded into annoyance. Unfortunately, Gillian had begun to accept Malus' offer to serve him. In doing so, that would mean he would have to cut ties with his newly formed friends. If he were to commit to serving Malus, it would be best for him to pretend the others never existed. A cruel but necessary thing for Gillian to do if he was going to be happy. He would cut ties and with it lose the guilt he carried inside. It was a good idea, in theory. *Can I really just move on? Can I really just forget about Jessie? About Eva and Andy? I still remember watching Richard fall into the Devil's Kettle. I don't know that I could ever forget that... Even if I tried.* Gillian thought as he pondered these things. However, if he was going to survive and live his best life within the castle, under Malus' rule, denying his friends was a must.

"I have no desire to hear your message. It no longer concerns me," Gillian snapped. His confidence became elevated now that he knew he was in no danger of being found out.

"What?! You have too. For Jessie's sake," Isabell said with panic in her voice.

"I heard what Jessie had to say about me. He will never forgive me anyways. Why should I even care any more..." Gillian said defeatedly, thinking back to Malus' chambers and the words Jessie threw at him out of anger.

"Jessie is in danger. They all are. And only you can help them!" Mischka pleaded.

"I'm sorry, but I cannot risk my own life any longer," Gillian said. Before Isabell could get the words out that Gillian needed to hear, a loud blow from a trumpet came from within the castle's walls.

"But..." Isabell stammered.

"But nothing. We must be off. You know that was an assembly horn. The King has summoned all within the castle walls," Gillian ordered as he took one step towards Isabell. All around them, they could hear the commotion of the stables. Every stable boy and every Pegasus stopped what they were doing and began to filter out of the stable yard and into the inside of the Castle walls. "I wonder what this is about?" Gillian mumbled quietly as he slipped past Isabell and followed the crowd of Pegasi towards the courtyard.

"This is what I am trying to tell you about!" Isabell shouted. However, she immediately regretted it, because all eyes from passersby were glued to her. She knew she had to be more careful with her words. If anyone found out she was trying to help the prisoners, she would be punished or forced to join the prisoners in their fate.

Isabell put her head down with Mischka on her shoulder, concealed by her long blonde hair, and trailed behind Gillian, trying her best to catch up to him.

"You don't understand," Isabell whispered forcefully as she got within earshot of Gillian. He paused for a moment, which allowed Isabell to come up beside him. "You know the King is evil." This statement only made Gillian roll his eyes and pick up his pace. He didn't want to hear it. He knew that the King was evil; in fact, he knew Malus was evil, but at this point, he wanted to save his own life. He was a hero and a legend among his comrades. He was choosing to ignore what was right and indulge in the wrong.

Gillian continued to ignore her as she pleaded behind him. As they entered through the Castle's outer walls, they began down the pathway that would bring them to the courtyard. Every creature under the covered pathway was headed in the same direction. Except for three titans, who had oddly been walking against the current of creatures and were heading towards the dungeons.

"Oh no…" Mischka whispered, understanding that the mission of those three titans was to retrieve Andy and Eva. "Hurry!" she squeaked into Isabell's ears. Isabell pushed forward through the crowd of creatures until she was right beside Gillian again.

"They are innocent!" she whispered. Again, he ignored them and pushed on, getting away from them again. Mischka, in a last effort, spoke up.

"Gillian, they are going to kill Eva and Andy!" A tear formed on Isabell's cheek as she heard the words from Mischka's mouth. However, Gillian acted unfazed.

"Did you hear her?" Isabell screamed in terror. Again, the creatures looked at the distraught young servant girl, but this time Isabell did not care. Gillian too looked back at her outcry. At first, he wondered who she was talking about, but then soon remembered the little mouse hiding beneath her golden locks.

"The mouse? No, I didn't hear a thing." Which was the truth, because of the crowd of creatures, Gillian had not heard a word. "I don't have time for this," Gillian grumbled, trying his best to calmly get away from Isabell and the dreaded mouse.

Up until this point, Gillian had been calm and as polite as possible. However, Isabell began to create a scene, and he wanted no part in it. So in an outburst, Gillian lifted his wing quickly from his body and bumped Isabell with it. Sending Isabell across the hallway into the castle wall. Then he merged into the crowd.

Isabell glanced towards the dungeon and watched as the three Titans turned and entered the dungeon. *I have to hurry. Please, Great White Eagle, help me convince him.* She cried in thought. She pushed off the wall and immediately weaved herself back into the crowd.

—

Deep within the dungeon, the three traitors and Phillip had heard the horn blast. Andy and Eva had never heard it before, but Phillip knew exactly what it was for. The King was summoning all the creatures of the castle for an important announcement. The announcement was the execution of Andy and Eva. Luckily, Andy and Eva did not know this otherwise, they would have been panicking. Instead, their curiosity ran rampant as they listened to the commotion of creatures stomping above.

Suddenly, the three Titans that had passed Isabell above appeared within the dungeon. Quietly, they marched forward until they stood before Andy and Eva's cell door. As Thomas unlocked it, the other two Titans drew their swords and pointed them at Andy and Eva.

"Hey! What's going on?" Jessie barked from the cell behind the Titans.

"If you try anything, your friends here will get it," Thomas warned from over his shoulder to the lone boy. Since Jessie was unaware that his friends were scheduled for execution, he obeyed the Titan's threat for fear of his friends' lives.

"Thomas! Don't do this, Thomas!" Phillip pleaded.

"Oh, shut it! You had your chance to be a hero," Thomas scolded Phillip, causing shame to flood over him. It is true, if Phillip wanted to be a hero, he could have busted out of his prison cell long ago, overpowered Simon, and helped them escape. But he was too much of a coward, and now it was too late. Even if he had mustered up the courage, it would be him against three Titans, who were armed, and Simon. So Phillip just sank into his cell, masking his shame with the shadows of the evening.

As Andy, Eva, and Jessie protested the Titan's advances, Phillip tuned out the commotion, covering his ears and rocking back and forth in the corner. Soon, the Titans had seized Andy and Eva, forcing their arms behind their backs and placing them in cuffs.

"Where are you taking us?" Andy demanded to know.

"Leave them alone!" Jessie barked.

"Lock the gate, will you?" Thomas said as he walked past Simon, tossing him the keys. Closely behind Thomas were the other two Titans, with Andy and Eva gripped in their clutches. Jessie shook violently at his cell door. Kicking the iron bar and shouting at the Titans, demanding they bring his friends back.

Just before Thomas reached the stairs, Phillip burst out of his corner and pressed himself against the cell door. Again, he pleaded with Thomas, an old friend. "Please, Thomas. You know this is wrong."

This time, instead of a hot-tempered insult, Thomas paused, taking a deep breath. He turned to Phillip, looking between the other two Titans, and let out a heavy sigh. "Phillip, you know I don't have a choice." Thomas turned and led the way out of the Dungeons. Slowly, the clanking of armor faded away.

"What are they doing?" Jessie asked frantically.

Phillip sighed and looked at Jessie. Phillip's eyes had welled up, and tears were ready to let loose. He had seen prisoners come and go, and this part of the going was never easy. In fact, this time was much worse, for Andy and Eva were innocent teenagers. They didn't deserve what was coming, and Phillip felt guilty that he hadn't done anything to stop it. Knowing the fate of Andy and Eva, Phillip gazed at Jessie, whose face was painted with a worrisome scowl. Knowing that Jessie deserved to know, Phillip gulped hard and revealed the truth of the matter.

"They are going to execute your friends for treason," Phillip said. His heart felt heavy because his plan to save them failed.

"What! They can't do this!" Jessie cried, falling to his knees in heartbreak.

Chapter 15
Lost in the Castle

Isabell's heart pounded. She had become so distraught. So scared for Andy and Eva, that the voices of the crowd pressing around her muddled into a silent blur. The mission to convince Gillian to help was so intense that even with the crowd's chatter, the only thing Isabell could hear was her own heartbeat and her heavy breathing. *It's not too late, I must try again.* She thought as her head swiveled sharply so she could scan the crowd for Gillian.

Apparently, news had gone out about a very important announcement, for amongst the crowd were goblins from Sod-Omen, a handful of Dwarves, and almost all the creatures from within the castle walls. Titans, servants, and Pegasi all gather in the courtyard. The courtyard was overrun with creatures, making it almost impossible for Isabell to squeeze through.

Everywhere she looked, she knew someone, and many of those creatures tried to talk with her, but she didn't have time; she would just wave and force a smile and then push on. Even more daunting was what she saw to her left as she pushed forward. The dreaded execution stage was set and ready for its victims. A handful of Titans stood before it in a half-moon shape, each holding onto spears. They were the buffer between the crowd and the stage. The stage itself elevated the Executioner, who was sitting quietly, in all black, face hidden from the crowd, with his double-sided ax laid across his lap. Isabell's eyes naturally raised to the balcony that overlooked them all. At the moment, the King was not present, which gave Isabell a bit of relief. Thinking to herself, *I still have time...* However, her mission was still in jeopardy, and the war banners of blood-red with the black pegasi stitched into them were a reminder of the great tragedy that lay in wait just around the corner.

Just then, the doors of the King's chambers opened up and trumpets began to blast. The King, accompanied by Malus, presented themselves. *This is bad, so very bad!* Isabell cried to herself in panic.

The King was dressed in his ceremonial battle gear and approached the railing. He looked proud and powerful, gleaming with greed. The torches ablaze beside him reflected light off his golden breastplate, and a blood-red cape draped down behind him. Isabell also couldn't help but notice his golden crown. It was so beautiful and dazzled with the most beautiful gems she had ever seen.

Even Malus wore a golden helmet. It was similar to the battle gear the Pegasi guards would wear, but his was gold and had a sharp point protruding from the forehead. In addition, Malus had golden clasps cuffed like bracelets along the front ridge of his massive black wings, and ornamental golden feathers clipped into his Primary and Secondary feathers. He looked impressive without any of his ceremonial battle gear on, but now he looked downright unstoppable.

Isabell was almost mesmerized by the black beast. His beauty always surpassed every other Pegasus around them, which was probably why many of the Pegasi desired to earn their black markings, because they hoped to one day look as beautiful as he was. However, in doing so, they were going against the good nature that was within them and becoming more evil with every stain on the hide. At this point, Isabell barely knew Malus. All of her dealings were with the King, and all of the announcements were made by the King, so Isabell thought of Malus as the muscle, the behind-the-scenes guy. However, the true nature of King Fraust and Malus' relationship was unknown to most. Yet, it would be only a matter of time before the creatures of Regnum learned who really made the decisions around the kingdom.

"Isabell, we must keep moving. Lives are at stake. Innocent lives!" Mischka screeched when she noticed that Isabell had become distracted by Malus' beautiful, gold-laced hide.

Isabell shook her head and snapped back into her mission. "Excuse me, excuse me!" She uttered as she squeezed past a Goblin. She raised herself up on her tippy toes and peered around. Mischka, too, parted Isabell's hair and looked about.

"There!" Mischka whispered. Isabell looked, and there in front of them was a Pegasus. Mischka had noted Gillian's markings from before and knew it was him. Slowly, Isabell crept forward, coming up beside Gillian. However, he was unaware that it was her in the pressing crowd. They stood just off to the right of the stage, maybe four or five rows of creatures back. Oddly enough, they could not see the executioner from where they were, for a large blood-red banner hung down, hiding him from their view. Isabell thought nothing of it because from their location in the crowd, they could clearly see the King and Malus from above, and they were the biggest threat to Andy and Eva at the moment.

"Gillian," Isabell whispered.

He looked over his shoulder at the girl and the mouse. Scoffing, he said, "You again, I thought I told you to stay out of all of this?"

"You don't understand!" Mischka said it loud enough that others around them looked to see what she was talking about. But she didn't care; something needed to happen, and it needed to happen now.

The dreaded sound of trumpets blared, and the crowd hushed. The King was about to begin his announcement, the execution ceremony had begun. Isabell's heart sank, and Mischka's blood ran cold.

"Friends and Allies. People of Regnum! Welcome!" King Fraust said joyfully.

Just then, the crowd roared with excitement. The Pegasi and Titans began to chant, "Long live the King, Long live the King!"

It was expected for the servants to join in on the chant, and Isabell, under normal circumstances, obliged. But for the first time in Isabell's life, she refrained from the chant. She was sick to her stomach, knowing what the King had planned. He was cruel and evil, and she couldn't stand it any longer.

The crowd's roar grew louder, deafening even. In that moment, it felt like the courtyard walls were squeezing in on Isabell as she felt the crowd around her swaying like the sea. It was the most uncomfortable she had ever felt in a crowd before. She wanted to curl up in a ball and cry on the cobbled stone beneath her feet. But she knew she couldn't. For her friend's sake, she needed to stay strong. Luckily for her, the King raised his arms into the air and slowly let them sink until his hands came to rest on the balcony. The crowd's volume became mute instantly.

"As you all know, the last few days have been quite… exciting." The King began raising his eyebrows. "However, it weighs on my heart to announce that such events must be met with some consequences." He said, in a way that made him almost sound genuinely upset.

"Don't you see? Consequences," Isabell sputtered towards Gillian.

"Would you stop? Her consequence has been made known to me. Eva will be a servant to the King. And I'm sure Andy will become a stable boy," Gillian said. He was informed that those were the consequences that they would receive, but he had again been lied to. He did not actually know the fate that was set for Andy and Eva.

Malus stood behind the King, but Gillian's side conversation with Isabell did not go unnoticed. Malus could see their disturbance and began to watch them closely.

"Three traitors have been captured. They are prisoners because they have broken my law. No, they have broken the laws of Regnum, which is *our* law!" The King announced over the crowd. This made many in the crowd begin to murmur. Rumors had spread about it, but many were hoping that the King would give them first-hand insight on the situation that had occurred days ago. "Many have counseled me to make these traitors servants for the Castle," The King said.

Gillian then looked over his shoulder again at Isabell and Mischka and said, "See?"

"But is that fair to our servants? To let such dangerous criminals serve alongside them?" the King asked.

Gillian was still looking at Isabell, but heard the words of the King. His ears swiveled sharply toward the balcony to soak up his every word. King Fraust's tone indicated to Gillian that his mind had changed, and Gillian's heart began to thump.

"I need you to listen to me," Mischka said. But Gillian ignored her. His ears were glued to the King's announcement.

"What example does showing mercy to these traitors give to the other creatures daring enough to enter into the Forbidden Circle? Is it not the law that no one enters into that forbidden land? And yet these three had? Tell me, why is there such a law?" The King asked. However, the crowd remained silent. "It is the *law*, because it is what keeps all of you safe!" The King said a bit more aggressively.

Gillian was torn; he believed that Andy and Eva deserved some punishment, after all, they willingly broke the law. Yet, so did he. *Becoming a servant would be enough… What is the King planning… It is true, many creatures might follow their lead, thinking it's safe to enter the Forbidden Circle. But it's not! I know firsthand how dangerous it was, especially the Uada Hollow. The King is right, the law protects the creatures whether they like it or not…* Gillian thought. He wanted no harm to fall on his friends, so he was happy with what he had been told, that they would become servants. However, the King's tone began to indicate that Isabell and the mouse's desperate attempt for his help was not an empty request.

"That is why the laws must be enforced. These traitors must be punished. But there is only one punishment that fits this dreadful crime," The King barked.

The crowd became loud. Everyone began whispering to their neighbor and putting their own thoughts into what this punishment would be. For Gillian, his heart began to race with fear. He thought about all the punishments he had ever seen and feared that it would be execution. He began to sweat, and his head began to spin. *He wouldn't, he can't, they don't deserve that. If they deserve that, so do I!* Gillian thought.

"Gillian?" Isabell asked, Gillian was stuck in his own thoughts and beginning to panic, and Isabell could see it on his face. His eyes were wide, and the sweat beaded up above his brow.

Now, there is something catastrophic that can sometimes happen in intense situations like this. Gillian seemed to lose himself in the moment. Although the next few things that happened all happened at once, for Gillian, it was as if time slowed to a stop. It was as if the crowd around him turned into a gentle wave, and their voices were muffled by a ringing that pierced Gillian's ear.

His eyes shifted from the King to the crowd. The crowd began to jump and shout, their movements turned from a gentle wave to a raging sea. They raised their fists in agreement with the King's words. Gillian's mouth hung open in disbelief, and his eyes traveled the ocean of creatures. Then, his eyes became trapped by something that stepped out onto the open stage. Gillian felt sick already, but what he saw caused his heart to sink deeper than it had ever sunk before, and a cold shiver shot down his spine while a swell of heat festered in his forehead.

For the first time in Gillian's life, he came to realize something terrible. The thing that caught his eye was nothing new, in fact, it was something he had seen many times before. What he saw was the executioner. As he gazed at the creature, who was clothed in ragged and tattered black garments, he realized he had seen him recently. Not the executioner but a creature that looked just like him. Deep within the Uada Hollow, Gillian remembered seeing the dreaded Messorems. His whole life, right under his nose, the King and Malus had disguised the executioner as one of the most vile and dangerous creatures in all the land. Even the executioner's face was covered by a heavy black hood. Gillian became weak. *All this time! All this time, the man who executed prisoners was dressed up just like a Messorem. That is wretched!*

Realizing this meant Isabell was telling the truth. The King was going to kill Andy and Eva.

Slowly, the grip of the moment began to break loose. The ringing in his ear quieted, and in a muffled voice behind him, he could hear Isabell and Mischka saying his name, but it was like a slow, distant echo in which he could not quite understand.

Then the words from King Fraust stunned him to the core.

"To maintain order in the Kingdom of Regnum, I sentence Eva Huntsberg and Andy from the orphanage to death."

...to death echoed in Gillian's head. Gillian's weak legs almost failed him, and he stumbled back.

"Gillian, we have to save them. This is it, this is the last chance we have!" Isabell cried, pulling on his wings with tears in her eyes.

She was right; if Gillian did not do anything at this exact moment, it would be too late. The Titans, ordered to fetch Andy and Eva, had just arrived at the top of the Dungeon stairs. With only a quick walk down the covered pathway, Andy and Eva would be brought before the crowd of creatures and face certain death.

Gillian regretted being so stubborn but had no time now to apologize, so he began to push through the crowd. At first, he was trying to be stealthy, but he realized that was getting him nowhere. In order to get to the dungeons quickly, he began to push creatures out of his way. He opened his wings, shoving creatures back, creating a path for himself. A scene had broken out, and he was at the center of it.

"Get out of my way! Move!" he ordered.

The disruption within the crowd caught the King's eye. "Stop him!" The King began to shout. Malus rushed to the rail and peered down. He realized that Gillian was going to betray him. He knew now that Gillian was going to serve the Great White Eagle. This heroic act of saving two pesky humans was proof of it.

"Seize him!" Malus shouted from the balcony. Gillian glanced up at him for only a moment, and then lowered his head and pushed through the crowd even harder, knowing that his window of opportunity would soon close in on him.

To his surprise, the crowd moved out of his way, but it was only so the Titans could easily surround him. They all drew their swords and pointed them at Gillian. Yet, none of that stopped him. Without hesitation, Gillian stretched his wings out and thrusted them to the ground, lifting himself up and over the Titans. Thinking he was in the clear, Gillian let out a little whinny. But before his feet could safely hit the ground, Gillian felt a great force from above him, which caused him to abruptly crash into the cobbled stone below. It was Zolton. At Malus' order, he leaped into the air and aimed to take out Gillian. Ever since he had to babysit Gillian on the mission to the Forbidden Circle, Zolton had not trusted him and had been waiting for this moment.

Gillian quickly jumped to his feet and faced Zolton. Behind him were a string of Titans with spears in their hands. Zolton lurched forward, but Gillian quickly responded by rearing up and thumping Zolton's chest with his front hooves.

Zolton pulled back just enough to avoid new blows from Gillian. A Titan took a turn and rushed in with a spear aimed at Gillian, but Gillian extended his right wing and rotated his entire body. In doing so, the tip of the spear missed his chest, and his wing scooped the Titan off his feet and threw him into the archway that led up the stairs into the castle. This dodge set him in the right direction. Facing the covered pathway, he could see Eva and Andy coming his way, being led by three Titans. Gillian rushed down the pathway, as he raced towards them, Eva could see the panic in his eyes.

"Gillian?" Eva asked, wondering what was going on. Eva and Andy had heard the commotion, yet still did not know what was lying in wait around the corner.

"Let them go!" Gillian ordered with a snort.

Thomas then stepped forward. "Gillian, move aside!" Gilllian could hear the herd of Titans ambushing him from behind. So, instead of halting to plead with Thomas, he lowered his head and charged. It all happened so quickly, Thomas was unable to draw his sword. Defenseless, Gillian charged in. With a lowered head, Gillian collided with Thomas. Quickly, Gillian flicked his head back, lifting Thomas right off his feet, sending him through the air. By the time Thomas found the ground again, he had been thrown over Gillian's back and into the oncoming group of Titans.

The two other Titans that had been holding onto Eva and Andy let go of them and drew their swords. This was the chance Gillian hoped for. Both Titans raised their swords above their heads and rushed Gillian. Gillian flicked his wings out to the side and barreled forward. The ridge of his wings clotheslined the Titans, and their armor crashed into the ground like a tower of pots tipping over. Luckily, Andy and Eva had more time to react, so as Gillian approached them, they were able to duck under his wings and allow Gillian to pass by them, no harm done.

"Run!" Gillian said as he tucked his wings tightly into his body and turned to face the Titans, who were finding their feet.

Andy and Eva scrambled back toward the dungeons, putting themselves behind Gillian for protection.

"I'll hold them off… Go!" Gillian shouted as he charged the horde of Titans.

Without hesitation, Andy and Eva darted north. They raced past the archway that led into the Pegasi stables, then they slipped past the dungeon. Everything in them wanted to try and rescue Jessie, but they knew time was of the essence. So, with heavy hearts, they both rushed by and did not look back.

At a fast pace, they were approaching the back corner of the castle. Once they arrived there, the maze in which Malus gazed upon each day would be before them, and the castle to their backs. With perfect timing, they rounded the castle, bringing them out from under the covered pathway and out into the open air. In the exact moment they were coming out from under the covered pathway, a Pegasus was aiming to enter. However, the Pegasus was just as shocked to see them as Andy and Eva were to see him. With a shriek, Eva and Andy ducked, and the Pegasus, being surprised, hesitated just enough before attempting to clasp down on the two prisons with his wings, and his momentum carried him over them. They were safe, but only for a split second. The Pegasus may have missed on his first attempt, but he was not about to give up. As soon as his hooves hit the ground, he swirled around and let out a forceful snort. This left Andy with very little time to think. He felt trapped. In front of him was a Pegasus, behind him a castle barrier wall, to his right a garden of some sort with tall hedges, and to his left the castle itself. He really wanted to get away from the castle, but his gut told him to avoid the garden. He was unsure of what was in there, and truthfully, he was lucky he felt this way. Going in there would have caused him to get lost and exposed them to Pegasi from above. Not to mention the powerful calling the wishing well in the center of the maze had on all creatures. So, Andy lurched for the door that rested on the face of the Castle. His heart skipped in relief as the door swung open by his hand.

"Quick, get in!" Andy exclaimed to Eva. Without a second to waste, she and Andy ducked into the castle and slammed the door behind them. The Pegasus pawed at the door. Again, they lucked out; here they found themselves in the kitchen of the castle, and because only the human servants were tasked with meal preparation, a rope was never tied to the outside of the door. Normally, a rope was tied to the door, so Pegasi could bite down on it and swing the door open. Now, the only thing this Pegasus could do was beat on the door with his hooves and hope that the door would get knocked down.

Leaned against the wall was a wooden board, and on the door, there were two L-shaped pegs into which the board fit perfectly, securing them inside and preventing the door from being knocked down.

As they turned around, they were met with the faces of three servant girls. One girl stood with her mouth dropped open. She was at a table in the center of the room, with a knife in her hand and vegetables spread out on the table before her. The second girl was standing beside the fireplace where a hog was being roasted rotisserie style. Her eyes were wide and frightened from the abrupt entrance of Andy and Eva and the vicious thumping on the outside of the door.

The third girl, however, did not react the same way. Instead, she quickly made her way toward Andy and Eva.

"Come this way, quickly now!" She ordered as she placed her hand on their arms to direct them towards a walk-in pantry. The poorly lit pantry was filled with bags of flour, potatoes, and freshly hung meats. There were pots and pans and all of the royal china stacked chaotically on shelves that lined the walls. "Isabell said you were good people. We heard the King's announcement. Stay in here until I say so." She said as she lifted the top off a giant kettle, which was stuffed in the back corner of the pantry.

Andy looked at Eva and gestured as if to say. "After you." Eva crawled in, followed by Andy. Once they plopped down, the servant girl placed the lid back on the kettle, hiding them both from sight.

It's ironic that we are finding a safe harbor in a kettle, when it was the Devil's Kettle that got us into this mess… Eva thought as she tried to quiet her breathing in the darkness of the covered kettle.

The pounding on the door continued. As the helpful servant girl made her way to the door she grabbed a few pots and pans that were on the preparation table and knocked them on the floor and then she flicked her hands at the other two girls and said "Shoo! Be on your way." and the other girls dropped what they were doing and disappeared without question.

"Goodness me! I'm coming," she hollered out at the beast.

As she went to lift the wooden board from the door, she paused for a moment. She took her hands and messed up her hair, scraped some dirt off the ground, and smudged it on her face. She had a plan.

Shortly after she lifted the board, the door flung open. On the other side was the Pegasus and now two Titans. Immediately, the two Titans rushed into the kitchen. They saw the servant girl who looked as if she had been roughed up, and pots and pans on the floor of the kitchen.

"Where are they?" They asked impatiently. Then the two Titans began to search the kitchen. When one of the Titans began to make their way towards the pantry, the servant girl grew tense. As he poked his nose into the pantry, she responded to his question, hoping to direct him away from the pantry and the two traitors hiding inside.

"They came in here and knocked all these dishes to the ground. I tried to stop them, but they pushed me to the ground." The servant girl said as she put her hand on her head, the way one would if they had just knocked it into something.

"Where did they go?" One Titan asked.

"That way!" she said as she pointed to a doorway that led into the heart of the castle.

Simultaneously, the two Titans exited the room in search of the escaped prisoners. The Pegasi who had nosed in the doorway backed out and flew off, hoping he could catch them trying to exit the castle.

As the Titan's armor clanked off down the hallway, the servant girl peeked out of the kitchen to make sure the coast was clear. Once she was certain that she was alone, she grabbed something that was hanging on the wall, and then she made her way into the pantry.

From within the kettle, it was as dark as a night sky without the moon. As the servant girl took the lid off, a small sliver of brightness shone in, but within seconds, the lid had been removed, and Andy and Eva were exposed. They could see the servant girl's soft face peering at them. In one hand she held the lid to the giant kettle, but with the other she held a hatchet.

"Please don't hurt us," Andy begged, seeing the blade.

"I won't hurt you. But we must get those cuffs loose," she said with a smile. Now Andy knew why she had the hatchet, so he followed her eagerly, excited to get the cold iron cuffs off his tender wrists.

She led them over to the preparation table and pushed aside the vegetables that were being prepared. "Put your hands here..." she said while pointing to the table. Eva did as she was asked. "Spread your wrists as far as you can," she ordered. Eva did just that. As far as the cuffs would let her.

Eva trusted the servant girl, after all, she helped them hide from the Titans that were hot on their trail. But when the young girl raised the hatchet into the air, Eva couldn't help but clench her teeth and look away as the hatchet swung down towards her hands.

Thump! The hatchet sheared through the chains that kept the cuffs together, causing Eva's hands to become free from each other.

"Your turn," the servant girl said to Andy. As she did the same thing to Andy, he looked away, but instead of closing his eyes, he peered around the room. The kitchen looked dirty and dingy, reminding him of the dungeon. Rock walls and small windows that barely let in any light. Pans hung from pegs that were nailed into the room's ceiling, and the burning fireplace made it miserably hot. Soon, Andy's arms were free from each other as well.

"Thank you, we owe you our lives," Andy said.

"I'm sorry I can't get the cuff off of your wrists, but at least you're free to use your arms," she said with a smile.

"What is your name?" Eva asked.

"Jenny," the servant girl said.

"Thank you, thank you, thank you, Jenny. I will never forget you," Eva said as she wrapped the servant girl in a bear hug. Eva was so thankful to be free that she hugged her like they had been friends all their lives.

"You must be on your way now. The guards could come back any second now," Jenny said.

"Where should we go?" Eva asked.

"Follow me," Jenny said as she began to lead them into the castle. They left the kitchen and hung a sharp left. Down a hallway, she led them. On their right, there was an archway, and inside Eva recognized the throne room, where she was able to see her mother. This archway accessed the throne room from behind.

As they continued, many doorways lined the left side of the hall. Some doors were open, and you could see bedrooms inside. Clearly, they were in the servant's quarters.

Suddenly, the faint sound of voices echoed from behind them. Without a word, Jenny pulled them into an open door on their left and shut it quietly behind them. If you have ever been trying to hide or stay quiet while your heart is racing, you would know that in that moment, the silence of the bedroom screamed. Although not a word was spoken, each of them could hear their heartbeat as if it were being shouted from a rooftop. Their heavy breathing quivered as they tried to calm it down, and as they crowded into the tiny room, the shuffling of blankets on one of the beds as they pressed deeper into the room made them feel like their cover would be blown. Jenny stood stiff as a statue with her finger pressed to her lips. *Shhhh* is what she indicated. In a very short time, they could hear outside the door a pair of Titans' armor clanking down the hallway. Everything was so still that their heartbeats thumped, and to them, it sounded like someone was pounding a drum. Thankfully, that was not the case, and the Titans had no clue they were hiding in the room beside them.

"I think they went this way," one shouted right outside their door. Then they rushed off.

"Whoa, that was so close… They are everywhere… How will we escape?" Eva whispered in fear. Just then, a faint thump sounded from down the hallway.

Jenny looked around the room. Then again, the thump echoed, but this time it sounded closer. "Here, put these on." She scraped up a dirty shirt from the floor and tossed it to Andy. At that moment, he didn't really think about it, however, he threw the shirt on immediately. Now wearing two stable boy shirts, one he had received when they first arrived, and now a second as a disguise. It was pointless, since they were basically the same shirt; however, in time, he would be glad he did.

Then Jenny reached into a cubby and pulled out another cream colored shirt and gave it to Eva. There was a hat on the floor which she set on Eva's head and pulled it down so the brim of the hat covered her face.

Thump, again, louder than before.

"Here, these too," Andy said as he pulled a pair of baggy brown pants out of the same cubby and handed it to Eva. After a brief moment, both looked like servant boys.

"There, now we look like servants," Andy whispered.

"Good thinking, Jenny," Eva said.

Just then, the thump came to life. A Titan had been making his way down the hallway, kicking down any closed doors. This time, it was the room they were in.

"Freeze! In the name of the King," he ordered.

They were all terrified and felt like their hearts were trying to escape out of their bodies through their throats. But to their relief, the Titan asked. "Have you seen the prisoners?"

Andy and Eva's hearts settled back down into their chests, and the three responded simultaneously. "No! Haven't seen them."

"If you see them, report them at once," he ordered.

"Yes, sir!" Andy blurted as he straightened out and raised one hand to his eyebrow to salute the Titan. With complete faith in Andy, the Titan vanished down the hall without wasting another second.

"Phew!" Eva said as she wiped her brow.

"Let's get you out of here. Thankfully, that Titan was dull. The next one might just recognize a girl in a boy's clothing." Jenny said, tucking Eva's long hair into the back of her baggy shirt.

Slipping out of the room, they continued back down the hallway. Jenny led the way in the direction that Andy and Eva hoped would be freedom.

Passing a second archway that peered in on the backside of the throne, they came to the end of the hall. A heavy wooden door with three iron hinges hung before them. Through this door, they would find themselves out of the castle and into the evening air.

As Jenny pushed the door open, they could see the darkness of dusk falling onto the land. Quickly, Jenny poked her head out of the doorway to check to see if the coast was clear.

But it wasn't. The whole castle grounds were crawling with Titans and Pegasi searching for Andy and Eva. However, it seemed that their disguises were working. Just then, two Titans crossed past the open door and peered in at them. They quickly disregarded them as servants, lifted their eyes to scan the hallway behind them, and continued onward down the covered pathway outside the castle.

"This is it. I can't bring you any further. Straight ahead is the stable yard." Jenny explained.

"The stables for the horses?" Eva asked.

"Yes."

Both Andy and Eva looked across the outside pathway and through the archway that fed into the stable yard. They could see the well where they were forced to wash up in, and some of the stable barns behind it.

"It's getting real dark now, so use the shadows to your advantage," Jenny said as she closed the door to muffle their conversation from the outside.

"Beyond the stable barns is a hay mound. That is the outside edge of the castle. The only thing stopping you from escaping from there is the open pastures. You might want to make sure it gets really dark before you try and run through the open field."

"Okay, thank you," Andy said.

"We owe you our lives," Eva said as she hugged Jenny goodbye. Jenny didn't say anything. She just squeezed Eva tightly and nodded. Then she turned and headed back to the kitchen.

Chapter 16
Hay Mound Haven

"Ready?" Andy whispered, with one hand on the door, and with the other, he reached for Eva's hand. She nodded and squeezed his hand tightly, then pulled the brim of her hat down again to hide her face.

Forcefully, Andy pushed the door open, and they stepped out into the cool crisp air of the evening. As he looked to his right, he could see Titans scrambling about in the courtyard. Peering left, he could see a

Titan questioning a stable boy near the rear of the castle, near the washroom.

Lurching forward, they passed through the archway and could feel the dirt of the stable yard shift beneath their feet. The stars above glistened in the dark sky. But snapping their chins down, they kept their eyes to the ground, for above them were Pegasi searching the castle grounds from the air.

Again, Titans could be seen speaking with servant boys, and Andy knew they needed to hide quickly before they too became subjects of questioning. *We were lucky before, but how many times until a Titan figures us out?* Andy thought anxiously.

As they scurried through the stable yard, they could hear the sound of voices around the corner of the barn. Avoiding any contact, they tucked themselves against the adjacent side of the barn, keeping to the shadows. They leaned against the barn's front door and listened to the conversation. Andy felt safe in the shadows and thought no one had seen them.

"Have you seen the prisoners? A boy and girl about your age?" they overhead a Titan asking from around the corner of the barn.

"No..." a servant boy said. Little did Andy and Eva know, but the servant boy being questioned was the young boy who Simon had ripped his shirt for them to use as a washcloth.

"If you see them, you report them. Understand me?"

"Yes, of course," the boy said, with a terrified quiver in his voice.

Then the Titan's armor could be heard clanking, and he was coming their way. Eva's eyes grew wide as she peered at Andy, wondering what to do.

Quickly, Andy pried the barn door open, and the two of them slipped into the barn. Hoping they acted quickly enough, they pressed against the inside wall of the barn.

Outside, the clanking of the Titan's armor came to a sudden halt.

Oh no… he must have seen us. Eva thought to herself. Then, in a desperate cry for help, she began to speak with her inner voice. These thoughts were directed to the Great White Eagle himself. *Please save us, protect us from the Guards, just as you did when you saved us from the Messorems. I trust in you.* She said in her head, hoping the Great White Eagle would somehow hear her. But quietly, the Titan slowly opened the barn's door. As a sliver of light grew inside the dark barn, Eva thought that this was the end. But then, the sliver of silver light halted.

"Hey, you!" the voice of a servant boy shouted.

Slowly, the barn door settled shut, and Andy and Eva were in darkness once again.

"What is it, boy?" The Titan asked.

"I believe they have found the prisoners. I heard a commotion in the courtyard."

"Good," the Titan barked as he trotted off.

Eva let out a sigh of relief as the clanking of armor faded away into silence. *Thank you,* her inner voice said. Whether it was a coincidence or the Great White Eagle intervening, she was grateful.

"I think the coast is clea…" Andy started as he was abruptly interrupted. The door swung open, and the silhouette of the servant boy slipped in, the door closing quickly behind him.

At first, they were terrified, thinking the servant would turn them over to the Titans. But they're nerves settled once the boy began to talk. "You're the prisoners, aren't you?"

Andy gulped hard but answered truthfully. "Yes…"

"So you know Isabell?"

"Oh yes!" Eva said as a smile grew across her face, but then it vanished just as quickly. "Why, who wants to know?" Eva realized that if the wrong people learned that Isabell helped them, Isabell could be in danger.

"Well, I'm Hector. I would assume that she was trying to help you?"

"She might have been," Andy said cautiously.

"Well, she came to me to help find Gillian… the royal guard who helped you escape? Considering she wanted to find him, and shortly after he helped you escape, I have to imagine she had something to do with it." Hector said, piecing together the events of the evening. However, Eva and Andy's silence hinted at the fact that they still didn't trust him. "Oh, don't worry. I'm a friend. Isabell and I go way back."

Both Eva and Andy sighed. They were relieved that this Hector guy seemed to be a friend. After all, he did get the Titan to leave when he could have easily turned his back and looked away.

"If you're a friend of Isabell's… can you help us?" Andy asked. Hector pondered the question. The truth of the matter was, Hector had a crush on Isabell. That's why he always went to her for favors and why he was willing to help her with her top-secret mission.

If I help her friends, maybe she will finally like me. Hector thought to himself. "Hmmm, I suppose I can," he finally said.

"Oh- thank you! Thank you!" Eva quietly exclaimed.

"We were told to try and escape through the pasture, once it got dark enough," Eva explained.

"Hmm, I don't think that will be happening any time soon," Hector grumbled.

"What? Why!" Andy demanded. Awaiting Hector's response, they all hushed their voices as they could hear footsteps thumping outside the barn.

Then, they heard a Titan shout, "Check the barns. I'll take this one, you check those over there."

The three panicked. "That's why!" Hector said, "This place is crawling with Titans out for your heads. There is no way you would make it across the pastures in a full moon…"

"What do we do?" Eva cried.

"Quick, follow me." Hector led them through the dark to one of the stalls. "Hey, Lucky, it's me, Hector." To Andy and Eva's surprise, the horse responded with a soft whinny.

Hector opened the stall's gate and quickly pulled Andy and Eva in behind him, and latched the gate behind them. As the barn door was opened, an orange flame illuminated the stables, causing the shadows to dance in the quiet barn. Hector patted Lucky on the back side of his leg, and the horse instantly lay down. Apparently, Hector had trained his horse to lie down with one simple pat. Both Andy and Eva were impressed as they watched it unfold from their crouched position.

Then Hector waved the two of them over and motioned behind the horse. "Get down…" Hector whispered.

As the Titan moved along the stables, he used his torch to shed light into each stable, looking for the prisoners.

"After the coast is clear, meet me on the far side of the stables, by the hay mound," Hector softly ordered Andy.

Soon, the dancing flame on the torch was staring Hector in the face. But to the Titan's surprise, Hector looked to be napping with his horse. Hector had sat down, leaned back against Lucky's belly, and stretched out his arms in both directions, resting them on the horse's side.

Because Lucky was lying down, the torch cast a shadow behind him, and Andy and Eva remained out of sight.

"What are you doing here?" the Titan asked

"Can you not see that I'm taking a nap?"

"The castle is on lockdown, this is no time for games. The escaped prisoners are dangerous," the Titan announced. Eva was shocked to hear the Titan say that she was dangerous. Her eyebrows slanted towards her nose, and her jaw dropped open in disbelief.

"Dangerous?! Ha! I heard they are just a couple of kids. You ain't scared of no kids, are you?" Hector said, mocking the tough-looking Titan.

"Until I get a good look at them, I must assume they are dangerous..." the Titan said, taking their threat to the kingdom very seriously.

"Oh, relax, would you? They're just a couple of scared kids!" Hector said nonchalantly.

"How do you know? Harboring fugitives is a punishable offense!" the Titan threatened, becoming suspicious of Hector's knowledge of the escapees.

Realizing the Titan's growing suspicion, Hector covered his tracks. "Slow your roll, mister. I saw them when they were first brought in. Since then, I've been with Lucky. Haven't I, boy?" Hector said, reaching over and scratching his horse between the ears, causing the sleepy horse to whinny gently.

"Alright then," the Titan said hesitantly, "back to your chambers!"

"You got it, Sarg! Right after I finish tucking ole Lucky in," Hector said with a smile.

"It's a horse. He'll be fine," the Titan argued.

"Eh, em. He's my horse, and he doesn't sleep too well, 'less I tuck him in."

"Looks like he's falling asleep just fine." Hector looked over, and his horse's eyes were closed, and his head was beginning to bob, the way one does when they are beginning to fall asleep.

"Oh, trust me," Hector said as he gave Lucky a solid tap on the neck, causing the sleepy horse's eyes to shoot wide open. With a gentle, sluggish turn of his nose, Lucky began to nibble at Hector's arm, "The horse has a routine."

"Well, fine. But after you're done *tucking* him in, off to your chambers. That's an order!" the Titan said.

"Understood!" Hector said, jumping to his feet.

Slowly, the Titan crept along, extending his torch into the stables in search of the prisoners. Some of the horses whinnied or snorted when the bright light entered their stall. But soon, he had searched each and every stall, but had no luck finding them.

While the Titan was checking the stalls, Hector crouched down and whispered back to Andy and Eva, who were still hiding behind the horse, "I'll meet you near the hay mound." Then spun around, exited the barn, and let the Titan escort him out of the stable yard.

Although Andy and Eva found themselves in the dark again, they were in the clear. As they stood up, Lucky hoisted himself to his feet as well. Eva wrapped her arms around Lucky's neck and ruffled his mane and scratched behind his ears.

Andy began to walk towards the stall's gate, but stopped in front of Lucky, guided by the moonlight that slipped in through the cracks of the barn wood, he reached out his hand and scratched the horse on the head.

"Thanks, Lucky," he said. As he opened the stall's gate, he whispered back to Eva, "Come on, let's go."

She patted the horse one last time on the neck and ducked under his chin and scrambled to Andy's side. Shuffling their feet along the ground and feeling with their hands out in front of them, through the dark, they navigated the barn. Finally, Andy's hands felt the firm, seasoned wood of the barn's back wall. The flaky paint began to crumble under the weight of his hands, and the coarse grains of the barn's lumber brushed his fingertips. Eva was a bit shorter than he was, so when she came to the wall, a small round hole that formed from a knot in the wood popping out over the years looked her in the eye. Through it, she could see outside, softly lit by the moonlight above.

Seeing with his hands, Andy felt for a door. He had to side-step a few times before he found the door, and he had to feel around a bit before he found the latch.

"Okay, we will head straight east until we find the hay mound. Ready?"

"Not yet." Through the hole in the barn wall, Eva could see a shadow towering across the ground from around the corner of the stable. As she watched the shadow grow longer, she soon saw a Titan appear from her left. Holding her breath, she leaned back from the hole in the wall and sank into the darkness of the stable. The small hole acted like a moon spotlight. With its help, Andy could see that Eva had a finger hovering over her lips, silently telling him to keep quiet.

The Titan's armor clanked by and faded out to their right. Once all was silent again, Eva leaned back to the hole and peered out. "Go!" she forcefully whispered, seeing that the coast was clear.

Carefully, Andy flipped the latch on the door, causing the door to pop open a sliver. Wasting no more time, Andy swung the door open and rushed outside. Allowing Eva to follow, he gently shut the door behind them. Making sure he didn't leave a trail of clues for the royal guard to follow. Then the two bolted across the open yard towards the east. The only building left between them and the rolling hills of the pasture was a small square building.

"That has to be it," Andy said in between breaths. Approaching the building, Andy swiveled his head, looking out for any Titan or Pegasus that would be searching for them. But for the first time, the stable yard seemed to be empty. The shadow hung off to the right side of the barn in a slim sliver. Leaving the majority of this small building's shadow resting on its far side. Darting to their right, Andy and Eva slipped into the shadow beside the building and rounded its corner to the far east side.

"Here it is!" Andy said finding this building was the hay mound. A three-sided shelter, much like the Pegasi stables, where they stuffed hay into to keep it out of the rain.

Both of them stood looking out at the pastures. Hector was right… There was no way they would make it across the pastures in this bright moonlight. Any Pegasi flying above would see them, even if they were half asleep.

Suddenly, a cold rush flooded down his spine, that feeling you get when you sense you're in big trouble. Someone had a sudden grip on his arm and yanked Andy into the mound of hay that was behind him.

"Andy?" Eva shrieked quietly, afraid they were in danger.

Soon, Hector's head poked out of the hay mound, and he smiled at Eva, who felt a sense of relief flood her body.

As Hector emerged from the stack of hay, he shook like a dog, causing stocks of hay to shake loose and float to the ground around him.

"You guys hide here," he said. Andy still lay within the haystack.

"How long will that be?" Andy asked, sounding muffled from within the heart of the haystack.

"I don't know, at least until I can figure out how to get you two out of here."

"Oh... dear," Eva said, very unenthused to have to anxiously wait within this hay mound haven.

"You don't have much of a choice, I'm afraid. You will never make it across the pastures with the moon as bright as it is tonight," Hector explained plainly.

"He's right... It would look suspicious seeing two kids in servants' closes running across the pastures this late," Andy said, swimming his way to the surface and poking his head out. Eva didn't like the thought of crawling into the itchy hay mound, but couldn't think of any other options. This would have to do.

"Fine..." Eva said with a look of disgust as she tiptoed into the hay mound and cautiously buried herself within it.

"Goodbye for now," Hector whispered, and the servant boy vanished into the night.

Eva crawled deeper into the hay mound until she ran into Andy. The two of them pushed and kicked the hay around them until they had made a pocket big enough for them to sit in comfortably.

Unfortunately, as they settled in, Eva sensed the presence of an oncoming sneeze. *Oh no... I knew this would happen.* She thought.

You see, just like in the clearing, dust, this time from the hay, began to nuzzle itself into her nostrils. Hay was something that always triggered her allergies, and now was not an ideal time for a reaction. That's why she was so hesitant to enter into it in the first place. However, uncontrollably, she began to sneeze. She pulled her shirt up over her nose to act as a mask, but it was too little, too late.

Thankfully, for their sake, they had burrowed deep enough into the heart of the hay mound that the hay dampened her high-pitched shrieks. After a brutal sneeze attack, she was finally able to refrain. However, if you have ever experienced allergies, you know just how miserable Eva felt. Her breathing became laborious, her eyes itched and watered, and her throat began to hurt. It became so bad that tears ran down her rosy cheeks. Not from crying, but as a reaction to the hay fever that had set in. Andy knew she wasn't trying to blow their cover, and he could hear her breathing become more laborious as time went on. He felt terrible for her, but couldn't help but worry that someone might hear them.

"How are you doing? I can hear your breathing drag," Andy asked quietly, in between each wheeze of Eva's breath. Although he couldn't actually see her, he had seen her in the past have spurts like this. He could imagine her soft face reddened and watering eyes.

Poor Eva, I wish I could make it better for her. He thought empathetically.

"I don't know how much longer I can hold out. My throat is itchy, my mouth is dry. My eyes hurt even with them closed," she said miserably.

Andy thought hard on how he could make it more comfortable for Eva. He wished it were he who was suffering instead of her, but that wasn't the case. Suddenly, an idea popped into his head. He began to claw at the hay above him, and the pocket they had created began to collapse. Eva began to cough from the dust. "What are you doing?"

She asked, unimpressed that an avalanche of hay began to rain down on her.

"Climb with me," he said calmly, reaching out towards Eva, finding her arm, and helping hoist her upwards.

The two began to pull the hay above them down, and then stomped it down below them. Slowly, they began to bring themselves closer to the top of the pile from within it.

The sweat on their faces collected dust. While grime and stalks of hay found their way into every place imaginable.

Finally, a gush of cool air splashed against their faces. The roof of the building floated only inches above their heads. High enough in the mound now that their heads were exposed to the pastures beyond the stable yard, but deep enough towards the back of the hay barn that anyone passing by on foot would not be able to see them up in the hay mound.

"I hope this fresh air will help…Maybe it won't be as bad," Andy said. The moonlight seeped through the cracks of the three-sided structure and illuminated Andy's face by leaving streaks of pale light across his face. Eva could see his soft smile and knew he was doing everything he could to make her comfortable.

"Thank you, Andrew," she said softly. The two turned their heads and looked into the pasture. Eva's breathing was still cumbersome, but she felt much better with the fresh air of the night cooling her flushed face.

A soft breeze rustled the hay and lulled the two to sleep.

"Pst! Psst!" Hector was outside the hay mound and woke them up. Unbeknownst to them, they had been asleep for a few hours, while Hector schemed on a way to help them escape.

Andy and Eva slid down the hay until they tumbled to the ground before Hector. They itched and scratched and pulled hay out of their hair and clothing.

Silhouetted, Hector stood before them, and in front of him, he had a two-wheeled cart with handles for him to wheel around.

"What is that smell?" Andy said, covering his nose with his shirt. Luckily for Eva, her hay fever caused her nose to plug, and she could not smell the strong smell coming from the pile heaped up on top of the cart.

"Your chariot awaits!" Hector said, smiling in the darkness.

"Is that manure?" Andy asked.

"Sure is!" Hector said with a grin big enough to see in the dark.

"You want me to ride in that?" Eva said disgustedly.

"Hey, I said I'd get you out of here, I didn't say it would be pretty."

"Thank you, this will do, we are very grateful for your help," Andy said humbly, understanding that this was their only real chance of escaping the castle grounds.

Eva looked at the pile of dung with disgust but mustered up the strength to crawl onto the wagon. The dung squished between her fingers as she propped herself into the wagon, and she could feel it shift beneath her as she lay back onto the wagon's platform.

"Eww Eww Eww!" She squeaked.

Hector grabbed a pitchfork and began to put fresh hay over top of them, and then began to mix the horse dung with it to hide them beneath it. He did his best to keep any of the dung from landing near their faces, but mixed it thoroughly enough that the fresh hay looked like it had been used already.

Then, before Andy and Eva knew it, they could feel the cart being moved along the bumpy ground.

Before long, they knew they had reached the courtyard, for the cobblestone that made up the courtyard floor caused the wheels of the cart to make a loud chattering noise as it rolled along. Not to mention, their ride became more uncomfortable as the cart jiggled over the uneven cobblestones.

It was late enough in the evening by now that most of the chaos had settled. From within the mixture of hay and dung, Andy and Eva could not see, but Hector could see the increased number of guards who had taken positions within the lookout towers that loomed over the castle walls. Hector just kept his head down. With any other servant, this plan may not have worked, but Hector was always doing his duties at odd times; many of the Titans knew him for his unorthodox timing of his chores and duties. So, although it was a ridiculous time of the night to be hauling dung out of the castle walls, none of the Titans thought much of it. In fact, Hector had done this in the past, normally it was to escape the castle for a few hours while everyone was asleep. He felt less pressure to return so quickly and found it to be freeing.

"Hector!" A sudden voice shouted from a distance. The cart stopped in its tracks.

"Hey there… Thomas." Hector said with a very airy voice.

"Is this really a time to be cleaning stalls? There are prisoners on the loose."

"Well, sir… My job is to keep the stalls clean. With all the disturbances today, I did get behind schedule."

"The prisoners did not escape until after dark. Aren't you supposed to clean the stalls during the day, when the horses are out in the pastures?" Thomas asked, unimpressed that Hector neglected his daily duties.

"I did, however, I always wait until the cool of the day to bring the manure out to the manure pit, and since there was a disturbance, I am just now getting to that part," Hector said with a side of snark.

"You need to make sure your duties are done before the sun falls below the horizon," Thomas ordered. He was one of the Titans who lost the prisoners, and feeling pressure from a servant boy only made him feel worse.

"Like I said, I would have had it done…" Hector said, knowing Thomas was involved with the escape.

"No excuses, Servant!" Thomas said, feeling even less hospitable.

"With all due respect…Sir… I did not let them escape."

Thomas became enraged. "Hector!…" However, Thomas paused, chest puffed and breath held, he closed his eyes and then breathed out slowly. He felt angry, but more so, he felt like a failure, disappointed that he had failed at his job. He was scared of the King's temper and what he might do to him if the prisoners were not found.

But this wasn't who Thomas really was. Thomas was a kind man who only cared to do what was best. Much like Gillian, Thomas desired to help others and felt that serving the King was the best way to do that.

"Be on with it then!" he ordered Hector with a sadness lingering in his voice. Thomas, then, rushed to the castle gates, waved his hand at the Titan attending the gate, who lifted the heavy door, and Thomas vanished into the night as the wooden gate thumped back down, once again, sealing the castle shut. Hector shook his head, gripped the handles on the two-wheel cart, and worked toward the gate himself.

Whew... Both Andy and Eva thought as they felt the cart moving again. It was only a few seconds later that the cart came to another stop. This time, they could hear another voice from way above them.

"Working late, I see?" a Titan asked from the lookout tower.

"Yes, sir," Hector said. "You know me, burning the midnight oil!" he said with a smile.

"Be careful, young man. There are treasonous criminals on the loose," the Titan warned. Andy could tell that Hector was well-liked by some of the Titans and clearly disliked by others. Luckily for them and their escape, the Titan watching the gate knew and liked Hector well.

"I heard they ain't nothing but a couple of kids. You ain't scared of a couple kids are you?" he asked, poking some fun at the Titan.

"Ah, Hector," the Titan chuckled, "Always with the jokes. Do me a favor?"

"What's that?"

"Make it quick? Stakes are high tonight. I can feel the tension in the air. Dump your load and hurry back. No lollygaggin tonight. Alright?"

Hector smiled at the guard. The rumor mill had been hard at work, and all the Titans and creatures of the castle truly believed Andy and Eva were dangerous. "You got it, Hank. Be back soon!"

The Titan nodded across the archway to the Titan station in the tower on the other side of the large wooden gate. Simultaneously, they both rotated their own wooden cranks, which looked much like the steering wheel of a pirate's ship. Wrapped around the crank were steel chains, which were used to hoist up the castle gate. Slowly, the chains chattered as the heavy wooden door creaked open. Iron spikes were fixed to the bottom of the door and hung like icicles from the arch once the door had been lifted open.

"Thank you!" Hector said cheerfully and brought the two-wheeled cart through the archway out into the streets of Regnum.

Andy began to grow very suspicious. Growing up an orphan, Andy learned to read people. He listened to their words, their actions, and had come to learn that a person's smooth words indicated a lot about the person. He had been promised many things by men with smooth words, and they always failed to deliver. Saying only what he wanted to hear instead of being honest with him. Unfortunately, Hector was giving Andy this same vibe. Hector was smooth with his words, trusted by both Titans and servants alike. It seemed to him that Hector did what was best for Hector. Saying what he needed to at any given time to get what he wanted. He was grateful for Hector's help, but Andy was not ready to trust him beyond this. *He is so smooth and charming. He talked to the Titans like they were friends, yet he is helping us escape, which is betraying the Titans… If the Titans shouldn't trust him, why should we? Andy* thought.

However, their escape depended on Hector. So, for now, Andy hoped that it was in Hector's best interest to help them. Once they escaped, Andy aimed to never have to rely on him again. These thoughts, Andy decided to keep to himself, because he knew that Eva would not understand. After all, it was only a gut feeling. Andy had no real evidence.

Although they were out of the castle, all three remained quiet. It was the late hours of the night, and there was not a candle burning in any of the houses they passed by. Their ride seemed to last forever. Knowing each step Hector took brought them further away, made them more and more anxious to get out of the cart of horse manure.

Suddenly, the cart tipped forward. All the contents of the cart began to slide off, including Andy and Eva.

Without warning, they were plopped into a large compost pile. This was Regnum's community compost pile. Manure, hay, straw, and food scraps were piled around them. It smelled horrible, so much so that all of them couldn't help but gag. King Fraust ordered years ago that all of the castle's dung would be dumped here. Just beyond the main village, into the slums. Slowly, the village folk embraced it and added their own food scraps to it, creating a community compost pile. The poor folk in the slums hated it, but the compost proved useful in the village gardens. It helped yield greater crop production, which helped keep the King and his Titans off their backs when it came time for their weekly contributions to the castle. So, ultimately, it proved to be one of the only helpful laws that King Fraust had put into place for the laymen of Regnum, and now it had provided Andy and Eva with an escape.

"Alright, you're free. Isabell is gonna be so grateful! Good luck!" Hector said. Before Andy and Eva could even thank him, he backed up the cart and rushed off. Both Andy and Eva thought it was odd, but they were not about to chase him down to thank him.

Isabell will be so grateful I saved her friends! She will be mine in no time! Hector thought joyfully as he headed back to the castle, eager to tell Isabell of his heroic act. He hoped that this would finally win her heart and the two could fall in love. He was a very dramatic boy about it, but considering there was very little he cared about, Isabell became an obsession for the boy.

Andy stood up and began to scrape any compost from his leg and back. Afraid to even know what was sticking to him.

"This is disgusting…" Eva groaned.

"Yeah, it is…" Andy chuckled a bit. "But we are free. Let's go. I think it will be best to follow the Calvary loop," he suggested.

"Not yet, I have to see my parents. They have to know I'm okay," Eva said.

"Eva! We can't!"

"You don't have to come, but I'm going!" she said with determination in her voice.

"The first place I would send guards if I were King would be your parents. Where else would a scared little girl go?"

"I'm not a little girl!" she scolded.

"You know what I mean… Besides your house, it's that way," Andy said as he pointed towards the castle, which was the exact opposite direction he wanted to go.

"Well, I have to try. To tell them I love them one last time, then we can go to the Elves. Please, Andy?" she begged.

"Fine, but we have to be quick. Stick to the shadows," he commanded.

Eva darted off into the night. Sliding alongside buildings with her back to the wall, she peeked around every corner before moving on to the next building. The night was very helpful in masking them as they snuck through the village to Eva's home.

Finally, they came to an alleyway that would run behind her house. Slowing down, they crept quietly, looking for any Titans or Pegasi that could be lurking about.

As they rounded the last corner, Eva halted in her tracks so abruptly that Andy couldn't stop fast enough and crashed into her.

"What is it?" he whispered, wondering why she stopped. However, he soon learned why. Eva never said a word, but as Andy looked, he could see through the window of Eva's house. Andy could see Eva's mother seated at the dining room table with Eva's father standing behind her.

Quickly, Andy pulled Eva back around the corner into the shadows. Eva was stunned because her parents were not alone. In the nick of time, Andy had gotten them out of sight before a Titan passed by the window.

"We have to go," Andy whispered.

"But my parents…what will happen to them?"

"I don't know, but I do know what will happen to us if we get caught."

Eva turned and leaned into Andy, and he hugged her tightly as she began to weep. However, she knew he was right, they had to keep moving.

With heavy hearts, they were off into the night.

Chapter 17
Repercussions

"Hold him down!"

"Tighten the ropes!" men grumbled and shouted as they leaned back, putting all their weight into pulling on ropes that bridged over Gillian. Slowly, Gillian lost his strength. Multiple ropes pressed him down, pinning him and his wings to the ground.

As he struggled to break free, a large shadow crept up on him and consumed the moonlight. As the helpless Pegasus' eyes darted up to see, he could see Zolton towering over him.

"I knew you would betray us," he said with a smirk on his face. Gillian threatened Zolton's status within the castle, and being proved right puffed his ego. Even though chaos had broken out because of Gillian's betrayal, Zolton was happy knowing he would still be Malus' unchallenged right hand, Pegasus.

As Gillian lost his strength, his will to fight fled as well. It was now that he had begun to question all of his choices. *What have I done?* He thought as the images of his rescue attempt flashed through his mind. He wondered if saving the humans, who were strangers only a week or so ago, was worth the trouble he now found himself in. They were traitors to the King after all... Yet, before long, more images and thoughts raced through his mind. Every lie Malus had told him rang in his ear, the images of the Messorems darting in and out of the Devil's kettle played out in his head, and the strong bond that he had formed with Jessie and the late Richard tugged at his heart. It was these thoughts that allowed him to know that what he did was the right choice. Even if it cost him his wings, he couldn't let Andy and Eva be killed.

The truth of the matter was that he had chosen to sacrifice himself for his new human friends, and even though he was bound by ropes and physically giving up, he had hoped that those two would escape.

Soon, his thoughts became drowned out by the eruption of shouting around him. All the creatures present for the King's announcement exploded into chatter. Some in confusion, some in anger, and others in disbelief. It's an odd thing; that is to say that when creatures are led to believe something or even unwilling to learn the truth, something as heroic as the act in which Gillian just performed can seem like something entirely different. Treasonous, uncalled for, or even pure evil. This was exactly the case. Many of the creatures present stood behind the King, they had ignored his temper and his shady dealings in exchange for safety and status within the kingdom.

So much so that they had convinced themselves that King Fraust was a good man. So when Gillian saved the lives of Andy and Eva, all the creatures reacted in chaos. Some in anger, for Gillian's apparent betrayal, while others were confused as to why Gillian would do such a traitorous act against the kingdom of Regnum. Yet, none of what those creatures thought mattered, because what Gillian did was the right thing to do, even though his world would now crumble down around him.

Then a halter was forced onto Gillian's snout with a thick rope fastened to the bottom of it. Gillian did not resist. He felt that at this point, there was no use. He knew his decision had consequences and was willing to accept them peacefully.

It's not that he wasn't scared of what was to come, but he knew it was no use worrying about it. He just hoped it would be over quickly, whatever it was. All he could think about now was whether or not Andy and Eva would be okay.

I hope they can escape! Please, get as far from here as you can! Gillian hoped in his mind. Slowly, the wonder of whether they would escape shaped into a plea. *Please, Great White Eagle. If you can hear me, please let them escape!* Gillian had done all he could; now he just had to trust that the Great White Eagle would take care of them.

"Hold him tight, but let the traitor to his feet!" Zolton ordered from afar. With the command, the ropes loosened. Slowly, Gillian propped himself up onto his hooves. Then, without hesitation, the Titans tossed ropes beneath Gillian's belly, then threw them back over his back, binding his wings tightly to his body.

Gillian felt like a muzzled dog. Without the use of his wings and a halter around his snout, Gillian had officially become a prisoner of Regnum.

"Gillian… How you have disappointed me." A stern, yet familiar voice came sharply from Gillian's left. Unable to turn his head, Gillian's eyes darted to see Malus standing at the bottom of the castle stairs within the archway. Behind him was the King, with a deep scowl on his face. Seeing Malus caused a cold flash of chills to shoot down his spine. "I had strong hope that you would have served me. I could have made you great in all the land." Malus said as he began pacing around Gillian. A tactic he often used to intimidate prisoners.

"But instead, you choose to betray me?" King Fraust spewed, adding even more pressure to this intense questioning.

Gillian didn't respond. As daunting as both these creatures were, he had seen this tactic used a hundred times before. He knew that the words of Malus and the King were more of a spectacle for the loyal Titans and Pegasi than they were words for him.

Suddenly, the King's tone took a sharp turn. "You will be happy to know that your traitorous friends have yet to be found… They may even escape." King Fraust said, in a way to try to convince Gillian that he wasn't even upset about the escape.

What is his angle? Gillian questioned.

"Who knows, there may yet be mercy for you, Gillian. Just tell us where they went." Malus said, playing along with the King's charade.

There it is! Gillian said, knowing now that the King was pretending to play nice, only to try and get information out of him. It was another classic tactic he had seen dozens of times. However, because Gillian had seen this done with other traitors before, he knew that the King never kept his word. Whether or not Gillian told the King anything useful, the King would have him punished.

"Even if I knew their plan, I wouldn't tell you. I have made my decision. Do what you must," Gillian ordered, confident in his defeat.

"Bring him to the Dungeons. Leave his wings bound and the halter in place," King Fraust ordered. He understood that Gillian knew all their tricks and knew it was a waste of time to even try. "We will make our decision by dawn. Until then, enjoy your stay in the dungeons, Gillian." The King whipped around, causing his cape to swirl with him, much like a long dress would when worn by a young girl dancer. Then he was off. Malus, too, in an effort to be dramatic, flicked out his wings, causing a great gust of wind, and lifted himself up to the balcony that overlooked the courtyard.

"Oh, and… make sure to cuff his ankles," Malus shouted over his shoulder.

"Yes, Sire," Thomas shouted.

The crowd around him erupted into an angry outburst. They shouted nasty names, threw stones toward him, and even spat in his direction. Even as he was led around the corner, down the covered pathway, and down into the depths of the dungeon, he could hear the crowd echoing threats in his direction. It was the most humiliating thing that had ever happened to him.

Things began to change, to look different. Not physically, but emotionally, the castle began to change for Gillian. For example, as Gillian was led into the dungeon, he began to see it through the eyes of a prisoner. Before, the dungeon may have looked dirty, but it was harmless for him. However, on this grim night, the shadows hung like demons and reminded him of the danger he felt when surrounded by the Messorems at the mouth of the Devil's Kettle. This dark dungeon had now become Gillian's very own nightmare. Uncertainty loomed in the air, seeping in like a hazy fog on a heavy, damp night. Gillian's mane stood on end, and he was chilled to the bone by the creepy shadows and cold reality of the unknown fate which lay ahead.

Just then, a familiar voice echoed in the gloomy air.

"Gillian…? Is that you?"

"Jessie?" Gillian asked. Just hearing Jessie's voice lifted his spirits. The same way we excitedly greet a long-time friend, Gillian's heart warmed just enough to bring him a sense of comfort in the lonely place.

The Titans remained quiet as they led Gillian into his cell, which was directly across the hallway from Jessie.

Jessie watched, gripping the iron bars with concern as Thomas led Gillian into the cell. Gillian slowly followed his commands. His ears drooped, and the light in his eyes dimmed.

"Turn around and spread your legs a bit," Thomas ordered. Gillian did as asked. "Thank you, Gillian…" he said solemnly. After all he and Gillian had served together, chaining up Gillian was a difficult and sad task for Thomas to do.

Simon handed Thomas a key that had a leather string attached. The Titan looped the string around his neck. The key hung down and swayed on his breastplate. Then Simon handed him the ankle clasps. Without any resistance from Gillian, Thomas locked him up. Each ankle cuff had a chain that stretched out with clasps that clung to the iron bars of the prison cell.

Before leaving, Thomas looked Gillian in the eyes. As he sighed, he gave him a soft smile, then softly scratched Gillian behind the ear. "I'm sorry, Gillian." Then he turned away and headed out of the dungeon. The truth of the matter was that Thomas was conflicted himself. The order to take Gillian, a comrade, to the dungeon as a prisoner had saddened him greatly. Yet, he witnessed with his own eyes that Gillian betrayed the king. Thomas, along with many others within the Kingdom, was terribly confused. *Why would a Noble Pegasus turn on the King? It just doesn't make sense.* This thought raced through Thomas's head. He headed towards the staircase but halted when he heard Gillian's voice.

"They're innocent. That's why I did it," Gillian said softly.

Thomas never turned around, he just hesitated before rushing out of sight.

Simon walked over and looked up at Gillian. Wings bound by ropes, a halter still clamped on his snout, and ankle cuffs chaining him to the prison itself, Gillian was trapped. This old oaf was dumb, but smart enough to know how to make matters worse when it came to torture. So, instead of locking the prison cell door, Simon opened it all the way, leaving the cell door completely open. However, Simon knew Gillian could not fly or move his hooves, so leaving the door open, taunted Gillian with an impossible escape. Thus, making matters worse for Gillian's already heavy heart. Simons let out a disgusting belly laugh and walked back to his chair at the bottom of the staircase.

Jessie pressed against the iron bars. He did not know what had happened and was completely unaware that Andy and Eva had escaped, but he could clearly see that Gillian was in trouble. Jessie's heart thumped heavily for his friend.

"Gillian…" Jessie began, "I'm really sorry. I never meant… Well, I did, but… I forgive you," he stuttered. Jessie was referring to all the nasty things he said while in the clearing. He had regretted his words as soon as they left his lips, but in that moment, Gillian's betrayal had angered Jessie. But now, after time spent in the dungeon and all the mourning he had endured, Jessie was grateful to have the chance to apologize to his friend, despite the hard feelings from before. Clearly, Gillian's imprisonment meant Gillian was being punished for the events that unfolded. That made Jessie feel like he and Gillian were once again on the same side. The side of truth.

"The other two?" Philip butted in before Gillian had a chance to respond. "What happened to the other two? Did the king go through with it?" Jessie's eyes opened wide. Seeing Gillian in chains made him forget about his friends for a brief moment, but Phillip's question brought panic to Jessie.

"Please, Gillian, please tell me they're alright?" Jessie cried.

"I… I, um…" Gillian said slowly. "I saved them."

"Oh, thank the Great White Eagle…" Phillip said, with a great sigh of relief.

"Oh, that's great! Just wonderful!" Jessie said as he jumped into the air.

"Yeah, it's *real* great," Gillian said in an unhappy tone.

"… but you had to sacrifice yourself?" Jessie asked gently. Gillian gave no response. "Oh Gillian, what will they do to you?" he cried, feeling the weight of Gillian's heroic actions and the repercussions that would come with it.

"The Alatum punishment…" Phillip said quietly, tucked away in the shadows of the night. Although Gillian knew that Alatum's punishment was the obvious punishment he would receive from King Fraust, actually hearing it out loud from Phillip felt like a dagger had been driven into his heart.

"We can save you! Just like you saved Andy and Eva! We have to," Jessie exclaimed.

"I don't think so…" Gillian muttered.

"Come on, there has to be a way! Tell him, Phillip," Jessie said, trying to find some positivity.

"I'm sorry, Jessie, but I don't think so… not this time."

"No, it can't be," Jessie insisted. Meanwhile, Simon kicked back in his chair and painted a long smirk across his face. He listened to every word Phillip said and gained confidence that there would be no more escapes.

"I think it's finally time to accept my consequences," Gillian admitted.

The dungeons fell quiet, for no one knew what to say. Frankly, there was nothing to say. It seemed that what was going to happen couldn't be stopped.

A sick churning knot rolled in the pit of his stomach. Phillip had not felt this much concern for another creature in years, he had almost forgotten that he was even capable of caring for others. His heart felt heavy for Gillian, yet joyous at the news that Andy and Eva had escaped. However, his biggest concern yet was the fate of young Jessie.

Phillip's life had been messy, corrupted even. All thanks to Malus. Phillip knew that Malus was a lying and deceiving creature who would promise anything in exchange for utter loyalty. He also knew that if you wouldn't willingly do as he asked, he would find a way to make you. Phillip understood that Jessie was in more danger than the young boy could ever imagine, and if he was left alone with Malus, Jessie would fall and make the same life-crumbling mistakes that Phillip himself had.

I must protect Jessie. I must help him resist Malus and all his tainted promises. I cannot let Malus ruin Jessie's life the way he has mine. Phillip thought. However, his thoughts were disrupted by the clanking of Titan's armor.

Lifting his eyes to the staircase, an orange glow from a torch illuminated the stairwell. Moments later, Phillip could see Thomas entering the Dungeon. "Phillip, the King would like to see you," he announced.

Being so bogged down by thoughts, Phillip didn't even think about the command. Without careful thought, Phillip stood up and quickly walked to the cell's door. Then, without waiting for Thomas to come and 'open' the door, Phillip casually pushed the iron cell door. As the door creaked open, Phillip realized what he had just revealed to Jessie. His body tensed up, while holding his breath, his eyes darted towards Jessie.

Jessie stood with his eyes wide, and his mouth hung open in shock. Jessie had discovered one of Phillip's secrets: his prison cell was never locked. In one simple and small mistake, Phillip had become a complete stranger to Jessie. All trust had been shattered. Jessie was in shock, and Phillip didn't know what to say. So, as Thomas waved Phillip along, Phillip lowered his head and shamefully rushed out of the dungeon. Simon followed closely behind, and now it was just Gillian and Jessie.

"What...? I mean, who...? I mean, what the who, just happened?" Jessie stammered. A concoction of anger, confusion, and hurt boiled inside of him.

"Did you not know that Phillip is the King's brother?" Gillian asked, shocked to learn that this was news for Jessie.

Jessie's jaw dropped to the floor. "How...? I mean, what...? I mean this whole time?" Jessie turned his back to Gillian and tapped his pointer finger on his bottom lip. He wanted to scream and to shout and cry all at the same time, but couldn't do any of them. "Why would he have kept that from us? Is he a spy for his brother?" Jessie asked, turning back towards Gillian.

"I doubt it. Phillip has openly admitted his hate for his brother. And well... the King has not refrained from his opinions either. There is a strong mutual hate."

"How can you be sure?" Jessie asked.

"I guess I can't be... But Phillip has been here as long as King Fraust has been King. And honestly, they have hated one another this whole time. They have had spats, fist fights, and have tried to leverage us and the servants against one another throughout the years… So, if they are pretending, they are really good actors," Gillian explained.

"You've got to be kidding me! The nerve!" Jessie said, stomping his feet in anger. Gillian just looked away. It was kind of an awkward moment, and he wasn't sure what to say. "What's his angle?" Jessie asked aggressively.

"Angle?"

"Yeah, like why hide his identity from us? To get information out of us? Did he really want to help us save Andy and Eva, or did he set us up? Will he tell the King that Isabell helped us?" Jessie asked in a panic, worried that Isabell may soon find herself in danger all because of Phillip and his secret identity.

"Jessie, calm down. Isabell knows that Phillip is the King's brother. We all do. That's not a secret. So be comforted knowing that Isabell trusted Phillip enough to help them," Gillian said. "If Phillip is pretending to hate his brother, I would be shocked. In the last five years, Phillip has only left the dungeon for three things. Ale, an occasional visit to Sod-Omen, and by the demand of his brother."

"Hmf…" Jessie huffed in disbelief.

"Look, Phillip is miserable. You can see it on his face, the way he acts, and the fact that he lives down here with his prison cell door left unlocked should tell you all you need to know."

"I… I just can't trust him anymore." Jessie tried to process everything that had happened in the last few days, and he remembered what Eva had said when she was first brought down to the dungeon. She said, *We aren't to trust the King or his brother, either for that matter.* Jessie's thoughts raced. *Is Phillip really the King's brother? If he is, Eva's mom said he cannot be trusted. But why did he help us? Why does he want to find the Great White Eagle? Does he really want to?* After a few minutes of trying to process this traumatic discovery, Jessie had one question that he just had to ask. "What I don't understand is, why would the King's brother live like this? Why stay down here? He could have anything he wanted. A king-sized bed! A feast every night! A status above the rest… I don't understand why he would live in ratty clothes and sleep on the cold, hard stones of the dungeons…" Jessie asked Gillian, who stood across the hallway from him.

"I don't think we will ever know. Some say his brother forces him to live down here, to punish him for something they did when they were younger. While others say it's all just an act, a way for him to gain pity from others." Gillian shrugged.

"Hmm. Well, I want answers!" Jessie exclaimed.

"I'm sure you will get them. Phillip will be back. He always comes back. This filthy dungeon is his home," Gillian said, understanding Jessie's anger.

"Thanks Gillian…" - there was a short pause - "Gillian?" Jessie said, softening his heart. "Andy and Eva owe their lives to you. And for that, I hope you know that if there was anything I could do for you, I would."

"There is," Gillian said softly.

"What is it? Anything!"

"If you ever get out of here, spread the truth. Make sure all the Earth knows that the Great White Eagle is real. Make sure they know that Malus has lied to us all."

"So, you believe? I remember you saying you didn't believe in the Great White Eagle. Remember? It was when you tried a Nectorsuckle."

"I was wrong. I had been lied to. The last few days have opened my eyes to the Truth. Not to mention that even Malus admitted that he lied to me. He himself confessed that the Great White Eagle is real," Gillian said.

This news made Jessie's eyes twinkle. A great wave of hope rushed over him. He knew now in his heart that he had to find the Great White Eagle. Only he could help. "But how can I spread the truth? I'm stuck in here…"

"I guess that's not my problem, is it?" Gillian said with a soft smile. The blatantly honest response caused both boys to let out a chuckle. "But if you can do that for me, it will be worth whatever punishment I receive."

"If I ever find a way out of here, after I find the Great White Eagle and save my brother, I promise I will remember you and tell the whole world the truth!" Jessie said, with a soft smile.

"There's one other thing…" Gillian said softly.

"What?"

"If you do find him, the Great White Eagle, I mean, would you tell him I'm sorry? That I'm sorry for ever doubting him?"

"Yes, you have my word."

"Thank you, Jessie. You are truly a great and noble friend."

The conversation ended there. Both of the creatures remained silent, while their thoughts ran rampant. Eventually, Jessie could hear Gillian begin to breathe heavily, long breaths dragged along until he began to audibly snore. Just like many horses tend to do, Gillian was standing, but fast asleep. Eventually, Jessie's thoughts became a blur, and he found himself curled up on the floor, drifting off to sleep.

Chapter 18
One Last Gift

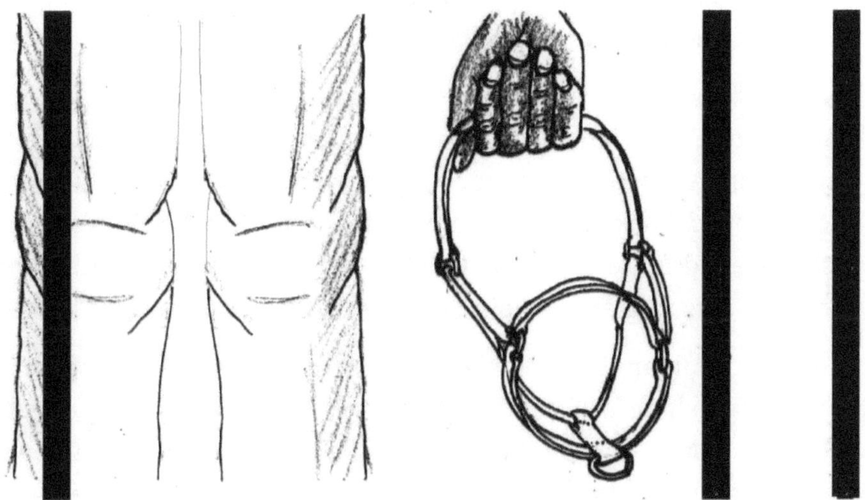

Suddenly, Jessie could hear voices at the base of the stairs. It was Phillip and Simon. As he opened his eyes, Jessie could hear that they began to argue, but he was unsure what it was about. He rubbed his eyes and then quickly scrambled to his feet. Making his way over to the iron bars, Jessie pressed his face into the bars, trying to see what was going on.

In the stillness of the night, Jessie saw Gillian turn his head, he too was awake. Just then, Phillip and Simon's argument grew into an altercation. As Phillip tried to slip by Simon, the big oaf placed his hand on Phillip's chest. Phillip leaned to his right and set something down on Simon's chair. He did it so gently that Jessie thought Phillip aimed to reason with Simon. Phillip straightened up and lifted his chin while looking Simon dead in the eyes. Then out of nowhere, Phillip socked Simon right in the jaw.

Simon took one step back, and his eyes opened wide. For a moment, he couldn't believe Phillip had hit him. He rubbed his jaw, shook his head, and narrowed his eyes. With an angry growl, Simon lunged forwards, his large hands landed on Phillip's shoulders and drove the old man backwards until Phillip was pinned against the cold iron bars of one of the prison cells.

Phillip clenched his fist and began beating on the arms of Simon. Finally, Simon's straightened arms were bent, and Phillip broke free from the pin. Again, Phillip clipped Simon in the jaw, but this time, as Simon stepped back, Phillip wrapped his heel behind Simon's heel, causing the big brute to crash straight onto his back. But not before Simon was able to grab Phillip's cloak, bringing him down with him.

Onto the floor they tumbled, rolling this way and that. Simon threw his fair share of fists, but Phillip was much faster. He dodged punch after punch. Finally, Phillip was able to slip around to Simon's backside and wrap an arm around his neck. Simon flailed and tried elbowing Phillip. He even leaned back, pinning Phillip against the iron bars again, but Phillip remained calm and, most importantly, in control. Slowly but surely, Simon fell unconscious.

Phillip grunted as he pushed the large dungeon keeper off of him. Standing up, he dusted himself off and then snatched the keys that were hanging off of Simon's belt.

"Is he… ah… dead?" Jessie asked. Shocked at the whole debacle.

"No, he is just sleeping, he will wake up soon, that's why we have to hurry," Phillip said as he swiftly made his way towards Jessie's cell door. As Phillip wiggled a key into the lock of Jessie's cell door, his face was illuminated by the moonlight. Vertical shadows cast by the iron bars laid evenly spaced upon Phillip.

"You want me to go with you? No way! Not until I have answers!"

"We don't have time! As soon as Simon wakes up, he will alert the whole castle." Phillip pushed open the cell door.

"Why should I trust you? You might be leading me to my death, bringing me to the King. To your brother!" Jessie said angrily.

"You told him, huh?" Phillip asked as he turned around and looked at Gillian.

"I didn't know it was such a big secret, your majesty," Gillian said to Phillip.

"Don't call me that! I might be his brother, but I do not belong to this kingdom. I reject it and everything it stands for," he said angrily to Gillian. "We must go! NOW!" he ordered, growing impatient.

"I refuse. At least I know who Malus is, and he doesn't hide it. But with you. How can I be sure of anything?" Jessie asked with his arms crossed, tapping his foot on the ground. He remained in his cell. Phillip ignored Jessie's pout, he dropped to his knees. Using the set of keys from Simon, he pried at the locks of the cuffs on Gillian's ankles.

"Gillian. None of these keys work." Phillip said.

"Thomas has the key, or at least he did. I saw it around his neck." Gillian said as he thought back to when Thomas said, 'I'm sorry," before leaving the dungeon.

"Then we go get it!" Jessie exclaimed.

"We don't have time! Thomas probably gave it to Malus, or the King, or who knows who has it. It would be a wild goose chase!" Phillip said.

"I'm not leaving without Gillian! He saved Andy and Eva," Jessie huffed.

"Jessie! Listen to Phillip. I know you don't trust him, but this is your only chance at escaping! Leave now! Before it's too late." Gillian said solemnly.

"I'd rather be stuck here than to leave a friend behind," Jessie said stiffly.

"Jessie… You must go… How will you keep your promise if you don't?" Gillian said, with drooped ears.

Jessie ignored Gillian but rushed out of his cell, snatching the keys from Phillip. Quickly, he knelt down at Gillian's hooves and began to try each key.

"We have to go! Isabell is waiting for us," Phillip again demanded, placing his hands on his hips in annoyance.

"Isabell?" Jessie's tone changed immediately once he heard her name.

"Jessie, go! I'll be okay! Just remember your promise! Tell all the land. The Great White Eagle is real!" Gillian said, lowering his head and nudging Jessie away.

Phillip, sensing Jessie was finally ready to go, rushed over to Simon, thankfully he was still unconscious. So he picked up the item he had set down before. Suddenly, Simon slowly began to wiggle his fingers as he began to come too.

"Jessie, we have to go now!" Phillip said in a commanding voice.

Jessie shot to his feet, looking Gillian in the eye. Both Jessie and Gillian had tears rolling down their cheeks. Jessie lunged forward, wrapping his friend in a hug, and Gillian tucked Jessie close with his snout. Jessie scratched his neck, behind the ears, and quickly with nimble fingers undid the silver buckles that kept Gillian's halter in place. One last gift before he left, Jessie removed the uncomfortable halter from Gillian's snout and scratched him.

"Thank you... Now get!" Gillian said, flicking his nose out.

Soon, the two were off into the night. Dashing up the stairs, they entered the cool crisp night air, leaving Gillian behind.

"This way," Phillip whispered.

"Okay," Jessie said softly.

Hanging a sharp right, they found themselves rushing down the same hallway that Andy and Eva had hours before. Once they arrived at the back of the castle, they could see the hedges of the Maze outlined by the moonlight.

As Jessie's eyes adjusted to the night, he saw someone standing around the corner in the shadows. They had a knapsack, tied to a stick which was bent over their shoulder.

"Isabell!" Jessie said excitedly.

"Did anyone follow you here?" Phillip pressed the pale young girl.

"I don't think so. I did what you asked," she said as she handed the knapsack full of bread to Phillip.

"Good. We must be off," Phillip said. By her body language, Jessie sensed Isabell would not be joining them.

"Wait! Without Isabell?" he asked Phillip.

"Yes, Jessie. I wish I could come with you. But my sister... I can't let anything happen to her," she explained to him again.

Although Jessie was sad, he knew she was right. Without another word, he embraced her in a hug, and both had tears streaming down their faces. Although he had only known Isabell for a short few days, leaving her behind was as hard as it was to leave Gillian. He felt scared and worried that he would never see her again.

"I know that we barely know each other, but somehow I know you have a heart of gold," Isabell said as she looked into Jessie's eyes. She reached up and softly wiped Jessie's tears away.

"I promise, I'll come back for you," Jessie said, reaching up and cupping her hand. Even though the night was darkened, Jessie could see Isabell's cheeks swell a rosy red. She smiled at him and rubbed her tears away.

"Go," She said gently. "Hurry. I'll be here waiting." Isabell squeezed Jessie in the arm and smiled again.

"Goodbye Isabell," Jessie said as he turned, grabbed the knapsack held out for him to carry, and then followed Phillip into the dark Maze.

Chapter 19
The Light

This is the first time Jessie had seen the maze up close. He had never experienced the power of the Wishing Well and had to follow Phillip blindly. Putting trust in Phillip was still a little difficult for Jessie, but the alternative was to remain a prisoner.

Luckily, this was not Phillip's first time here. For many years, he had studied the maze, carefully following each pathway from afar by tracing them with his eyes. Occasionally, Phillip had even wandered the maze itself. He read all the books about it and knew the lore; he knew that it was something more than a well, that it reflected life as they knew it.

Only one time before had Phillip entered the maze with the intent of actually finding the proper way out. Only once had he aimed to find the Great White Eagle beyond the maze. However, that attempt resulted in him staring into the Wishing Well.

It wasn't that he had gotten lost. In fact, he knew the maze almost better than anyone. But its pull, its promise to fulfill his greatest desire, always won out. Phillip knew the risk of even attempting it, the chance of being caught like a fly was large. However, this was their only option.

Malus knew no creature had ever been able to successfully make it through the maze, therefore, he never wasted any manpower guarding it. Making the maze an obvious route for escaping, though no one ever had. Except Phillip and Jessie would have to be the first to succeed. It was their only chance to escape. They were desperate and out of options. Somehow, they would have to resist the Wishing Well's call.

In the dark mask of the night's shadows, they raced down the straight hall-like pathway. Jessie was confused. I thought this was a maze…

"What kind of a maze is this?" Jessie asked between breaths. "It only goes straight."

"It's complicated," Phillip responded. Jessie rolled his eyes because his thoughts contradicted that statement.

"My friendship with Gillian is complicated. This is just a straight path," Jessie said sarcastically.

"This maze has only one way out, and it's down this straightaway," Phillip said, slowing his pace a bit as the hedges of the maze began to crowd in around them.

"Why is it so easy?" Jessie thought out loud.

"It's far from easy… no creature has ever made it through."

"I don't understand…" Jessie said, slowing to a stop. He already didn't trust Phillip, and now the older man wasn't making any sense. *What kind of danger has this man gotten me into?* He thought.

"Look, this maze is more than a maze. It's truth."

"How hard did the dungeon keeper hit you?"

"Jessie, I will explain later. We have to keep moving. Every second we are in this maze, we risk getting stuck here."

"What's the big deal?"

"Fine, I'll tell you. But as we go!" Phillip said as he started moving down the straight pathway. Jessie hurried along with him. "Do you know what the scrolls say about our life's journey?" Phillip asked. Jessie gasped for breath, but he gave no response, so Phillip continued. "It says that the way to the Great White Eagle is a path that is straight and narrow. We are warned not to venture off the path."

"Oh yeah, I've heard that!" Jessie said, remembering the old saying.

"So, you get that every other path will not lead you to him?" Phillip asked.

"Yeah, I suppose I understand what you're saying. My mamma always told me to do good, don't lie, cheat, or steal."

"Right, the straight and narrow," Phillip confirmed.

"So this maze represents that?"

"No, this maze is real… The legends say that if any creature makes it through this maze, they will find the Great White Eagle."

"Really?" Jessie exclaimed, excited to find the Great White Eagle.

"That is only if we make it through without being drawn to the Wishing Well," Phillip said, with a quiver in his voice.

"A Wishing Well?" Jessie asked, stopping in his tracks. Phillip kept going.

Jessie couldn't see anything; the walls of the maze had narrowed so much that there was just enough room for Jessie's shoulders to pass through. In fact, in only a few steps, Phillip had gained enough distance that the branches of the bushes around him engulfed him, blocking him completely from Jessie's sight. He could only hear his voice from ahead.

"It calls to you, to all creatures, it's dangerous. The Well promises you your greatest desires," the muffled voice of Phillip said.

My brother! Jessie thought.

However, Phillip had realized that Jessie was not on his tail. He spun back around to retrieve Jessie. Coming upon the boy as Jessie turned around and stared off into the darkness, as if in a trance. Phillip reached out and gripped Jessie on the shoulder. "The bargain comes at a cost, you will never find the Great White Eagle!" Phillip explained. Phillip's hand shocked Jessie. He turned, looked at Phillip, and blinked his eyes.

Suddenly, the two raced off again. Visibly, the path began to grow more difficult with each step. The bushes were not trimmed and had straggly branches that whacked him in the face. The ground began to grow rough. Bumps and rocks made their footing uneasy. Soon, Jessie could feel his feet colliding with exposed roots. They caused him to lose his footing, but only for a moment before throwing him into the bushes. Quickly, he sprang back down the path following Phillip. Slowly, he could feel the bushes consume the space.

Fear began to grow inside of him, and doubt that they would make it out of the maze draped its shadow over his heart. Jessie could feel a dark desire forming. *If I could just find the Well, I wouldn't need the Great White Eagle.* That thought scared Jessie. *No! Just keep going. But what if this path closes in? What if there is no way out? What if there's no way to find the Great White Eagle, and it's all a trick?* Jessie thought. His anxiety grew, and Jessie began to panic, struggling to breathe in this tight, untamed place.

If I just go back, the path will become easier again… I want my brother back, I want him safe… Then my brother and I can find the Great White Eagle together. Maybe even try the maze again… His thoughts seemed to be overpowering his mission.

Come on, Jessie! Fight it! He again thought to himself, convincing himself to press on. In only five or six steps, Jessie pushed through some branches only to crash into Phillip. Who, for some reason, had stopped dead in his tracks.

"Do you hear that?" Phillip asked.

"Hear what?" But just as he responded, he began to hear his name being called from somewhere within the maze.

"It's the Well," Phillip said, almost hypnotized.

Somehow, voices were calling to both of them. But they each heard something different. They each heard their own desires. Slowly, Phillip turned and bumped into Jessie as if the Wishing Well was pulling him like a magnet.

Jessie instinctively put his hands out to stop Phillip, but even then Jessie could feel a force tugging at his own body. Although his mind understood the danger of giving in to the Wishing Well's call, it seemed as if he had lost all control over his own body and began giving in to the force that pulled at him. Slowly, he too turned towards the well, even taking small steps in that direction.

Just then, the hounds barked from within the castle's courtyard. It startled both of them, but seemed not to have an effect on their trance. It seemed that nothing could prevent them from being trapped by the Well. The strides of Jessie's steps became longer, and Phillip was right behind him. Jessie wanted his brother back. He wanted the death of his brother to be erased, and the Well whispered empty promises. The truth of the matter was that only the Great White Eagle could bring new life, and deep down Jessie understood that. But at this moment, Jessie didn't care. Every ounce of his being was being tugged towards the Wishing Well deep within the heart of the maze.

Again, the hounds barked, this time closer than before.

Phillip's toe caught the uneven ground, but even that could not withstand the inevitable pull the Wishing Well had. The bushes around them were thick and for a moment prevented them from crossing over, but as the Well called to them, their will to find it took over. Jessie couldn't help it any longer. He had decided to break the branches and bust through the bush in an effort to find the Wishing Well.

That was until something unexpected happened. A black raven must have been perched on the branches within the hedge, for at the last possible moment, before it would have been too late, it burst forth. Its loud squawk grabbed their attention, and its flapping wings halted their movement. The raven itself wouldn't have been enough to snap them out of their trance, but as Jessie swung his arms at the bird, trying to move it out of his way, the bird ducked and weaved itself around to Jessie's backside. Being convinced that the raven was an enemy who was trying to stop him from gaining his deepest desire, Jessie turned around to strike the bird down. Phillip, disgruntled from the raven, had fallen into the hedge, but the bird fled down the narrowing pathway towards the No Man's Land Mountains. Jessie's eyes followed the bird's silhouette as it swooped low, beneath the low-hanging branches that crowded the pathway. Unbeknownst to Jessie, the desire of his heart had become corrupt, and he hated the bird in that moment for disrupting his journey to the Well. Soon Jessie noticed a soft yellowish glow begin to seep under the brush and bring light into the darkness.

Phillip crawled out of the hedge, still determined to find the Well, but as he looked at Jessie's face, the growing glow of light swelled in Jessie's eyes, causing Phillip to snap out of the trance. Phillip turned to see. He had always known there was a crystal at the end of the maze, he had seen its soft glow every time he had entered the maze before. However, this time, something was different. As if the crystal wielded some great power that extinguished the spell the Wishing Well cast on them, it shone brighter than ever before. At first, the crystal blazed its color, blue to Phillip and yellow to Jessie; however, as its brightness intensified, the color shifted to an almost blinding clear white. It was so bright and so powerful that its light seemed to penetrate their hearts. Never before had Phillip seen the light at the end of the maze do this. All around them, the maze became illuminated. The shaggy shadows of branches seemed to shrink, and the path before them almost seemed to widen before their very eyes. In fact, it seemed that by the power of the crystal, the maze seemed to begin healing itself. Now that they could see clearly, they noticed that there were many holes and broken branches along the maze, where other creatures, including Phillip, had given in to the call of the Well and broken through the hedge. But to Phillip's surprise, those holes began to close.

In an instant, the focus on their own desires had been washed away, and a new desire to follow the light took hold.

This time, when the hounds barked, they were near the entrance of the Maze. Being revived, Jessie could no longer ignore their presence. Jessie glanced back. The light was so bright it penetrated the entire pathway, and Jessie could see the black hounds barreling towards them.

"Run!" Jessie said as he began to shove Phillip forward. The two raced off toward the light. As they grew closer to the light, their eyes seemed to adjust, and they could see the crystal at the mouth of the maze. It was resting on a stone pedestal, carved in the image of an eagle. The bird's wings were spread out so that the tips of its wings raised high, as if it were about to take flight. The stone sculpture was a magnificent piece of art. However, its beauty had nothing on the magnificence of the Eagle's Heart crystal. The crystal rested in the beak of the sculpture.

"I can't believe it!" Phillip shouted with excitement. With his back turned to Jessie, Phillip reached out and plucked the crystal out of the statue's beak.

"What?" Jessie asked. Slowly, Phillip turned around, and Jessie could see the shape of the crystal.

"Behold the key!" Phillip said as the crystal's glow lit up his smile.

Jessie was excited, but for a moment, he was puzzled. What does a key have to do with anything?

As if reading Jessie's mind, Phillip handed Jessie the key and then held out the item he had been carrying since the dungeons. It was wrapped in a thin blanket of elk hide. As Phillip peeled back a layer of the blanket, the corner of a book was exposed. Instantly, Jessie saw the golden stitching of the book and knew it was the Book of Truth.

"You mean this crystal is the key needed to open the Book of Truth?"

"Sure looks like it!" Phillip said as he rewrapped the book tightly in the blanket, making sure the key was wrapped securely as well.

With the key wrapped within the elk hide, darkness fell instantly upon them all. The spooky feeling of the maze returned, and out of the darkness, the hounds barked again. Peering back down the straight path of the maze, they were surprised to see that the raggedy branches had reappeared, making the maze even narrower than before. As a result, the hounds became entangled and caught. Their jaws snapped at the branches that held them back.

"We gotta go!" Phillip announced as he took off towards the No Man's Land Mountains. Jessie followed closely behind. For a minute, the hounds continued to bark and yelp, yet in an eerie instant, they became quiet. Yet, Phillip and Jessie pressed on. There was no time to look back, whether the hounds were still after them or not.

Far beyond, at the base of the No Man's Land Mountains, there was another yellow light shimmering.

Neither one had to say another word. They both began running away from the castle and towards the new light. Jessie's mind was boggled. Why did the hounds stop? Did their masters call them? Why have no Titans or Pegasi followed them? *Clearly, they know we are missing.*

The light came from a farm that lay at the foot of the No Man's Mountain. From the edge of the maze, it was hard to tell, but as they raced up the gradual slope, they could see it better. Boulders were scattered about, growing larger the closer they got to the foothills of the mountain. The ground swayed up and down with little hills and mounds, but always held an incline. It was mostly thick, matted grass that covered the ground, with the occasional islands of smooth-faced slabs of rock hidden in a sea of green. Very few trees stood about, and if they did, they were small, scraggly trees whose leaves had already fallen off. They ran and ran and ran, and with each step they could feel the air growing colder.

The No Man's Land Mountains were known for their harsh winters and uninhabitable conditions. As they reached the halfway point between the castle and the foot of the mountains, they could feel the shift in weather. The clear sky above them began to fill with dark clouds, and the wind began to blow. However, they remained hopeful as they raced towards the pulsating glow.

At first, Phillip was leading the way, but very quickly Jessie zoomed past him and would quite often have to stop and wait for the older man to catch up. During one of his waits, Jessie again took notice that not one Titan or Pegasi had followed them. *Alright! They don't know what hit them!* He thought excitedly.

With the lack of pursuers, he felt it was time he gave the older man a break. "I guess all that ale and dungeon time is hard on your endurance, old man!" Jessie chuckled as he stood next to a large boulder planted in the rolling prairie of the mountain base.

Finally catching up to Jessie, Phillip bent over, put one hand on the boulder, and began coughing. Slowly, his coughing changed into laughter. Then his laughter grew so hard that he reverted to coughing again.

"What's the matter with you?" Jessie asked while looking back towards the castle, searching for any of the King's men who would be after them.

"I feel so alive!"

"Really? You sound like you're about to die."

"I haven't felt this free in years, my boy!" Phillip expressed as he slowly straightened himself up and put his hands on his hips. He then arched his back, and it sounded as if every vertebra in his back popped.

"Oh man, was that your back? You'd better take it easy," Jessie said, poking fun at Phillip's old man bones.

"Ahh!" Phillip groaned with satisfaction. "You know… back in my younger years, I could have beaten you."

"You're dreamin, buddy!" And with that, both burst into joyous laughter. After they settled down, Phillip turned and scoped out the vast ground behind them. Placing one hand above his brow he searched the dark night for anyone who could be on their tail.

"It seems we have outrun the castle," Phillip said proudly, "Not too bad for an old man after all," he said, which sparked a smile from Jessie.

"Yeah, it's weird. That seemed way too easy."

"Easy? All that running about killed me!" He chuckled. "It seems weird, but I bet it was the maze."

"The maze?" Jessie thought about it.

"Remember, I said no creature had ever made it through before?" Phillip asked.

"Yeah, but if you believed that to be true, why'd we even try it?" Jessie asked.

Phillip shrugged, "I had a hunch."

"You risked our entire escape on a hunch?" Jessie said, growing a bit excited. "Are you crazy?"

"Hey now! It worked, didn't it?" Phillip said calmly.

"Barely…" Jessie scoffed.

"I bet no one has followed us because they are all crowded around the well, consumed by its spell," Phillip said. "Honestly, I had hope because of this…" Phillip said as he set down the bundle of elk hide. Peeling the corner of the blanket away, the golden thread of the Book of Truth glistened in the glow of the crystal key beside it.

Phillip reached into his pocket and pulled out a bottle of ale. Tugging at the cork, it opened with a loud pop. Knocking his head back, Phillip took a big swig, then extended the bottle to Jessie.

"No, thank you…" Jessie respectfully declined. His father, years ago, before he passed away, taught him the value of a sober mind.

"When the King…" Phillip started, but the sour look on Jessie's face made him rephrase his words, "When my brother called me to his chambers, I had not planned on trying to escape. But that's when I noticed the book on his bedside table. Then a plan unravelled. Many times I had been lured to the Wishing Well, and one other time I specifically tried to get through the maze, but I failed. I guess I doubted myself, or maybe I doubted the Great White Eagle…" Phillip said. Jessie softened his heart as he listened to Phillip open up. "But when I met you and your friends, I remembered what life was like, back when things were simple. The hope you guys have reminded me that I used to have hope, too. Having friends who have your back no matter what… I remember that. But for me, it was lost long ago. You guys gave me hope. Hope that there is still good left in this world, maybe even a chance for me to do good again… before it's too late. When I saw the Book… a great treasure which is believed to be a source of knowledge from the Great White Eagle himself. When I saw it in… my brother's room… this escape plan popped into my head."

"Just like that? Poof, a brilliant plan that relied solely on blind faith?" Jessie asked, still shocked that Phillip would risk their lives on a whim.

"Pretty much… I am a Lector, you know, understanding dreams and thoughts are kind of my thing," Phillip explained.

"Hmf…" Jessie shrugged.

"Oh man! What a rush!" Phillip said with glee. "Can you believe that this key was right under our noses all this time?"

"No one ever found it before? Not even Malus? It seems pretty stupid that it hasn't ever been discovered."

"That's right, pretty dumb and yet, quite simply brilliant if you ask me... I think it's because every Titan, every Pegasus, Centaur, Elf, or Dwarf that has ever attempted to make it through the maze always ended up at the Wishing Well," Phillip rambled.

Just hearing the words Wishing Well caused Jessie's mind to be drawn back to it. *How did we really make it through the maze? I felt the pull, I had given up, I lost all my control...*

"Do you really think it was the book that helped us through it?" Jessie asked.

"Hmm, now that we actually made it through? No... I don't."

"Me neither, it was the crystal..."

"I think you are right... I was a goner. Honestly, I feel like I blacked out, lost all control," Phillip explained. That brought relief to Jessie. He was glad to hear that the terrible feeling he let overtake him in the maze was not just experienced by him. That he wasn't alone in the darkness. Phillip continued, "When I saw the light in your eyes, all the darkness melted away. My mind was clear again, free even!"

"There is something special about these crystals," Jessie said with a soft joy in his heart.

"You got that right, the stories are true. These crystals make me feel like the Great White Eagle is near. I can feel it, even now."

High above them, the clouds became dense. A loud crack of thunder clashed overhead. Looking up, they realized that a storm was brewing. They needed to find shelter and fast.

"Well, that crystal ain't gonna protect us from a thunderstorm. Looks like the light is coming from a farm place up ahead," Phillip said. Jessie understood, and with that, they were off. Although they were now on the run from both the King and the brewing storm overhead, they traveled at a much slower pace.

Baffled by the events of the night, Phillip chuckled. "I used to believe it was impossible to get through that maze. Yet, here we are!"

"I still can't believe you risked it all on a feeling," Jessie said.

"Ha… I guess you could call it faith. But you know, the more I think about it, my gut feeling about our escape makes more and more sense. Especially the more I think about it."

"How so?" questioned Jessie.

"Just think about it, everything has changed. Your friend's dream has been had by many Somniators before, including my brother. However, until the girl, none have ever said when. But her dream revealed a time. The Great White Eagle's followers have been waiting for this time their whole lives. The Great White Eagle has told us, through your friend, that it's time!"

"Huh…" Jessie said, trying to wrap his head around it all.

"Plus, we have the Book of Truth. It's all falling into place."

"This is really big, isn't it?" Jessie said, as he looked up into the night sky, thinking about the weight of what was to come. The clouds looked angrier now. They swirled and churned as the thunder rumbled. Occasionally, streaks of lightning shot across the sky.

"It really is." The future was uncertain, but he was excited for what was to come. A newfound hope swelled up within him, and a shot at redemption waited to be grasped out on the horizon. *It is time, time that all things are made right again,* Phillip thought.

They walked for about an hour before they found themselves on the edge of a small farm. Leaning against the outer fence, they peered into the farmyard. They could see a small cottage home. It was built with rocks and mortar, and the roof was lined with yellow straw. A small chimney poked out the top and a consistent stream of smoke swirled in the air. The whole farm was surrounded by wooden fencing, rustic yet sturdy. The fence contained all the buildings and corralled a flock of sheep that were grazing the pastures of its confines.

At the center of the yard was a water well, with a bucket on a string waiting to be let down. Opposite of the cottage was a barn. This was where light was shown from. It had a hay mound up above, and side doors for the sheep to roam in and out of. The double-wide door, which opened up towards the yard and the cottage, clearly used by the owners of the farm, was sealed shut.

"I bet there is a crystal inside," Phillip said. Seeing that there was a glow seeping out of the barn that looked very similar to the crystal key, Jessie agreed.

As raindrops began to fall, the wind began to grow stronger. They would have to find shelter in the barn. In an attempt to remain unseen, they crawled over the fence and began a cautious journey to the barn. In the distance, a blast of a ram's horn sounded off.

Chapter 20
Castle of Chaos

Chaos had been unleashed within the castle. Amidst the chaos, Hector had become aware of some major intel concerning Phillip and Jessie.

Desperately, King Fraust wanted his brother found, and along with him, the boy Jessie. Not only had one set of prisoners escaped, but now a second set. The King had every available man, hound, and Pegasus searching for them.

Phillip's plan to escape through the Maze behind the castle had worked better than he could have hoped. Even though the hounds were simple creatures, unable to speak even to a Somniator, they found themselves circling the well, barking at its entrapment. Like them, the Titans assigned to follow the hounds found themselves at the well, unable to withstand its call. Not even a Pegasus who had attempted to fly over the maze was able to pass. With half of the King's men searching for Eva and Andy and some of his men ensnared by the well, Phillip and Jessie had gained a substantial head start.

Before the escape of Jessie, Hector had returned from the Village of Regnum. After dumping his load of horse manure, along with Andy and Eva, outside the castle walls, Hector was filled with confidence, hope even, that Isabell would be forever grateful for his help. He had decided that he was going to tell Isabell how he felt, and that the only reason he helped Andy and Eva escape was because he had always loved her. That he did it for her.

Hector raced to her room and knocked on her door. However, as he knocked, the unlatched door creaked open. Isabell was not there. What on earth is she still up at this hour for? Hector thought. Just then, he saw movement down the hall. The silhouette vanished around the corner, into the kitchen. Isabell.

He quietly headed that way, the halls were darker than usual, and the kitchen was lit by only one torch.

"Isabell?" Hector asked. Isabell's heart jumped, and she flinched, knocking over a couple of items on the countertop. Realizing who it was, she took a deep breath and quieted the chattering pots and pans.

"Hector. What are you doing here?" she asked.

"I need to talk to you, I saved your friends," he said, "Wait, what are you doing? It's late?" Hector asked, changing his tone, wondering why she was bundling up loaves of bread in a knapsack. "Are you running away?"

"No! Why would you think that?" she asked, as her voice quivered.

"You're packing a knapsack? If it's not for you, who is it for?" Hector questioned.

"I was asked to gather it for someone," Isabell said, remaining secretive.

"By who?"

"Someone with status within the Castle," Isabell said, still trying to shake the questions.

"The King?"

"No, but close."

"Huh…" Hector said.

"What friends? Do you mean Andy and Eva?" Isabell asked, changing the subject.

"Oh yes, they are safe. Free!" Hector whispered in an excited tone. A large smile formed on his face.

"Wonderful! Thank you, Hector. Thank you!" Isabell said. She quickly gave him a hug.

"Isabell, there is something I want to tell you," Hector said, trying to regain her focus since she had gone back to wrapping the elk hide cloth around the loaves of bread. At his words, she paused and looked up. "Isabell, I want you to know that I… I umm, I love you," he stuttered. He felt his face become flushed with heat.

Isabell's mouth dropped open. She didn't know what to say. Her face turned red with embarrassment because she had not felt the same. She considered him a friend, but that was all.

"Hector… I, I'm grateful for what you've done," she spoke softly, and his face lit up with joy, "But I don't feel the same…" she said quietly. Instantly, his smile vanished. The truth of the matter was that Isabell's heart was held by someone else.

"I'm sorry! Forget I said anything!" Hector said defensively. He swirled around and rushed out of the kitchen.

"Hector!" she called out, but he did not stop. Isabell felt terrible, but had no time to waste. She finished wrapping the loaves of bread in an elk hide knapsack, tied it to a stick. Then left the kitchen out the back door. It was there she would wait for Phillip, just as he had asked her to.

At first, Hector regretted the way he just walked away, so in a split second, he turned around to try again, but by the time he returned, she was already gone. This enraged Hector, and again he stormed off into the heart of the castle.

In the dead silence of the castle, Hector heard something. A struggle. The sound of two men fighting whispered in the night. Changing his course, Hector headed towards the dungeons. As he reached the top of the dungeon's stairs, he could tell that the struggle had stopped, but now he could hear the murmur of whispers.

Tap! Tap! Tap! Footsteps started up the stairway. Panicked, Hector ran towards the Pegasi stables archway and slipped around the corner to hide out of sight.

Listening closely, he realized that Phillip was one of the men, but when he heard the second voice, he understood what was happening. Phillip is helping Jessie escape. Hector began to follow cautiously from a safe distance, staying in the shadows. Although he could not hear what they were saying, he could see Jessie's back poking out from around the corner.

Suddenly, someone wrapped their arms around Jessie. As Hector watched closely, the moon shone just bright enough that Isabell's face became illuminated.

As if his blood began to boil under his skin, Hector clenched his fist, began grinding his teeth, and a flash of jealous heat flooded his body. *How could you, Isabell! Betray me like this?* A tear swelled in his eye and rolled down his cheek. The love that he had for Isabell became a hot anger and hatred. He knew he would lose a fight against both Jessie and Phillip, so instead, Hector did the only thing he could think of.

Thump! Thump! Thump! Hector pounded on a door.

"Come in!" Malus said from within his chambers.

Hector shoved the door open, "Sire! Jessie has escaped!"

"Has he now?" Malus questioned.

"Look for yourself!" Hector said, pointing to the heavy black curtains. Malus extended his wing and peeked out at the maze. To his surprise, Phillip was leading Jessie down the straight path of the Maze.

"Haha!" Malus said, a giant grin rose on his face. Hector was shocked to hear a joyous laugh from the all black steed.

"We must catch them!" Hector said, still filled with anger.

"Don't worry about it, young Hector," Malus said calmly.

"But they are getting away!"

"They won't get far. No creature has ever made it through that maze before. In a few minutes, I will have to go get them from the edge of the well," Malus said, closing the curtain again.

"Malus, don't you see? We must catch him, he must be punished!"

"Why does it matter to you?"

"Because, he… he broke the law!" Hector stuttered.

"And you have never broken any laws?"

"Well, not willingly."

"Oh, so your naps in the hay mound are just you… Doing your job?" Malus said. Hector felt a lump in his throat. He thought no one else had known about it.

"What is the real reason you have found yourself here, late at night? Why do you want a boy you know nothing about to be punished? What is in it for you?" Malus asked smoothly.

"Nothing! I just want to serve the kingdom," Hector insisted.

"So you want fame? Glory?"

"No, no, not that…" Hector assured him.

"But there is a reason?"

"Well, there's this girl…"

"Ahh, yes, love. It's a powerful thing. Let me guess, this girl doesn't feel the same way about you, but instead she fancies the boy Jessie?" Malus asked as if he already knew the answer. He had seen this scenario played out hundreds of times before. Many of the creatures that sought his favor were often driven by love.

"How did you know?…" Hector asked. His anger faded as embarrassment rushed in. Hearing it out loud made him think he was crazy, but even still, his heart felt what it felt.

"This girl, who is she?" Malus asked.

"Her name is Isabell Butler," Hector said, looking at his feet. Thinking of her beautiful blonde hair.

"Isabell? The servant girl?" Malus said with some surprise. "Interesting! Interesting indeed! There is a table to your left, there should be a box of matches. Would you light the torch on the wall beside you?" Malus asked. Gently, Hector felt around in the darkness until his fingers came upon a little box. With one swipe, a small flame glowed in the darkness. Soon, with the torch's help, there was light in Malus' chambers. "Tell me, was Miss Butler involved in the boy's escape?"

Do I put Isabell in danger? Do I tell Malus what I saw? Hector thought about what Malus might do to Isabell if he knew she helped them escape. He was angry at her, but he still hoped she would love him back one day. "No, Sire," he said.

Just then, the hounds barked. Simon had warned the Titans of Jessie and Phillip's escape. Malus opened the curtain and peered out at the Maze. He could see both Phillip and Jessie giving in to the pull of the Wishing Well. "Ah, right on time!" Malus said, having confidence that the escapees would fall victim, just as every other creature had before.

"You may leave. I will go and get the boy soon, rest assured," Malus said. Hector blinked heavily. Then bowed and rushed off to his room. The hounds barked again.

Malus stood in his room, relaxed. Joyous, even. Eyes closed, he thought about the many times creatures had ventured into the Maze, only to be captured by the call of the Wishing Well. Then, Malus would go retrieve them, hear their greatest desires, and plot to manipulate them. The best part was that he could always work out a deal that benefited himself. He already had leverage over Jessie, and now he would gain even more.

Again, the hounds barked. This time, Malus could tell that they were right outside his window at the edge of the maze. As he peered into the Maze, he expected to see two men standing at the Wishing Well. Instead, he saw the Eagle's Heart crystal's glow flare up and the silhouettes of Jessie and Phillip racing towards the exit of the maze.

But how? Malus asked himself. "HOW!" he shouted. Then, like a burning blaze, he shot out of his chambers and rushed towards the maze. By the time he had gotten there, Phillip and Jessie were rushing towards the No Man's Land Mountains, and the hounds huddled about the Wishing Well. Phillip and Jessie had escaped.

Frustrated, Malus spun about and went to find King Fraust.

King Fraust was unwilling to pull men off the search for Eva and Andy because Eva was a bigger threat to his own life. So, luckily for Jessie and Phillip, half of the King's men searched for Andy and Eva, a handful were trapped at the Wishing Well, and the others were off duty.

By the time the off-duty men were aroused, and made aware of the dreadful situation at hand. The sky had grown angry; gloomy clouds had rolled in overhead, the wind picked up, and the flags on top of the watchtower bellowed out and whipped with the wind. The air temperature instantly dropped, and the wind shifted direction. As if in an instant, the sky echoed with booms of thunder, and lightning splintered in the sky.

"Malus, would you get those buffoons out of the Maze?" the King asked, as the wind swayed his beard and his cloak danced behind him. Seeming to be the only creature unfazed by the maze, Malus lifted himself into the air and over the castle. He would have retrieved them earlier, but he was so mad that he left them there to suffer.

In the midst of the courtyard, the King watched as his men frantically rushed about. The flame of their torches danced and flickered violently as the wind grew stronger. A storm was brewing, one like they had never seen before.

"You!" King Fraust ordered. A Titan rushed over to him and stood straight as a board. "Gather a group of men, circle the castle, find the boy and the girl!"

"But, sir, the storm? If we get caught…" the Titan began, but the scowl on King Fraust's face made him halt his sentence. "Right away, your majesty." Then the Titan bowed and rushed to find a group of men willing to join him on his mission.

Just then, four Titans and Zolton, who had been out all night searching, trudged through the castle door. "Zolton!" King Fraust announced. "Any luck?"

"No, your majesty," he said with a tired voice.

"They must be found!" The King said, "I need you to search along the Great Northern River."

"But sir, the men, myself included, are exhausted," Zolton pleaded.

"Does it look like I care?" King Fraust said, clenching his teeth.

"Surely you know that storm could prove dangerous! These weary men might die or catch pneumonia! What good are they as sick men?"

The King was growing angry, impatient even. His rule over Regnum had never been in such disarray. All of his prisoners had escaped, and now Gillian had betrayed him. What would the masses say? *If the girl doesn't kill me, will the kingdom seize this opportunity to unite and overthrow me? Three prisoners, merely children, escaped! They must think I'm a fool! I must find them!* Timothy's thoughts boiled in his head.

"Your order is to go find the prisoners. Do you aim to join Gillian in the dungeons?" The King shouted.

"No, your majesty. We will be off, right away," Zolton said, lowering his head and dropping his ears as he turned away.

Then the loudest crack of thunder rumbled in the sky, so greatly that the castle ground seemed to shake. Slowly, cold drops of rain fell to the earth.

"Halt!" The king shouted in all his anguish. His voice boomed above the wind, and the entire courtyard stopped in their tracks. *If I send men out in this storm, they will not trust my judgment. I will lose their support faster if I force them to go into the storm…* He thought again, changing his mind from just moments ago.

"You are right, the storm could prove to be dangerous for us all. We must prepare for the worst. Batten down the hatches, blow warning horns, and prepare for the storm.

"Yes, sir!" The crowd shouted in relief, and frantically, they were off.

Again, the air temperature dropped drastically. King Fraust pulled his cloak in tight and headed towards the dungeons. The pitter-patter of rain fell on the covered pathway above King Fraust's head. By the time he had reached the dungeon stairway, the stable yard behind him had been covered by polka dots of rain. The dust had been drowned by the moisture of the night. A light rain had fallen on them.

"Your Majesty!" Simon said as he jumped to his feet and stood at attention in the presence of the King. "Phillip jumped me, he knocked me out!" Simon pleaded, trying to find mercy from the angry King.

"LEAVE US!" King Fraust shouted, as his breath was seen in the cold air. The winds of the storm had blown the crisp mountain air down into the plains of Regnum. Simon, cowardly, scurried up the stairs.

Stomping down the hall, King Fraust marched to Gillian's prison cell.

"Where are they!" he shouted at Gillian. Full of rage, the King bent down before Gillian and picked up the halter that Jessie had removed hours ago. "I command you to tell me where they have gone!" he continued.

"I do not know. They didn't tell me anything," Gillian responded.

"You expect me to believe you? Your words mean nothing to me! You have betrayed me once; how easy it would be to do it again."

"I am telling you the truth! I do not know where they have gone. But you are right, I would not tell you even if I did," Gillian said, lifting his snout into the air.

"You traitors, you are ruining everything! What will the people say, what will they do? An example must be set!" The King spoke out loud as he paced the hallway of the dungeon. "And *you're* going to be it." Then King Fraust stormed off towards the stairs. As he vanished from sight, his voice could be heard echoing down the stairwell. "Mark my words, Gillian, tomorrow at dusk, the ax will fall upon your wings."

Gillian gulped hard. It was settled, the King had made his decision, and the Alatum punishment was in order.

The wind whistled into the dungeon, the thunder clashed, and the lightning flickered. The rain fell harder. So much so that a flash flood took hold and fountains of rain water began to rush into the dungeon through the little windows, up above Gillian's head. It wouldn't be long, and he would be forced to stand in inches of rainwater.

Everyone panicked and did the best they could to prepare for the storm. The stable boys scrambled from their chambers into the barnyards. They began to bring in any horses that were left out to graze for the night. They made sure all windows and doors were secured and that the horses would be safe during the storm.

Servant girls were frantically trying to pull down any banners that were left out from the scheduled execution and bring anything that the wind could take from the castle's courtyard into the storage closets within the castle.

Meanwhile, the King, with Malus and many of their highest Sergeants, fled to the storm cellar. It was a small room near the kitchen in the heart of the castle. Servants huddled in their rooms, hoping the storm would pass quickly. But it wasn't going to. This was going to be one of the most violent storms that King Fraust had seen since he became king all those years ago.

Chapter 21
The Shepherd Boy

Guided by the light that seeped out of every crevice of the barn, Jessie and Phillip tiptoed across the sheep's pasture. There was something different about the light coming from the barn, and they hoped that it was an Eagle's Heart crystal awaiting them. Along with it, they hoped for shelter from the storm. However, in a split second, the storm hit so hard that they found themselves in the midst of a downpour.

The sheep in the field all trampled to the barn and bullied their way inside. The booming sky startled Jessie and Phillip and forced them from a tiptoe into a full-on sprint. Shelter was more important now than trying not to get caught. The wind was blistering cold, and they found themselves soaked, splashing through puddles in the pasture.

They headed for the barn doors on the front of the structure, but as they ran, they noticed a candle being lit in the small cottage across the yard. Still hoping to avoid being seen, they veered off to their left. The sheep plowed and shoved about, leaving no room for Jessie and Phillip to crawl into the half doors left open for the sheep. Instead, they found themselves on the south side of the barn, above them was a loft door. That was their only hope of safety from the storm roaring down on them.

Things took a turn for the worse, soon they could feel little balls of ice pecking them. Hail began to rain down from the rumbling sky. The wind whipped sideways, forcing the rain and hail to pound into the side of the barn. The balls of ice cracked loudly upon the faded red siding.

"Quick, on my shoulders!" Phillip shouted at Jessie, who could barely hear him over the voice of the storm.

Jessie planted his foot into Phillip's laced fingers, and he hoisted Jessie up. Jessie then stepped up onto Phillip's shoulders. Phillip tried to steady Jessie as best he could, but the wind was making it difficult.

Jessie tried to pry the haymound hatch door open with his fingers but couldn't get it to budge. Wiping the rain from his eyes, he pressed his face against the barnwood and looked through the crack between the haymound hatch and the barn frame. He could see a wooden latch on the inside. He tried to wiggle his finger between the crack, but could barely reach. The wind howled and pushed against the hatch, making it impossible for Jessie to wiggle the latch free.

"I can't get it!" he shouted out over the roar of the storm.

Barely hearing what Jessie said, Phillip stepped back, preparing to let Jessie down, when a great gust of wind barreled along the barn. Taking more steps than planned, he tried to counter the strength of the gust, but Phillip tripped, sending both of them tumbling to the ground.

The soaked ground around them looked white, as it was laced with marble-sized hail.

"Mischka? Mischka?!" Phillip screamed frantically over the roaring storm.

Mischka? Jessie thought. *She's here?*

But then he saw her. During their tumble, Mischka had been tucked under Phillip's hair, clinging to the back of his shirt collar, but the impact with the ground jolted her, and her grip was lost. Being so small, in such a vicious storm, caused her body to tumble and roll much further into the night than Phillip or Jessie.

"Mischka!" Phillip shouted again, he saw her off in the distance, and scrambled to his feet. The little mouse shook like a dog after jumping in a puddle. At first, Jessie did not realize how dangerous this storm was for a little mouse like her. For him, the rain was annoying, and the hail stung, but for the little brown mouse, this storm was life-threatening.

When Jessie realized just how big each ball of ice was compared to Mischka, he understood that in comparison, it was as if large white boulders were being flung out of the sky at her. He jumped to his feet and watched anxiously as Phillip ran towards Mischka, and Mischka towards Phillip.

As if meteorites were crashing into the ground around her, balls of ice smashed the earth, leaving craters to her left and her right. She dodged and weaved and scurried along as fast as she could. Water and mud splashed in every direction. It was the scariest thing Mischka had ever had to face.

"Mischka! Here!" Phillip cried, knowing the severity of her situation. The thunder roared in victory overhead.

Moments, only seconds, is all she needed to reach the safety of Phillip's hands, but as the lightning illuminated the water-soaked ground, the small brown mouse never reached him. Instead, at the very last second, a marble-sized ball of ice sailed through the air, striking Mischka on the head. Her little furry leg collapsed, and she moved no more.

"Nooo!" Phillip cried. Dropping to his knees and crawling to her aid. The mud stained his pants and splashed up his arms as the rain ran down his face. "Mischka, I'm here," he said as he cradled her in his palms. He used his hand to shade her body from the storm, but she gave no response. "No, no, no!" he cried.

Jessie, watching the tragedy unfold from behind, lost it. Tears burst forth from his eyes. *Not you too…* he thought as he remembered the death of his brother. Using his arms as an umbrella to shield his head from the hail, he began sobbing.

Crack! Thunder echoed overhead and lightning flickered.

Longer than usual the lightning seem to illuminate the sky, so much so that Jessie took notice, peering up he realized that the yellow glow that came from within the barn was shining down on them, and the hatch they tried to get open moments ago was now wide open and the silhouette of a young boy peered out with his hand extended down to Jessie.

"Phillip!" Jessie shouted to his friend over the storm. Phillip swiveled around to see.

"Outside is no place to be in a storm like this!" the young boy said.

Jessie reached up and clasped hands with the boy, and he hoisted him up into the loft of the barn. The rain and hail still pounded outside. Then the boy reached out for Phillip, and Jessie reached down too. Gently, Phillip slipped Mischka's limp body into the palm of Jessie's hand, and he quickly pulled her out of the storm. Then the young boy pulled Phillip up. As he fell into the barn, he rolled away from the hatch. The young boy pulled hard on the hatch door until the wind grabbed it and slammed it shut. Fixing the latch in place, the sound of the raging storm outside became muffled. Instead, the comforting series of sheep bleats took its place.

"My daddy warned me, it was gonna be a real bad storm. He sure was right about that one, wasn't he?" the boy said with a smile.

Phillip and Jessie just blinked at him. They were terrified. The wind outside was relentless, pushing on the frame of the barn. The old wooden structure creaked and groaned. Jessie and Phillip just shivered against the slanted roof of the barn, traumatized by everything that had just happened. Phillip's best friend had been killed by the storm, and Jessie was afraid that although this boy saved them from the storm, he would surely turn them into the King, once again forcing him to be a prisoner.

However, the young boy never changed his tone. In fact, he seemed to be completely unfazed by them. Almost as if he had expected them, or had helped strangers one hundred times before.

Recovering Mischka's body from Jessie, Phillip just peered down at his dear little furry friend's body. Jessie just stared wide-eyed at the boy. The boy wore a well-loved rain jacket. As he pulled his hood down, Jessie could see his face. Pale skin with hundreds of freckles that ran across his cheeks and nose. He wore a smile and had short red hair.

"My name's Uriah. Welcome! My barn is your barn. You're welcome to weather the storm here for the night," he said. He crawled over to the lip of the loft and swung his legs over the side. Then slipped off and vanished from sight.

Surprised that the boy had just jumped out of the loft, Jessie scrambled over to the edge to see if the boy, Uriah, was alright. He was. The boy had landed in a big pile of hay that was in the sheep's pen and was already making his way over the wooden fence, out of their pen. From above, Jessie scanned the barn. It was a rectangle, and they had entered from the rear. A hay loft hovered over both the back third of the barn as well as the front third. Leaving a section open in the middle. The front loft was stuffed full of hay. From the wooden platform to the very peak of the barn, hay was stacked tightly. On the back loft, the one they were perched in, there was some hay, but it looked as if most of it had been fed already, or brought down into the pile below.

"Come on down here! I'll stoke the fire. Let's get you dried off!" Uriah said. He grabbed an iron fire poker and stirred up the glowing embers left in the large stone fireplace.

Slowly, Jessie began to crawl down from the hay loft. He used a wooden ladder instead of jumping. To his surprise, the lighting of the barn was not a mysterious Eagle's Heart Crystal, but a few torches fixed to the upright support beams of the barn. In fact, there was no sight of a crystal, and its warm glow seemed to be gone.

The ground level of the barn was different from above. The floor was soft dirt that had been beaten into a sandy pulp over the years. Almost as if he were walking on a sandy beach. The double door of the barn was straight ahead, sheltered under the front loft. But directly beside the door on the right, the sheep pen began. Taking up three-quarters of the ground floor, the sheep's pen made an L shape. Consuming the entire right side of the barn and the entire back, leaving only a square area open on the front left of the barn. Farm tools and other equipment rested in that corner under the loft, while the stone chimney was fixed to the wall near the Sheep's pen, near the center of the long left wall of the barn. This allowed its tall chimney to sneak up past the front loft and poke out of the barn's roof. Its heat radiated out to the barn. The base of it was wide and sturdy, and the sheep's wooden fence corralled alongside it. Unsurprisingly, the sheep did all they could to huddle next to that part of the fence.

As sheep do, they bleated loudly. The young boy had gotten flames dancing in the fireplace, so he leaned over the wooden fence to pat the sheep on their heads. As if comforting them, he whispered softly to the sheep. "It's only a storm, it'll pass." Oddly enough, a few sheep he patted, hushed their cries.

The storm still waged outside, but there was something special about this barn that made Jessie feel safe.

Uriah looked back towards the two new strangers. Jessie's eyes were fixed on him, but Phillip stood at the base of the ladder with his hands cupped, and tears streamed down his face.

"What's that there you're holding, my friend?" Uriah inquired. The kindness this young boy seemed to have surpassed any creature Phillip had ever met. Innocent, sweet, and kind. He looked to be only twelve or thirteen.

Phillip couldn't answer but instead, took a few steps forward, passing Jessie, and elevated his hands to show him Mischka's body.

"Oh my, who is this poor little mouse? Not just a simple creature, I suppose?" Uriah asked.

"How did you know she wasn't simple?" Jessie asked, shocked that this young boy knew anything about talking creatures at all. *Being just a young boy, secluded in the countryside, how did he even know about animals that could communicate? Does he even know about Somniators?* Jessie pondered.

"I had a hunch, I suppose," Uriah said with a smile. "Why don't you boys come on over. Fires burning!" Jessie and Phillip walked slowly over to the fire. The warmth felt amazing on their soaked skin. "What's her name?" Uriah asked.

"Mischka..." Phillip whimpered.

"Mischka? What a cool name!" Uriah started cheerfully.

Phillip was confused... *Can he not see that she's dead?* However, before he could ask the boy, as if reading Phillip's mind, Uriah spoke up.

"Don't worry. Your friend is just sleeping, in time she will wake up," he said.

"Sleeping?! How can you say that? She's gone!" Phillip sobbed.

Uriah, very calmly, went over to the corner and found two wooden stools and placed them around the fire for Jessie and Phillip. He already had one close by, so he sat as well.

"Have some faith, Phillip!" Uriah said.

"How did you...? Who are..." Phillip sniffled. *How did he know my name? Who is this boy?* He thought to himself. The boy's calmness now alarmed Phillip. *Does he work for my brother? A spy?*

"Please put, Mischka, is it?" Uriah asked. Phillip just nodded. "Put her down here." Phillip's eyes followed Uriah's finger to the floor. To his surprise, he noticed a small lamb wrapped in a wool blanket at the foot of the fireplace. "This here is Rascal!" Uriah said as he bent over and pulled the lamb out of the blanket and cradled it in his lap. "I named him that cause he sure is a little rascal. He had run off again, just before the storm hit! Sure was good, I found him when I did. It's mighty cold out there. I just got dry, myself!" Uriah rambled. Jessie was intrigued by the boy, but Phillip was wary of trusting him. *He sure knows a lot about me...*

"You mean you went out looking for him? One little sheep? All the while, a storm was raining down on you? The rain? The wind and hail?" Jessie asked, confused. *Why would he risk his own safety for one little sheep when the rest of his flock, who hadn't run away, were in the barn, safe? It's the little lamb's own fault, he would have gotten what he deserved.* Jessie thought to himself.

"Why, of course I did! I AM their shepherd, what shepherd wouldn't leave his whole herd in search of one lost sheep? That's my job, you see. No matter how much of a rascal he is!" Uriah said as he scratched the sleeping lamb behind the ear.

"Well, that seems ridiculous to me!" Jessie said, laughing. However, the cuteness of the lamb won him over.

Gradually, the storm outside grew even more ferocious, the hail doubled in size and pounded the roof of the barn.

"Wow, I don't know if I have ever seen a storm this bad before, could cause a lot of damage," Jessie said nervously.

"I'd say! But I wouldn't worry. We get a lot of storms up here. Being so close to the No Man's Mountains and all," Uriah said calmly. Again, Phillip and Jessie were surprised at his relaxed state. "You think this barn will hold up?" Phillip asked, looking around at the old barn wood that held the structure together.

"For sure, Phillip," there it was again, *No one told him my name, how does he know me...* "You just gotta trust in the Great White Eagle!" he said.

"You know the Great White Eagle?" Jessie asked, intrigued by the boy.

"Course I do! That's who you are looking for, aren't you?" Uriah asked.

"Who are you?!" Phillip asked, standing up from his stool. He stepped back, nervous about the boy. "How do you know me? How do you know we are looking for the Great White Eagle?" Jessie sensed Phillip's concern, and he too stood up and stepped back.

"I'm sorry, I don't mean to scare you. Please sit down." Uriah said in the most sincere way. Cautiously, they both listened to Uriah. "No one ever comes this way unless they are looking for the Great White Eagle…" he said.

"So… you know him? You know where he is?" Jessie asked again.

"Yes, sir. Me and the Big E are tight! He's like my pa, but from the heavens. You know?" Uriah said.

"Ummm… No, not really," Jessie admitted, scratching his head.

"Well, it's like this. When I'm scared or worried, I talk to him. Or when I don't know what to do, I ask him for advice," Uriah said.

"You ask the Great White Eagle that?" Phillip asked. "Are you a Somniator?"

"No." Uriah chuckled. "You just have to trust him. Believe he will provide. If you can do that, I promise he will always be with you. Just like he is with me."

"The Great White Eagle is here? With you? Right now?" Phillip asked. He frantically began looking around the barn for the feathered creature.

"Course, he is!" Uriah said.

"Where?!" Both Jessie and Phillip asked excitedly.

"Right here!" Uriah said as he pointed to his chest.

"Huh?" Jessie asked, more confused than ever.

"He's in my heart, he is all around me. He is, and I am," the boy said.

Suddenly, the storm outside buckled down twice as hard. The wind howled, the barn wood creaked, and the hail pelted the earth. The thunder grumbled so continuously that Jessie and Phillip cowered in fear. Suddenly, the front doors of the barn burst open from the wind. A cold gust pierced through the barn, and every torch went out. Even the fireplace went cold.

It was eerie and cold. A chill fell on the barn.

Phillip and Jessie tried to look at one another, but the darkness made it impossible to see. But then the most peculiar thing occurred. Out of the corner of Phillip's eye, a soft blue glow fell into the picture frame that was the barn doors. In the midst of the falling hail, another blue crystal fell. Then another, and another. Slowly, the balls of ice faded, and the small round glowing crystals took over. Jessie saw the same thing, only the crystals shone a warm yellow instead.

Like a dream, the ground filled with small, grape-sized crystals. A soft glow blanketed the ground like a fresh covering of snow. It was the most surreal and magical thing they had ever witnessed. Thunder still grumbled, but softer now than before. The blue light, for Phillip (yellow for Jessie), seeped into the darkness of the barn and cast a faint light on their faces. It was beautiful.

Then lightning illuminated the sky, and as the gray clouds went dark again, so did the crystals on the ground. Everything was dark once again.

"Did you see..." But before Jessie could finish his sentence, an even brighter light flashed boldly behind them.

Spinning around to see where the light was coming from, they could not believe their eyes. At the heart of the great light, they saw Uriah, and in the palm of his hands, he held Mischka.

Like thunder, Uriah's words boomed. "If you will it!"

Then the light grew all the more intense, so much so that they covered their eyes, but even then the light seeped through their fingers, and neither of them could withstand it any longer. In an instant, Jessie and Phillip both collapsed into unconsciousness.

Chapter 22
In Plain Sight

"I can't believe the Titans are at my home. Do you think they will harm my parents?" Eva whispered as she and Andy snuck through the night.

"I really hope not," Andy sympathized with her. Although he had only met Eva's parents a few times, and they had never been under great circumstances, he cared for Eva. Therefore, he cared for her parents. "We will get help. We will save them all. Jessie and Gillian, and your parents too," Andy said, knowing full well that two teenagers wouldn't be able to stop the King's army on their own.

Eva smiled at Andy. The moon light illuminated her affection and Andy swung his arm over her shoulder and pulled her in for a gentle side hug.

"Come on," he said, as he darted out into the open street that paved its way down the heart of Regnum's village. "If I were a royal guard," he started as he puffed out his chest, pretending to be a tough, ruthless guard. "I would be looking for two kids sneaking around in the shadows."

"We are two kids sneaking around in the shadows, and they are looking for us…" Eva said hesitantly, looking at Andy in the moonlight as she herself hid in the shadows of a house.

"Exactly, so let's not act like those kids," Andy said as he smiled and held out his hand in Eva's direction.

Eva was terrified. She could see the Titans off in the distance, checking all the streets. Frankly, it was only a matter of time before they overturned every shadow and found them. *Maybe Andy is right? Maybe hiding in plain sight would be our best option. Just like dressing as a servant in the castle,* she thought, as she lurched forward and grabbed Andy's hand.

The two began to nervously skip down the village road towards the slums of Regnum. At first, it was nerve-racking. If they got caught, it would be the end of them. Making it out of Regnum into the Forbidden Forest would be their only chance of relief. However, the streets were crawling with Titans and Pegasi. If they were found creeping through the shadows, every Titan would know that they were the fugitives. However, Andy's plan was to just act like regular kids, breaking curfew.

Soon, their forced skipping turned real, and the two of them couldn't help but get into it. They skipped higher and thumped their feet on the ground. As if they were on their way home after school, acting like the kids they were again. Not on the run, but breaking curfew and looking for a slap on the wrists. They couldn't help but giggle.

Soon, they caught a Titan's ear. Sneaking along a dark alleyway, the Titan crept over to see. The Titan was Thomas. Peering out, he saw them. He had seen their faces first hand, being one of the guards who had escorted them to their near execution, and they each still wore the iron cuffs around their wrists. Although they tried to hide it as they skipped along, he caught sight of them. His heart pounded. He was conflicted. He reached for the hilt of his sword, but could only think of one thing. Gillian's words. *They're innocent, that's why…* rang in his head.

Closer they came, heading straight towards him. One quick leap out of the shadows and a call for backup, and they would be captured. Thomas would redeem his failure and be in good standing with the King once again. Quietly, Thomas slowly pulled his sword from its sheath. Every step Andy and Eva took, more and more of his sword was exposed. Then he stopped. He couldn't do it. He believed Gillian, he believed that these two kids were innocent. In that exact moment, Andy and Eva skipped past him, unaware that Thomas lay in the shadows.

As they made their way down the street towards the slums of Regnum, Thomas slid his sword back into place. Suddenly, two other Titans snuck up beside Thomas.

"Did you get a good look at em?" one of them asked, drawing his sword.

"I did. Just a couple kids playing. You know how kids are, always breaking curfew and looking for trouble. Keep searching the shadows, watch the houses, and keep an eye out for suspicious activities. Those prisoners have to be around here somewhere," Thomas ordered.

"Yes, sir!" The Titans responded. They rushed off into the shadows and continued to search for Andy and Eva. Thomas felt relieved. Relieved that the Titans hadn't come any sooner. Relieved that he had not been caught aiding their escape. Relieved that he had done the right thing. He leaned back against the house. Closed his eyes and breathed deeply.

Andy and Eva had heard the commotion when the two other Titans came to Thomas' side. Andy thought his plan was working. As he and Eva skipped away, he looked over his shoulder and saw a Titan peek down the street at them. However, they never came his way. Never ordered him to stop. Nothing.

So, he tugged at Eva's arm and smiled. "It's working!" he whispered joyfully, and the two giggled with glee and skipped even faster, even higher.

They skipped until they again had reached the slums of Regnum. Once there, the streets seemed to be crowded by evil shadows. It didn't take long for the rush of excitement to wear off and they were back to a serious mission. Quietly they crept through the streets, on high alert.

To Andy, this was home. The buildings, the strange noises lurking about, and all the stray animals scrounging for food in the trash were familiar to him. To Eva, it was quite spooky. She stuck close by Andy, not wanting to be separated for even a second. Most of the time, Eva made Andy meet her anywhere but the Slums of Regnum. She thought the people were filthy and dangerous.

"I wonder…" Andy said as he pinched his chin between his thumb and pointer finger. Before Eva could question his words, he dashed off the street and rounded the backside of a tall, dark building.

"Andrew! Andrew!" Eva whispered harshly. "Don't leave me like that!" she scolded him, as she raced after him. "What are you doing?" she asked when she finally caught up with him.

"This is the orphanage," he whispered. Eva had not paid much attention to the buildings around her, instead she was hoping to pass through the slums of Regnum without any unnecessary stops. "Mrs. Rosewood had a strict curfew," Andy explained, "But as you know, I always bent the rules."

"Yeah, so?" she asked, still frustrated that he left her alone in the slums.

"Mrs. Rosewood always locked the doors after ten. But I used to sneak through the windows. She would always get mad when I woke up the other kids while sneaking back in at night."

"That's great, but what does it have to do with us now? Let's get out of here. This place gives me the creeps," Eva said, rubbing her arms, trying to smooth out the goosebumps that formed on her skin.

"She knew she could never get me to stop sneaking out, so she made me a deal. She promised not to get mad if I snuck out, as long as I remained outside until she unlocked the door in the morning," Andy said.

"Huh…" Eva said, silently judging Andy for being barbaric.

"Eventually, I think she felt bad for me. Either that or she had a soft spot for me. But one night, I came to these back steps, and there was a wooden box. Inside was a blanket and some…" Andy explained, as he opened the wooden box, "Ahh, yes! Some bread," and he pulled out both the blanket and bread.

"That's awfully nice of her."

"She was the closest thing I ever had to having a mother," Andy said as he began to tear little pieces of mold off the bread and tossed them to the ground.

"I'm sorry," Eva said, thinking about how hard it would have been growing up without either of her parents. Her goosebumps never went away, instead, she began to shiver.

"It's okay. Here…" Andy said as he flung the blanket over Eva's shoulders and rubbed her arms to try and warm her up. Eva's cheeks became rosy. Which made him feel awkward, the kind of awkward you feel when you like someone.

Not knowing what to say as he gazed into her brown eyes, he said the first thing that popped into his mind.

"Man, you stink!" he said with a smile. You could say that was his way of flirting, but clearly that area of his life needed a bit of work. She giggled and pushed him away, but she knew he was just trying to be funny and lighten the mood.

"Yeah, well you stink too!" she giggled softly. The scent of their manure bath during their escape still stained their servant boy disguises.

Andy shared the rest of the bread with Eva, and the two were on their way.

"We should get moving. It looks like a storm is moving in." Eva said as she pointed up into the sky. The clouds of what looked like a vicious storm had begun to roll in from the north. The faint sound of thunder rolled.

"I think you are right. We need to find shelter. But not here. Let's get out of Regnum and look," Andy suggested, and the two were off. Luckily for them, the Orphanage was one of the first buildings you came across when entering Regnum, so getting out of the slums would be accomplished soon.

They hopped back on the dirt road that led out of Regnum. This was the same road they had been paraded in on a few days prior. If they continued straight, it would bring them back to the clearing that had started it all. However, as they raced out of the village, past the farms on the outskirts of Regnum, they found themselves at a crossroads.

A wooden post stood in the corner of the crossroads. Attached to it were different boards facing different directions. Each one had words engraved into it. It was hard to see what it read in the dark, but Andy and Eva had both passed by it many times on their smaller adventures.

The top board faced Regnum, and it said Calvary Loop. The next one down said Gravis Terra, and it had an arrow pointing to the west. Below that, one that read Borrian with an arrow to the East. The final one read The Forbidden Forest, with an arrow pointing straight ahead. As they came alongside the sign, there were four more boards. These signs were for those coming from Gravis Terra, aiding directions for those traveling.

"This way," Andy said, as he pointed towards Gravis Terra.

"To the Elves," Eva said, knowing that that was their plan all along, and Gravis Terra was home to the Elves.

"Yes. We will follow the road, walk along the edge, staying just inside the shelter of the forest. Hopefully we can find a hollowed tree before the storm hits…" Andy said as he listened to the sky grumble.

The Calvary Loop was a road built to connect the three civil regions. From the Centaur's village, the edge of Regnum, and into the heart of the Ruth Valley, the Calvary Loop ran, allowing easy travel for creatures. This made trade among the communities easier, and for

Andy and Eva, it made finding their way to Gravis Terra in the dark an easier task.

The moonlight became scarce as the storm clouds rolled overhead. Thunder and lightning loomed above as sprinkles began to rain down and kick up the dust on the road.

Leaving Regnum behind, they rushed to the edge of the forest and dipped into the shadows. At first, the canopy of the Forbidden Forest shielded them from sprinkles, but as it began to rain harder, the leaves became heavy, bending from the weight. Soon, droplets rolled off the leaves and dripped onto their heads and shoulders. The crack of thunder boomed louder.

The storm had hit Regnum by now, and although the clouds had consumed the light, Andy knew by the wind and the dropping temperatures that the storm would soon be full force upon them.

"Eva, we have to find cover. Fast!" he shouted over the howl of the wind.

"But where?" she asked as she looked deeper into the Forbidden Forest. With the moon behind the clouds, the forest looked darker than ever.

"There!" Andy shouted. Eva followed Andy's finger. He was pointing to a stone bridge. The stone bridge stretched across the Northern River and just might do the trick in keeping them out of the rain that was on its way.

Leaving the cover of the forest, they darted out onto the gravel of the Calvary loop. Racing against the storm, they ran as hard as they could. Rain pounded down around them. In a mad dash, they slipped under the bridge. It arched up and shielded them from the rain.

Andy and Eva huddled under the blanket at the foundation of the bridge; there was just enough room for them between the rushing river and the bridge itself for them to curl up out of reach of the storm.

"Think we will find any trolls under this bridge?" Andy said jokingly, trying to make light of the heavy situation. The rain fell so hard they had to yell at each other to hear, even though they were sitting beside one another.

"Andrew! You know there are no such things," Eva said as she yawned. Her yawn was contagious, and Andy too began to yawn.

They were beyond exhausted, not to mention filthy.

It's incredible that either one of them would be able to fall asleep, considering the weight they had on their shoulders. Escaping the castle was only a small part of the chaos that had unfolded that night. Andy and Eva both worried about their friends. As far as they knew, Jessie was still locked in the dungeons of the castle. Phillip's secrets were still unknown to them, and as for Gillian, they didn't even want to think about what was going to happen to him.

Andy wondered how he would ever keep the promise he made to Eva. *I can barely believe that we have escaped, how can I possibly believe we will rescue her parents… How could I possibly rescue Jessie?* He thought.

However, life as Andy and Eva knew it had changed. Jessie and Phillip were on the run, with the Book of Truth in their possession, and they had even found the key. A lot of good things had happened, but they knew nothing about it.

Outside in the cold, they found themselves stuck again. Anxiety filled their hearts.

"Trust in the Great White Eagle. Like we did in the Uada Hollow, like we did in the Dungeons, like we have to do now," Andy said softly.

They were cold, wet, and on the run. *What else can we do?* Eva wondered. From the beginning, this journey had been dangerous, now things seemed worse. "Trust in the Eagle..." she repeated sluggishly. She closed her eyes and let her head lean back against the stone base of the bridge. It rained so hard that the splashing of the river and the constant thump of rain drowned out the thunder. They both fell asleep.

Chapter 23
Mischka's Morning Miracle

When Jessie and Phillip awoke, it was the next morning, and the storm had passed. Jessie pushed himself off the ground and looked around the barn. The front door was closed, and all the sheep were gone. It was silent. Only the orange glow of embers remained in the fireplace.

Remembering all that had transpired the night before, Jessie swirled his head about looking for Uriah, but Uriah had vanished.

"What was that last night?" Phillip asked, holding his head, which was pounding.

"Did Uriah have a crystal?" Jessie asked.

"It looked like he was the crystal… I have never seen a light that bright before," Phillip said as he slowly crawled to his feet. His bones and muscles ached. He hadn't had that much exercise in years, and his body was feeling it. Phillip walked over to the barn doors and opened them. He was expecting to see the ground covered in crystals from the night before. To his surprise, a great brightness flooded into the barn.

Overnight, the rain and hail turned to snow, covering the ground with a blanket of white. The cold wind rushed in and sent shivers through the hollow of the barn. As goose bumps formed on their skin, they quickly swung the barn door shut. Jessie scurried to the stone fireplace and stoked the embers. Phillip came alongside him and rubbed his hands together.

"Man, what a weird night…" Jessie said.

"A sad night…" Phillip said solemnly. He thought about his little furry friend. *She deserves a proper burial,* he thought to himself. "Where is she?" he mustered the strength to ask.

"I saw Uriah holding her last night… Maybe he took her with him?" Jessie suggested.

"Why would he take her?" Phillip said with a tear rolling down her cheek. Jessie shrugged and lowered his head. He didn't know what to say. Uriah was gone, and Mischka's little brown body was nowhere in sight.

Both of their eyes stopped at the heart of the barn. The night before, Uriah stood there holding Mischka in his hands and a great light overpowered them all, causing both Jessie and Phillip to black out. However, this morning, Uriah was gone, but in his place a pile of garments lay in a heap on the ground.

Feeling warmed up from the embers of the fireplace, Phillip walked over to the garments and knelt down beside them. As he started to sift through them, he heard a faint squeak.

"Did you hear that?" Phillip asked. Jessie ran up and knelt beside him.

Suddenly, he heard it again. A muffled squeak from within the pile of clothing.

"Mischka?!" Phillip asked excitedly. Hope filled his heart. Peeling away the layers of clothes, Phillip searched for the sound. Finally, he uncovered a little brown mouse. She twitched her nose, and her whiskers wiggled. "Mischka! Mischka! You're alive!" Phillip cried with joy. He held out his palm, and Mischka jumped into his hand. Phillip ran his pointer finger over her head and down her back.

"But how?" Jessie gasped. He remembered Uriah saying that Mischka was only sleeping, but he clearly saw the chunk of hail hit Mischka. He saw she was dead. *How can this be?* he thought.

"The Eagle!" Mischka squeaked. "The Great White Eagle brought me back!"

"Are you sure?" Jessie asked. *If it was really him, then he really can save my brother!* Jessie thought about the possibility, and hope flooded through him.

"As sure as I was dead and now made alive! It was the Great White Eagle who rescued me!"

"Rescued?" Phillip asked. "What do you mean?"

"Oh, Phillip, it was dreadful," Mischka squeaked, shivering at the thought of it.

"How so?" Jessie said. He stood up, rushed over to the stone fireplace, and threw on another log. "Come over here! No sense in being cold!"

Then he settled in next to the new flame that danced in the fireplace. Phillip set Mischka down on the stones near the fireplace's brim. Now it looked as if she was on a stage telling her story for all to hear. Before she began, her nose began to twitch and her sniffer lifted into the air.

"Do you think I could have some bread?" she asked, referring to the knapsack that Isabell had prepared for them.

"Oh, yes, you must be starving!" Phillip said. He reached down and unwrapped the bread from the elk hide.

The bread was soggy, but all of them were famished. Phillip broke the bread into small pieces and distributed them.

Mischka nibbled at the bread as she told Jessie and Phillip what had happened to her.

"The last thing I remember before everything went black was running to you," Mischka said, and everyone looked down at their feet because they knew what happened after that. "But then, almost instantly, I woke up, but I was in another place."

"Where?" Jessie inquired.

"A forest. One I've never been to before. The trees there were massive, and their trunks looked as if they were painted black or something."

"Do you think you left this world? Did you go to Caelum?" Jessie asked.

"I don't know Jessie, those trees she described sound like Blackwood trees."

"If that was Caelum, then all the stories about how beautiful and wonderful it is are wrong. This place was terribly scary and awful," she squeaked.

"Sounds to me like you ended up in the Blackwood forest," Phillip said, "But that seems odd."

"You know this place?" Mischka asked.

"Yes, actually. The Blackwood forest is in the forbidden circle!" Jessie said, thinking back to when he, his brother, Andy, and Eva all rode on the back of Maizey through the forest.

"Hmmm, that makes sense then," Mischka said, thinking deeply.

"How so?" Phillip asked. Going to a place in their world after dying didn't seem to make any sense.

"Because of what I saw there," she continued. "Not only was the forest dark with long shadows, but there were spooky noises too. At first, I thought it was just the leaves rustling. That's what I wanted it to be, but then it sounded more like whispers."

"You must have been terrified, Mischka. I know firsthand how scary and dark it is there at night. But I still don't understand…" Philip said.

"I'm getting there!" the little mouse scolded her old friend. She settled back in to tell her story. "All of a sudden, I heard the hoot of an owl!" she said, with a quiver in her voice. Jessie and Phillip stared at her with a blank look. They did not understand just how scary an owl is for a mouse. "Owls are silent killers! They swoop down without a sound and take their prey. One of them dreadful beasts snatched up my uncle Slim and carried him off."

"I've never seen an owl, but I've heard they can flap their wings without making any noise at all, and they have great night vision, which makes them great hunters!" Jessie said excitedly, fascinated by the winged creature. "No offense, Mischka!" he said, catching the glare she began to give him.

"But that's just it. They can spot a mouse from way up in the treetops in total darkness, but this one never saw me. I was obviously an easy meal. Right in the middle of the forest, no trees to hide behind, no long grass, nothing but the open air. To make things worse, the ground was covered by fallen leaves. Any movement would cause a stir," Mischka explained.

"What do you mean it never saw you?" Phillip asked.

"I mean, it never saw me. I saw it perched in the tree, but then it left its perch and began to swoop down toward me. I was terrified, I thought I was a goner... Again! I ran as fast as I could, hoping that somehow I could outrun the owl. But it began to close in on me."

"Then what?" Jessie said, scooting closer to hear her story.

"Then, *SWOOSH,* it glided right over me! I think I could have jumped up and touched its talons; that's how close it got to me. Quietly, the owl re-perched in a tree. I froze and watched him closely."

"So you mean, it really didn't see you..." Phillip asked, just as shocked as she was.

"Maybe it wasn't hungry..." Jessie said with a soft smile. But again Mischka glared at him. She did not think it was as funny as he did.

"At first, I didn't understand. How could he have not seen me? I thought. But then I heard a terrified scream coming from within the forest," Mischka said.

"A scream? You were not alone?" Phillip asked.

"No, not at all. I looked around, but didn't see her at first. But the weirdest part was that the owl didn't flinch. He didn't swivel his head or even ruffle his feathers at the girl's scream.

"So, it couldn't hear or see anything?" Jessie said. "Sounds like a real impressive hunter," he said sarcastically.

"That's just it, seconds later the owl swooped down and snatched up a rodent," Mischka explained.

"Weird…" Phillip said.

"Like I said, I didn't understand… at first. But then I saw her. The girl who screamed. She was all white and almost seemed to glow," she explained.

"You mean, she was a ghost?" Jessie said, leaning back with wide eyes.

"Umhm… That's when I looked down at my own paws and realized that I, too, was all white, just like a ghost."

So the noises Maizey hears at night sometimes really are ghosts? Jessie thought, but then his mind retraced his journey to the Devil's Kettle. He remembered the night in the house of rubble when he looked out the window and saw the Messorems dragging ghosts towards the Devil's Kettle. He remembered that his mother's ghost was one of them. "Wait a minute… Why did the girl scream?" Jessie asked. He had a hunch that he knew exactly why.

"Something was chasing it…" Mischka said, with a quiver.

"What was it?" Phillip asked. "Did it wear all black?" he asked. Phillip, too, was beginning to know exactly what happened. Considering he and his brother had been to the Devil's Kettle as well, it was all beginning to make sense for him, too.

"Tattered clothing? No face?!" Jessie stuttered.

"Why yes, how did you know?" Mischka said, shocked that they knew exactly what she had seen.

"They are called Messorems," Phillip said.

"Yes, and when I was at the Devil's Kettle… I saw them and the ghosts of many creatures…" Jessie swallowed hard. That night was tragic for him, and he wished he could forget.

"There were many ghosts when I was there, too. Not just the girl, but many other creatures dashed through the woods. An elf, a couple of beavers, a dwarf, two centaurs, and a few others. All of them ran just as fast as they could. That's when I first saw the Messorem. Oh, Phillip, it was terrifying…"

"I know, Mischka… I know," Phillip said in a comforting voice.

"But you made it? Your back? The Messorem must not have caught you?" Jessie said, eager to learn what happened to Mischka.

"Barely… I froze. I was so scared, so confused that although my brain told me to run, my legs wouldn't budge. The Messorem headed straight for me. Its boney hands swung a chain over its head like a lasso."

"Then what?" Jessie asked. Phillip smacked Jessie on the arm and gave him a scolding look. "Sorry…" Jessie mumbled.

"The Messorem threw its chain at me. I remember seeing the cold iron chain links crash around me. Just like a lasso, I knew the Messorem could yank on his chain, and the chain would squeeze in. Binding me tight," Mischka said, recalling what happened. Both Jessie and Phillip shivered at her words. Both had actually been bound by a Messorem on their separate journeys. The cold steel squeezing every ounce of strength out of them was not a pleasant memory to recall.

"I really thought I was going to be captured by it. I couldn't move. But then suddenly my biggest nightmare came true."

"What? What's more scary than a Messorem?"

"Out of nowhere, I was snatched off the ground… My heart jumped right out of my chest, and I screamed like a little field mouse.

I thought that the owl had finally seen me and snatched me up for lunch."

"But it wasn't the owl, was it… It was the…" Phillip began.

"Yes, Phillip! It was the Great White Eagle! Can you believe it! I have to admit I didn't think your escape plan was actually going to amount to anything. I figured it was another drunken attempt to redeem yourself… Hehe, sorry…" she squeaked.

"It's okay, why should you have faith in me?" Phillip asked his little friend.

"But Phillip, we have to keep going, I think we are really going to find him." Without even thinking, Jessie swallowed up the last of the bread Isabell had packed them.

"You're sure it was really him?" Phillip asked, sceptical of his own plan.

"I have no doubt in my mind. The Great White Eagle saved me from the Messorems, and he brought me back to life."

"What was he like?" Jessie asked.

"Majestic and powerful, yet gentle," Michka began. "He carried me all the way here. Out of the forest, over the slums and village of Regnum, high above the castle, and all the way to this little barn. It was as if the roof peeled away and a great green light glowed from the heart of the barn. It was so bright that I could not even see anything in the barn."

"Uriah?" Phillip questioned, looking at Jessie. Jessie nodded his head in agreement.

"Right before he dropped me, he said. 'Your time has not yet come. You have much to do. I have brought you back so that the works of the Great White Eagle may be made known among all creatures."

"What work does he want you to do?" Phillip asked.

"I don't know… but I'm sure it will be revealed in a dream. I am a Somniator after all."

"This is so great!" Jessie said excitedly. "If he brought Mischka back, he can bring back my brother!"

"I guess so!" Phillip said. However, as the words left his mouth, a funny feeling struck him. Similar to all the times he had revelations about Somniator dreams, this feeling told him something. The words *"Your time has not yet come. You have much to do."* Echoed faintly in his head. *Will he really bring Richard back?* Phillip wondered. It was obvious he had the power to do it, but for some unknown reason, Phillip had an uneasy feeling about it.

He tried to shake the feeling, but couldn't. Although he felt like there was more to discuss, he didn't want to ruin the moment. Mischka was alive! Phillip was overjoyed that his best friend was alive and well. He kicked back and enjoyed the moment. They were free, together, and warmed by the fire. It was a glimpse of happiness that he hadn't felt in a long time. For some reason, Phillip felt attached to Jessie, as if he were a younger brother or a son, even. There was much to Phillip's story that was still unrevealed, but his story connected him to the boy more than Jessie knew.

Oddly enough, Jessie felt the same connection. Phillip was older, wiser, and seemed to understand him more than any of his friends could. Although Phillip had betrayed them, he felt safe and comforted while with him.

Mischka's morning miracle filled them all with hope, joy, wonder, and amazement.

Chapter 24
The Rock

Soon, Phillip stood up from beside the fire and stretched out his limbs. Curious about the pile of clothing, he knelt down beside it and began to sift through it again.

Jessie too stood, but instead, he wandered over to the barn door and swung it open. The snow was so bright that Jessie had to squint to see anything clearly.

"I wonder where Uriah and the sheep went?" Jessie asked. "There are no tracks…" The wind from outside was cold against Jessie's skin, but the mysterious disappearance of Uriah and the sheep piqued his curiosity. He stepped out into the snow and peered out into the barnyard.

To his surprise, there were no tracks, not one, and no sign of Uriah or the sheep. *Odd…* he thought.

"Maybe they left before the snow hit?" Phillip said, still shuffling through the clothing. "Do you remember seeing any of this here last night?" he asked, but did not wait for a response. "There is enough clothing for both of us to bundle up. Coats, gloves, wool-lined pants, fur hats- and even two pairs of elk hide boots." Phillip said, astonished. Even more so, the garments looked to be his size.

Jessie didn't pay much attention to the clothing, because he was mesmerized by the beauty of the snow. As he gazed out into the pasture, the pure white snow covered the fence posts like frosting on a cookie. Like a story book, the cottage looked like a cut-out in the snow. The wind blew and the snow swirled about, drifting into banks of snow against the water well at the heart of the farm yard.

Taking another step into the cold, Jessie peered around the barn towards the castle. The snow-covered ground extended out a ways, but off in the distance, a scribbled line was visible. The snow halted, being too warm further south to stick, the snow melted, leaving the green slopes of the foothills. It was an odd feeling, looking down upon Regnum. Normally, Jessie had always looked up at the mountains and seen snow, but now he was standing in the snow looking down at the green grass of Regnum. Life as he knew it seemed to be backwards.

Suddenly, Jessie saw something move near the edge of the castle.

"I wonder where these came from? Or why they were left here?" Phillip asked, still concerned about the clothing.

Jessie squinted, trying to see clearly. "Ahhh, Phillip," Jessie said nervously.

"Yeah?"

"We gotta go!"

"What is it?" Phillip said. As he stood up, he had the coat in his hand. Casually slipping one arm into a sleeve, he put the coat on and joined Jessie outside.

Phillip's eyes grew wide as he saw what Jessie had seen. Poking out from above a rolling hill, the blood red banners of King's cavalry flapped in the wind. Slowly but surely, more and more of them were exposed. First the flags, then their heads, and finally the horses they rode on. Only a fifteen or twenty-minute ride out, the King's men were on their way.

"Quick, gear up!" Phillip said, rushing back to the pile of clothing.

"We don't have time for that! We have to go!" Jessie exclaimed. Like most young boys, Jessie always felt he would tough out the cold.

"Jessie, put the clothes on!" Phillip ordered in a stern fatherly voice.

"Fine, but if I'm captured while trying to put on some winter pants, I'm blaming you," Jessie said, as he hopped around trying to pull the winter leggings on.

In just a few minutes, the mysterious gift of clothing was put on. Phillip patted himself down, making sure he was covered head to toe, to ensure their best chance of survival in the blistering cold mountain range known as No Man's Land.

Then Phillip rushed over to the fireplace. Laid out on the soft ground was the elk hide. "Where is the bread?" Phillip asked. Jessie gulped hard. It was, in that moment, that he realized he had made a grave mistake. In the excitement of Mischka's Miracle, Jessie had gobbled up every last crumb of their bread reserves.

"There is no more…" Jessie admitted, with a shaky voice.

"What do you mean there is no more?" Phillip shouted.

"We ate it all," Jessie explained.

"We? I only had one little piece," Phillip grumbled.

"Well… I was hungry."

"Yeah, well…" Philip began, but before he could finish, Mischka scampered up his leg and plunged into a heavy lapel pocket on Phillip's jacket.

"Enough!" she scolded, "We don't have time for this! The cavalry will be here in a matter of minutes."

"Fine," Phillip huffed, "Grab the Book of Truth."

Jessie sheepishly handed the Book of Truth to Phillip. With it, he wrapped the key and his bottle of ale in the elk hide and tied it to the knapsack stick. Throwing it over his shoulder, Phillip led them out of the warm barn and into the untamed mountains.

Blistering cold, slippery slopes, and jagged rocks, hidden by the fresh blanket of snow, lay in wait. If the Titans couldn't capture them, they would have to find a way to survive the mountain range. Not far beyond the farm did the ground become rocky. It was here that a majority of the boulders and slabs of rocks had peeled away from the tallest cliffs of the mountains and fallen to the hills below. Knowing the cavalry was hot on their trail, they rushed along, finding the ground difficult to navigate and surprisingly slippery, they were forced to slow down or else face an injury that would surely get them caught.

Not only did the fresh snow hide the dangers beneath, but it also left a trail of footprints for the cavalry to follow. Hoping to escape into the mountains, their hearts were set on finding the Great White Eagle. *Maybe, just maybe,* Phillip thought, *we can outrun the cavalry long enough to find the Great White Eagle. He will protect us.*

Without realizing it, they had already gained great elevation. The hump of the mountain brought them quickly upwards. Coming to the first ridge, it was a tall, smooth-faced ridge that ran east and west. There was no way over it, so Phillip led Jessie along its edge. Slowly, the ridge's height lowered until they could hop over it. Running parallel to it was a second ridge, with a small ravine between them that would allow them to climb higher into the mountain. As they reached a new height, they looked down.

Below them, they could see the King's cavalry searching the farmyard. "Keep moving!" Phillip ordered. "It's only a matter of time before they follow our tracks."

Already panting hard, Jessie reached out and scraped some snow off a rocky lip next to him and held it to his lips. Slowly, the cold snow melted, and he drank. Realizing just how cold the snow was, he was grateful Phillip made him dress warmly. The mountain range stood tall all around them. Layers upon layers of rock towered high. They did not know where they were going, but if their direction brought them higher up, they were happy with it. With their backs to the castle, they waded into the mountain range. Pillars shot up beside them as mountain spurs stretched out gradually towards the farm below. Some places were bare where the wind had blown the snow away, while others brought it into sheltered areas where the snow was more than a foot deep.

The higher they climbed, the more jagged and tall the rock formations grew. Carved by hundreds of years of weathering, sharp pillars towered around them as they climbed. Using any and every crevasse they could manage to wedge themselves through, they continued up.

There were no trails, no beaten paths, only free climbs that became more difficult with each ridge they capped.

If Jessie were honest with himself, he would have to admit that he had underestimated the mountains. From afar, they look majestic and beautiful, and he thought he could climb it with ease. Thinking, *I could climb that!* However, now, in the heart of it, more than once, he had wondered how they would go on. Every ridge or peak they faced seemed like its very own mountain, but every time they crested one, another much larger peak waited on the other side.

Jessie bit his tongue. He wanted to turn back, give himself up, or find another way, but he remained quiet. He had to trust that Phillip would lead them safely. For his late brother's sake, they had to find the Great White Eagle. But this task was daunting. Many times, they would look around and see only walls of rock in every direction. A small opening here, a quick scale there, and worse, a few times they would have to backtrack because the rock walls were too steep. It seemed like there was no quick way to navigate the mountain, for the rocks were jagged, unpredictable, and uncharted. This put them at a disadvantage because while they were trying to find a way up the mountain, the Titans just had to follow their tracks. They didn't have to guess or stop to look for ways to climb. The trail had already been made for them.

They were exhausted, sweating, and most of all growing hungry. Jessie's stomach grumbled, but he didn't say a word. He knew Phillip blamed him for eating most of the bread, but the lack of food was really dragging Jessie down. He felt tired and sluggish. Each step he took was a battle in his mind. *Keep going. Keep going,* he convinced himself.

To Jessie's surprise, Phillip suggested they take a break at the next peak. The older man was just as tired, but knew of the danger that stalked them from behind. So, until now, he had pushed them forward without any breaks.

Trudging and slipping on the slopes, they climbed. It was the most strenuous thing Jessie had ever had to do. When they finally reached the next peak, both Phillip and Jessie had crawled on their hands and knees the last stretch. The ground angled upward sharply, and walking was not an option. Digging their numb toes and frozen fingers into the hardened snow, they pulled themselves onto the peak.

Their blood pumped through their veins, but their ears and noses all stung from the cold. However, despite being completely exhausted, what lay before them made all the work worth it.

The view set before them was breathtaking. Partly because they were out of breath from the climb, but also because the mountain range in front of them was indescribable.

A lofty mountain saddle stretched out before them. Like a shallow bowl, the mountain dipped in front of them. Higher peaks on their left bridged down into a long ridge that ran to meet them where they stood. To their right was a raised valley that disappeared into the cloudy skyline. The mountain saddle before them looked as if it used to be the end of the valley, but had sunk deep into the mountain. A sheer cliff remained between the two. Over time, rock gave way, and a landslide of scree, small loose rocks, formed. Sloping from the valley above to the mountain saddle below. Like a frozen waterfall, they rested silently in the blistering cold wind.

Scree Falls, Phillip thought, as he took in the majestic view. There was also a large shard of rock hanging in the balance above the landslide of scree. Frozen in place, it looked as if it had broken off the valley's peak and slid down the valley itself years ago. Half of the huge rock hovered over the scree landslide, while half of it clung to the base of the valley. Like a boat teetering on the edge of a waterfall, the shard of rock rested.

Now, the ridge that they stood on extended to their right, but was met by raised cliffs and jagged rocks. So, to their left and their right, the terrain looked difficult. Their only hope would be to go down into the saddle and head north.

Luckily, across the mountain saddle to the north, the snow covered the ground. From where they stood, the blanket of white seemed to stretch out north forever, blending into the horizon. *Gradual and clean!* Jessie thought, filled with relief.

Resting from the vigorous journey, they soaked in every inch of the landscape. Every fold, layer, and point. It didn't take long before they began to cool down and needed to get moving again. By now, the sun was beyond high noon. The last thing they needed was to find themselves without shelter at nightfall.

Standing up, trying to regain some of the warmth they had lost, they turned around and looked behind them. To their surprise, many of the mountain peaks behind them also stretched up higher than they were now. When navigating them, they took routes around their bases that gradually brought them to where they were now. They scanned the mountain range and realized there was so much more to the mountain than they knew. When you are crawling your way up, sunk into valleys, crevices, and other low areas, you miss seeing a lot of the mountain itself. Off to the left, tall skinny towers poked up. Like arrows resting in a quiver, they shot up in clusters. There was so much to see that they could spend hours looking. Bracing themselves against the wind, they looked downward between the peaks, pillars, and rock formations and could see a glimpse of Regnum and the Castle. Like little specks of sand, the village could be seen in the very faraway distance.

"They look like ants," Mischka squeaked, peeking out of Phillip's lapel pocket. Although the pocket held plenty of warmth for her to survive, her whiskers were covered with frost.

"Ironic…" Phillip said, peering down at his small friend.

"I feel like an ant!" Jessie said. "This mountain is huge!"

"Beautiful…" Mischka squeaked. Never in her life had she imagined she would ever see anything like it. With her tiny legs, it would have taken her years to scamper this far. However, by the Great White Eagles' graces here, she was. *Magnificent!* She thought.

"The scrolls say the Great White Eagle carved the mountains. He must have huge talons!" Phillip said.

"You got that right! Look at those deep cuts," Jessie said, pointing to a set of ravines below, filling in with blowing snow as they spoke. *I wish Richard was here… I wish Andy was here…* Jessie thought. A sad look fell on his face.

"What is it?" Phillip asked. Recognizing the pain in his eyes, Phillip placed a hand on Jessie's shoulder and squeezed.

"I just miss… I miss my friends. I hope Andy and Eva are alright," Jessie said. "I wish they could see this."

"If they escaped the castle grounds, your friends have a chance!" Phillip said. But his words held a sting. *If…* rung in Jessie's ear.

"Do you think they did?" Jessie asked.

Seeing that Jessie was worried about his friends, Phillip chose his next words carefully. He knew Jessie needed hope more than he needed to worry. "I'm sure they did."

"Then they must be on their way to the Elves," Jessie said with confidence.

"Ahh, yes. That is a good place for them to go. The Elves will protect them."

"Yeah?" Jessie questioned.

"Pious beings they are. They will do right by the Great White Eagle. They will do right by your friends," Phillip assured him.

Just then, they heard an echo. Unsure exactly where the noise came from, since the echo of the muffled voices bounced off the mountainside into every direction, they peered down below them.

"The King's men," Mischka suggested. She was right. Seconds later, a Titan appeared on the top of a peak that rested far below them. As the bird flies, he was only a few hundred yards away; however, because of the ups and downs of the mountain, the Titan had to travel at least a mile on foot.

Realizing that brought peace to Phillip. He remained calm. "We should be off now. Let's go straight north. It looks like easy terrain," Phillip suggested.

"I like the sound of that," Jessie said with a smile.

Phillip was surprised by how far behind the Titans seemed to be. Considering he was an old out-of-shape man, he assumed the Titans, in peak physical condition, would have closed in on them. However, the odds were stacked against the Titans. The jagged rising and falling terrain made it impossible for the horses to climb, rendering them useless once they arrived at the base of the mountain. This forced the Titans that rode them to travel on foot. Although these men were agile in battle, their clanking armor, cold as ice to the touch, made it very difficult for them to scale rocks and cliffs. It slowed them down tremendously. Although bulky, their armor was the only thing holding in their body heat. So, taking it off would cause them to freeze in the rigidly cold temperatures of the No Man's Land Mountain range.

Even the Pegasi struggled in the weather. Although they were able to fly ahead of the Titans, the moisture in the air clung to their wings, and ice formed on their feathers. It became too heavy for them to fly continually, so they had to find places to land and break the ice off their feathers. This all gave Phillip, Mischka, and Jessie time to get ahead of them.

Jessie looked back to see a Pegasus join a Titan. Using the hilt of his sword, the Titan beat at the Pegasus' wings, shedding the ice.

Quickly, Jessie and Phillip slid down the slope towards the mountain saddle. Unfortunately, the snow in the mountain saddle was deep. In some places, it drifted waist deep. The mountain air caused the snow to crystallize. This made their trek worse. One step, the snow surface held their weight, while the next, they plunged through the crust waist deep. If you have ever walked through snow like this, you know it's the worst kind. To make matters worse, the snow down in the saddle blew steadily, making blizzard-like conditions.

Straight across they trudged. By the time they had reached halfway across, Mischka peeked up, looking over Phillip's shoulder, and could see through the blowing snow a Titan dismounting a Pegasus. Then another set, one Titan and one Pegasus. The Titans chipped away at the newly formed ice on the Pegasi's wings.

It's a different feeling when those hunting you are within sight. Even though they were hundreds of yards ahead of them, knowing the enemy could see them made everything dire. As they trudged along, they became winded, but pushed through. Finally, the waist-deep snow lowered to almost no snow at all. In some spots, they could even see that the wind had brushed the face of the mountain bare. This allowed them to run; Jessie in front and Phillip close behind. The further they ran, the more blind they became. The wind whipped and caused whiteout conditions. They could only see ten feet in front of them now, and the Titans behind them faded into white. But they kept running. Their eyes watered from the wind, and they felt tiny pellets of ice plaster their face. Mischka became nervous and scared. She ducked down deep into Phillip's pocket.

Jessie stared straight forward, looking for anything to get them out of the wind. Suddenly, he saw a dark void only feet in front of him. With snow still blowing, it was hard to make out exactly what he was coming up to, but with each step closer, the void grew before him. Suddenly, he realized what it was. Trying to dig his heels into the snow-covered ground to stop, Jessie felt no traction. Leaning backwards, he fell onto his backside, but still his forward momentum continued. An uncontrollable slide had taken effect. "Phillip!" he shouted. However, Phillip too was in a deadly slide behind him.

Reaching to his waist, Phillip had tucked a dagger away before their journey had begun. Quickly, he yanked it out from under his jacket and stabbed the dagger into the ice-covered mountain. It carved deep into the ice, slowing Phillip down. At the very last second, Phillip reached out and grabbed the collar of Jessie's jacket, and the dagger bit into the ice hard, jolting them both to a dead stop.

Breathless, Jessie scooted back from the ledge. The dark void he saw had been a massive gorge. Below, the Great Northern River rested. The top of the river was frozen while water rushed beneath. A handful of rocks forced out over the edge from Jessie's slide and tumbled down. As if he had hung at the edge for minutes, he saw them fall. Down, down, and still further down before they shattered against the ice of the river below.

Their eyes had deceived them. Back on the peak, when they overlooked the saddle of the mountain, the blowing snow masked the gorge, making it look like a gradual slope to the mountain peak beyond. That mistake had almost cost them their lives.

Jessie shook. Not from the cold but from imagining if he had been the rocks that he had watched crash into the gorge below.

"Jessie… Jessie. We have to go!" Phillip said as he shook Jessie and helped him to stand.

"Go where?" Jessie asked.

Phillip thought about the landscape. *Good question…* He thought. He closed his eyes and imagined the view. To the left, the mountain peaks staggered straight up. Maybe if they had followed the ridge, they could have found a way up or around them, but now they would have to scale from the bases. Any second, the Titans could be on their tails. That would not do. That was when he remembered the Scree falls. *It will be dangerous. But what other choice is there?* He thought. Having to make a choice, he decided they would scale the scree. "This way. Grab my shoulder. We can't afford to get separated!" he shouted over the wind.

Jessie did. He placed his hand on Phillip's shoulder and followed closely behind. Carefully, Phillip ran east. Using the edge of the gorge as a guide in the blistering cold blizzard, they walked swiftly. More than once, the ground was plagued with large cracks that they had to go around. The gorge's edge weaved in and out and was laced with drop-offs, large boulders, and unforeseen dangers.

The only good thing to come from this winter misery was that the wind blew so hard that their tracks had been brushed away within minutes. Any Titan or Pegasus that followed would have no visual trace of them.

After nearly half an hour Phillip began to see traces of the scree. Small shards of rock were scattered along the ground. But, finally, they were at Scree Fall's base.

As they scaled higher, the bluff they were on sheltered them from the wind. Being high enough now, they could see back to the peak they once stood on. Standing watch were a Pegasus and two Titans who had caught up with them. They each held something in their hand... a weapon. Seeing Jessie and Phillip, they rushed along the top of the ridge, avoiding the saddle as long as they could, before being forced down towards the base of the scree. The bluff protected them from the wind, and they could still see each other clearly.

Just then, Jessie stepped on a rock that gave way. The rock shifted beneath his weight, and a small chain reaction began to take place. The rock beneath his foot shifted slightly, which caused several more to readjust. Freezing in fear, Jessie held his breath until everything was still again.

"Jessie! Careful! The last thing we need is an avalanche of rocks." Phillip shouted. However, Phillip knew that he was just as capable of stepping on the wrong loose rock as Jessie was. If they were not careful, they could cause an avalanche of rock and snow, burying them alive.

Slowly, they climbed the volatile mountain's edge, slow but steady. Peering down behind them, the two Titans and the Pegasus had reached the bottom of the scree. If the Pegasus had not been hunting them down, Jessie would have felt bad for the creature. Its head dropped down, and its wings drooped to the rocky mountain ground. It looked exhausted, defeated, and weighed down by the ice on its wings.

Then, directly below them, two more Titans emerged from the blowing snow and stood at the base of the scree. Resting for just a moment, they gazed up at Phillip and Jessie. Hate was in their eyes. Pushing forward, the exhausted Titans began up the scree. With the armor as extra weight, their climbing was abrupt. Each step they took rocks gave way below them. Their lack of caution began to cause rocks to shift and tumble in a chain reaction. So much so that the rocks beneath Jessie and Phillips' feet began to shift because of it.

Almost to the top, Jessie and Phillip heard a deep creak. Looking up, the shadow from the massive rock that hung in the balance over the scree falls cast down on them. The creak came from it. *Oh no. If the rocks shift enough, that teetering rock will come down on us all...* Phillip feared.

It creaked and moaned as the rocks began to shift at the Titan's careless movements.

"We have to hurry!" Phillip cried.

Just then, something struck a rock in front of Phillip, and it splintered into pieces. Frantic, he looked down at the Titans. The fresh Titans who stood watch and had come to the scree by way of the ridge held bows in their hands. Before Phillip could warn Jessie, a second arrow struck just above Jessie's head.

There was no time to waste. Becoming more and more careless, they scrambled up the side of the scree. Two Titans pursued, while two Titans stood beside the exhausted Pegasi and fired arrows. Some arrows ricocheted off the rocks while others would get wedged in between them, but thankfully, none struck Jessie or Phillip. As they scurried higher, the arrows became less and less accurate.

Although they were out of reach of the arrow's sting, they were still in grave danger of what the arrows caused next. Every arrow disrupted the scree, causing an uncontrollable chain reaction. The massive rock shifted suddenly, sounding off a loud pop, causing a few rocks to spit out from beneath it. Once still, the balanced rock was now beginning to teeter on the edge.

As they reached the very top, they stepped away from the massive rock. Shouting down to the Titans, Phillip warned them. "Stop! You are all in danger!" he shouted. Standing beside it, he could see just how much it was rocking back and forth.

The weight of the rock shifted once more, this time shattering the rocks beneath it. It then slid forward two feet before halting. With it, the ground shook. Phillip peered down at the Titans. Both Pegasi had regained enough strength to take flight and were on their way towards them. "Go back! Save yourselves!" Phillip hollered. But it was too late. Like rolling thunder from an incoming storm, a deep hum bellowed behind them.

At first, small rocks tumbled at high speeds down the mountain valley. They flung so fast that they completely cleared the bluff and vanished deep into the blowing snow behind the Titans. But the small rocks grew. Larger ones began coming, and with them, they could see layers of snow begin to shift high up on the mountain valley. As if the earth itself was cracking, the sheets of snow separated from one another. Then, tumbling, hundreds of small snowballs led a charge. Following close behind was a wave of snow. In their carelessness, the Titans had triggered an avalanche that could claim them all. The snow would sweep them all away.

That was when a large rock, tumbling down the valley, struck the massive rock that hung over the scree falls. Like an explosion, the tumbling rock shattered into a million pieces and caused Phillip and Jessie to fall to the ground. More rocks zinged by, followed by tumbling snow. The collision forced the balancing rock to tip further, now, there was no stopping it. With loud chattering echoes, the rock's weight shifted, crushing the frozen scree beneath it. No longer supported by firm, frozen rocks, the larger rock hung in the balance no more and began to slide. Panicked, Phillip and Jessie crawled behind a large protruding rock that rested on the bluff's edge, not too far from the once teetering rock, and clung to one another. They couldn't watch. Clenching their eyes shut, the avalanche came full force.

For minutes, they sat in fear. The avalanche howled around them. Phillip, completely shocked they were still alive, opened his eyes. He could see nothing. Snow crashed down all around them. However, the rock acted like a force field protecting them from the deadly act of nature. Jessie leaned into Phillip even more. Gripping him harder, he couldn't look.

Then, as if nothing had happened, the mountain was quiet. The wind whistled, but the snow had settled around them. The sun shone high above them, and the skies were crystal blue.

"What just happened…" Jessie said in disbelief.

"Is this real? Jessie, are you really alive? Am I really alive?" Phillip asked, squaring up with Jessie and cupping his face in his hands. They both wore massive smiles as they looked into each other's eyes. "Haha!" Phillip began to chuckle. His chuckle, like a rolling snowball, steadily grew until it was a deep belly laugh. Next thing they knew, Phillip and Jessie were jumping and dancing with joy. Shouting, "We're alive! We're alive!" Phillip was so excited that he ran over to the rock that saved their life. *Mwah!* He kissed it!

Their excitement lasted for a minute, until they looked over the bluff. Below the saddle of the mountain was filled with snow, and there was no life left. Their spark of joy fizzled out, and the smiles faded into a soft frown. Quickly, a tear rolled down Phillip's cheek.

"I'm sorry, Phillip," Jessie said. "We are lucky we aren't down there with them…" Jessie said solemnly. He was right, but Phillip knew every last one of the men and Pegasi that had chased them. Now they were gone.

"Come on, we best get going. It will be dark soon," Phillip said.

"Phillip?" Jessie asked, "Where's the knapsack?" realizing he did not have it, nor did Phillip.

"I'm sorry, Jessie, but I lost it… It was either you or the knapsack," Phillip said. When they had almost slipped into the gorge, Phillip used one hand to wield his dagger, while his other hand caught Jessie. That left the knapsack in the wind. Within it, the Book of Truth and its key were lost.

"Thank you… Phillip," Jessie said. Then he, Mischka, and Phillip headed up the valley in search of the Great White Eagle.

Chapter 25
Preparations

"**Y**our majesty!" Felix, the Royal Pegasus guard, cried out as he landed his flight in a soft trot before the king.

"Felix! Please tell me you have brought good news," the king responded. He had spent most of the morning pacing back and forth in the courtyard awaiting good news. He hoped his men would find the traitors.

"I'm afraid not," Felix said, bowing low.

"Then why have you returned?" The King asked, irritated. He knew Felix was assigned to follow the trail of his brother and Jessie. "Has my brother outwitted you?"

"We found them, but..." Felix began.

"But what?! Where are they?" the king shouted, cutting him off. The servants in the courtyard quickly left the area. They had been cleaning up the castle after the vicious storm, but could tell by the king's tone that they would be safer if they were not in his presence.

"In the No Man's Mountain Range, Sire," Felix said as his ears drooped.

"Did you go after them?" he pressed.

"We did, Your Majesty." Felix again began, before being cut off.

"And?"

"My whole platoon died in those mountains... I am the only one left," Felix said, saddened by the loss of his friends.

"How is it possible that a coward like my brother and one boy were able to kill countless trained Titans and a few Pegasi?" the King asked, inching closer to Felix.

"No, there was an avalanche, Sire. Your brother warned us to turn back. He tried to save us," Felix said. He remembered seeing the cloud of snow rushing down the mountain and hearing the echo of Phillip's voice. He had been one of the Pegasi in pursuit, but at the last second, he had pulled up and retreated. Being forced away by the wind gust, he watched his brothers in arms vanish beneath the snow. Scared for his life, knowing his wings would freeze up for good if he didn't return instantly, he rushed back down the mountain.

"You will not speak of my brother's warning..." the King ordered. Felix gulped hard. "Do you hear me?" the King asked for assurance.

"Yes..." Felix said.

"My brother will hang for this!" he said as he swirled around and began to think to himself. Everything within Felix wanted him to stand up for Phillip, but he knew if he did, he would be labeled a traitor himself. He knew that what happened to his comrades was not Phillip's fault. In fact, Felix had realized that it was the Titans who had caused it all. Their arrows dislodged the rocks, which caused the avalanche to come down. Felix knew that if he disobeyed the King in this matter that he himself could receive the Alatum punishment.

Rubbing his chin, the King had an idea. He turned back around and faced Felix. "I want the names of those men! And the Pegasi too!" he ordered.

"Yes, Sire. I will find a Titan to write them down for me," Felix responded with a low bow.

"Gather another group of men. Twice the Pegasi! You will lead them to my brother," the King ordered.

"But Sire, if I may speak freely," Felix begged.

"What is it!" he snapped.

"Those mountains are dangerous. It took half a day to climb it ourselves. There was no sign that your brother survived the avalanche himself. If he's not dead already, surely he and the boy won't survive the night. I'm afraid your brother is dead... buried by the snow..." Felix said softly. The King looked him in the eye. Realizing that his brother might be dead caught him off guard, and his eyes began to swell with tears. "I'm sorry. I'm sorry for your loss..." Felix said, sensing the King's tears.

However, not wanting to seem weak, he cleared his throat and snapped back at Felix. "You shut your snout. My brother is not dead!" the King blurted. "But I suppose you are right. It would be a waste to lose more good men. Instead, post guards along the base of the mountain range. If he survives… when he comes down from those treacherous mountains, we will be waiting," he said.

"Yes, your Majesty," Felix said. Then the King turned away once again. As he was leaving, he shouted back towards the Pegasus.

"Get me those names by tonight, and I promise the Kingdom will know your name. A hero, one that escaped the clutches of my murderous brother," the King said as he marched away.

The King was angry, hurt, and if he was honest with himself, worried for his brother. The truth of the matter is that if King Fraust had wanted Phillip dead, he would have done it years ago. However, a soft spot remained in his hardening heart for him. Although there was one soft spot, Timothy Fraust was still angry at the prisoners and his brother. If he's not dead, I'll find him. I'll lock him up with no free range to the castle. He's my brother, but he betrayed me. He must suffer the consequences, King Fraust thought.

The eventful days had left him unstable. Anger flared in his heart, and a desire to regain control over his subjects. Eagerly, he thought of what he must do. I'll send a message to all who think they will try to follow these traitors' footsteps. Gillian will be their example. He was the first to try and be a hero. He will pay.

Eager to set his plan in motion, the King rushed around the castle grounds. Ensuring everything would be prim and proper for the evening's festivities, he had planned.

"Get this castle into shape, there is a very important ceremony tonight. Many special guests and announcements," he ordered, clapping his hands as if to push the servants along and hurry them up. The storm from the night before left the castle grounds a mess. Tree branches, leaves, and other debris lay scattered about.

He made sure every hallway, barn, closet, and corner had been swept and put in order. He would make sure that the whole land, Regnum and beyond, knew he was a powerful King. He would make sure no creature dared go against his rule.

Next, he made his way to the Pegasi stable yard, checking in with Zolton, he pressed him. "You will be setting out to the foothills of No Man's Land shortly, I assume?"

"Yes, Sire. You will be happy to know we have extended our search radius into the Forbidden Forest for the boy and the girl. We have doubled our guard in the clearings and will search every inch of legal ground," he said. Legal as in everything but the Forbidden Circle itself. Zolton had been Malus's right-hand Pegasus long enough that he knew the King desired to find Andy and Eva more than Jessie, so he assured the King that even though his new orders were to establish a line along the base of the mountains, he had not forgotten about the other two traitors.

"Very good, Zolton. Malus is lucky to have such a dedicated and trustworthy steed at his side!" the King praised him. Zolton lifted his head high and smiled down at the King with pride. "Your orders at the mountains?" the King inquired. They were his orders, but he liked hearing them back from the mouths of his men. This assured him that they were received well.

"Multiple brigades will set up camp along the base of the No Man's Mountains. Each group is an arrow's shot away from the others. Our first grouping will be on this side of the Mountain Lake, and the last grouping in front of the Originem Mountain range near the start of the Acies forest," Zolton said.

"Very good! The No Man's Land Mountains are unforgiving, so if my brother has any sense, he will have to turn back and come down. That's where you will be waiting for him!" King Fraust said with pride in his plan.

"Yes, your majesty. A beautiful plan."

"Very good, carry on," the King said, satisfied with his conversation.

The King's next stop was the kitchen. You cannot have a magnificent announcement with special guests without a feast to go with it.

"Servant girl!" the King shouted joyfully.

"Yes, your majesty," she said, putting down her work and curtsying low before the king. She never looked him in the eye, instead, she stared at the floor.

"Tonight, there will be an extravagant ceremony. I need you to prepare food for the whole kingdom. Pork, Beef, and Chicken! A meal to remember!"

"Yes, your majesty."

"We will have dwarves, goblins, and humans as well. We should have fresh vegetables, fruits, rock bread, and wine!" he said.

"Yes, your majesty," she said with a nervous quiver in her voice. Such a feast with only a few hours to prepare would be impossible. However, she was afraid to say anything to the king.

As he left the kitchen, the servant girl began to frantically gather anything in the kitchen that could help her prepare. Moments later, Isabell came in.

"What's the matter, Jenny?" Isabell asked, seeing the panicked look in her eyes and her flushed red cheeks.

"The King," she said, rolling her eyes.

"What has he done now?" Isabell asked.

"He has ordered me to prepare a feast," she said, not stopping her work.

"Oh? When is it?" Isabell inquired.

"Tonight…" Jenny said with a tear rolling down her cheek. Isabell understood immediately the undertaking that job was.

"I'll go get help. We can do this," she assured her friend. Then quickly she disappeared to find other servant girls to help. She even recruited some of the stable boys to go and gather the meat, vegetables, and fruits from the village.

Walking into the Throne room, the King settled into his Throne. Two Titans stood beside him. One on his right and the other on his left. They stood like statues.

"Fetch me Ashby," he said. Ashby was the event organizer.

"Yes, Sire," the Titan on his left said. With a quick bow, he was off. Minutes later, Ashby arrived. The man was short and thin. He held himself with great poise, and you could tell by looking at him that he was arrogant. Wearing green leggings and a stiff tunic, cut off at the arms, it went down to his knees. The tunic was golden with a diamond-patterned stitch all over. His under tunic was a long-sleeved shirt made with the same green material as his leggings. Both his legs and arms seemed to protrude from beneath his golden tunic. He also wore a white ruffled scarf around his neck. His face was clean-shaven except for a mustache. It was elegant, stretched out from either cheek, and it had been carefully curled back towards his face. Making large O's. His black hair was slicked back, and he held a small staff, made of a beautiful dark walnut wood, with the handle on top laced with gold. In addition, Ashby had a writing quill resting behind his ear and a dried square of elk hide tucked in his armpit.

"You called," he said in a deep, yet flamboyant way.

"Yes, yes! We are to have a party tonight!" the King said.

"Oh? And the occasion?" he said, interest piqued.

"A celebration of victory!" the King announced.

"I see," he said, pulling the small square hide from under his arm and the writing quill out from behind his ear. "And who shall I invite?" he asked, ready to write down the details.

"Invite the whole kingdom of Regnum. I want the Goblins of Sodomen and even a few of the important Dwarves. I want a Jester for entertainment, music, and oh… I'll need the executioner," The king said, as he strolled away from the organizer.

"Ohh," Ashby chuckled, "I do love a good show." Ashby was an evil little man. He soaked in the luxuries of King Fraust's good favor and enjoyed watching others suffer.

This will be a spectacle no one will ever forget. The King thought with anger in his heart.

"Anything else, Sire?" Ashby asked.

"Yes, make sure Rachael and William Huntsberg have front row seats," the King ordered.

He had decided that he was done being walked over. He was king after all, and his subjects needed to learn that they must obey him. He had a message to deliver, and he needed to make sure certain individuals heard him loud and clear.

"Very well," Ashby said, then with a bow, "Your Majesty." Ashby turned and left the King's presence to begin at once the preparation of the evening.

That afternoon, the castle buzzed with work. Servants, stable boys, Ashby, and all the King's men prepared. Each with their own orders. They work diligently not to disappoint an already volatile king.

Late that afternoon, Malus stretched his wings and he went to meet the army at the base of the mountain. The No Man's Land mountains scared him, not because of its harsh conditions, but because all the legends say that this is where the Great White Eagle would be found. The last thing he wanted was the Great White Eagle's return. Malus had great influence over all the creatures, but compared to the Great White Eagle, he was nothing.

However, with half of the Kingdom's army standing watch at the base of the mountain, he felt sure that if the Great White Eagle showed himself, the King's army could hold him off long enough to escape.

As dramatic as King Fraust had been, Malus knew that the King was not overreacting. Malus had been around since the beginning. He had seen the fall of Peacekeepers, the rise of kings and their downfalls, and had seen the Babble and the King's Wars through. He had a hand in pretty much all of it, and because of it, he sensed the wave of turmoil that was headed towards the Kingdom of Regnum.

He knew that Andy, Eva, and Jessie were all a key part of it, too. Like a story book unfolding before his eyes, Malus knew the damage they could cause. His only hope of maintaining his power and influence over all creatures was Jessie.

He needed to find Jessie and convince the boy to serve him, knowing Jessie's greatest desire, Malus could use it as leverage. After all, that's what he had done with King Fraust long before he was king. Without Jessie, Malus could lose it all. Jessie was desperate to get his brother back, so desperate that he would be willing to do anything. Malus planned to exploit this and use him to carry out some very nasty things, all to ensure his power and status among creatures.

Jessie had acted out. Misbehaved. For that, he would need to be punished. That was Malus' intention for this journey. Over the years, Malus had held onto power. He had learned many useful tactics that leveraged control over other creatures. Some creatures caved easily, while others took more convincing. Malus had learned Jessie was one who would need more convincing, and a direct approach would not do. He would aim to inflict pain on others because of his lack of compliance. Eventually, Malus would make sure all creatures knew that because Jessie refused to cooperate with the rule of the land, the consequence was that others would suffer on his behalf. A tactic that the black steed had used in the past to break the spirit of his enemies.

If he could break Jessie's spirit and find him before he found the Great White Eagle, Malus could still find an advantage over the boy. But he must act quickly.

Swooping down, he landed at Zolton's camp. Zolton had set up his men at the base of the Crusade Falls. It was where the Northern River poured out over the high cliffs of the No Man's Land mountain into the foothills of Regnum.

"Zolton!" he shouted, as he came to a stop.

"Yes, Great one?"

"How many men can you spare?" Malus asked.

"My orders were…" Zolton began to protest.

"Your orders from the King were, but you have new orders from me."

Clearing his throat and straightening out, "Yes, Sire," he said.

"So, how many men can you spare?" Malus asked.

"If I may, my lord…" Zolton said, lowering his head with caution.

"Continue…" Malus said, knowing by Zolton's tone the next words would be blunt.

"It is likely Phillip is dead," Zolton said.

"I agree, but let's hope not. I need the boy alive," Malus said.

"I understand, Sire. If…they are alive and make it down off the mountains, how will two men, one of them merely a boy, fight an army?" he asked.

"Precisely, so, how many men can you spare?" he asked Zolton. Malus was clearly asking Zolton to abandon King Fraust's orders for Malus.

"I will gather a group of twenty, Sire."

"Very good," Malus said. Zolton lowered his head and turned to gather a group. "Zolton," he said, causing Zolton to turn back around. "A storm is coming. I've seen days like these before. Chaos, maybe even war."

"You have my complete fealty and service," Zolton affirmed.

"Good. Gather your men and meet me at the most Eastern clearing of Regnum," he ordered. Again, Zolton bowed. This time, Malus let him leave.

Looking up into the mountains, Malus shivered at the thought of the Great White Eagle. Then he lifted himself into the air and headed toward the clearing he had instructed Zolton to meet him at.

Murmurs spread throughout the land. Invites for the ceremony that evening had already been sent out, and so had the rumors of all the escapes. The village of Regnum was well aware that all three traitors had escaped the night before. Confirmed by the increased number of Titan patrols and the accumulating army at the base of No Man's Land Mountains. The people of Regnum knew something big was about to happen.

All would be known for sure in a few hours, at King Fraust's ceremony.

Chapter 26
The Lamb, the Bread, and the Doorway

The sun had slipped below the highest peaks of the mountain, and the temperature dropped. The wind was relentless and blew steadily into their faces. Finally, after hours of fighting forward, Phillip collapsed to the ground. He rolled onto his back and looked up into the darkening sky. He was exhausted and could not move. The snow blew across the rocky ground and whirled around them. Jessie fell to his butt and looked back at Phillip.

"I can't go on," Phillip said. "I'm too old for this."

"Come on, Phillip, we are close. I can feel it," Jessie said, trying to convince him.

"Maybe we should find shelter..." Mischka suggested. As she poked her head out of Phillip's pocket, she had to burrow through some snow that had snuck in with her.

"Go on without me! Leave me here to die!" he said.

"Stop that!" Jessie scolded as he crawled to his feet and came back to Phillip's side.

The cold wind bit their faces. "All I wanted was forgiveness! I came all this way! But I was wrong. What a fool!" Phillip cried. His tears began to freeze on his face.

"Listen to me!" Jessie said, trying to prop Phillip up. "We are not going to die! Remember the High Priest said if we seek the Great White Eagle, we will find life!"

"Jessie, you naive boy! Look around, we've seeked him. Where is he?" he said. "Stupid fool I am. How could I have believed we would actually find him?"

"You're wrong, Phillip! We will find him. We have to!" Jessie said, refusing to believe their journey had been for nothing. "Don't you remember?" Jessie said, reaching down, he tried to pull Phillip's cap down below his ears. However, Phillip, in a tantrum, pushed his hands away.

"Remember what?" he said dramatically.

"The maze? You said yourself that it was a miracle we made it through. And what about Mischka? The Great White Eagle brought her back," Jessie said.

As if the cold, blistering wind had wiped Phillip's memory clean, Jessie's words warmed his heart and reminded him of all they had been through.

"Jessie, but how can we go on? I am weak, I have no strength, and no food to regain it. If we don't starve to death, we will freeze to death," he said.

Jessie looked around. He, too, was starving and weak with hunger. A day in the mountains on an empty stomach would leave anyone faint. His pockets were all full of snow, his fingers and toes numb, and a nasty blister had formed on his big toe.

Then he thought he saw a glimpse of something. He shook his head and focused on the bush in the distance. Again, something moved. *Am I seeing things? Is it just snow?* He asked himself. "Do you see that?" Jessie asked.

Phillip propped himself up and looked in that direction. Squinting, he used one hand to block the blowing snow. "I do! And it looks to be moving?!" Phillip said with a curious excitement.

They scrambled to their feet and rushed over to it. Caught in a bush, a lamb had been snagged. Even more surprising, something else had been caught by the bush. Covering their faces from the blowing snow, they were in complete shock at what they found.

Tangled in the branches of the bush was a long stick, tied tightly to the end of that stick was an elk hide knapsack. Even more strange, a set of footprints sat in the snow. From off in the distance, looking to be left by a small boy, the prints marched right up to the bush, but beyond the bush, only the evidence of a bird's talons marked the snow. However, seconds later, the wind brushed the mountainside clean, and all the prints were gone.

"I don't believe it!" Jessie exclaimed. Immediately, Phillip pulled out his dagger. "What are you doing?"

"What does it look like?" Phillip said. "We have to eat."

"I guess… but what if this lamb belongs to someone?" he asked.

"Who do you think lives up here?" Phillip asked, looking out at the dimming horizon. Bare it was, covered by blowing snow.

"What if the lamb wandered up here?" Jessie thought out loud.

"Jessie, we barely survived it this far. A feeble lamb would not have. This lamb was put here," Phillip said confidently.

"By who?"

"By the only creature capable of it. Look, it's our knapsack, I'm sure of it. Look inside." Phillip commanded.

Untangling it from the bush, Jessie peeled back the corner of the elk hide. Inside was the Book of Truth. "You're right. But how?" he asked.

"Exactly. What creature would be up here in the first place? What creature could have found this knapsack at the bottom of the gorge and knew it was ours? You tell me which creature!" Phillip said, as hope began to refuel in his heart.

"The Great White Eagle?"

"It has to be!" Phillip said with glee.

Mischka, who had been safely in Phillip's pocket, had poked her head to see all that was going on. With the discovery of the lamb and the knapsack, she had grown excited. She crawled out of Phillip's pocket to investigate the bush a bit closer, but in doing so, she put herself in danger. A great gust of wind overpowered her, and she was blown off into the wind. Tumbling out of sight, she disappeared behind a large boulder. Panicked, Phillip started her way.

"Phillip, I'll go. Take care of the lamb… If we lose it, we will surely not survive the night," Jessie said, understanding just how important the lamb's meat would be for their survival. Phillip nodded, and instantly Jessie was off into the dusk.

Uncontrollably, Mischka tumbled along the mountainside. Until she came to a sudden stop, her body thumped against something. Shaking her head, she looked up. *I cannot believe it,* she thought.

Following the direction of the wind, Jessie searched for Mischka, and then he saw it too. *No way!* He thought. Fixated on what he saw, he did not see Mischka leaning up against the base of it. Rushing over, he grabbed onto the iron latch, slid it open, and the heavy wooden door flung open. With it, the wind pushed Mischka inside. Catching a glimpse of her body tumbling, Jessie called out. "Mischka?" he shouted over the whistling wind.

"I'm here!" she squeaked.

"What is this place?" he asked.

"I don't know, but it's home for the night. The light was growing dim, but they could see just enough to know it was everything they needed and more. Yet another miracle.

The cave was very shallow, but at the center of the cave, there was a fire pit. Surrounding that were logs arranged for seating. Stacked along the back wall was firewood, cut and ready to be burned.

"Stay here! I'll go get Phillip!" Jessie exclaimed. He was smiling, but from within the cave, Mischka could only see his silhouette against the gray skyline.

Racing as fast as he could, he found Phillip. By now, the grim deed was done. "Phillip! Phillip!" Jessie said gleefully.

"What is it?" Phillip said. Jessie reached down and grabbed the knapsack.

"It's a freaking fire pit!" Jessie shouted with joy. But before Phillip could question him, he was off running back to the mysterious cave.

Wiping clean the blade of his dagger on his pant leg, he placed it back in the sheath at his belt. Then he picked up the lamb and followed Jessie.

Seeing the cave from a distance, Phillip felt excitement grow. Soon, he was running and almost beat Jessie inside.

"There is actually a fire pit! And wood!" Jessie said, pointing to everything within the cave. It was better than a fire pit, it was also a shelter. With a safe place like this to rest their heads, they were going to live.

Phillip knew the most important thing for them to do now was to start a fire. Feeling around the fire pit, he found two rocks that he could use to create a spark. Then he glanced over at the logs lined along the back of the cave.

"Jessie, grab me a log."

"Yes, Sir!" Jessie said with excitement.

Once Jessie handed him the log, Phillip's excitement grew. "Alright! A birch tree even!" he said. "Birch trees are fantastic fire-starting trees. Their bark is like thin layers of paper, and naturally, they have a sort of chemical that repels water and is highly flammable."

With the birch log, he began to peel the white paper-like layers of bark off and set them to the side. Beneath those, a stringy fiber-like bark remained. Next, he stripped a handful of those from the log. Then, using his fingers, he mulched them up until they were fuzzy. He laid one sheet of white bark down like a platform, then balled the fuzzy strips on top.

Quickly, he struck the rocks together and created a spark. As if waiting its whole life to be lit on fire, the ball of fuzzy bark burst forth with flames. Then, using the rest of the paper-like bark, Phillip gently created a teepee structure over the dancing flames. In no time at all, the flames had grown, consuming the birch bark, and now they could build it up and warm themselves.

Leaving Jessie in charge of watching the fire, Phillip prepared the lamb.

"I'm gonna need the knapsack stick," Phillip said to Jessie. Untying the elk hide sack from the stick, he handed it over to Phillip. Feeling the book inside, Jessie desired to look at its beautiful gold stitching again. Holding it in his hands, the beautiful golden stitching brought his mind back to the first time he had ever seen the book. In the house of rubble, he and his brother had been in the middle of a lightweight wrestling championship showdown, a rematch, of course. That was when Eva and Andy had found it.

"We found this book," Andy had said. "But it has a lock on it."

"Eh, reading sucks anyways," his brother said.

"Guess the lock saved us from having to read it," Jessie had added.

The memory brought back a flood of emotions. A time when things were simple. His brother was still alive, and he was with his friends. At the time, Jessie couldn't have cared less about the book, but now it seemed like one of the most important things in his possession. Now, here Jessie sat with the Book of Truth, and they had found the key to open it.

The pain of missing his brother and being separated from his friends welled up in his chest. Tears began to run down his cheeks. Whipping them away, he set the book down beside him, and reached down and flipped the elk hide wide open. To his amazement, besides the Book of Truth, he also found three loaves of bread.

"Phillip! Mischka!" he said, holding up the bread.

"Where did it come from? Wait a minute! Where's my ale?" Phillip asked.

"Phillip!" Mischka scolded, "It's about time you quit drinking that anyway."

Suddenly, Phillip burst forth with a great belly laugh. "You are right, my dear friend! Tonight we feast on bread and lamb!" he said. They all knew exactly where it came from. The same creature who had put the knapsack in the bush, the same creature who gave them more bread. It had to have been the Great White Eagle. They were getting close to finding him, they could all feel it. They were so overjoyed that they had not at all realized that the Key was missing. At least in the present moment, they were happy, warm, and content.

While Phillip roasted the lamb over the fire, Jessie broke off pieces of bread to share. This time, he only used up one loaf and saved the others for the next day.

Night had finally fallen on the mountains and left the outside in complete darkness. However, within the cave, the fire flickered and left no darkness. Only the shadows of Phillip, Jessie, and little Mischka danced on the walls behind them.

The heavy door sealed well and only a small draft squeezed in, but the fire kept them so warm, their jackets soon lay on the floor beside them.

They all ate to satisfaction and were merry.

Chapter 27
"I Used to be You, Don't Become Me."

Deep into the night, the three sat around the fire, telling stories and sharing laughs. Eventually, Mischka suggested they clean up.

"Make sure things are ready to go, in case we are found by Titans or Pegasi. A quick escape is vital."

The elk hide sack rested on the cave floor, and two loaves of bread rested on top of it (the third had been eaten!). However, one corner of the hide was folded over. While trying to pick the sack up, that corner unfolded, and something fell out and rolled across the ground. Immediately, they knew what it was. In the size and shape of a toothpick, an Eagle's Heart crystal rolled to a stop.

Mischka scampered quickly over to the mouse-sized crystal and gazed upon its soft green glow. "Can it be?" she squealed.

"Mischka, what is it?" Phillip asked the little mouse about the small, pointy crystal she was holding in her paw.

"This is called a Mapier. The human version is the rapier sword, but these were designed just for mice!" Mischka said proudly.

"No offense, but what could such a small creature use a sword for?" Jessie asked. Phillip began to chuckle in the corner because he knew the question Jessie asked was very offensive to a proud mouse like Mischka Meese.

"You listen here! We may be small, but the mice were the Centaurs' closest allies during the Babble Wars! Read a history book!" she spouted.

"Ahh Jessie," Phillip said as he sat back down beside him and put his arm around his shoulder. "You see, the design of the Mapier sword is long, slim, and sharp. But it has small leather straps that allow the mouse to fasten it to their tail. Leaving all four of their paws free for maneuvering on the battlefield."

"Exactly right! Want to go a round or two, little boy?" Mischka said as she slipped the Mapier over her tail and began to fasten it.

"Oh no! I did not mean to offend you, Mischka!" Jessie responded, worried Mischka was about to teach him a lesson.

"I know you didn't, but from here on out, don't disrespect the mouse!" she squeaked.

"Yes, ma'am!" Jessie saluted, and all three chuckled.

"I Used to be You, Don't Become Me."

"I think this confirms it!" Phillip announced.

"What?" Mischka asked, waving her tail about with her new sword.

"This was all because of the Great White Eagle," Phillip said proudly.

"You think?" Jessie asked.

"Every time one of these crystals shows up, it feels like the Great White Eagle's presence was here too," Phillip explained. Both Jessie and Mischka understood that because they had witnessed it themselves. "And now we have another crystal! That lamb and the knapsack wasn't in that bush by chance. I believe the Great White Eagle put them there."

"But why a weapon?" Mischka pondered.

"The scrolls warn of dark days…hmmm, 'Upon Thy return, ye shall wage wars of ye spirits.' or something like that," Phillip said, trying to recite some verse pertaining to the Great White Eagle's return.

"So there will be a war?" Jessie said. He didn't want to fight in a war. When he was in the Forbidden Circle, he and Andy had even considered staying there, escaping the duties the King would force them to do.

"I don't know for sure, but if I know my brother, if he doesn't catch us, or Andy and Eva, he will tear this Kingdom apart looking for us," Phillip said.

The cave grew quiet for a moment.

"Phillip?"

"Yeah, Jessie?"

"Who are you really?" he asked very softly. Phillip could tell that by the tenderness in Jessie's voice that he was hurt by Phillip's secret. When they left the dungeon, Jessie was mad at him, unwilling to trust him, but now, after all they had been through, Jessie just seemed to be hurt that he had kept something so big from him.

"There was a time that I was you…" Phillip began. "I was in the exact same shoes you are wearing." He paused for a moment, but Jessie leaned in. "When I was younger, almost twenty years ago, my brother and I were the best of friends."

"Hard to believe you two used to get along…" Mischka chuckled softly.

"I know…" Phillip smiled, "We didn't always hate one another. In fact, there was a time when I would have done anything for Timothy."

Jessie swallowed hard, he knew that was him now. "I understand that, I would do anything to get my brother back," Jessie said lightly.

"That's just it, it's a dangerous mindset. Desperation that is," Phillip said, which offended Jessie.

"I'm not desperate!" Jessie snapped.

"I'm sorry, I didn't know anyone would try to find the Great White Eagle in the No Man's Land Mountains out of anything but desperation…" Phillip said sarcastically. "Besides, I was desperate."

"What do you mean? What happened?" Jessie asked.

"I lost my brother as well," Phillip said solemnly.

"You mean, like to the Devil's Kettle?" he asked in disbelief.

"Yes… Exactly like you."

"What happened?" Jessie asked.

"Oh so much… I don't think we need to cover it all," Phillip said. However, Mischka swung her tail and poked Phillip in the leg.

"I Used to be You, Don't Become Me."

"It's high time you be honest with the boy!" she scolded Phillip.

"Fine… I suppose if I expect you to trust me, I best be honest with you," he started. "Timothy made a deal with Malus. He promised him glory… that's all he ever wanted was recognition and status," Phillip said, rolling his eyes. "In exchange, my brother was to go to the Devil's Kettle and find the Book of Truth and the key that belonged to it."

"Really? Malus wanted the Book of Truth? But why?" Jessie asked.

"Who knows, it is supposed to contain a great deal of knowledge. Knowledge is power, you know. But anyways, my brother convinced me and three others to go along."

"You knew about the deal, and you went along with him?" Jessie spouted.

"Of course not. My brother was always into schemes, trying to become famous. A stunt into the Forbidden Circle was not out of the ordinary for him. We had actually gone into the Blackwood forest a few times before. Just never beyond the Centrum's Core."

"Okay, but why are you telling me this? If your brother fell in and he is back, then you obviously found a way to bring him back… How?" Jessie said, wanting the end of the story.

"He's getting there! Be patient!" Mischka snapped at Jessie. "It all matters."

"Okay, I'm sorry, continue please," Jessie said, slouching back.

"There were five of us. Timothy, me, Peter, Rachael, and Emma…" Phillip's voice softened when he said Emma's name.

"Who is Emma?" Jessie asked.

"She never made it out of the Uada Hollow…" he said.

"Oh…" Jessie said, remembering the terrible night he and his friends had themselves been in the Uada Hollow. He could sympathize with Phillip.

"However, Peter was Peter Adams," Phillip explained.

"Like the Peacekeeper, chosen bloodline, Peter?" Jessie asked.

"Yes, and Rachael is your friend Eva's mom," he continued.

"What?! You were friends with Peter Adams and Eva's mom? What are the odds?" Jessie said.

"Exactly, do you see now why this is all important?" Mischka said.

"I'm starting too… So what happened next?" Jessie asked.

"Well, I started to sense things were off with my brother after Emma died. The group wanted to turn back, tell her family what had happened. But my brother refused. He went on and on about finally seeing the Devil's Kettle. He said he would go on with or without the group. But I couldn't let him go alone. Not after the attack of Messorems the night before." Phillip explained.

"Remember, only Timothy knew about his deal with Malus at this point," Mischka said.

"Right. However, Peter sensed something was off with Timothy as well. So he refused to let us go alone. Then it was settled. All four of us would go and see the Devil's Kettle," Phillip said. "It wasn't until we found the Book of Truth that things really went sideways. Peter wished to bring it to the Elves. Pious creatures they are. They would use it for good. But Timothy became violent because he wanted to bring it to Malus. Our group was on the brink of violence," Phillip explained.

"Violence?" Jessie asked.

"Oh yes, and there was. Peter and Timothy began to throw fists. Timothy was my brother, but more than once, he had gotten us both into trouble trying to seek glory. Knowing Peter was right, I couldn't take it anymore. My brother was stricken with greed, it made me sick. So, while they fought, I grabbed the book, ran to the crest of the waterfall that filled the lake of the Devil's Kettle, and threw the book over the edge. Down Corkscrew Canyon, it fell and plunged into the water. I hoped it would all be over with once the book was gone, but it wasn't," he said solemnly.

"Oh, I hate this part," Mischka squeaked. Having heard the story before, she knew what came next.

"When my brother saw me throw the book over the edge, my brother escaped his fight with Peter and leapt off the cliff. I watched the currents pull him toward the Devil's Kettle. I tried to run down and save him, but by the time I got there, he was gone…" Phillip said, tears welling up in his eyes.

"I'm sorry, Phillip, I know just how you feel…" Jessie said.

"Yes, Jessie, but listen to me. You cannot make a deal with Malus. If the Great White Eagle brings your brother back, then great, but if he doesn't, you must promise not to listen to Malus…" Phillip said.

"The Great White Eagle will bring my brother back! Won't he? He brought back Mischka, so why not Richard?" Jessie spoke with a lump in his throat.

"Sometimes things don't always go our way… just prepare yourself for that."

"I'm getting my brother back!" Jessie snapped, "If the Great White Eagle won't, I'll find someone else who will!" he said in a fit of rage.

"No, Jessie! You cannot trust Malus. What he wants is never worth the cost!" Phillip said.

"He never said what he wanted. Obviously, you took Malus' deal, it couldn't have been that bad!" Jessie spouted angrily.

"I did, and it was that bad!" Phillip protested.

"What did he make you do? Find the Book of Truth again?"

"No, Jessie, he had me kill Peter Adams!" Phillip shouted. Standing to his feet, Phillip became distraught. The terrible memories of all he did flooded back to him.

"You killed Peter Adams? But he was your friend?" Jessie asked, shifting away from Phillip.

"Yes, yes, I did, and I have regretted it ever since. Why do you think I live in the dungeons? I can hardly stand myself," Phillip said.

"How could you?" Jessie asked bluntly.

"Desperation Jessie… just like you," Phillip said, looking Jessie dead in the eye.

"I could never harm anyone!" Jessie protested.

"I didn't think I could either. And I didn't for years, but after years of desperation, my desires won…" Phillip said.

"You were weak!" Jessie said, thinking he would never stoop that low.

"You're right…" Phillip said. Jessie was expecting protest from Phillip, but the heartfelt submission caught Jessie off guard, indicating that Phillip really was sorry for all he had done.

"What finally convinced you to give in?" Jessie inquired.

"A girl," Phillip said with a soft smile, thinking back about the beautiful young girl he had fallen in love with all those years ago. "Morana," he said, as tears streamed down his cheeks.

"Who was she?" Jessie asked.

"She was the most beautiful girl I had ever laid eyes on. She found me in my misery and loved me, despite all I had been through. I told her everything, and she still stayed by my side," Phillip said. The thought of Isabell popped into Jessie's mind. If he was honest with himself, he was quite smitten with her.

"I asked her to marry me," Phillip said. "I was healing, ready to move on from the death of my brother. I had separated myself from Rachael and Peter because of what Malus wanted me to do, so she was all I had left. Morana was my escape, my chance to start over," Phillip said, "But one night she went to the Village of Regnum to stock up on supplies and didn't come back. The next day, Titans arrived at my door."

"What did they want?" Jessie asked.

"They took me to the castle, specifically Malus' room. From there, I could see Morana tied up in the heart of the Maze. She had been beaten..." Phillip said.

"By Malus?" Jessie asked. But Phillip continued his story.

"Malus told me that if I did not do what he asked, he would kill Morana."

"Why didn't he just kill Peter himself, or have someone else do it?" Jessie asked.

"Malus never gets his hooves dirty. He always manipulates creatures to be destructive. He convinces us to tear each other apart, so he doesn't have to. All the while he maintains power over us," Phillip said, grinding his teeth together.

"Why did he even care about Peter in the first place?" Jessie asked.

"He was of the Great White Eagle's chosen bloodline," Mischka said.

"With Peter gone, the bloodline would be too. The Great White Eagle is Malus' greatest enemy."

"So you caved?" Jessie asked. Suddenly, Jessie felt bad for Phillip. What he did was not at all okay, however, Jessie thought of Isabell. *If anything were to happen to her…* he couldn't even think about it.

"Yes, that night, reeking of ale, I set Peter Adams' house ablaze."

"They have told the story of that fire at the Village gatherings…" Jessie said, hearing of them in the past. "But everyone thought it was an accident."

"Well, it wasn't! Peter, his wife, and his newborn son Esok all died because of me!" Phillip sobbed.

"What happened to Morana?" Jessie asked.

"Oh, this is the worst! Just the worst!" Mischka said squeamishly. Her harsh reaction surprised Jessie.

"Well then, what happened? What about Morana?" Jessie asked.

"Well… it turns out she worked for Malus. The whole thing was a ruse. She never loved me, and Malus never harmed her. They faked the whole thing to get me to save her and kill Peter…" Phillip said, completely and utterly defeated.

"What! That's despicable," Jessie said, standing up and clenching his fists out of anger.

"Yes… It was," Phillip said.

"When the Great White Eagle brings my brother back, the three of us will get revenge on Malus," Jessie announced. Hearing Phillip's story made him angry. Not at Phillip, he now understood him, but at Malus for making him do it. None of it was okay, Phillip was still guilty, but if Malus could manipulate Phillip, what's stopping him from trying it on Jessie? Thinking that Malus might try to corrupt Isabell or worse, actually hurt her to get leverage over him, made his blood boil. "Malus must be stopped!" Jessie announced.

"I Used to be You, Don't Become Me."

"Eckhem! The four of us will!" Mischka said, making sure they knew she would have their backs.

"Jessie, you understand that I messed up. I made the wrong choices. You get that right?" Phillip asked. "That's why I'm here, I want to find the Great White Eagle to ask his forgiveness. What I've done can only be forgiven by him…"

"Sure, but Malus made you do it," Jessie said.

"No! I chose to. I still had a choice in it all. I was selfish and look what's come of it!" Phillip said. However, Jessie did not hear his warning, instead, he was set on revenge against Malus. "Listen to me, Jessie. When… I mean, if you are faced with these same choices I was, you cannot give in," Phillip warned.

"But I won't, the Great White Eagle will make everything right again," Jessie announced confidently.

"But what if he doesn't?" Phillip asked. Jessie looked coldly into his eyes. "Will you do what's right, and accept things as they are? Before you hurt someone else?"

"I won't have to," Jessie said. Turning away, another tear streamed down his cheek. He didn't want to even think about that possibility. *The Great White Eagle will bring my brother back! But what if… No! He will…he has to*, Jessie thought.

"I used to be you, Jessie… I don't want you to become me…" Phillip said. Silence fell heavily on the cave high up on the mountain tops. The fire crackled, and the wind whistled outside. Phillip settled next to the fire, curling up on the floor, and he used his coat as a blanket. "It's been a long day. We need to get some sleep," Phillip said as he rested his head and closed his eyes.

Jessie wanted to cry. To shout. But he was exhausted. Curling up across the fire from Phillip, he too drifted off into a deep sleep.

Chapter 28
An Example for All to See

While Jessie, Phillip, and Mischka talked in the warm safety of the mysterious cave, high in the peaks of the No Man's Land Mountains, Gillian stood in the dungeons. Still standing in a few inches of water from the storm the night before, he watched as the light of the day crested the horizon.

Then, trumpets blared. The King's special ceremony had commenced.

The gates of the castle swung open, and the people of Regnum began to flood in. Titans, Pegasi, servants, Goblins, and Dwarves piled into the courtyard.

Many creatures were curious as to what announcement the King had. Many rumors about escapes, the Forbidden Circle, and even the Great White Eagle floated around. However, as soon as they entered the courtyard, they knew this announcement was going to be grim. The courtyard was dressed for an Alatum Punishment. It was the only time that a garden of burning coals was placed in the center of the yard. Wing clamps rested on either side of the stage. Hanging from the King's balcony were blood red banners with the image of a black pegasus stitched into them.

There were also Titans arrayed on both sides of the stage in full armor, holding spears, and additional archers stationed in the castle's watch towers hovering above the crowd.

Soon, the Executioner presented himself before the crowd. The crowd hushed at his presence. As he walked towards the burning garden of coals, the crowd parted, giving him plenty of room to walk. Then he drug his double-bladed axe through the coals. Slowly but surely, the razor-sharp edges began to glow orange from heat.

Just then, a series of small trumpets played a majestic sequence. The crowd hushed at its tune.

"Attention! Attention!" A Titan commanded. "Your King."

He pointed to the balcony above them, and the king stepped forward from within his chambers. Normally, Malus would have followed the King out onto the balcony, but he was nowhere to be found. On his secret mission, even the King was unaware of his plans. Yet, with or without Malus, the King was driven to deliver his message. Tonight, he was to set an example for all to see.

Most of the crowd began to clap and cheer, but a common villager from the slums of Regnum began to boo and mock the king. He began to taunt him. "Where is Malus, your puppet master?"

As if planning for this exact moment, the king looked to one of the towers and flicked his wrist. Out of nowhere, an arrow zoomed from the tower and struck the man dead. Titans quickly carried him away. The crowd gasped and murmured at what had just occurred. As if it were nothing, the King calmly faced the crowd.

"Anyone else… care to disrespect me?" King Fraust said nonchalantly. "I have called you all here tonight to address recent events." The King began. "I am quite sure that there are many rumors and lips full of gossip, but I am here to set them straight," he announced. The crowd murmured again.

"You may have heard that I have lost control over my subjects… You may have heard I am no longer respected by the people… You *might* have even heard I have lost my strength as a leader, that I have become weak… but I suggest you get one thing straight. The only thing I have lost is my PATIENCE!" he shouted.

Then a group of three men began to shout and boo the king. These were not the rumors they had heard. They had heard of the prisoners' escape, their journey to the Devil's Kettle, and Gillian's betrayal. In hearing the King twist the crowd's thoughts with threatening words, they knew he was about to sway the people with false words, aimed at a power grab. But the King's fuse was shorter than ever, and in response to their protest, the King looked to his Titans next to the stage, nodded, and the three protesting men were flogged and tossed out of the courtyard.

"I open my doors to you all, welcome you into my home, and this is the thanks I get?" the King asked the crowd. "I am not evil, or cruel as many of you presume, but you must understand there are laws and laws keep order. Without order, there is chaos. The things I must do, the things you see as cruel, are all the heavy responsibilities of a King. So, I ask you, kindly, to respect me for the grim things I must do to maintain order for all our sakes." The crowd remained silent. "Now, as for the traitors!"

"They are just kids!" Rachael Huntsberg shouted. The King glared at her, but left her be.

"These four children broke the law and betrayed the castle."

"Yers pass, we dwarves mined fur gold en dah Furbidden Circle! What's dah big deal?" a burly Dwarf asked.

"The big deal? The big deal is that four children went in and only three came back! The big deal is that two of my bravest Pegasi went in to rescue them and only one came back! THIS is why we have laws! To protect us all!" the king said, building strength in his voice with every word. This time, the crowd murmured in agreement with the words. Hearing that creatures had died gave strength to the King's law and convinced many that the laws were actually there to protect them. "This is why those who break the law must be punished, to remind those who dare to push the nets of safety, that there are consequences," he said. "A good and loyal Pegasus, committed to protecting you all, died because of these traitors' carelessness."

"Our hearts go out to Vincent's family!" A Pegasus guard shouted from the edges of the crowd. Like an echo, all the loyal Titans and Pegasi shouted. "Hear! Hear!"

"Surely one mistake could be forgiven?" A Chief Elf with a blue sash asked from within the crowd.

"Perhaps… However, it is not only one offense, my dear subjects," King Fraust said. The crowd was shocked to hear this. As far as they knew, the teenagers had only broken one law. "You have heard by now that these prisoners have escaped." Again, the crowd murmured in agreement. "But what you may not have heard is that they have left in their wake destruction." The crowd gasped in disbelief. "Only hours ago, reports came in that a traitor by the name of Jessie LeRoy, accompanied by my murderous brother, killed an entire brigade. At least four men and one Pegasus perished at their hands!" The crowd erupted into chatter. Disbelief and shock spread throughout.

"Your brother? Murderous?" a castle gardener said.

"Phillip? The drunkard?" a Titan chirped.

"That drunken fool, he couldn't kill a fat dwarf stuffing his pockets with gold!" A goblin smarted off. He had seen Phillip in the taverns of Sod-Omen many times and knew just how pathetic he was.

"Yous bess watchya words, ya freckled fairy!" The dwarves present took great offense at his words.

"My brother? Do you care to know just how capable he is of murder? Do you remember all those years ago, the fire that killed Peter Adams? The fire was no accident, it was my brother who set their house ablaze!" King Fraust announced, and the whole crowd burst with gasps. Many doubted the king's words, while many others were baffled by the news. Peter was a staple of the community; they all knew he was of the favored bloodline. His death brought despair to all the followers of the Eagle. Many of their own hopes of the Great White Eagle's return died with him.

"Liar!" A woman shouted.

"If you don't believe me, believe him." The king responded as he nodded behind him. Simon stepped forwards nervously to the balcony's edge.

He looked at the King, and the King nodded. Simon looked over the crowd and spoke in a nervously rushed fashion. "It's true. Phillip is a killer. He tried to kill me, but only choked me enough to knock me out! He helped the boy escape. He's dangerous!" Simon rambled.

"Simon is a fool!" another shouted from the crowd.

"Big dumb fool!" another shouted. Simon had been a filthy, unsympathetic brute his whole life. Many of the people of Regnum knew him, and only because the castle had taken many of them prisoner for absurd and harmless crimes. Simon never batted an eye at the King's unfair rulings; Simon never cared about anyone but himself.

"These are just the facts. What I tell you is true, Phillip and the boy have murdered an entire brigade, all except for one brave Pegasus." Right on cue, Felix lifted himself into the air and accompanied the King on the balcony.

"Go on, tell them what happened," the King said.

"Well.. I… I ummm. I was with one other Pegasus and four Titans who were pursuing Phillip and the boy into the No Man's Land Mountains," he began as the crowd again murmured, this time about the dangers of those dreadful mountains. "When there was an avalanche that killed all of my comrades."

"Echem…" The king said, his chest puffed and his face firm.

"Oh, umm, the avalanche was caused by Phillip," Felix said, and before he could say anything else, the King stepped in front of him and cut him off.

"You see! Phillip is a murderer, he must be stopped! And again, the traitors have not only put themselves at risk but have also claimed the lives of innocent creatures. Tell me how that is fair?" the King asked, pressing the crowd below. Some shook their heads in disagreement, some in disbelief, but most shook their heads at the tragic loss of life.

"If that's not enough, these traitors have caused more destruction." The crowd was again shocked to hear.

"These traitors carry with them an enticing but dangerous ideology. One of false hope and it causes disorder," the King announced.

"What is it?" a man shouted from the crowd.

"I dare not even say, for it brings with it corruption!" King Fraust snapped. "What you do need to know is that they broke the law and deserve to be punished. However, they have convinced one of our own to betray the Kingdom! Their sly words have brought disorder. Again, without order, none of us are safe from the dangers of this world," The King continued to paint Eva, Andy, and Jessie poorly.

"That is why anyone who is found guilty of harboring any of the traitors will be put to death! There is no one above the law. Not a man, Dwarf or Elf, nor a Titan, not even a Pegasus!" the King shouted.

Eva's mom and dad were in the crowd and began to sob at the news. They had been watched closely by Titans since their daughter had escaped, and they feared they would never see her again. The crowd erupted louder than before.

"Quiet! Quiet!" The Titan commanded. At his words, Titans filtered into the crowd, looking to quiet the loudest of creatures.

"That is why, as a reminder, tonight will be concluded with an Alatum Punishment!" The crowd hushed. Everyone knew that an Alatum Punishment was worse than death for a Pegasus. Proud creatures, valued as top citizens in the land, are belittled to the lowest of lows. Slaves to the Dwarves, merely horses once their wings are taken away. "Not one creature, not even those of the castle, are above the law!" he announced his grim warning. "I present to you Gillian from the lineage of Manuel, Traitor to the Kingdom of Regnum." The King said as the Titan led Gillian by a lead rope in front of the crowd and up onto the stage for everyone to see. The peasants of Regnum, along with the special guests, were in disbelief. It was rare for a Pegasus to betray the kingdom, but for those who knew Gillian, they still wondered why he threw it all away for a couple of traitorous kids.

Although rare, the stage was built for Alatum Punishments. Four iron loops were positioned to tie each hoof of a Pegasus. In addition, a fifth iron loop was bolted front and center on the stage. Using it, the Titan leading Gillian slipped the end of the lead rope through the iron ring and walked it out. When the time came, he could lean back and force Gillian's snout to the ground. Immediately, Titans tied Gillian's legs to the four loops, prohibiting him from kicking or rearing up.

Looking out at the crowd, he looked at all of the faces. The humans of Regnum all looked worried, the Titans confused, the Pegasi angry, and the Dwarves looked joyful. They would be receiving a new slave after all.

But the face that hurt Gillian the most was his own. Below the stage, a pail of water sat undisturbed. It would later be used to clean the Executioner's axe. The perfectly still water reflected his image back at him. There it was, the black gash that stretched across his face, which was his first 'noble' marking. When he first saw it, he was in the clearing. At first, it brought him so much joy. He was excited to earn his very first and dreamed of one day being covered with spots all over. But as he earned more, he barely recognized himself. The things he had done that earned those marks were not good or noble at all, but instead, the black stains marked him with all he had done wrong.

The crowd cast their judgments upon Gillian. However, none of them knew the truth, not really. Gillian had done what was right, although to most it looked so, so wrong. His choice was much bigger than saving Andy and Eva, it was a matter of something more. Gillian had chosen to give his life to the Great White Eagle, instead of serving Malus. Although bound by ropes and chains, about to lose his wings, Gillian was comforted, knowing he had finally done the right thing.

After a few minutes, Asher walked onto the stage. Dressed in fancy garments and a baggy hat to match, he unrolled a scroll and began to read from it.

"The Pegasus Gillian, from the lineage of Manuel, is hereby charged with treason of the highest degree and of murder in the third degree. In series, his failure to protect the border of the Forbidden Circle has resulted in the deaths of one, Vincent II, from the lineage of Cohen, and one, Richard LeRoy. In addition, he has aided the escape of two prisoners. By order of King Fraust, I sentenced him to the Alatum Punishment. After which, he will live out the rest of his days as a slave for the Dwarves," he said. Then he rolled up the scroll, bowed to the King, and exited the stage.

The crowd began to move; some had no interest in seeing what came next, but the Titans had been ordered to allow no one to leave. King Fraust wanted everyone to witness. Gillian was to be an example for all to see.

Titans unbound Gillian's wings, then using the wooden clamps, pinched down on them. Ropes tied to the clamps allowed the Titans to pull out his wings to either side of Gillian. At the same time, the Titan holding the lead rope leaned back. Now prepared for the Alatum punishment, Gillian had both wings forced out to his side as far as they would go, and his nose had been forced to the iron loop on the wood stage by his lead rope. There was no escape, and the time had come.

Although the crowd of people was forced to witness this terrible thing, I cannot in good conscience explain in detail what happened next. Instead, I will only tell you what you need to know.

On that dreadful night, Gillian did, in fact, become a wingless Pegasus. Although he had rescued Andy and Eva, there was no one there to rescue him. He became a hero in the eyes of justice, he was labeled a traitor in the eyes of the world. Physically and emotionally, it was the most pain he had ever felt. What once was, was lost. But his journey was far from over.

Chapter 29
I AM

Late into the night, the fire had died down in the cave high on the mountains. Only embers glistened in the night, and the wind howled relentlessly outside. However, Phillip, Jessie, and Mischka slept undisturbed.

That was until Mischka began to receive a dream. Being a Somniator, this was not abnormal for her. However, in the midst of the darkness, she still tossed and turned as the Great White Eagle revealed to her another message by dream.

This dream was odd, different from others. Instead of a seemingly unfamiliar scene, everything she saw in this dream was familiar, as if the Great White Eagle was showing her the past. People, places, and things from a very recent past. The images flooded into her head, more vivid and brighter than ever before. Usually, the dreams she received meant nothing to her, as if encrypted or foreign to her, which was why a Lector had always been needed. However, this dream seemed clearer than most. Not that she knew what it meant, really, but she had witnessed many of these memories with her own eyes. Not all of them, of course, but enough to recognize that what the Great White Eagle wanted to show them was related to their most recent journey, the one that led them high into the No Man's Land Mountains and into the very cave they were in now.

A flash of the snow arching over the rock that Phillip and Jessie huddled behind as the avalanche crashed down around them. Then the image streaked into the lamb caught in the bush, then the door on the mountainside, then the bread. Then three other images flashed in her mind; however, these three she did not recognize. She saw a man in an elegant white robe, whose skin was of a dark complexion. He stood in the dungeons. Then the image quickly changed to a great light, one that squashed the darkness, but was too bright to see anything around her, but then her dream changed again to a young boy holding a lamb in his arms.

Again, they all flashed. Over and over, they played, each time, as if she could see them in more depth. At first, it was only a still picture of each, then the images played out in chaotic snippets, then she saw more, and by the next time each example arrived, she could hear different things. Sounds, even words, were added to the motion pictures. Until finally, the flashing halted, and each memory played out slowly and clearly for Mischka.

The first to play out was the man in the elegant white robe. His voice was deep. "I am the High Priest," he said, "Seek this world and you will find death, but if you seek the Great White Eagle, you will find life." Then the scene faded away like dust in the wind, but soon the second memory settled in. A darkness flooded around Mischka, in the distance, voices spoke her name, until suddenly a great green light overtook the darkness. Hedges to her left and right were illuminated, and instantly the eerie voices from afar became hushed. But then she heard the Great White Eagle's voice, seeming to come from the light itself. "I am the way, the truth, and the light," it said, faintly. Eager to find the Great White Eagle, Mischka scurried towards the light. However, once again, the light crumbled like sand being blown by a great wind, fading into the next dream. At first, it was a young boy leaning out of the loft. At a blink's speed, they were safe from the storm inside the barn, then at another blink, they were around the fireplace, with the sheep in the boy's arms. "What shepherd doesn't leave his whole herd for one lost sheep?" he said, petting the lamb. Once more, she blinked, and the boy was now at the heart of the barn, holding something in his palms and lifting it to the sky. "If you will it," he said, and again the image drifted away like dust. Slowly, the dust transitioned into snow. Blowing across the mountain saddle. She realized, as if watching from afar, that the avalanche was in progress. Completely covered, the rock where Phillip, Jessie, and she had been tucked behind was nowhere in sight. Not until the snow came to a complete rest and the swirling snow came to a rest did Mischka see her and her friends appear by the rock.

To her surprise, high above them, the Great White Eagle flew in circles. "I AM!" he boomed. Again, the wind picked up and blew the snow until that memory drifted into the next. This time, when the snow settled, Mischka saw the door. Something began to occur which had never happened to her before, this dream caused her to feel what she saw. Quickly, her little feet began to freeze, the tips of her ears began to sting from the wind, and the whiskers grew heavy with ice. She had become so cold that she struggled to breathe. By a great gust of wind, the door blew open, and Mischka tumbled inside. As if magically, the second she entered inside, all of the pain, the coldness, and misery vanished, and she couldn't remember a time when she had felt better. The fire pit within was blazing away, many creatures sat around the fire, and before them was the Great White Eagle himself. She couldn't make out what he was saying, but she could hear all the creatures laughing. They were joyous, merry, and at peace. Then the Great White Eagle held in his wings the elk hide knapsack. He peeled back the corners, and from it came loaves of bread. "Take and eat, whoever eats from me, will never hunger," he said. Then, he broke the loaves of bread up and fed every creature there. Until every creature had their fill. Mischka blinked, and it seemed as if hours had passed. Suddenly, a creature in the crowd spoke up, a bit angry. "You said that if we ate from you, we would never hunger! I ate your bread, but I am hungry again!" he said. Mischka was confused; she, too, had eaten the bread but again felt hungry. Never before had a dream felt real; she had felt cold, then better than ever. She felt full and now hungry once again. *What is going on?* Mischka thought. Then the Great White Eagle stood up. "You seek fulfillment in your belly, but I seek fulfillment of your heart." Then he burst out of the cave onto the snowy mountain top. Angry, the crowd of creatures chased after him. Torches lit in their hands. Clubs, pitchforks, and axes. Mischka tried to follow, but her little legs caused her to fall behind. The snow again erased the image before her, but like static, a new, final memory came to be. Mischka saw, caught in a bush, the lamb. Like a booming crack of thunder, the Great White Eagle's voice echoed on the mountain top. "I AM, and I will be," he said.

With that, Mischka was abruptly awakened by a rush of cold air that swooped in the doorway. Jessie had opened it to the new day, and they were greeted by the crisp mountain air. The whipping wind of the night before had died down, and the sun had risen above the Eastern Mountain peaks of Borrain. From this beautiful spot, they could see all the land. Regnum, the steps of the Pious Mountains in Gravis Terra, the Centaurs village, the soot-covered face of the Nani Mountains in the Eastern Region of Borrian, and even the faraway mountain tops of Terribbia, including the flat top of the Eagle's Plateau. It was a glorious sight. Both Phillip and Jessie were taken by the view. When Phillip realized Mischka was awake and had not taken interest in the view, he knew she had had a dream the night before.

"Mischka, what was it?" Phillip questioned her. "Jessie shut the door, Mischka doesn't need the cold right now!" he ordered, and the two of them slipped back into the cave. Someone had added logs to the fire before she had awoken.

"I had another dream, but this one was different."

"Different how?" Phillip asked.

"In so many ways. It was brighter, more vivid, and not something from the future. Instead, things you and I, and Jessie saw in the past. The recent past. And Phillip, I could actually feel things for some of it. The cold and hunger!" she squeaked.

"Is it not normal to receive dreams about the past?" Jessie asked.

"No! Most dreams are about something to come, like with your friend, Eva. She dreamt of what was to come. The reaping of the weeds or evil doers and the return of the Great White Eagle. None of it has happened, but will soon prove to be true," Phillip explained.

"Oh, okay, so then what did you dream of?" Jessie asked Mischka.

"They were memories. Things of our past."

"That is odd. Please, Mischka, tell me your dream," Phillip encouraged her.

Mischka then went on and told him how she had seen snippets and sections of the encounter with the High Priest, the Shepherd boy, the great light, the rushing of snow around the rock, the door, the bread, and the lamb. She told them what she heard, what she saw, and what she felt with each encounter.

"What do you think the Great White Eagle meant by saying, 'I AM'?"

Phillips' eyes grew wide. Unlike his brother's dream about the axe and the old Oak tree, in which he had a good idea about what it meant but still hadn't figured out all the pieces, this dream was plain as day, as if the Great White Eagle had explained it to him directly.

"What is it?" Mischka said, recognizing his excitement.

"This journey! How could I have missed it?" Phillip said with excitement. "I thought it was all strange, but they were all clues. If we had just opened our eyes to see."

"What? What did we miss?" Jessie questioned.

"I AM! It means he is!" Phillip said.

"What?" Mischka asked.

"Every strange thing we encountered was the Great White Eagle himself," Phillip clarified.

"Well, sure, I believe he had a hand in getting us here," Jessie said.

"No, I mean, he is the High Priest, he is the light, he is the shepherd, the rock, the bread, the door, and the lamb!" Phillip said.

"What are you talking about?" Jessie said aggressively.

"Let him finish," Mischka suggested.

"A high priest's duties are that he guides and provides knowledge and understanding for his people. It is he who is responsible for the people. Who has greater knowledge and understanding than the Great White Eagle himself?" Phillip began to explain.

"So, you think he was the Key then? Clearly, the crystal key was the light we saw?" Jessie asked.

"No, no, he is the light. No darkness and no evil can withstand his light. He brings all things into the light, so that good can overcome evil," Phillip explained.

"And Uriah? You mean to tell me that some random boy was the Great White Eagle too?" Jessie asked.

"Not just a boy but a shepherd. A protector of his flock. He would sacrifice his life for one lost sheep. Don't you remember his words?" Phillip said, becoming more and more excited. Jessie nodded but was flabbergasted at the explanations. *Sacrifice himself? But he is the Great White Eagle; what does a couple of sheep matter?* Jessie thought.

"The next memory was the rock. The rock never spoke but was silent and sturdy. It did not budge, nor did it move. While everything else around us was being squashed and crumbled that rock did not move," Phillip said.

"So he is the rock, for all our sakes. Never changing, never budging, always there to protect?" Mischka asked.

"Exactly!" Phillip exclaimed.

"But what about the bread? Why did the Great White Eagle lie to those creatures in her dream?" Jessie asked.

"He did not lie! Instead, those creatures did not understand. Just like the bread we magically received in our knapsack, the bread they ate filled their bellies. However, that's not what the Great White Eagle spoke of," Phillip said.

"Then what?" Mischka asked.

"He wants to fill our hearts! Take me for example, oh this is so good!" Phillip began, "Before this journey, I was nothing but a beggar. A drunk! Worthless and a coward. I was a broken man who had done terrible things. I wished I were dead. I hungered for something I thought I lost."

"What did you hunger for?" Jessie asked.

"Completeness. Forgiveness. A new start," Phillip said. "This whole time we have been searching for the Great White Eagle. Instead of focusing on myself, I looked to him. He has fed my heart. For the first time in a long time I feel free, complete, and hopeful!" Phillip was now wearing a giant smile and a sparkle twinkled in his eyes.

"So, he is also a door?" Jessie asked.

"Yes, Jessie. Think about it, Mischka, for the first time ever, felt something real in her dreams. Standing outside the door, she was cold and miserable. However once she passed through the door, she was safe. The Great White Eagle is that door. When we pass through to the otherside, with him, we are saved from the world of misery!"

"No longer cold? No longer miserable?!" Mischka said. She was beginning to understand that each one of these encounters was more than just something physical, but they represented a truth that existed everywhere.

"I just don't get it…" Jessie said, a bit frustrated. He tried to think of the Great White Eagle as just a light, or a rock, or some bread, but he did not understand that those things represent much more than the physical item.

"He said 'I AM!'" Phillip said, clasping Jessie on the shoulders. "He is the high priest, having all truth and knowledge. He is the shepherd, we are his flock and he would leave the masses in search of one! He is the rock, he will not be moved and we are protected by him. He is the door, only through him can we escape all evils of the world!

He is the bread, when we look at him, our hearts are filled!" Phillip said with great glee.

"You never explained the lamb caught in the bush? What does that mean?" Jessie asked. Phillip's face went dim.

"Well… that one is not so exciting…" Phillip admitted.

"What do you mean?" Mischka asked.

"Well you remember how I said the shepherd would give up his own life for one of his lost sheep?" Phillip asked.

"What's that have to do with the Lamb in the bush?" Jessie asked, still not understanding the spiritual side of it all.

"Wait a minute… You mean to tell me…" Mischka began, but paused.

"What? What is it?" Jessie asked.

"Jessie, you remember what we did to the lamb?" Phillip began. "It had to die, so that we could live," he explained.

Suddenly, the door of the cave swung open, and a bright white light shone in upon them. A deep voice boomed from outside the cave, "You have traveled far seeking me, yet I was with you all along."

Slowly they stepped out of the cave into the open air and their eyes began to adjust and they could finally see who was standing before them.

"Who are you?" Mischka squeaked.

Perched before them was a significantly large eagle, but he was brown, not white. He had a few specks of white covering his feathers, but even his head was brown and his sharp beak was yellow. He had fierce eyes and long, tall feathers, and he had normal eagle-looking feet; yellow with razor sharp black talons. The only abnormal thing about him was that he was much larger than a normal eagle. As big as an adult Pegasus, if not bigger, and he could speak the common tongue.

"My child," he said with a great laugh, "Do you not remember me?" the eagle asked. Instantly, Mischka's Mapier sword, still strapped to her tail, began to glow vividly. As if his words removed a veil from their eyes, they saw him and they knew that he was the Great White Eagle. Phillip began to sob and fell to his knees and Mischka bowed low.

"Is it really you?" Jessie asked, stepping forward. The Great White Eagle nodded. "But you don't look like him?" Jessie was a bit sceptical because nothing about the Great White Eagle was making sense.

"I don't? What did you expect?" the Great White Eagle asked.

"I expected you to be white!" Jessie announced.

"Hmmm, who says I need to be white?" he asked.

"Well… everybody?" Jessie asked.

"Huh… What if I were pink? Or green?" the Great White Eagle asked with a chuckle. However Jessie did not think it was as funny. But then the Great White Eagle looked down at Phillip, with compassion in his eyes. "Phillip Fraust. Why must you carry so much guilt and shame on your shoulders?" But Phillip did not respond. He could not even look at the Great White Eagle. He was too ashamed of all he had done.

"I know you feel guilt and shame for killing Peter Adams," the Great White Eagle said, and Phillip sobbed harder.

"Wait, can you save my brother?" Jessie pressed, cutting the Great White Eagle and Phillip's moment short.

"I can give him a new life."

"That's so great!" Jessie said, jumping up and down for joy.

"Be careful in your understanding. I will give your brother life, but not as you know it to be," The Great White Eagle said as if to warn Jessie to think deeply about his words.

"Wonderful! Just wonderful!" Jessie said, completely disregarding the Great White Eagle's warning. He was just so happy to hear the words "life" and "his brother" in the same sentence.

"Phillip, you understand, don't you?" the Great White Eagle asked, concerning Richard. Phillip calmed his sobbing but never looked up. He just nodded. "How do you feel, little Mischka?" he said, changing the subject.

"I feel great... Thank you." She said in a humble manner realizing that he was the one who brought her back.

"Wonderful!" the Great White Eagle said.

"Now I must be off, I have much to do and very little time to do it. I must bid you farewell. Continue eastward, you will find the mouth of a cave. That is where your journey continues," The Great White Eagle said. He spread his wings, preparing to lift himself off the ground.

"Before you go... What should we call you? Or would you prefer us to call you the Great White Eagle?" Mischka asked.

"You can call me Salus (Saul-oose). Oh, and Phillip?" the Eagle asked for his attention.

"Yes? What is it? Anything!" His sobbing had calmed, and he was eager to serve the Great White Eagle.

"I forgive you. Now, go forth, not for your own glory but for that of the Great White Eagle," Salus said.

Before Phillip sobbed because of the shame, the guilt, and his unworthiness to stand before the Great White Eagle. But, when he heard those words, *I forgive you,* he sobbed tears of joy. He began this journey for exactly that, forgiveness from the one creature who could forgive him. When he finally met him, he was too ashamed to ask for it. Yet, Salus knew. He knew that's what Phillip wanted, that's what Phillip needed. Like the warm breeze of a warm spring day that melts the snow away, the forgiveness from Salus caused Phillip's pain, guilt, shame, and desperation to melt into a feeling of joy, happiness, and a heart filled with peace.

Without another word, he thrust his wings towards the ground and was instantly in the air. As he flew away he shouted one last time to the three creatures standing exposed to the mountain side. "You will soon realize that something is missing. Know that I am bringing it somewhere safe. When you find it again, you can use it. I shall keep it safe until then." By now the Great White Eagle was off in the distance and within seconds disappeared into the clouds.

"Can you believe it? The Great White Eagle has returned!" Mischka said.

"Just like Eva's dream predicted!" Jessie said, excited about his brother's new life.

"So many of us have been waiting for this moment!" Phillip hollered from the mountain top. "And you heard him, I'm forgiven. But better yet, I feel forgiven!"

"I cannot wait to see my brother again! Onward to the cave!" Jessie shouted. He raced back into the cave, grabbed the knapsack with the Book of Truth and the loaves of bread. Threw his jacket on, and started on his way.

Phillip knelt down to allow Mischka into his palm and the two spoke quietly.

"This is so exciting! He really has returned!" Mishcka squeaked.

"It is, but I am afraid for Jessie. And what are we missing?" Phillip admitted.

"Why? Salus told us he would give Richard a new life," Mischka said.

"Right, but I don't think it means what we think. He didn't say he would bring him back. Just that he would give him a new life," Phillip asked.

"You think there is something more to it?" Mischka asked.

"I do… Just like Salus is the light, meaning more than a physical light, and he is the rock. I think that what he is speaking of might be different than what we think," Phillip said anxiously.

"How do we tell him?" Mischka asked, watching Jessie happily gather together their stuff.

"I don't think we can. He must come to understand it himself. Besides, I could be completely wrong about it all. I think it's best we let things happen as they may," Phillip suggested.

"What are you two babbling about! We have orders to follow!" Jessie said with a smile. With that, Phillip gathered his winter gear. Running, he caught up with Jessie who was already out onto an open ridge in search of their next journey. Still puzzled, he pondered the Great White Eagle's last words. At last, he knew what they were missing.

The Key! He said to himself.

Chapter 30
Esok Adams

A new mother sat in a wooden rocking chair holding her new baby. She wrapped the baby tightly in cloth and rocked him to sleep gently. Her husband, Peter Adams, stood behind her and they both peered down at the baby. They were a happy couple. They had a brand new baby and a humble quiet home. The fireplace crackled away, keeping them all warm. Neither of them said a word but just embraced the moment. Soon, the baby's fussing quieted, and he was asleep.

Mr. and Mrs. Adams brought the baby into the nursery and laid him down in a crib. Dangling above the baby was a series of creatures hung by strings. Elves, dwarves, Pegasi, Titans, Centaurs, and Beavers were the figures that floated above.

Mr. and Mrs. Adams settled in their rooms for the night.

Later on, in the dead of night, someone lit their home on fire. The flames clung to the side of the house and quietly burned away at the house's structure. Fast asleep, like the rest of the village, they had no idea what was happening.

Unfortunately, by the time the flames burned hot and awoke them, it was too late. The flames had grown and consumed the roof. The structure became weak and could no longer support the rafters. Its structure began to crumble. The roof collapsed, blocking their bedroom door trapping them inside. Knowing their baby was in the room over, they pushed and pulled at the door trying to rescue the baby. The smoke was so heavy that by the time either of them thought to jump out the window, they had grown too weak and collapsed on the floor. They never made it out of the house.

However, the baby had a different outcome. He watched as the house burned down around him. Orange flames blazed, and the heat produced brought tears to his eyes. He was incapable of saving himself. He became scared at the roaring fire burning brightly around him. Suddenly, he was hoisted out of his crib. Too young to know what had saved him, the baby was rescued from the fire. Each stride of the hero brought him further from certain death.

The villagers mourned the deaths of Peter, his wife, and their baby boy Esok. They tore down the house and planted a tree in remembrance of the Great White Eagle's chosen bloodline.

Years later, the tree had grown. Its branches sprawled out in every direction, providing shade beneath them. With it, the boy who had been saved by the fire had also grown.

Now, the boy found himself standing within a dimly lit tunnel. Before him stood a grand wooden door, with the image of an iron eagle, holding in its clutches an iron ring, used for knocking. He reached for the ring, but before he could knock, the door creaked open and there stood a very old elf. He was dressed in a light blue long-sleeved tunic which covered his knees, gray pants beneath. Golden buttons were sewn on the front of his tunic. He had silky white hair, which hung straight, although tucked behind his pointy ears, and his white beard hung down to his brown belt. Then the old, stern elf graced his lips with a smile, and soft wrinkles formed near his eyes.

"Esok Adams! I have been waiting for you!" He said.

Instantly, Eva opened her eyes, and she awoke from her dream.

A Note From the Author

I hope you enjoyed the second book in The Tale of the Devil's Kettle series. A lot has happened, and much more rests on the horizon, but I wanted to take a moment to reflect on what you have read. Throughout the first and second books, laced within the story, you will find spiritual truths grounded in biblical teachings. My stories intend to entertain, inspire, and bring readers to Christ. However, I felt compelled to leave you with this: Do not take my story as biblical truth; instead, I encourage you to dig into the bible yourself! Although there are themes that I believe to be true within my story, I encourage you to discover those themes within the Bible from God's Word directly!

Good vs. evil, finding one's faith, and discovering the characteristics of Jesus Christ in relation to our own lives are some of the themes explored in the story. However, there are some themes that are to be taken only for storytelling purposes. One such theme is that of the afterlife. I do not have any real knowledge or understanding of what the afterlife looks like or consists of, and the way I depict it within my story should only be taken for entertainment purposes. Again, I must encourage you to read through the bible yourself to discover the promise that God gave us through Jesus Christ, about our "afterlife."

Thank you again for reading my story. Make sure to check out the rest of the series to see what happens next! God bless you.

About the Author

The writer, **For His Glory**, comes from a small town in the Midwest. He began working at fifteen years old, and since then has started his own small business. His most prized accomplishment is that he got married to the girl of his dreams.

His favorite hobby growing up was Taekwondo. He earned his black belt at the early age of eight years old, and has continued to teach the art alongside his father and wife. Recently earning the Rank of 4th Dan. (Master instructor Status.)

Although he had many accomplishments, life gave him many setbacks. Many times, he found himself failing to be the strong Christian man he aimed to be. However, his writing became a way to remind himself that all he did should be done for God's Glory.

He hopes that his stories can be entertaining but also that it may inspire those who read it, to dig into their own faith no matter what failures or setbacks life throws their way.